CAPTAIN'S ORDERS

CAPTAIN'S ORDERS

KARA KEEN

To Scott – You believe in me more than I believe in myself.

ACKNOWLEDGEMENTS

The power behind this book and my life is my husband Scott! Without him, there would be no confidence, no persistence, no focus and certainly no web presence, mortgage, taxes or health insurance. His support made it possible to sit, day after day, on my screen porch and write this book. And thanks to my family and friends, who provide the best reasons to grow as a person.

Thanks to Faith Freewoman, my editor, who highlights my strengths and many wicked weaknesses with great kindness and accuracy. Denice, busy mom and great writer, you're a terrific beta reader and cheerleader. Thanks to Amanda and to Nick and the gang at Writers of Chantilly who had great suggestions for the story. Thanks to all you readers who dared to try a new author, enjoy!

CHAPTER ONE

COLE CARLETON LIKED to check out the passengers in the lounge while they waited to board his cruise ship, *Sunset*. It gave him an advantage over his brother Jack (essential between competitive siblings) and a chance to anticipate what problems and pleasures might be ahead on their voyage.

Wearing jeans and a T-shirt and carrying a duffel from his London shore leave, he fit right in with the passengers instead of looking like the captain of a ship with 3,000 passengers and 1,000 crew members. He was hoping to absorb the excitement while people checked in, their heady anticipation of an eleven-day luxury cruise around the UK.

Truth be told, he'd gotten a little blasé about the whole cruise business. It wasn't the intensity that bothered him, the challenge of keeping 4,000 people safe and 3,000 of them entertained. He loved that part of the job. It was...something else, a nagging feeling of being alone despite being constantly surrounded by people.

"And what part of cruising are you tired of?" Jack had asked him before shore leave. "Gourmet meals 24/7, seeing the world, the best gym on the high seas, women throwing themselves at us on every trip. If you asked most guys, they'd say we have the world by the balls!"

"Yeah," Cole frowned. "There's that last one. Don't you feel like shit sometimes? These ladies get off the ship and never think of us again."

"Au contraire!" said Jack, busting out his perpetual grin. "I think every time they're in bed by themselves, they think about us…a lot! And some of them come back for more!"

The young co-captains had a reputation on internet message boards for the attentive "customer service" they provided for single ladies on the high seas. They'd been profiled in the *Wall Street Journal*, the *Observer*, and *Le Monde* newspapers, but the full page in *USA Today* was the real kicker. A big photo showed the brothers smiling, captain's jackets unbuttoned, grinding a dance on either side of a lovely passenger who was wearing Jack's hat.

After they were interviewed by an attractive female host on *The Today Show*, she did an extensive feature covering her cruise hosted by—you guessed it—the Carleton brothers. The cruise line had been delighted—gave them a raise, in fact!

But Cole was tired of the lover-boy lifestyle. "You're okay with these women chewing you up like a fucking piece of man-cake on the buffet?"

"Okay with it? I love it! Bring on the frequent flyers, I say!" It was obvious Jack enjoyed flirting with every passenger in a skirt. It fit right in with his persona, the party guy who'll show a girl a good time—*this* week. Behind the mask, he was a shrewd judge of people and a quick study who'd schooled Cole through the maritime exams for their captains' licenses. When it came to women, though, Jack liked to leave emotion at the door. Numbness and indifference were easier than the effort and risk of an actual relationship. When the main event was over, he was out the door, leaving the cuddling to Cole.

And control was not an issue for either brother once the

bedroom door was closed. They shared…many things, including the ability to lead women down the edgy road to ecstasy.

But Cole had been feeling something else lately, a relentless loop running in his mind, especially after hooking up with someone. *It's always the same. You see someone, the eye contact thing, the flirting thing, hanging out, laughing, drinking. You hook up late at night and wake up alone the next day, feeling disconnected and lonely. Repeat. Drink, hook up, wake up alone. Repeat. What if there were something different? Something real I'm missing.*

He occasionally caught a glimpse of it in the eyes of older couples on the ship celebrating their 40th, 50th, sometimes 60th or 70th anniversaries. "What's your secret?" he'd ask them when he brought a bottle of champagne to their table. Some men would joke "Answer every question with 'Whatever you say, dear,'" but most couples talked about trust, honesty, support and the ability to laugh and have fun. They had a special glow and seemed to share an entire universe of growth, history and humor.

But right now, in this job, the single ladies kept coming, sailing after sailing. The twin thing was a big draw for women, always had been, even when they were teenagers. In their years as cruise ship captains, the brothers had teamed up with one woman, two—including a ridiculously high number of stunning twin sisters—and sometimes even more women. For a while it had felt like living the dream.

Recently though, after a few particularly wild nights, it'd started to feel more like a nightmare. Dressing in the bathroom of some woman's suite…again. Creeping back to his room and sleeping alone…again. *I'm the fling, the guy women sleep with before they meet "the one." My sisters think Jack and I are assholes. Are they right? If I find my "one," will I lie to her about my number? What is it anyway, have I slept with over 50 women? Fuck. If I tell the truth, will she feel I have no respect for women, no respect for myself?* Shoulders squared, arm stretched out as he pointed at his reflection in the mirror, Cole had vowed to end his casual hook-ups. *No more of that crazy shit. I'm done with it.*

*

He pulled his baseball cap down to avoid being recognized, dreading being back on board and dealing with problems extending way beyond getting the giant floating hotel from here to there. Could there be problems in such a fun, luxurious atmosphere? Yeah…

The tall, stacked redhead greeting the first-class passengers was one problem. Jeannette Taylor, the ship's entertainment director. Even though Cole and Jack had a no-fucking-shipmates policy, she'd made a play for them and ended up in the middle of the famous Carleton Brothers' Sandwich. Then for a while she'd expected to be on their regular menu. Big, big problem.

Cole watched as an older guy shouted in German, gesturing wildly at Jeannette. She expertly steered him over to the bar and calmed him, putting a glass of champagne in his hand. Leaning in so the obnoxious German could easily ogle her cleavage, she smiled and nodded while she listened to his complaints. *Nice work*, Cole thought when Jeannette led the German to the special elevator leading to the ship's largest suites. It wasn't officially time to board yet, but it was smart of her to hustle the high-maintenance rich guy out of the public eye and into his cushy suite. His unfortunate entourage, a tall guy with a shaved head and a pretty girl teetering along in ultra-high heels, followed close behind.

A white-haired gentleman a few yards away struggled to hoist his luggage onto a cart, and Cole considered whether to help him. He decided against it when the fellow's lady love handed him her bag and rewarded his efforts with a glowing smile. Grinning from under the bill of his cap, Cole looked forward to bringing a bottle of champagne to their table and asking their secret.

"Oooph," Cole had the wind knocked out of him when a big Middle Eastern guy stiff-armed him against the wall. *Problems, here come more problems.*

"Coming through," announced the well-dressed man behind him, barging through the other passengers as if they barely existed. Just as Cole was on the verge of protesting the rude behavior, he recognized them. The fashionable asshole was the Saudi prince the *Sunset*'s officers had been briefed about. Following close behind were his burly bodyguards and his burka-shrouded wives. They were bound for the Celestial Suite, the ship's largest and most luxurious. A tricky problem with this group was that other passengers felt uncomfortable when the women were herded around the ship like sad ghosts in their long black coverings.

Adding insult to injury, one of the sheikh's bodyguards threw the older couple's suitcases off the luggage cart, piled on the bags from the sheikh's wives, and pushed the cart toward the elevator. The sweet elderly couple looked dismayed for only a moment before Jeannette returned, bringing a porter and whisking them away from the ill-mannered offenders.

But who's this sweet thing? He watched as a tall girl with long dark hair and mile-long legs bounced back to her seat after registering. The woman had curves, something he didn't usually see in the leggy ones, and her teasing jiggle intrigued him. There was a quiet confidence in her long stride, strength in her posture, and she gave him a playful smile when he caught her eye. *Those eyes, long lashes pulling me into big brown eyes. And the lips, shit, full lips begging for a kiss.*

There was a prickly feeling at the back of his neck, an awareness that made it a struggle to look away from her. His anti-hookup vow flew right out of his mind and he grinned when she glanced back at him. Blushing a little, she looked down and then leaned back in her seat, staring intently at the private boarding lounge.

Still, her killer smile and a vision of her sweet ass, naked and ready for him to stroke and explore, distracted him from making his move. Long enough for a sophisticated-looking guy to sit down next to her, take her hand, and kiss it. *Dammit.*

CHAPTER TWO

TANIA SHEVCHENKO FORCED herself to stop trading glances with the tall guy in the baseball cap. *I am not here to see anyone but my sister,* she thought, *but why was Oksana with that German man over there?* A month ago, a single five-minute call from her sister had revealed enough to bring her to this cruise ship docked near London, 3,500 miles from her home in New Jersey. The panic she'd heard in her sister's voice then made her cautious about approaching her now.

Tania watched the first class passengers, positioning herself so Oksana could *not* see her, but wondering why her sister seemed to willingly follow the German to the elevator. It was only when Tania smelled a Russian cigarette—if her nose remembered correctly—that she turned away to face a pale, slender man. His tight-cut blazer and expensive brown shoes screamed "European."

"Qu'est-ce que tu fais ici, ma belle?" the handsome man asked. She immediately stiffened, disliking his blank eyes and disdainful tone. Why was he questioning her eligibility to be on the cruise? His question implied she didn't belong here.

"Je suis un passager sur ce bateau, Monsieur, et vous?" She answered his use of the familiar "tu" with a polite but distant "vous" as she asserted her identity as just another vacationer on the ship. Although well-dressed and articulate, this guy made her skin crawl. Her pulse quickened and she looked around for a way to escape.

"Moi aussi. Je m'appelle Ivan Fedorov, et tu?"

His French sounded awful and she wasn't impressed. She answered as graciously as possible in her slightly accented English, "I'm Tania. Let's speak English, Ivan, shall we?" He kissed her hand again and held tight until she pulled her hand back and stood, crossing her arms over her chest.

"You're from Ukraine, right Tania?" he said, standing to loom over her.

"Yes." Maybe one-word answers would make him go away.

"You're very beautiful. Do you have a boyfriend on the ship?"

"Uh…yes. Yes, I do." She blushed and ducked her head a little when she said it, and realized she had to agree with her American friends. She was the Worst. Liar. Ever.

He stepped close to her and tucked a stray lock of her hair behind her ear. "Such a shame. I could introduce you to some very powerful men who know exactly how to treat a woman like you, Tania."

Her hands balled into fists at her side and in a low voice she asked, "And exactly what kind of woman *am* I, Ivan? Do you think you are my friend and I'm your piece of ass 'cause I'm from Ukraine, you Russian asshole?"

"Whoa, whoa, little hellcat." He chuckled and rubbed her back, as if he were trying to soothe an angry child. She pulled away and held her shaking hands up, alarmed by his creepy persistence.

"I think you should probably take your hands off her and sit somewhere else, sir. She seems upset by your conversation. Is that right, ma'am?" The tall man in the Phillies baseball cap got in Ivan's face and spoke softly, shielding Tania and ending the scary encounter. The Russian turned on his heel and stalked away without a glance.

Trembling, Tania felt her brave front disintegrate when she sank down into a seat and looked up at the handsome stranger. "Thank you. Thank you very much." The seat next to Tania filled up with well over six feet of gorgeous, hard-bodied male when he squeezed himself into the little plastic chair.

"Hi, I'm Cole, Cole Carleton. Are you okay?" When she nodded and offered her hand he shook it warmly. "Where are you from?"

"Tania Shevchenko, I'm from New Jersey," she said.

She fought an overwhelming urge to stare at him. It was like looking at one of those men's cologne ads featuring a perfect model with broad shoulders, intense blue eyes and perfect white teeth. And it was obvious he "worked out," as her college friends would say. He had the big, American-style smile she'd grown to love while living in the States, and the smile spread to his eyes when his big, strong hand surrounded hers. *Many possibilities, hands like that. Long, strong hands… they might show me things I don't know about or help me do what I came here to do. Maybe both.*

"But originally from…Russia, I guess…right?" He was still smiling, holding her hand. She decided she might need to stop shaking hands with men; they didn't seem to want to let go. But in this case it might not be a bad thing.

"Yes. I came to New Jersey from Ukraine eight years ago to become a nursing student. I know Americans think Russia and Ukraine are the same place, but Ukraine became independent in 1991."

His scorching blue eyes burned a hole in her from under the baseball cap, his gaze bold and direct. She managed not to flinch and something in his eyes softened, a flirty smile playing on his lips.

Pushing up the brim of his Phillies cap a little, she said, "I went to the Phillies World Series game! I love American baseball!" Her laugh warmed up the space around them while she pulled her hand away and took a good look at his chiseled, handsome face. "I was at the game because the first one got rained out. My friend had to work and gave me her ticket. Then I got to go in the clubhouse and I poured a bottle of champagne on Ryan Howard and Utley butted my head, it was amazing!"

Cole seemed confused, "He…he butted your head?" After a beat, he smiled when he got it. "Oh…a head butt, you and Utley celebrated with a head butt! Cool!"

"Yes, yes, it was lots of fun!" Her face lit up and his steady blue gaze seemed to assess her from top to bottom…whether appraising or devouring, she wasn't sure.

*

"Wow, a French-speaking crazed Phillies fan. How often do you run into one of those?" Cole asked after a few moments.

She tilted her head, her eyes questioning.

Glancing over at the Russian, Cole said, "I heard you speak French to Mr. Asshole, the guy who was bugging you. Where did you learn?"

"In Ukraine schools, we learn English and French."

"Yeah…well, I'm sure you've noticed that in the US we're lucky if we speak intelligible English. So…are you traveling alone this trip?" Cole asked, nodding fervently. *Please say yes. Whisper sexy French things in my ear. Soon.*

"Yes," she said, blushing. "I'm…uh…it is my first cruise." A young woman traveling alone on a cruise was unusual, but there was something steely and challenging in her gaze. "How about you?" she asked.

"I'm…I work on the ship…I'm a crewmember. " He'd considered lying, pretending to be a passenger, but he was always so busy onboard he decided he'd better own up to it right away. In his mind, he was already working out ways to spend time with her, something he generally didn't do. Some of the elite-class passengers had already boarded the ship and would soon notice the attractive single woman among them, so he decided to start monopolizing her time right now.

"Let's see your boarding materials. I'll bet I can get you an upgrade." He pulled her toward the crew entrance, easily carrying her bags, but wishing he could throw *her* over his shoulder as well, caveman-style. She was tall, probably around five-nine, but her height gave him a closer view of her sweet lips and almond-shaped brown eyes. There was a naïve directness about her, a sexy swing to her hips that made him want to stamp MINE on her forehead and learn her secrets.

Jeannette, the ship's Entertainment Director, blocked the entrance. "Hey, Cole, you know you're not supposed to bring passengers through this entrance, sweetheart." Her smile was tight, one hand on her elegantly suited hip, as she looked back and forth from Cole to the girl with an assessing gaze.

"And you, as always, will save my ass and not tell a soul!" Cole winked and put a finger to his lips, choosing to charm the woman rather than piss her off. "See you on deck!"

*

Tania studied the interaction but lowered her eyes while she passed the woman glaring at her. "Don't make enemies for free," her mother had always taught her and she was careful not to challenge this lady. *You never know when you might need a friend.* Besides, she had absolutely no idea where this tall, determined man was taking her.

They were the only ones in the elevator, but he stood close after putting her luggage down. They looked at the floor, very aware of each other and the energy filling the small space. Cole had seemed easy and outgoing a few minutes ago, yet he suddenly seemed at a loss for words.

Her skin prickled when she felt his eyes on her and when she reached up to smooth her hair she dared herself to stare at him. *Wow, this man is…beautiful. The size of him and the way he stands, long legs apart, his muscles busting out of his T-shirt. A tall woman like me appreciates a man like this. Wait.* Any *woman appreciates a man like this, as we've seen from Miz Sweetheart at the door.* The chemistry arcing between them was heating up her skin, and it was obvious from his smoldering gaze that he felt it too.

They heard music, and Cole seemed to change his mind and pressed a different button. Pulling her out into the ship's sun-filled atrium lobby, he stashed her stuff behind a group of musicians playing a dreamy 1940's tune. The gorgeous space was filled with the priority passengers, most of whom were already enjoying flutes of champagne, elegant appetizers and dancing.

Would the German be here? Was her sister here? "I have to go to the ladies' room," she said, breaking his spell and disengaging her heart from the sexy stranger who only had to glance her way to make her forget why she was here. Staying in the shadows on the edge of the atrium, she stopped behind every pillar and studied the crowd. No sign of Oksana or the German. It took her ten minutes to go all the way around the sunlit space and check the room from every angle before she was satisfied. When she returned, Cole was talking and joking with the band leader and some of the musicians. She was hoping the effect he had on her would diminish once she walked away, but instead she felt as light-headed as a lovesick teenager just looking at him.

Grabbing champagne for her, he wound one arm around her waist and gazed into her face while she sipped the bubbly and they swayed to the music. She was sure her sister wasn't in the room, so she felt free to focus on her good-looking new friend. "Well, I guess you know how to get the party started," she said, one eyebrow raised. *You would think I would be wary, after the slimy Russian guy. But no, I couldn't wait for this one to touch me.*

She was kind of amazed at herself, letting him drag her around the ship like this. She'd spent much of her life being careful, being in control, this was...different for her. Fun. *This is what my friends do all the time, relax and see where things go. Fun. Maybe I should try it more often. Or maybe I'm comfortable with this guy, the way he makes me feel. Feelings, fun ---pffft! I have to concentrate, focus...remember why I'm here.*

They danced and talked, kind of flirting and kind of just making each other laugh. He told her a Halloween story about his sister, how when she was little he hid under her bed, yelled "Boo!" and grabbed her ankle. He realized he'd literally scared the piss out of her when his hand came away wet. She'd gotten him back!

His dimple was adorable, and she dug up her own funny story just to see his dimple flash again. "On my first Halloween in America, my new roommate went next door for a while and came back as a zombie vampire! I locked myself in our bathroom, so frightened I was in tears. She got me to open the door a little bit so I could see it was her voice coming out of the zombie vampire."

When she put her glass of champagne down, he took her hand and kissed it, then turning it over so she felt him on the palm, then his lips on her pulse, moving gently up her arm. His kisses were wet, a little tongue, a little teeth, no hurry, no worry who was watching. Tania blushed crimson when he got to the crook of her elbow, giving it a sexy suck and a kiss before he placed her hand behind his neck and drew her in. *Holy cow, this guy knows what he's doing! But what the heck am I doing?! Fun, having fun,* she reminded herself, taking a deep breath, *making a friend, an important friend.*

When Tania drained another champagne, Cole put his face in her hair. His scent was citrus and soap, his chest warm and hard.

Tania wanted to curl up against him and never leave, a tiny yawn escaping despite her best efforts. He rubbed her back, chuckling a little. "I'm sure you're tired from traveling, but I didn't want you to miss this, it's such a great little party, a great way to kick off your cruise. And of course the best thing about dancing is it's an excuse to get to know you better and…to hold you in my arms."

She nodded into his chest when he twined her hair around his fingers. "I like the holding too," she whispered, her voice husky as she snuggled against him and ran her hand up his muscular arm. His thumb was tracing a little circle over a sensitive spot behind her ear. *Mmmmm.* She fought the urge to purr like a love-starved kitten. It was fun being in this new persona, acting like a woman who knew how to flirt and have a good time.

The skin below his sleeve felt good and she let her hand slide up over the sexy tattoo peeking out from under his shirt where his bicep flexed and bunched under her touch. She moved her hands up, tracing the muscles of his shoulders and up to his neck. What she really wanted to do was move her hand *down,* tracing the ridges of his abs, continuing down to his… *He's right. Dancing means holding each other, and holding him is making me dizzy and really, really stupid.*

"Did you fly overnight from New York?" he asked. From the tight, controlled sound of his voice, it seemed her touch was affecting him and he was trying to dial it back a little. When she nodded again, blinking up at him, so tired she could barely speak, he rolled his eyes. "I've taken that flight lots of times. Sucks, doesn't it?"

He looked down in surprise when Tania quivered with laughter. "I was planning to sleep the whole way, but then this man sat next to me and he smelled *bad!*" Now she was laughing out loud, and he joined her. "The flight was so full there were no extra seats, so I couldn't change. In the hospital where I work, we put a dab of deodorant under our noses when something stinks, but I used cherry lip gloss and for a while I smelled only cherries." Cole was nodding and smiling along with her story; he'd obviously been where Tania was, at the point when you're so tired you *lose* it.

"Then the man took off his *shoes and socks*! I thought I would *die* from the smell!" Tania felt his hand move up her back, stabilizing her, while they both laughed so hard he actually needed to hold her up. She looked up at him, at the tears of laughter in his eyes matching hers. Having his strong arms around her was heaven, and dancing with him was the easiest thing she'd ever done, though her sister was the dancer in the family.

As their laughter subsided, his hand moved back down below her waist and pulled her in close again. He was …bossy. When he wanted something to happen, he just made it happen. And much to her surprise, she loved every minute of it. She wondered if he *wanted* her to feel how aroused he was, feel his erection straining against his jeans. Their bodies were close enough that she felt his heat through the thin fabric of her dress.

His breath was warm where he murmured against her neck. "Every person in this room is watching us, wishing they were having as good a time as we are. Every man wants his arms around you like mine are." Leaning back and looking around, she did catch a few people looking and felt herself flush. *People are watching us and I don't care!*

"C'mon, let's really give 'em something to talk about." In a heartbeat, his mouth was on hers, brushing her lips with his with a sweet kiss that begged to be more. She knew she was a little tipsy and a lot exhausted, but when he licked her lower lip he coaxed her lips apart and his tongue slipped inside. *Mmmm…strong, hot lips.* His hands held her hips as they continued to sway to the music. She felt her body pulsing with need, and she couldn't hold back a needy whimper. His tongue explored hers until she had trouble catching her breath and his arms, holding her, were so fierce and confident. Not usually the type to reveal herself in public, she arched into his possessive embrace as if she were drowning. *No, maybe not drowning, maybe lost. Lost in the very best kiss of my life.*

CHAPTER THREE

WHEN COLE WAS absolutely sure his kiss had claimed Tania, in her eyes and in the eyes of pretty much his entire staff, he dragged her off the dance floor and retrieved her bags. He wasn't completely sure *why* he'd kissed and dominated her in such a public way, but it felt right. Important.

Tania was the kind of woman men noticed, a tall, cool, classy-looking girl. Her baby doll lips and red-hot booty gave her an understated sexiness. Cole knew gossip traveled fast on a cruise ship and his message was loud and clear—*this one's mine!*

Back in the elevator, he stood across from her, wanting to keep touching her but determined not to scare her off. *Am I breaking my new no-hookup rule already? Maybe…but this feels different.*

"Where are we going?" she asked, her eyes on the numbers going up. "I thought my cabin was on the second floor."

Saved by the bell when the door opened on Deck Ten, he managed to repeat his lame upgrade story. "Yes, it was, but I…uh…like I said, I'm getting you an upgrade." He picked up her bags and steered her, his hand on the small of her back, through a small lounge with a computer workstation surrounded by four doors. Opening the third one and holding it for her, she entered a small cabin with its own bath and a stunning view of the ocean.

"And where is your room Cole?" She suddenly seemed anxious and unhappy, her hands fluttering at her sides.

"Mine is the other door, the one next to this one."

There was a long, heavy silence. Her fingers pressed against her forehead as if she had a headache. "I am not a prostitute, you know." When she looked up at him, her big brown eyes were filled with tears, her proud shoulders suddenly slack.

Cole hugged her, a stiff, sideways, brotherly hug, not the full-on press he'd wanted to continue since they were dancing. "Why would you say that Tania? Why would I think it?" He struggled to keep from stroking her silky hair, but allowed himself to bask in her fragrance, the sweet, peachy scent of her shampoo.

"Everyone thinks every girl from Ukraine is a hooker, and I'm not one of those." Her accent was more pronounced when she was upset. "I was hoping you don't... think of me that way."

"No, absolutely not, Tania. Really, no. This is a room where I can have people sleep when I have guests on the ship. My sister sleeps in this room when she visits us, for God's sake!" She nodded, happier then, making no move to break free from his arms or contradict him.

She seemed so damned comfortable with his touch and everything he said, he was knocked completely off his game. His thoughts ran away from him while he fantasized about her perfect, creamy skin, her breasts pressing against him, immediately triggering another unbrotherly hard-on he was sure she was aware of.

Okay, so yeah...he and Jack had let a few of their female friends sleep it off in here, and Jack was going to be pissed when he found out Cole brought a relative stranger to stay in their personal quarters. But he couldn't stand the thought of not being able to see her whenever he had a few minutes. They'd just met, but already he'd made her cry and he was obsessed with her. *What the hell?!*

Tania sat down on the bed and patted it for him to sit next to her. He did what she wanted, realizing she was sweet but not shy. *And there's something in her eyes...something I'm feeling too.* She smiled, wiping her eyes and sniffing away her tears. Sitting this close to her, he had to work hard not to let her full lips distract him from what she was saying.

"I'm sorry I cried," she said, "As you know, I did not sleep on the plane, I'm tired." Pausing, then choosing her words carefully, she locked eyes with him. "Will you tell me something, Cole? Are you married or are you with somebody, like the woman who called you sweetheart?"

"I am not married and have never been married, and no, that woman is not my girlfriend. I don't have a girlfriend."

"But you've had *lots* of girlfriends, yes? And they sleep with you because you're beautiful." His eyes widened and he took a deep breath when she took his cap off and ran her fingers through his longish sandy brown hair, twirling the part curled onto his neck around her finger. Now she was focusing on his mouth and when she licked her lips, well...

Cole was completely undone by her gaze, her lips, her touch, but he laughed anyway. "You're trouble, girl. That's what I'm going to call you, Trouble. You follow me and seem to trust me for absolutely no reason, and you're making me nuts. Why did you come with me?"

*

If she told him the whole truth, he'd run. Or worse, he'd throw her out. She was nobody, she had nothing, but she liked him, she... desired him. And she needed his help. Plus, she couldn't take her eyes off of him! Normally a hard-working, serious girl, Tania hadn't been with anyone, hadn't even been to a party in years.

But she was here for a reason. And though she wasn't sure why, she did trust him. She ignored his question, smiled and doubled back to hers.

"I notice you did not answer me about your girlfriends."

"Does it matter to you?" He turned to her and put a little kiss on her shoulder.

She felt the heat coming off him and leaned in a little. "It's yes, then. You've been with many women. And I'm okay about it." She felt the red-hot blush on her face. "Did I say it right?"

He pulled back and watched her face, a smile pulling at his lips. "You're good with it, you're okay about it, yeah." Cole's voice had a rich, deep sound that soothed and thrilled her at the same time. He raised an eyebrow and ran a finger along her chin. "Why?"

Now the heat spread from her face to her neck, and from there to places unknown, ones she would like him to know. "I…uh…I've only had one boyfriend. When I first came to the States, when I spoke very little English. He was a Ukrainian boy, and he was the only one I could talk to. I was with him for a few years, we had sex, but I never…uh…I never…." Her voice trailed off.

Tears burned her eyes because she didn't understand why she was even *telling* him about this. It was like some other woman's voice coming out of her mouth, completely unreal.

He put his hands on her shoulders and ducked, grinning, his gaze more intense. "Soooo…you've never had an orgasm. Is that what you're trying to say?"

Had she really asked this beautiful stranger to show her how to have an orgasm? *What am I doing?! This is insane! This isn't important, isn't why I am here.* But everything about him made her happy to be reckless and young for a change, seeking pleasure with this big, beautiful wolf of a man.

She nodded and looked down, red-faced. "My girlfriends say I've been re-virginized."

Cole nodded, suppressing a laugh 'cause she looked embarrassed. And her blushing was so funny. He couldn't remember ever meeting a women this pretty who was so innocent and easy to read. Beautiful women tended to learn how to mask their feelings, how to deflect unwelcome attention. He pulled back and looked closely at her again, examining her eyes for any trace of hesitation. There was an unmistakable fever in those big brown eyes, a heat.

"I can help you with that. You want me to, right?" He spoke softly, leaning down and smiling when she nodded, remembering her tears when their lips met. This wasn't how he'd imagined it would go; in a sense, she took charge when she asked about his experience with women and then revealed her history. Yet it fit right in with his desire to lead and take care of her pleasure…and enjoy the fact that she seemed to want a sexy experience as much as he did.

Had he reeled her in, or was it the other way around? He was usually firmly in control, and this was different, but he resolved to enjoy it and move the situation forward.

Cole leaned in to let her kiss him, just to be sure this was what *she* wanted. Her kiss was soft, but she smiled and put her hands on both sides of his face and held him close, just as he had done when they were dancing. He licked her full lower lip, and she moaned into him when he forced her lips open. The vibration pulsed through his body and made him want to tear her clothes off and tie her to the headboard. *Whoa, boy, she just told you she's re-virginized.*

"Let me show you." He laid her gently back on the bed, and she arched, curving into his hands. *Holy shit, she's trembling and I haven't even touched her yet.* He unbuttoned her dress, surprised to see the breasts he'd admired were unhampered by a bra. Her nipples were erect and pink and made his mouth water. He was dying to taste them and see if they were as sweet as they looked.

"Damn, girl, you drive me nuts, you are so beautiful." Beautiful, sweet and honest enough to tell him what she wanted. All thoughts flew out the window except for the need to touch her...everywhere.

She shivered, but the way she stretched her long, lean body out, arms open, told him it was a shiver of anticipation, not fear. He growled when he sealed his lips to her mouth again, loving the feel of her tongue exploring his mouth, licking him slowly, like he planned to do between her legs.

"Tania." He murmured her name against her lips, alternately nipping and kissing them while she quivered under his hands. "I have to confess. I've been thinking of all the ways I could make you come since we were dancing."

"So it felt like a...I felt like a...sure thing, is that how you say it?"

Cole reached up and stroked the side of her face. "No. I had no idea how this would go, and you surprised the hell out of me. The only sure thing was... I knew what I wanted."

He rolled and tugged on her tender nipples, triggering another shiver through her body. She gasped and tensed, drawing him in with her sweet sounds during this, his very first intimate touch.

Hoping it was the first of many times, he surrounded one of her nipples with his lips, ran his tongue around it and gave it a little nip. She twitched and wriggled her hips toward him. *Mmmm, she likes a little sting with her pleasure...so, so fucking hot.*

He brought her hand up to roll her nipple between her thumb and forefinger. "It feels good, doesn't it?" Her eyes were open, watching him, and she was responsive, whimpering her pleasure and moving her fingers to her other breast, pulling it and stroking the way he'd done. She opened her legs shamelessly, like she was aching for him, lifting her chest up to him, wanting more, and he wanted to lay her out and fuck her before he exploded.

But he didn't. Raising her skirt, he kissed and licked along the unbelievably soft skin of her thighs and ran his fingers over her panties. "You are so wet, sweetheart. You want me to do this, right?" She nodded, eyes wide, blinking up at him. Pulling her panties down over her feet and tossing them aside, he put his hand between her legs, spreading those lips and looking at her pussy, taking in her juicy pink folds.

"Fuck, you're amazing down here, too." His voice was hoarse while he slid one long, thick finger inside her. She gripped him eagerly, squirming and pushing into his hand. If he still had any doubts about what she wanted, she was shattering them with her body language. When he put another finger inside her, thrusting and twisting in and out and rubbing her clit with his thumb, her sexy little pleasure sounds let him know how turned on she was.

Turned on and freaking hot! She's nearly naked and those brown eyes are watching me finger-fuck her and she's spreading her legs wider... He couldn't help cataloging her reactions because they were kicking his ass, she was so sexy his brain was on fire.

She reached out for him, but he maneuvered the cock straining at his zipper away from her, guiding her hands back up to her breasts. He imagined coming deep inside her, feeling how hot and wet she would be...but he didn't.

The fact that she'd never had an orgasm told him she was afraid or ashamed to touch herself. "It's okay, there's nothing wrong with it," Cole murmured. "People do this, it's a good thing." His fingers circled the entrance to her slit, and he spread the wetness over her pussy and up to her clit while he guided her fingers there, his hand over hers, moving her fingers around again and again, then showing her how to touch her clit, how to massage it and press hard.

They were both sweating a little now, and he fought to push away the persistent image of sinking to the core of her, her sex pulsing around him, feeling her bucking against him.

But it didn't feel right yet. He wanted more time, wanted a next time with her. This first time he wanted to do only what she asked, and watch her experience it.

She was panting and trembling, her hips pleading for release, her toes curled. She seemed confused, in a holding pattern. Something inside her searched for the edge, reaching blindly to jump over the cliff. *Mmmm, next time I'll jump with you, sweet thing.*

"Let me finish you," he whispered, circling his fingers inside her, pressing hard against her cushy g-spot. He heard her gasp when he began licking her wet pussy at the same time, his broad shoulders widening her legs even further. She pitched against him, letting out a choppy cry. He felt the urgent need for his own release building, but focused more on enjoying her taste and keeping track of her breathing. A strangled moan revealed she was ready to come.

He wanted her to still feel him after this was over, think of him and the way he'd touched her.

Suddenly she stiffened, her body bowed, everything tight. She cried out, "Cole, Cole," her hips circling, the tension in her body a silent plea for permission to let go of the sudden, powerful wave rippling from her core.

"Tania, let it go. It's okay, give in to it, it's okay."

And he felt triumphant when she cried out, "OhGodOhGod! Mmmuuuuh!" when her hips lifted and her body went rigid with the intensity of her climax.

"Mmmm, yeah, I've got you," he murmured while he watched her, one hand cradling her head, the other stroking her belly to soothe her while the spasms faded.

It was strange, kind of dark and primitive, the way he felt

when he touched her. Different. When she calmed, he lay next to her, absorbing her tremors, kissing her thighs and belly and pulling down her skirt. Smiling to himself, surprised by his own tenderness, he pressed his face to her damp neck and kissed there before covering her with a blanket.

"Sleep now, Miss Trouble, you're tired, and I have to go to work."

Her brown eyes were huge. "You're leaving now? But I...I want to..."

"I'll see you later. We'll start again." He winked and was gone. And she did fall asleep, his tenderness filling her with warmth...and hope she had found an ally for her secret quest.

CHAPTER FOUR

"HEY GOOSE, NICE outfit!"

"Back atcha, Maverick!" Cole laughed when he spotted his brother, who was decked out in the white dress uniform they both wore to greet the passengers at the Sail-Away Deck Party. It was the usual hat and white jacket with gold buttons and captain's epaulets, but the jacket was shorter, more fitted. And the pants, especially commissioned from Italian designer Brioni, gave a hint of the toned ass and front bulge beneath the starched white fabric.

Their uniforms must have had the desired effect. When they introduced themselves to Ellora Lind, a famous sex therapist who would be lecturing during this cruise, she was almost too flustered to choke out a hello while she looked back and forth from one brother to the other. "Oh! Uh….hello. Uh…how do you…uh…do?" She might be a lady who gave lectures and talked to people for a living, but right then she seemed completely at a loss for words…but the hard-bodied identical brothers often had that effect on women.

Exchanging knowing glances, the Carleton brothers moved on, the ship's photographer following them around, capturing the passengers' surprise when they met their twin captains, and the ladies' delighted smiles while they posed with them.

It was costing SunShips a pretty penny to have two captains instead of the usual one, but they considered it a good investment because of the many television and magazine articles the brothers generated with their good looks and affable charm. Standing taller than anyone around them, the brothers worked the crowd while music played, champagne was passed, and confetti streamed from an air gun on the upper deck. Neither man held a drink, since they never consumed alcohol while they were on duty.

"Sorry, could I talk to you a minute?" Ellora Lind stepped between them, standing on tiptoe so her arms reached familiarly around both their shoulders while the photographer snapped a picture.

"Well, you seem like you're having a better time now," Jack said, reminding Cole of the woman's initial gawky greeting.

She bit her lower lip and looked up at them. "You know you guys are a real mind fuck, don't you?" Her English accent would make even the filthiest comment sound elegant.

"How so?" said Cole, eyebrow raised, letting his arm relax around her waist. He knew exactly what she was asking. They'd been doing their twin hottie routine since they were fifteen. But it was fun to let her dangle, make her say it out loud.

"I'm old enough to be your mother, but I'm not dead. And as you know, I'm a therapist and writer. I'm going to stalk you guys with my mind and soak you up, you're so sexy. What do you want me to call you in my articles?"

"He's Goose and I'm Maverick," said Jack.

"I'm prr-eetty sure those names are taken."

Cole leaned into her and said, "How 'bout Big and Bigger?"

"I like that, which one are you?" she sassed back, and the three of them collapsed in uproarious laughter while the photographer captured all. "Oh, fucking great, it's definitely the new wallpaper on my iPad," she said. "Well, ta, ta, be stalking you around."

He certainly met some interesting people on cruise ships, but

Cole wondered why no one seemed to notice he and his brother were more than party boys. They were also highly trained, experienced mariners, with degrees and certifications in maritime science from the top schools. In addition, they'd earned an excellent reputation for successfully handling passenger and crew situations, what the cruise line called administrative duties.

But in the end he was thankful he and Jack got to hang out together and have each other's backs. They'd been together in the Coast Guard Academy and in the service. They both had hated the lonely job of piloting oil tankers before they landed in this gig. After three years of sailing the Caribbean with SunShips, each of them moving up the ladder from Third, to First, to Chief Officer, they'd both been promoted to Captain and moved together to captain the *Sunset* through routes in Europe and Scandinavia for the past three years.

Even though computers did much of the navigation, an imperative and unbreakable SunShip rule was that the Captain must be on the bridge when the ship was leaving or entering port. Since Jack had conducted the officers' briefing and done the pre-sail checks, Cole rushed to the bridge to actually pilot the enormous ship away from the dock, leaving his brother to answer questions and mingle with the crowd. Still, after a dozen more photos, a couple of passengers asked anxiously who was steering the ship, a definite cue for Jack to go back to his room, take off his fancy uniform and help finish things up on the bridge.

When he got off the elevator, Jack went to the work station in the center of the lounge and entered his pass codes, logging in to record some of the guests' comments from the Sail-Away Party. Passenger feedback was precious, and it was amazing what you'd find out when people had a few glasses of free champagne.

Suddenly a pair of hands covered his eyes from behind and a

woman's low voice said, "Hey, I want to pay you back now. Your room or mine?" Her tone was sexy, an obvious invitation.

"Uh...mine. My room, for sure." He played along, wondering how she'd found this hallway. It wasn't the first time he'd been seduced and pulled into a room by a passenger, just the first time he'd been pulled into his *own* room. His erection swelled against the fitted uniform pants, and he hoped the woman behind him was as hot as her voice.

No problem there. When he stood and turned around, a beautiful young woman in a black slip dress stood smiling at him, her long legs leading to a pair of shiny black high heels. He didn't remember seeing her at the party—and he would've remembered. She held out her hand, linking her long, slim fingers with his when he led her to his door.

"What are you paying me back for?" he asked while he fumbled with his keys, finally getting the door open as she followed him in. He prayed she wasn't a staff member, but he'd met most of the newbies so...what the hell.

"At least tell me your n..." he began, but she laughed and spun him around against the closed door of his cabin, covering his mouth with hers and unbuttoning his jacket before he could ask her name. At times like this, he really loved life on a cruise ship.

"Just kiss me and let me suck your cock," she said in a husky whisper.

Well. In that case, what could a guy do but surrender gracefully?

He felt her breasts under the dress, no bra and probably not much else, the dark fabric in contrast with her stunning pale skin. When she undid his belt, stroking his dick through his pants, he stopped caring who she was or what she wanted to pay him back for and focused on getting both of them naked as soon as possible.

His mouth met hers again in a rush and her tongue stroked his fast and hot.

*

Tania reached around the back of his neck, taking control of the kiss and pulling him in. She felt his smile against her lips while she moved his hands to her shoulders.

Yes, smile handsome man, and see me. Show me a fantasy of me reflected in your eyes. See the me I never knew was here, I want to show her to you. Kiss me too hard and make me come.

He snatched the little straps on her dress and pulled them down past her shoulders, looking down and grinning when her breasts bobbed up, her hard nipples grazing the fabric. Gripping the dress when it snagged on her hips, he tugged it down until it pooled at her feet.

"Wow, you're…you're perfect!" His hungry gaze tightened her nipples even more, and she freed his erection from his boxers, grasping it tightly with both hands, stroking from root to tip, and she held on while he backed her toward the bed. He spun them around and sat on the edge while she climbed onto his lap, and she felt how damp her thong was when she straddled his thighs and pumped his hard, hot cock with her fists.

"Whoa, I can feel you, how wet you are already," he murmured while he steadied her, one broad hand between her shoulder blades, the other cupping her breast, pulling her nipple up and licking, nibbling until she gasped.

She loved being this close to his handsome face with her eyes open, intimate, breathing his breath, biting and licking each other's lips. She'd never done anything as daring and dirty as this, but his sinful kisses made her bold, and the way he sucked on her tongue made her eager to give him what she'd promised.

Like riding a bicycle, she hoped, and slid to the floor to pull his pants down and off his ankles, then fisting him and licking the drops of precum off the tip of his magnificent cock. When his hips jerked, she did it again, this time rolling the head with her tongue and then tracing the ridge from the tip down to his balls. *It's all coming back to me.* A choked cry and sharp intake of breath from above empowered her, and she pulled him into her mouth as far as he could go, bobbing over him, hand stroking his shaft.

But Jack's hand on her shoulder made her rock back and look up at him. He jerked his head at the door behind her and cleared his throat noisily.

*

Cole stood in the doorway, leaning against the frame with his arms crossed. He liked to watch —what man didn't? And watching Tania grip Jack's cock and circle it with her sweet lips made his balls draw up tight. He and Jack had done the sharing thing many times before, and he was usually okay with it, but this time felt…different, somehow. But still sexy as hell.

"Well, holy fuck bro! I see you've met Tania!" Cole beat down a sudden rush of white-hot anger, yet still stared hungrily at the intimate scene before him.

His dick pressed against his pants, announcing how unbelievably turned on he was by the sight of her kneeling there in nothing but her thong and high heels, her long, dark hair loose between her shoulder blades. The room smelled of sex, and she was flushed all over with the slight shine of sweat and desire. He felt an unfamiliar twinge of jealousy. *Jack felt those lips around his dick first, dammit. Wait—why do I feel this way?*

Tania's facial blush, the one he'd chuckled over, was now in full-body view, getting darker by the second and turning her pale skin a reddish-pink from her face to her gorgeous tits to her ankles. Her eyes were the size of plates, the most enormous brown eyes he'd ever seen, as she looked back and forth from Cole in the doorway to his brother sitting above her. "Oh, my God," she groaned, dropping her face into her hands.

Jack's chest was heaving, his expression somewhere between confused and agitated while he struggled to make sense of the situation. "She's a passenger, right? I came back here to change and she came up behind me and started kissing me, said she wanted to pay me back for something."

"And you went with it, is that right brother? Service with a smile?"

*

"I can't believe this!" Tania moaned again, taking off her shoes and crumpling her dress against her chest in a vain attempt to cover up. It felt weird to be here, peeking through her fingers at these two beautiful men, mirror images of each other. She'd had fantasies about men like this after seeing a movie with her friends, and she would imagine herself with the handsome hero.

And here she was, in real life, with *two* of them. But it didn't feel like this scene would have a happy ending, the end she'd wanted it to have. Sitting back on her heels, the tears streaking her cheeks, she looked up at them and said, "You guys are brothers? Twin brothers?!" She let the tears roll for a few moments, and the men nodded and remained still, as men will do when a woman is crying.

But the more she thought about what had happened, the angrier she got. She leaned back with her hands on her hips and then raised an elegant long arm with a finger pointing right at Jack. "You are an asshole, dammit!" she snarled. "You should have told me who you are, that you didn't know me!" Then she turned and hissed like an angry cat at Cole, pointing both hands at his chest, "And you! You should've told me you had this brother!" Then she slapped both hands against her thighs and crawled over to the edge of the bed, sat down and stared at the floor. It seemed the real world had arrived to drag her back down when she'd barely escaped.

The tears fell again, angry tears, her voice despairing. "This is it. I've come so far, worked so hard to get here, and now I've ruined everything. *Fini*, I'm done! I pulled those extra shifts, emptied a hundred bed pans, and now I've failed, I have…blown it, as my friends would say. Literally, I guess." She blushed again, looking at Jack. "Isn't it called a blow job?" Jack's lips twitched suspiciously when he nodded and looked away.

It wasn't until she rose to her feet, ready to put on her dress and vanish, that she saw them both shaking, clearly trying to suppress laughter. And she saw something she hadn't expected to see in their eyes—not anger, but… interest, desire. They weren't angry. As a matter of fact, when she saw the smile tugging at the corners of Cole's mouth, she also saw his gaze definitely travel along her body, moving down, and he licked his lips when he got to her erect nipples.

The nearness of two of the best-looking men she'd ever seen, two sets of searing blue eyes looking expectantly at her, sent a hot rush through her. She sat down again, her legs weakened by an achy, heavy feeling between them when she realized the question hanging in the air. *Do they really want to…share?*

"This is something you…do? Both of you at the same time with a girl?" she asked, searching their eyes.

"Yes." They both answered, smiled, then laughed at the same time. Cole stepped closer and closed the door behind him. Jack, his shirt closed but his erection jutting out below, let his thigh touch hers on the bed. He put his hand on her thigh, stroked it, and said "I really am sorry. I should have tried harder to figure it out, but you were…I mean, what guy wouldn't…" he stopped, sputtering. "You get what I mean, right?" His smile was sly, as if she was in on a joke.

Tania leaned forward, elbows resting on her knees, resting her chin on her hand, puzzled. Now she'd gone from angry to curious. She was right at eye level with the bulge in Cole's pants, and the air was sizzling with tension. *I seduced the wrong guy…kind of. I… did those things to a stranger. And I would have done a lot more. So now what?*

"But I don't get it," she said. "The men I've met don't like sharing even French fries, much less a woman." Her foot tapped nervously in the shiny high heels while she searched one breathtaking face, then the other.

A vision of what they might do began playing in her mind, an image of the three of them naked, and her body responded instantly, her panties even wetter than before, and her nipples standing painfully at attention. An involuntary blast of heat flushed through her, and she imagined watching herself, inhabiting a spirit on the ceiling who was watching Tania have wild, freaky sex with two men she'd just met.

Jack's answer was characteristically short, his voice low. "It's hot to watch."

Cole's intense stare followed the flush from her nipples to her mouth to her eyes. "What you're imagining right now, that's what's hot. Both of us pleasuring you at the same time, your whole body loose because we've made you come so many times." His smile reassured her. "I know it sounds strange. But have you ever thought…I mean, can you imagine it?"

His words hung in the air, tantalizing, and she answered. "I've never done…I mean except what I told you. This is way beyond… only my craziest girlfriend has done this. But I know you can…show me." Her voice shook and her hands trembled when she said it. *Am I fucking nuts? This is stupid, maybe the stupidest thing I have ever said.*

Jack grinned, the first to realize she was saying yes.

There was a buzz in the room and the excitement passing between the brothers made Tania's heart race. *It's embarrassing how much I...how I want this. How could I want this?*

Cole pulled her up to her feet and crashed into her mouth, his kiss deep. She shivered when she felt Jack's lips on her neck, one hand cupping her breast and the other stroking and squeezing her ass.

Closing her eyes, she felt four worshiping hands explore her secret places, the soft whisper of skin against skin punctuated by low murmurs of appreciation. Hot, hungry mouths followed the hands, kissing and licking, sucking and nipping as if she was an exotic dessert. Swaying a little, she spread her legs to steady herself and opened her eyes to be sure she wasn't dreaming.

Jack took the sides of her thong and slid it down her legs until she stepped out of it. Her legs were shaking—her whole body, in fact.

Cole caressed her shoulders, soothing her, and she looked in his eyes. "You're nervous. Do you want to do this?"

She nodded, eyes moist, throat tight.

"We won't hurt you."

"I'm okay," she whispered, looking down, cheeks flaming. She'd never, ever allowed herself to be this vulnerable and it was...liberating somehow!

Jack had stripped off his shirt and pulled her down facing away from him on his lap, his dick between her ass cheeks, his legs spread wide, taking hers wide with them. He pushed his hands under her arms and covered her breasts, stroking around and across them and down to her slit.

Cole undressed slowly, his chest tan and muscular, broad shoulders, perfect pecs, his sexy biceps flexing when he threw his clothes over a chair. She felt like a goddess because he watched her, his eyes hot as she wriggled and sighed from his brother's expert hands, her pussy spread wide for him.

"Keep your eyes open, I want to watch your eyes when you come this time Tania," he said, nodding at Jack while he unzipped his pants. Heat flushed her cheeks at the tone of his voice, so commanding and sexy. She gasped when the rigid length of Cole's erection pushed against black briefs, his tight, muscular thighs below. Circling her clit, Jack's strokes got intense and rhythmic, making little wet sounds as she began whimpering.

She felt herself drowning in sensation, only to fall further when Cole knelt and put first one and then two fingers in her opening, licking her nipple, then closing his lips around first one then the other. The feel of it, the awareness of urgent hands and hot breath in front and behind, built a wave inside her too big to contain.

She jerked and let out a soft cry, her orgasm short, made more intense by staring in Cole's eyes. When he pulled his fingers out and put them to his lips, tasting her, she shivered. It seemed so…kinky. But when he stepped out of his boxers, his cock long and hard with a little curve to it, she felt her pussy clutching with anticipation. His penis was as perfect as the rest of him.

"People, I'm dyin' here," Jack said, his voice strained, interrupting their stare-down. "Remember me, the guy who was getting her attention before?"

Shaking herself out of her sex coma, she got off his lap, turned, and held his cock in both hands, kneeling between his legs. Jack pulled her with him as he slid back on the bed, but as he was positioning her to straddle him, Cole pulled her hips to the side. Jack shot a questioning look at his brother.

"She…uh…it's been a while for her. We have to be careful." Cole's voice shook when he kissed and stroked her backside. While he touched between her legs, spreading her honey, Tania heard herself moan…and didn't give a damn.

"Sure. Sure, got it." Jack's eyes were blazing, his expression agitated. "Like I *wouldn't* be careful bro," he said, his voice flat.

Still, he took it down a notch and kissed her, stroking Tania's hair and speaking softly in her ear, telling her how many times she was going to come, and come hard, while Cole caressed her butt as he stood behind her at the edge of the bed. She licked her lips, waiting on all fours when Cole's long dick teased her, sliding back and forth across her wet opening. Slipping a condom on, he pressed slowly into her, one inch at a time. His restraint was driving her insane.

She spread her legs wider, opening herself to him and pleading, "Pllleeeaase. Please, Cole." He gripped her waist and entered her all the way this time, his hips and balls against her as he stilled, holding her tight to him. Her breath left her in a sharp burst when the fullness and pressure hit her brain. As her head flew up and she arched and pushed back, she turned and gave him a fuck-me look, wanting to give him every bit of the pleasure he had given her.

The bed dipped on the other side when Jack knelt and eased himself closer to her. "Your mouth is so sweet. Taste it, beautiful," Jack said, kneeling near her, taking his cock in his fist and stroking it while he spread his other hand wide behind her head. His tone was somewhere between a command and a request. "Suck it…," he said, "yeah, yeah," as he angled his way into her mouth, holding her steady. His hand wrapped around his base steadied him while he moved in and out of her mouth, almost as sweet as Cole's sexy rhythm behind her.

She wrapped her tongue around Jack's thick erection when he

went deep, hitting the back of her throat, then released him and licked his pulsing vein while he pulled almost all the way out. Circling her tongue around the tip, she gave him a wicked glance. She was feeling her power, remembering she used to be good at this, used to kind of enjoy it. Noticing his eyes focused intently on her, she sucked faster, enjoying Jack's moan and Cole's erotic sounds, his whispered encouragement, their skin slapping. Next stroke, as Jack reached deep, she took him even further, opening her throat. Behind her, Cole's fingers were spread out on her ass cheeks, gripping her tightly and probably marking her. Imagining it, wanting those red marks, she shook uncontrollably.

"Fuck it, she's swallowing me!" Jack groaned out in pleasure. She saw him fighting for control, abs pulled in tight. He jerked his hips back and forth, his fingers threaded through her hair, moving in her mouth while his expression got more fierce and intense. Pushing back frantically against Cole, she tensed her pussy, her lips, her behind, her whole body. She was desperate to have more of her around him, to have more of him in her, to feel every inch of him inside and out.

"Ohhh, hot and so tight," Cole hissed, his voice low and rough.

This was definitely the most insane thing she had ever done, but she felt beautiful, strong. Her old boyfriend had been quiet during sex, not putting his feelings out there. But *she* was doing this, driving them both over the edge with her body, her passion. Their moans and strained cries were because of her, *she* was making them as crazy as they were making her.

The thought made something tighten in her belly, a rush that kept growing, spreading like fire from the feel of one cock pushing deep in her mouth to the other one filling her pussy. When Cole reached around and stroked her clit, she gasped.

"Oh shit," he said, "I…she's so tight I feel her twitching around me. Come, ohhhh Trouble, come for me!" Tania fell to pieces for the third time in her life, her body shaking with an orgasm that made her go limp.

Still, Jack's scent and his hand stroking her cheek, the taste of him lingering in her mouth—they wound her back up immediately. His hand tightened under her chin. "Stay with me, baby, stay with me. I'm almost there." She took a deep breath through her nose and her cheeks hollowed when he raised his hips to slide in and out of her lips. "Beautiful, you're so fucking beautiful," he growled as his fingers tangled in her hair, bracing her while Cole spread his fingers on her hips and hammered into her from behind. She came alive again, wiggled and moaned around Jack's thick cock and bucked against Cole's thrusts, not sure if she wanted more or less or harder or…

*

"Dammit! Oh fuck!" Jack cried out when his hot semen hit the back of her mouth. He tried to ease back, but she held him in, the heat and suction of her mouth around him intensifying his orgasm. Watching her breasts swing from the force of Cole's assault on her cunt, he was breathing hard as he calmed down. A little awkward when he nuzzled her hair, he whispered "Didn't think I'd lose it so fast. You are amazing."

*

"Uhhmmm…."she said, seemingly incapable of actual speech. She licked her lips, closing her eyes and arching her back, pleading with Cole, saying his name. Cole responded with a growl when she called his name, *his* name. He powered into her, his hips slamming against her, his hands marking her ass the way she seemed to want it, making her feel possessed, consumed…claimed.

"Touch yourself, Tania, touch yourself like I showed you," he panted, "I want you to come with me." And the minute she did she lost it again, coming in waves this time, moaning through gritted teeth, and he jerked against her, both bodies spasming, both voices crying out, as Cole's thrusts grew slower, his touch gentler, stroking her hips but not coming out when his body came down over hers. They lay there, spent, and Cole slid the condom off, then spooned her.

Jack ran a finger gently over the curve of her jaw. He was hard as granite again from watching them come, and he looked at Cole, desire and a question in his eyes. Cole didn't move at first, then she felt him shake his head no against the pillow.

But a strange daring flowed through Tania, and she sat up, reached out and started stroking Jack's meaty dick, feeling her power and wanting more, wanting another orgasm, another experience. She had no idea where this brazen seductress had come from, but a force she couldn't explain possessed her, an urge to make up for a life lived too cautiously for too long.

Ignoring her move toward Jack, Cole asked, "Have you eaten, Tania? Are you hungry?" It seemed like he wanted to delay, to make her think before proceeding, and the truth was she *hadn't* eaten.

And she was suddenly hungry, keen to eat like she used to be when she was a kid, working on her grandparent's farm. "Yes, I am hungry," she said and smiled shyly. They laughed and Cole pulled some clothes on to go out in the hall and get food he kept in a fridge near their workstation.

Jack lay on his side on the bed, his head propped on his hand. "Ever had anal sex?" he asked her.

She felt her cheeks blaze when he moved her hand back onto his erection, and she nodded, eyes wide. "Did you like it?" he asked, his voice casual but his eyes intent on hers.

"N-n-n…o," she answered, remembering and going still on him. "It…he…hurt me. He insisted on trying it, my boyfriend, and he hurt me." She shrugged. "I guess for me it's an exit, not an entrance."

Jack let out a long breath, panting a little when she began to stroke him again. In a low voice, almost a whisper, he said "It can be really hot if you do it right, and we would do it right for you. You believe me, don't you?"

She nodded, looking down, her face and body hot with embarrassment and…*desire*? Another bolt of heat shot through her, and her body throbbed with an outrageous craving.

"Did he use lubricant?" Jack asked. "Were you turned on first? Did he prepare you?"

"Prepare her for what?" Cole asked when he shoved the door open with his foot and walked in with a beautiful tray of yogurt and berries. His shoulders relaxed when he saw Tania pull her hand away from Jack.

"Tania's considering the idea of having both of us inside her at the same time, but she had a bad experience with anal."

"Is that so?" Cole set the tray down in front of her, and she nodded, eyes wider, face even hotter than before.

Did I just say yes? Was I nodding to the bad experience or the other idea? Did he say both of them in me, both their giant cocks in me, at the same time? Who am I? Who is this dirty girl inside me? How can I be scared and turned on at the same time? And yet there was no denying that her nipples were hard again, and her pussy wet.

"Sooo…," Jack said to Tania, prompting her to continue the conversation.

"You're embarrassing her, back off." Cole spit out, sensing her panic and glancing at Jack. "Let her eat and think it over."

Jack shot his brother another irritated expression. "Are we in the same room here, bro? We're talking, she's telling us what she wants!"

"It's okay, I'm okay," Tania said, touching Jack's thigh, nodding at Cole. The berries tasted juicy, fresh and delicious, and the tang of the yogurt was intense on her tongue, her mouth probably as over-sensitive as the rest of her body. It felt like she was waking up from a long sleep, needing to stretch and taste everything around her. Since she'd been so focused on school, her friends, and her career the last few years, the passionate life had passed her by at a million miles an hour. Now she'd jumped in with both feet. And maybe with both... *Damn, I can not believe this is me! But, but...*

Knowing she was flushed scarlet from the roots of her hair to the tips of her toes, Tania ate quietly, remembering a college girl-friend of hers who'd done this, who'd bragged about having two guys inside her at the same time. "Didn't it hurt?" she'd asked back then, remembering her own painful experience with anal.

"Oh, my God, no! Well, it stung at first, but then it was incredible," the woman said, her eyes dreamy. Suddenly Tania had a now-or-never feeling, a tight, clutching sensation zinging her nipples again and another rush from her pussy, a convulsion of want, want, want. She was flexing inside, clenching the muscles she'd loved having close around his cock. *His...Cole's cock. Was he really into this?*

"You wouldn't hurt me, right? If I told you to stop, you would stop? Is it possible?"

"Of course, sweet thing. But you don't have to. You really don't."

She nodded yes. Looked at Cole, touched Jack...she knew she had to touch Jack to get his attention. And she licked her lips and nodded again. *I said yes, I actually said yes! Shit!*

*

Demanding her honesty with his piercing gaze, Cole was twisted up about it himself. It was fucked up to share her this way and yet mind-blowing at the same time. Those big brown eyes, feverish with desire, tipped up at the corners, those long legs and her gorgeous heart-shaped ass. Dear God, it was the first thing he'd noticed, and he wanted to feel her pucker around him, tight as a fist. She was a fit, slender woman, not much extra flesh on her except that sweet butt with its little jiggle. *It was obvious some idiot boyfriend hurt her, damn him to hell, whoever he was!*

To be sure, Cole said, "You have to say it, baby, you have to say it out loud."

"Yes. I'm saying yes. Do the things he said, the lubricant and… the things he said."

Cole fought his reaction, feeling like a schoolboy trying not to smile. *She's a nurse, for fuck's sake, she knows about lubricant. Okay, then. She wants to do this.* He moved the tray to a table and helped her stand, cupping her face while he kissed her, tasting the sweet berries she'd eaten. At first she shivered, her shoulders tense, but when he slid his warm hands down her back, circling and massaging her, she relaxed into him.

"See how this feels, baby, get on hands and knees and show me your amazing ass." Again, she climbed back onto the bed and did exactly what he said. It was bizarre, how natural it seemed to be for her. His brother lay on the bed underneath her, his lower legs hanging off the end, his hands playing with her breasts and her clit. When she leaned back, Jack rolled on a condom and pushed inside her with one strong thrust. "Oh, my God!" she whimpered, and Cole knew Jack was pleasuring her breasts with lips and fingers. She moaned and seemed to let go of the last of her tension, her breath coming in little puffs.

Her body tensed when Cole rubbed the slippery lube around her anus, massaging the forbidden opening, knowing she was a virgin there. A pleasure virgin. No man had ever made her feel the way he was going to make her feel when he penetrated her this time. He poured more lubricant on his palms and rubbed them together, warming the lube, and this time he put one finger in her, just a little, and she moaned. Shit, she was tight, so tight, squeezing him out.

"Relax, beautiful. Breathe out, a big breath. Now here's the secret." He took a deep breath himself, then out with a rush. "Bear down inside, and then push out. Down and out. Try it." *Damn, she opened to me, I can feel it! She did what I said. Fucking awesome.* He'd felt the technique used before but never thought to put it into words. The stakes were higher here, apparently.

And he put two fingers in this time, circling inside, willing her muscles to relax, reeelaaax. When he put three fingers in she fought it, writhing and panicking at the burning feeling. *Shit, I'm losing her!* Then suddenly, she bore down again, relaxed. Her soft groans brought his dick to a new level of excruciating hardness and, combined with the tantalizing view of her round, white ass…well, it was a good kind of overload.

"Oooohhhhmmmm!" her low moan was so hot, so needy, Cole almost lost his load right then and there. It was that killer low voice of hers, it…did it for him.

Jack was making her forget the assault from behind, using his teeth on her nipples, shaking her with his thrusts and swiveling his dick to push against her g spot while his thumb played with her clit. Sweating, his abs straining, he was tuning her up for the mind-bending sensation coming her way.

Cole sheathed his cock with a condom and lubricated it, his skin on fire, flinching from his own touch, pressing the tip of his cock into the tight pucker. He stroked her back, comforting her, leaving a little trail of goose bumps.

"Do it, Cole, you tease me," Tania choked out.

Still, his jaw was set while he penetrated one inch at a time, withdrawing and thrusting in a little more with each stroke. She spread her legs wider, bearing down and surrendering to the intense feeling of having her pussy and her ass penetrated at the same time.

"I'm coming all the way in now," Cole's voice was tight, and Jack was kissing her and stroking her soaked pussy with his hand while continuing to move inside her. When Cole thrust in, she gasped. He knew the full feeling was battling with the orgasm Jack was building with his fingers. Her eyes flew wide open and both men went completely still, giving her time to adjust.

Cole was balls-deep in her now, stretching her, and her body quivered, trying to escape the pressure. Leaning into her, he caressed her, murmuring praise and encouragement. "You're amazing, baby. Let it go, let us do the work."

*

Tania forgot the pressure when Jack bit her nipple again, hard, and the heat in her belly intensified as she came completely apart, screaming this time, slick with sweat, squeezing and pulling on them while they found themselves lost in a sea of sensation. Jack milked every last shiver of pleasure out of her, continuing to move his fingers on her wet flesh.

When she caught her breath, she realized how tight, how full she was, and she wondered what they were feeling, the two throbbing cocks filling her, stroking her, surrounding and filling her with friction and sounds and tastes that electrified her senses. She was too full to speak, full of excitement and emotion, not to mention two of the most gorgeous men on God's earth. Cole held her hips steady and the men began to slide in and out, taking turns, shaking her whole body with the force of their penetration.

Tania looked down at Jack's face, savage and clenched like a fist, his blue eyes blazing as he pounded into her, and felt the familiar tingle when arousal clenched in her belly again, thinking, *Can I really be coming again this soon?!* She thought she would die of insane wickedness, loving the hell out of Cole's hands fisting her hair, arching, pushing her breasts forward for Jack to slap, SLAP!

And I love it, I love the sting on my skin, love that he picks a different spot each time. Oh fuck, oh fuck! Beyond shocked at the white-hot pleasure she was experiencing, she let everything else go except taking it, feeling it, surrendering to it. It was driving her mad as she pictured herself stuffed full, swollen and sensitive.

Tania couldn't move herself at all, but she felt like the most powerful woman on earth, wrenching those moans and shivering cries from two powerful, imposing men. She clenched her soaked slit and ass tightly while she groaned, spasming around them, totally giving herself over to her orgasm when Jack stroked into her from below. She trembled with unexpected pleasure when he bumped against something deep inside her while she pushed her tight pucker up toward Cole.

*

"Hell, yeah, oh yeah!" Jack fell over the edge, screaming out his release, collapsing onto the bed with his hands cupping her breasts while Cole continued driving into her from behind. Opening his eyes, Jack stared up at her, at her body quivering, eyes flashing, her breathing coming in ragged bursts. "You…are so hot," he said in a strained voice when he stroked her face and rolled away. *And so into my brother.* He stripped off his condom, smiling while he dressed. He wanted to tell her again how amazing she was, but she and Cole were in their own little world.

*

Cole's hands were on Tania's neck, her shoulders, stroking her everywhere. He rolled her over on her side, pulling her knees up almost to her chest. Spooning her from behind, he fucked her ass like a wild man, loving her little pleasure/pain sounds, reaching his hand between her legs and stroking her hypersensitive clit. He molded himself against her, his grip tight, sliding his lips up her neck, her muscles clamping him so tightly he thought he'd lose it immediately. The strongest, strangest feeling overwhelmed him, a feeling of never wanting this to end.

"I wanted to be this close to you, feel you everywhere before I came" he growled. But he still fought it, holding her tightly, telling her how beautiful she was, and reaching his hand in, grinding into her wet slit until she let it go again, her head thrown back, pulsing against his fingers and his cock and calling his name. He was right behind her, roaring, biting her shoulder and leaving his passionate mark there as he continued to stroke into her, fast, deep and hard. Almost at the point of pain when he finally climaxed, he collapsed on the bed beside her. Pulling a blanket over them, he was still there, inside her, holding her to him when they both passed out. Jack was already asleep down the hall, his alarm set for 5 am.

CHAPTER FIVE

L E HAVRE, FRANCE was a beautiful, modern harbor, so beautifully laid out it was easy to dock the huge ship well before 7 am, but Jack still ran through a checklist in his mind while he rushed, alone, up to the bridge. He'd wanted to wake Cole as usual but didn't, knowing the gorgeous Ukrainian was probably still asleep in his arms. Unlike his brother, Jack never wanted to stay in bed with a lady after sex, it was too…personal. Intimate? Messy? Whatever.

"Maverick, my man, did you sleep well?" Cole was humming, already hustling around the bridge, obviously in a fine mood for 5:10 am.

"Kind of," Jack grunted. Never much of a morning person, he grabbed a cup of coffee and stirred it absent-mindedly. "What, no chop-busting? And…I'm surprised you're so chirpy, asshole. Thought you'd still be cuddling with Tania."

"Yeah, we were up pretty late. For a very amazing reason, luckily." Cole smiled to himself but didn't make eye contact with his grumpy brother, not really wanting to discuss Tania. Yet.

"Amazing. Fucking mind-blowing," Jack agreed. "I feel like maybe I dreamed it, like she's too good to be true, you know?" The lack of eye contact between the brothers spoke volumes. "I gotta say though, Cole. I wonder…why would somebody like her—she's smart, hot—why would she work so hard to come on a damn cruise?

You know, working private-duty nursing, emptying bed pans, like she said. That's some heavy shit, pardon the pun. Why would it even be on her radar? It's weird, don't you think?"

Cole didn't give a damn. She had walked into his life and lit it up like a Christmas tree. *And yet…damn Jack, he was right, it was strange. Fucking killjoy.* "Uh…I hear you. Let's see how it goes. I'm renting a car and driving to Omaha Beach with her today. Any problem if I leave you in charge and go be a tourist?"

They both knew he might be asking for more than the day off, but Jack waved him away and said, "Of course not, go!" The other officers were now buzzing around the bridge, making debarkation announcements and plans for loading cargo.

*

Tania had pretended to be asleep when Cole rolled out of bed at 4:30. She had seen the monograms on their jackets saying "Captain" and knew they had major responsibilities. She was thrilled in the middle of the night when Cole pulled her close and whispered he was taking the day off to spend it with her. Part of her wondered if he genuinely liked her or was only staking his claim to be competitive with his brother. That kind of thing happened between siblings sometimes.

She'd let this outrageous thing occur last night and the thought shocked her…again. Did they truly understand she'd been swept away, that she'd never, ever done anything like it before? Or did they *know*, because they often led women down that sensual path? She wasn't sure which reaction she preferred. Did Cole realize she hadn't done it lightly, that in the moment, for him, she'd been desperate to make up for her mistake?

She wasn't kidding herself, though. A guy like Cole would move on at the end of the trip, regardless of what happened between them over the next ten days. He might help her with her sister, he might not. Maybe he couldn't get involved. Tania wasn't naïve enough to think she was more than a pleasant affair for him. And there was another issue, another sad secret she kept close to her heart.

But she resolved to enjoy every minute in his arms, planning to remember it late at night when she was alone again, getting ready for an early shift at the hospital.

*

Tania was glowing with excitement when she and Cole walked by the fishmongers at the harbor in Le Havre, asking in French about the exotic seafood on display. It'd been a long time since Cole had gotten off the ship and acted like a tourist, and it felt like the right move with Tania by his side. She handled the rental car negotiation with the French agents, and laughed when he ground through the gears, admitting sheepishly that he hadn't driven a stick in a while.

Gracious but resigned in defeat, he pulled over. While she walked around to take the wheel, she made a sweeping gesture. "Ha, passenger alert! The great captain who steers your ship the size of a football field can't get this little Citroen out of the parking lot!"

Okay, that's embarrassing, but her laugh is so great, maybe it's worth it. Cole had *never* let anyone else drive except his brother, but it was cool to lean back and watch her. He was impressed with the way she expertly maneuvered the car in a tight three-point turn, wound through the narrow cobblestone streets, and flew over the magnificent Pont de Normandie, the beautiful cable bridge to the Normandy beaches. He was fascinated by her unrestrained joy at the sights and sounds of little villages, vineyards, and sheep farms. Her husky voice singing along with the French pop songs on the radio made him want to eat her alive, but he decided to stick with a neck massage.

When he massaged the velvet skin on her long, elegant neck, she pushed back into this hand, wanting more, purring like a cat. "When I was in school, the kids made fun of my neck, called me *zhyrafa*, the giraffe. The boys didn't like me because I was taller."

"Their loss, my gain," he said, expanding the massage to her shoulders. His smile was crooked as he considered putting his hands under her clothes while she was driving. It was weird the way he couldn't help touching her whenever they were together, felt compelled to mess with her body no matter what was happening or who was watching.

"What?" she asked, glancing at him. "What are you looking so tricky about? My grandmother used to tell us a story of the cat who swallowed the bird, and you look like the cat."

"I was imagining…touching you while you're driving. I'd enjoy it." He grinned and put one hand on her thigh. "And we tell a similar story, about the cat who swallowed the canary."

She gasped and then the blush started again, first on her chest, and then it spread in both directions, up into her neck and face and down through her shoulders and arms. "That is …hot." She exhaled sharply. "I…I think maybe I should pay attention to driving right now," she stammered. "You're bad. You make me…I'm hot all over right now!"

He crossed his arms and laughed softly, not wanting to embarrass her. "Okay, Miss Trouble. Hands off for now. But do you know what it does to me when you blush the way you just did?"

She took a quick glance at the erection straining his jeans to the breaking point. "Uh, I think I know, but I still have to drive." Her voice was breathy and full of sexy promises. Smiling while she turned back to watch the road, she said, "But maybe later, okay?"

It was confusing the way he wanted to touch her and fuck her and be with her all the time. Cole's nature was to be in charge, to make things go the way he wanted them to go. *Best to start right now, Jack be damned.* "Speaking of which…umm," Cole sat up straighter and cleared his throat. "How do you feel about last night? Was it good, or did we scare you?"

Still keeping her eyes straight ahead, Tania nodded, and said hoarsely, her voice shaking, "You scared shit out of me, but not the way you would think." She'd lapsed into her accent a little, pronouncing it "sheet."

"Ooooh-kaaay." He was trying to keep it light, wary of messing up whatever this thing was between them. Currently his plan was to do the dating thing in reverse – *first we had hot sex. Next, we'll date and get to know each other.* Now he wished he could take his question back and just enjoy the day.

There was a long silence. Her hands tightened on the wheel when she choked out, "When I saw you standing there and I was with your brother, I was scared that I messed it up with you, and I … when you…I can't stop thinking about it. You were gentle, and…strong. I never felt such pleasure. I never felt someone care for me and also make me…make me be like someone else, someone brave and special."

"Pull over." Cole said softly, stroking her cheek when he noticed the tears welling in her eyes. When they were safely on the shoulder, Cole put his arms around her and held her as close as the gearshift allowed, one hand pulling her close, the other rubbing her back while he whispered in her ear.

"You *are* someone special, how the hell can you not know it?" *She really has no idea how beautiful and sexy she is, how can that be?* He felt her nod and held her for a while longer, rubbing her back until he felt her body relax. Every time he felt he was moving things forward, she would say something so honest and out of the blue he was blown away. He decided to copy her gonzo style and go for it.

Cupping her face in his hands, he gazed into her eyes. "You are so special that I don't want to share you, not with my brother or anyone else. Is it okay with you?"

She nodded, stronger this time, and said, "I would like that." Tania paused, choosing her words. "But I'm not sad that it happened. For me it wasn't hard, because I pretended he was you. And it was...exciting, being with you and you." Laughing, she added, "Maybe one of the most exciting things of my life. But with you, things are always exciting, right?"

Now that she had him laughing, she threw him a curveball question. "Why *did* you share me with him?"

Cole took a deep breath and slid his hands down her arms, still holding her tightly. "When I saw you there, so damn sexy, kneeling in front of my brother...I...my brain just shut down. Part of me knew you thought he was me, but I was jealous of him, I would have done anything to have you. I swear I wasn't trying to trick you, I should've told you I have a twin, and I would've gotten around to it. I was a fool to let it happen. But I wanted you so badly and things just...moved forward." He blew out a breath. "Does any of this make sense?"

She thought a minute and then seemed to brighten. "A-okay!" she said, her eyes still damp from laughing so hard after almost crying, and she gave him a thumbs-up. "I heard A-okay in a movie once! It's from the '80's." She put her hands resolutely on the wheel now, looking ahead. "Should we go now? We have to go fast to be back in time for the ship, right?" He nodded, smiling, and she careened back onto the highway, passing cars right and left until they left the highway for the little villages of Normandy.

Once they passed the Peace Museum in Caen, they began seeing British, French, and American flags displayed on the quaint French homes and businesses in tribute to those who fought to protect and save this beautiful countryside and the world on June 6, 1944—the D-Day invasion.

"Did you want to stop at any of the other beaches?" he asked, curious to understand her single-minded focus on Omaha Beach, the "American beach," and cemetery.

"No, you'll see," she said while they parked and walked along the top of the cliffs. The beach was to their right, and a gardener was working on a flower bed to the left.

"These flowers are beautiful," Tania told the gardener. "Thank you for your hard work."

"Are you Americans?" he asked, dusting off his apron when he stood.

"Yes." They both answered, and laughed.

"Well, thank you, then, *monsieur et mademoiselle!* Thanks to you for my freedom," he said, and he put his hand over his heart and bowed.

It was a lovely, heartfelt gesture, and added to the emotional impact as they rounded a corner and saw over 9,000 white crosses and stars of David in the breathtaking American cemetery. Tears sprang to both their eyes and they looked at each other, each surprised to see the other was so moved.

"You're an American citizen? Good for you!" Cole was surprised at every turn by her determination.

"I filled out my citizenship papers the day after I arrived and started school. Before then, I thought I owed it to Ukraine to come back after school and work, since they paid for my scholarship. But the first day of nursing school, I found out the money was from a U.S. foundation."

The beautiful sunny day contrasted with the somber mood which had descended on her when they reached the cemetery. They walked along slowly, holding hands, as much to support each other as to connect.

"Do you think they knew they might die, or does each man think he will be the one to survive?" Tania mused while they walked down the center of the cemetery, not sure if there was an answer to her question. "We all work hard, but we don't have to give what these men gave on that day, do we? If a person doesn't feel pride and respect in this place, they have no heart."

Cole stopped at a grave marked with his last name, Carleton, wondering if they might be related somehow. "My grandfather was in the Navy in the Pacific during the war. He said during battle you don't think about dying, you're more concerned with the guys around you, and taking care of your friends and the guys in your unit you're responsible for. I think it was his way of telling us how important it was for Jack and me to look out for each other."

Looking at a piece of paper she'd taken out of her pocket, Tanya walked through the rows of crosses, counting. She stopped in front of one of the crosses and stood very still. When he caught up with her, Cole read the name on the cross – Vasyl Shevchenko, Sergeant, June 20, 1944, 29th Infantry, Maryland.

"Vasyl was my father's half-brother. He went to America to become an engineer and ended up in the army. He survived this invasion, but was killed later in the town of Saint-Lô."

"You must be proud. And sad, too."

"Yes. We are." A tear rolled down her cheek. "He left for America long before we were born, but my sister and I used to pretend Vasyl was our father, because our real father left us. If Vasyl was our father, at least his not being there would make sense. We didn't know anything about him except our mother's stories." She wiped her eyes again and said, "Sorry I'm so emotional these last few days. I am not usually like this."

"And where is your sister now?" Cole asked.

"She…uh…the last email I got from her was from Paris." *Which is true but it's not the whole truth*, Tania thought, and quickly changed the subject. "You mentioned a sister, so there is you and your brother and one sister?"

He took her hand and smiled. "There are four more of us Carleton kids, all girls. One older, one younger, and then the two youngest are twins." Rolling his eyes, he shrugged. "My parents fought constantly, but I've always thought the make-up sex must have been really, really good!"

Tania clapped her hand over her mouth, shoulders shaking, her eyes wide, trying not to laugh out loud in the cemetery. Cole had this effect on her. One minute she was crying over the memory of a childhood fantasy, the next minute laughing at the vision of the burly Carleton brothers surrounded by sisters.

Rubbing his face, Cole muttered, "Can I erase the make-up sex thing? It's such a gross thing to think about your parents, anyone's parents! Eecch!"

"My American friends would say it too, gross," Tania said, no longer laughing, her eyes downcast, "but my sister and I saw way too much of our mother's…shit like that." It was obvious to Cole it bugged her or she was ashamed of it.

They toured the museum and even managed to walk on the beach, their bare feet on the sand where many young men had sacrificed their futures. Still holding hands, they walked toward the parking lot and fell into step with two older women.

"Are you Americans?" they asked.

"Yes," Tania and Cole both answered, and laughed—together—again.

The one whose silver hair was wound into a braid and pinned up seemed unsteady on her feet. She was pale and sweating profusely, but managed to say thank you to them, adding "We're Dutch. If it weren't for you, we would be speaking German!"

They had a laugh about it, but Tania took her hand and asked "Are you okay? You seem ill, Madame."

The silver-haired lady looked panicky and then crumpled to the ground. Tania broke her fall and immediately lay her out straight to examine her. "Cole, call 112, that's the emergency number here," she said, looking at the sick woman's friend and asking "What's her name? Does she have a history of heart problems?"

"Yes, she does. Her name is Lena, Lena De Jong. I'm Elsa." Crying, the woman went through her friend's purse. "Her medications are in here. She took them today." Tania had already started CPR on Lena, checking her throat and alternating with compressions on her chest.

"The operator doesn't speak English, I'll hold the phone up," Cole said. In rapid French, Tania explained the situation and continued rhythmic chest compressions. Soon they heard sirens in the distance, coming closer.

A crowd gathered around them, and Cole made a path for the rescuers while Tania filled them in as they ran to the sleek blue and white ambulance. She asked Elsa which car was theirs and had her hand Lena's drugs to the medics before Elsa climbed in with her friend and they shut the doors and drove away.

Tania flagged down a security guard and showed him the women's car and told him what hospital they were being taken to.

"She's going to be all right," Tania said to Cole, leaning into him as they walked toward the car. "Her pulse was good, and she was responding a little while they settled her in."

Cole smiled and took a deep breath. "I don't know how to say this except to...say it. I'm impressed with how you handled what happened. I know you're a nurse, but you took total responsibility for her like a physician would, you took charge. Not that one is more important than the other, but have you ever considered becoming a doctor?"

"The scholarship was for nursing." She shrugged. "Other people have said this to me. But who would pay? It seems impossible, but thank you for saying it." Standing on her toes and throwing an arm around his neck, she kissed his cheek. "It means a lot coming from you."

She kept surprising him, being so easy to hang out with and yet so capable and talented—the driving, the languages, the emotion in the car, her desire for citizenship, her self-control during the emergency.

Whew, I've got it bad. Where the hell is this going so fast?

Cole had known he wanted her the first minute he saw her. But he hadn't expected to *like* her this much, or at times to *admire* her. He took a long look at her, drinking in her smiling eyes and bouncy walk, the matter-of-fact way she answered his questions. Seemed like she'd raised herself and her sister, made the most of her scholarship, and become an American citizen, pretty much without breathing hard. Real, difficult challenges, all of them, but she made it seem normal, nothing more than one foot in front of the other.

When they got back to the car, he took the driver's seat. "I watched you the whole way here, Super Girl. I've got this. I'm ready to drive this damn thing. Put your seat belt on and relax on the way back."

And he did okay, getting the feel of the narrow roads and moving quickly onto the highway. The minute they got up to speed she dozed off, the adrenaline finally gone, exhaustion in its place. They had just enough time to drive fast, drop off the car, and get back to the ship before it sailed. He pulled over and reclined her seat, covering her with his jacket. When he called his brother to check in, of course he got a wise-ass greeting.

"Hey Goose, how about a flyby here! We've gone through the pre-check and we're revving up the engines!" Jack could never resist a dig, especially if his brother was slacking off a bit. Which happened pretty much *never*. It was usually Cole covering *his* ass!

"Sorry Mav, no can do. I'll be up in time to dress for dinner with the big shots. Don't leave without me."

"No problem, really, you know I'm only bustin' you. So...how was it today? Was she weirded out about last night?"

"No. We talked. She's cool." *So cool I'm cutting you out, bro, but I'll tell you that in person. 'I'll see you at the Ice Lounge for the reception."*

CHAPTER SIX

INVITING SPECIAL GUESTS to the Captain's Table was a cruise tradition, and the *Sunset* kicked off every voyage with a small cocktail reception at the Ice Lounge, followed by a special dinner for the occupants of the ship's larger suites. Ivan, the Russian who had propositioned Tania in the boarding lounge, was there, but Cole saw and avoided him. The brothers were relieved when Saudi Prince Khalid Al Saud showed up without his entourage of wives, traveling light with one bodyguard and a stunning English girl, a brunette wearing western clothes.

"He's surprisingly cool, she's English, got her own suite, not one of the wives," whispered Jack, smiling while he led Cole over for an introduction. "His Highness Prince Khalid Al Saud and Amanda Leeds, this is my brother Cole," he said with a flourish. Like most people meeting them for the first time, Amanda and the royal looked from one brother to the other in amazement at their resemblance, and then laughed and shook their hands.

"What a beautiful necklace," Cole said to Amanda when they shook hands. It was hard not to notice the woman's heavy gold and diamond collar, and Khalid drew himself up, seeming proud the captain noticed it. The men exchanged glances while they shook hands, all three aware the collar meant Amanda was Khalid's sexual submissive, a trendy concept gaining eager acceptance in conservative

Saudi Arabia. Now the Saudis had an actual name for the women they kept on the side in addition to their many wives.

"Thank you," Amanda answered in her British accent, her smile not quite reaching her eyes. "It was a gift from Khalid."

Servers circulated among the elegantly dressed crowd, distributing expensive, ice-cold vodka in crystal glasses. The beautiful, upscale people filling the room were always vigilant in maintaining their slender figures, and the red raspberry vodka was perfect when served near-frozen and neat without fattening mixers. And if vodka didn't suit, Ice Lounge also featured a cocktail stylist to create the libation of any guest's dreams.

Several of the sexy dancers from the ship's theater circulated around the room, complementing the pulsing house music and the Art Deco-inspired décor. Ivan was mingling with each and every one of them, nodding, smiling and asking them about their training and where they were from. He laughed and seemed to listen intently when they shared stories of life at sea. Cole winced when he saw Ivan hand out his business cards.

"You see the guy over there with the dancers?" Cole spoke in a low voice to Tapar, the head of security for the ship. He nodded in Ivan's direction.

"Yeah," said Tapar. "Thin guy in the brown shoes?" The three Gurkha security officers onboard were known to be fierce, intelligent guards who made unruly drunks and unhappy gamblers disappear into their rooms in three seconds flat, quickly and without a fuss.

"Find out what he's saying to them, what's his pitch. When you talk to the dancers, ask for the business card back and give them your Gurkha stare, shake your head no." Tapar laughed, nodding. "Don't say anything, we don't want to get sued, just leave them with the idea he's bad now. And keep an eye on the creepy bastard, okay? Let me know what you find out."

"Got it." Tapar stood over against the wall, his arms crossed, watching, waiting for Ivan to walk away.

*

"I propose a toast," Jack said, and everyone held their glasses high. "To love, beautiful women, and a wonderful voyage!" A chorus of laughter and agreement in many languages rang out as the passengers drank and then entered the dining room.

When Khalid walked away from her with his bodyguard, Amanda tried to catch up to Cole while he was striding away, reaching into her cleavage and pulling out a note. "Do you have a special message for the captain, Amanda?" Ivan asked silkily. She froze when he stood in front of her, ripped it out of her hand, and opened it, reading it while he gripped her wrist.

"Let me go Ivan, you're hurting me!" Amanda said in a fierce whisper. The captain continued down the hall, oblivious to her plight.

"Please help me, I'm being held against my will." Ivan read, and yanked her closer, hissing in her face. "You stupid bitch! I told you what would happen if you tried to talk to anyone about our arrangement! I can't trust you now." Khalid and his bodyguard had returned, and Ivan thrust her toward them.

"I'm sorry, Your Highness, is it possible to have your man escort Amanda back to her room and remain there with her?" Ivan pasted on a smile as he walked with Khalid. "And you and I need to talk privately for a moment, if you don't mind. I'd like to walk you to the dining room." Amanda followed the bodyguard in the other direction, head lowered.

At a table in a roped-off area of the vast dining room, Cole saw he had been seated next to Emile Strauss, the German accompanied by a pretty blonde whose eyes remained fixed on her lap. Jack was seated across from them, next to Khalid. The other guests at the long table were frequent SunShips cruisers or just attractive passengers the sharp-eyed head waiter thought might add to the occasion with stimulating conversation.

Laughter rippled here, there, and everywhere while the special guests who hadn't met yet introduced themselves and sat down. The diners in the rest of the massive dining room—1,200 of them—cast longing looks in their direction, wishing they were among the chosen ones. And wasn't that the point? *Book more cruises with us, and you, too, can hang out with these beautiful people*, was the unspoken message.

Strauss's bodyguard, a giant of a young man with a shaved head, shifted from one foot to the other, looking this way and that, until Cole concluded he was uncertain about the seating arrangements. Shaking his hand warmly, Cole introduced himself, and the big man smiled appreciatively. "I'm Primo," he said, and asked in a low voice, "Is there somewhere nearby where I can be seated?"

"Absolutely," said Cole, and ushered Primo to a table some distance behind them where Tania and the ship's doctor and his wife were seated. "Primo, this is Tania Shevchenko and these are Dr. and Mrs. Santos, our medical officers."

"We're Felix and Anna, happy to meet you, Primo," the doctor said, standing and shaking both men's hands.

"I'd like to be on a romantic date right now with Tania," Cole said, "but as you can see, I'm working. I hope you'll take good care of her for me."

"We will," Felix and Anna said while Tania blushed, smiling. She was flattered by his words, both the acknowledgement that they were a couple and the implied warning to Primo that she was off-limits.

"Primo, you don't seem like a wine guy. Shall I have the waiter bring you something from the bar?" Cole asked before he walked away.

"That'd be great, thanks," said Primo, and he leaned back in his chair when the waiter brought the whiskey, his eyes checking the back of Strauss's head every few minutes.

*

Tania was struck by the way Cole treated everyone on the ship like a guest in his home. Though it wasn't possible, it felt like he must've been reading her mind, bringing someone who was in close contact with her sister right to Tania's table, relaxed, with a drink in his hand. "Primo, where are you from, and how did you come to work for...what's his name?" Tania asked in the most casual, nonchalant tone she could manage.

"Emile Strauss. I work for Herr Strauss when he's in London, which is where I'm based. Freelance security."

"And why do you live in London, Primo? You're American, right?" asked Felix Santos.

His face and shaved head reddening a little, Primo answered, "My mom lives in London, Dad in Las Vegas; he's Italian-American. I cover both sides of the ocean, but Europeans especially seem to think Italian-Americans are tough, great for security. The *Sopranos* effect, I guess."

They laughed, including Primo, and the table fell silent for a few moments while their food arrived. Tania had never seen food displayed this beautifully, carefully arranged on white plates ringed with gold. A gorgeous Beef Wellington wrapped in a golden brown puff pastry was served with sweet potatoes sliced thin and layered with gruyere cheese. Closing her eyes and inhaling deeply when she took her first bite, she was overtaken by the sensual pleasure of it as the tender beef melted on her tongue. The wine smelled like flowers when she lifted the glass to her face and the taste…well, it was a far cry from the Muscat her grandfather produced on his farm. *It is a big, beautiful world here, but I have to focus. I cannot waste this opportunity.* She fought a sudden urge to slap her own cheek, *Wake up!*

Not wanting to ask about her sister directly, Tania led with "I live in New Jersey now, but I'm originally from Ukraine."

Primo took the bait. "Really? That's interesting, because Herr Strauss's uh…companion is also from the Ukraine." There was an edge to his voice, and he didn't appear to be happy.

"That *is* interesting." Tania said, studying the food on her plate as if it were the most important thing on earth. *What makes him unhappy about my sister?*

Anna Santos, her brown eyes twinkling, patted Tania's hand and said to Primo, "You should introduce Tania to her. I know I am always happy to meet someone from the Philippines and see if we have people in common. Our countries are not as big as America, so it often works out. " *God bless you, sweet Anna,* Tania thought.

Primo's face flushed again, and he cleared his throat. "I'm not sure my employer would like that. I'm sorry. He's very…private."

"I'll tell you what, I will write her a little note and ask if we're *paisanos*, see if we went to school together, and you can give it to her. Sound okay?" she asked, trying not to sound as desperate as she felt, not wanting to lose her chance. Before he had a chance to say no, she'd scribbled a note in Ukrainian using the Cyrilic alphabet, telling her sister she was on the ship, wanted to help her, and to pretend they didn't know each other well when they met at the deck party tomorrow night.

She winked when she stuffed it in Primo's pocket, and as he stood to leave, he leaned close and said in a low voice, "I don't know if I can get it to her, but I'll try. She could really use a friend."

Tania nodded, feeling a tiny glimmer of hope. *He wants to help her. Good.*

*

American passengers loved being at the captain's table when the Carleton brothers were at the helm, in part because many other ship captains barely spoke English. The brothers had developed a repertoire of stories to tell, like the one about the little old lady who ate at the captain's table and then wrote a letter to the cruise line saying she had been "forced to eat with the crew." Then there were the usual cruise ship jokes, like "Be careful flushing our powerful toilets, last night I flushed and went down four floors." Or, "Our cabin stewards are so good, when you get up at night to go to the bathroom, you'll come back to find your bed made."

But for some reason guests loved their twin stories the most, like the time Jack and Cole got a new swing set and ended up being taken to the hospital emergency room with identical arm fractures. In high school they got identical SAT scores, and there was no way either one could have cheated, because they took the test sitting twenty desks apart in the same room.

A favorite story was of the April Fool's Day in middle school when the brothers switched places and seemed to breeze through the day with no one the wiser. Then the principal demanded over the PA system that Cole report to his office. Once there, he sternly threatened a lengthy series of after-school detention periods as a punishment for the twin switch—until Jack jumped out and yelled

"April Fools!" *with* the principal. One of the dinner guests would invariably pronounce that principal "the coolest ever," and Cole would bow to Jack for planning the best April Fool's joke ever.

Throughout the evening, lovely wines would flow, paired with fantastic menu items especially prepared for the captain's table gathering. At the end of the evening, a copy of the menu, signed by the chef and both captains, would be presented to each of the special guests.

When the diners were a little tipsy right before dessert, someone would invariably mention the internet posts by female passengers who claimed they'd "been with" one or both of the brothers, saying something along the lines of "I read online that you guys are quite a hit with the single ladies onboard."

Since he was bored shitless by then, Cole always looked forward to that moment, because they would both stand and Cole would flash a big smile, and say "We can't confirm or deny the rumors, but we do have to leave you now and get back to work."

It was a classy response, always greeted with a ripple of laughter and a great way to signal the end of the event. Etiquette seemed to dictate that no one could leave before the captains did, so it was a good time to exit and allow the passengers the option to stay or go on to the casino, the show, or any of the ship's other amusements.

Cole was hurrying away to spend time with Tania when he felt a hand on his arm. "Captain, ve enjoyed ze dinner vit you, especially my beeaa-uuu-tiful companion." Emile Strauss gestured to the blonde and said, in a low voice, "She vas vondering if you'd like to choin us in our suite for a few drinks."

CHAPTER SEVEN

"**H**E LITERALLY WAGGLED his eyebrows at me, like this," Cole laughed, doing his best creepy-old-guy imitation when he told the story to Tania back in his room. "It was weird, almost like he was trying to fix me up with her. Wonder what the relationship is?"

Tania shrugged, not meeting his eyes. She couldn't conceal anything from him when she was looking in his eyes. They stood together on his little balcony looking out at the sea, each holding a glass of wine. Candles flickered on every surface in Cole's room, his sweet attempt at the "romantic date" he'd promised earlier.

"Did you see her?" Cole continued. "The girl with Strauss. She didn't say anything, even though the sheikh, the guy across from her, said a few things to her. I'm not sure she speaks English." His voice lowered to a croon and he put his arms around Tania, surrounding her with his warmth, melting her tension with the glorious feel of his body against hers. "Something about her... reminded me of you, but the German said she was Ukrainian...so I guess that's why, right?"

Tania flinched and nodded into his chest, thinking *I have to tell him, I have to tell him.* Part of her wanted to hide, to pull away, but when Cole put his mouth on hers, her only thought was, *I want this to last forever.* She remembered thinking love songs longing for "one more night" were foolish, but now she totally understood.

Forgetting the past, living in the present, she vowed, *I'll tell him tomorrow. He is the best kisser ever. The best everything ever.*

He ran his fingers through her hair, spreading little tingles of delight while his lips opened over hers, kissing her thoroughly. Her heart went soft when his palms gripped her ass, claiming her, not asking permission. She loved knowing he was passionate about her, so wild, so masculine, kind of pushy and protective of her. So Cole. Had it really been only two days since they'd met?

When he's gone, I'll remember this, I'll remember the kissing. When he has forgotten me. Maybe "that Ukrainian girl," he will think. I will remember tasting him, consuming him. My chin will burn from his stubble, my fingers will remember brushing over his eyebrows and tangling in his hair. His lips, his tongue, those eyes bluer than the sky—I don't know about being on drugs, but surely this kissing is a drug, a narcotic keeping the rest of the world away, out of our minds. Yes, I'm out of my mind. But I don't care.

"This is so…unexpected. That this trip has turned into…this. Into…with you. The candles, the wine, everything," she said, her ear to his chest listening to his heartbeat. "I love it."

She was nervous, trembling again, but his words energized her. "I knew it the moment I saw you, I expected to learn every inch of you. And we're celebrating." He kissed her again, lighter, more tender this time. "I talked to Jack, told him how I feel about you. He'd figured it out already, he always knows every damn thing that's going on with me. He's okay with it."

How he feels about me? Tania was dumbfounded, speechless. *We just met, he doesn't know me. How can he know what he feels about me? And yet, here I am, memorizing every part of him, preparing for the day when he won't be around anymore. What does that say about how I feel?*

She nodded and pulled him inside, off the balcony, unbuttoning his shirt without breaking their kiss. Pushing his shirt off his shoulders, she ran her fingers through the hair on his chest, breathing deeply, committing the smell of his skin to memory. She inspected him, amazed by how the muscles in his chest and shoulders tapered down to his flat belly and narrow waist. He didn't seem to mind her staring at him, his little smile bringing out his one-sided dimple. This is what she'd wanted to do during dinner, especially when she caught him looking her way.

His face, his lips, his hair—she wanted to consume him, let him consume her, learn his face by heart. He was the most physically beautiful man she'd ever seen, his lean, muscular body wrapped in sexy, tanned skin, the right amount of body hair. Even his feet were sexy; she couldn't wait to see them again.

Last night he'd been behind her, stroking her behind and her breasts, entering her pussy and her ass. She hadn't been able to see his face, and she could already clearly distinguish between his face and Jack's. Tonight she didn't want to be more than six inches from him, watching him want her, watching him have her, watching him strain and groan and come.

*

Cole framed her face with his hands and pressed forward, willing himself to go slow, take his time. Not like last night, with Jack. *Which was awesome in a fucked-up way, but it would never, ever happen again. I'm not sharing this woman with anyone.* He locked her mouth in another kiss, finding the sensitive places inside, and then spoke without taking his lips from hers, pressing a smile against her. "I'm a persistent bastard, so you'd better get used to me. To you and me. Captain's orders."

Reaching under her dress, expecting to find panties, Cole was met with nothing but soft, silky skin, no panties at all. Just the sweetest, softest ass cheeks known to man, and he spread his hands wide, stroking and kneading them, his fingers pressing into her flesh, exposing her sex. His voice was low, lower than its usual deep tone, and husky. "Were you naked like this in the dining room? Nothing underneath?"

"Yes. Nothing under my dress." She spoke into his neck, pushing him toward a desk chair she'd placed in the center of the room. She shuddered as he urged her on and he hoped his expert hands would bring her inner sexy beast to fearless life, only for him this time.

Leaning down, he laughed soft and deep into her ear. "You're killing me, Tania. You're tearing me apart." Her relentless teasing made him want to throw her on his bed and fuck her like an animal, but after last night he realized…he knew she had to reclaim her power. She was obviously used to taking care of herself and others, to having some control. And he wanted her to have that control as much as she did. He felt the chair behind him.

She pressed down on his shoulders and he sat. After she straddled his legs, she pulled her dress off and stared brazenly right into his surprised eyes. "You screwed me last night, now I'm going to screw you," she purred.

Her hands at the back of his neck pulled him closer as she brushed the outline of his lips with her tongue. "What do you think of *your* orders, Captain?" she said, her chuckle deep and raspy. He let out a sharp hiss when she scraped his nipples with her nails, stroking his shoulders, his muscles flexing and bunching in response when she scratched a zigzag pattern down his arms.

Cole was stunned. He'd seen it happen in strip clubs, but he couldn't remember ever being straddled in a chair by a totally naked woman, especially one as strong and beautiful as Tania. There was something so wild and obscene about it, her wet pussy grinding against his dress slacks, her breasts pressing against him, he was compelled to lace his fingers through her hair, tasting and teasing her mouth when she parted her lips.

Forcing himself not to close his eyes, trying not to even blink, he felt her thighs straining while he watched her face, the perspiration at her hairline, her hair swinging over her shoulders. He couldn't keep his hands from roaming over her, pinching her nipples, squeezing the lush globes of her ass. When his fingers circled her sweet asshole, she sucked in a breath and licked her lips, as if she were remembering their ménage…in a good way. Her kisses were fierce, and he thought he would burst into flames when she stepped away and took her warmth with her.

*

She stripped his shoes and socks off in short order. Placing his bare feet wide apart on the floor, she stroked them, then pressed down, willing them to stay where she put them. *Sexy, wicked controlling man! Even now, he's just letting me do these things. I cannot imagine wanting anyone more.*

She crawled between his legs on her knees and unbuckled his belt, looking up at him with a naughty, naughty grin. While she pulled the zipper down, using her finger to trace the outline of his penis through his briefs, she bit out, "Okay, Captain, here's my next order. Lift your hips while I take your pants off." She surprised even herself when she remembered to take the condom out of his pocket as she pulled his pants and briefs down his long legs and threw them on the desk. Most of what she had done and said recently came from some wild, instinctual part of her brain she'd never visited before, a space where it was okay to be swept away and forget why she was on this ship.

He stared at her, his eyes burning bright with desire, his erection reaching up. He groaned when she wrapped her long fingers around him and licked the little slit at the top, playing with him, tracing the long vein with her tongue as if she had all night. As if he had all night, and it was no big deal that the cords of his neck stood out and his head was thrown back because he was ready to explode.

"I don't want to be so far from your face," she whispered, coming up from her knees and straddling him again, unwrapping the condom and pausing, her hand holding him at the base. "It feels so good, so hot and smooth, I hate to cover it up," she said, biting her lower lip.

"There's something else I want you to cover it with after this round," he choked out. He managed to give her a crooked smile as his hips, his thighs, and his dick jerked from the exquisite torture of her touch. She sighed and rolled the condom down the length of him.

Steadying herself, her feet flat on the floor, she locked eyes with him when he put his arms around her, one hand sliding down to her lower back. Trying to be in charge, she trembled when he possessed her mouth, biting her lower lip so much harder than she had bitten it, invading her with his tongue and sliding one hand along her thighs, stopping in the middle to spread the slick moisture from inside her. This felt so right, looking at his face, touching his hair while he controlled her from below, stroking her and kissing her like a man obsessed, imaginary sparks crackling on their skin as they breathed into each other.

She lowered herself and hissed into his mouth when his stiff cock grazed her sensitive secret parts. "Are you sore from last night, baby?" Cole asked, his voice rough and strained, looking into her face. "We can stop, we can do something else. It's okay."

"I. Don't. Want. To do. Something else." Determined, she lowered herself on him all at once and gasped. Yes, she was sensitive as hell but… "It hurts, it hurts a little, it feels so tight, but it's a good hurt. Do you know what I mean?"

"I fucking know all about what you mean," he moaned, gritting his teeth. She realized then how tense he was from holding himself back, his shoulders slick with sweat beneath her hands. While she slid inch by hard-earned inch up and down on him, she felt him relax and breathe deeply, moving his hips forward a little and tightening his hold on her bottom.

Then he met her, thrusting up as she came down and she gripped the back of the chair with both hands to push back at him, to meet him in the sweetest spot. Somehow he managed to put one hand between them and rub circles around her clit while she trembled and let her climax sweep over her, arching into him and whimpering out his name.

That's when the chair started to scrape along the floor and things moved faster and faster. Hearing her say his name turned him loose, gave him permission to push up into her and put his hands on her hips, his biceps flexing when he steadied her, supporting her quivering thighs as if she weighed nothing. When they were as close as possible, skin to skin, the feelings blazed though them, and they took sharp breaths, sensation and pleasure fusing them while they raced toward the edge. Sliding his hands up to her shoulder blades, he drew her close and moaned into her chest. Was he hiding a rush of feeling, holding himself back for…what?

Holding her still now, clamped down onto him without moving, he said her name, willing her to open her eyes and look at him. "You said you wanted to screw me. That was hot, but I'm not screwing you back. I'm *making love* to you, Tania. Don't pull away from me, don't hide, make love to me."

It scared her to realize he knew she was hiding something from him. But what really scared her was if she showed herself to him, showed him everything, her ugly and her beautiful, her shitty past and her gritty present, then he would leave her. It was something she'd never experienced and never wanted to. If you let people in, they had power over you. She'd learned that the hard way, when she was very young.

Her lips trembling, she looked down at him through tear-filled eyes. "I…I don't know if I know how. I've never…I don't think I've ever made love." But as she said the words, she knew they weren't completely true.

Sex with Cole was already more than sex, it was connected to a part of her she hadn't known existed. Taking a deep breath, her lips on his forehead, she whispered "I wanted to stay close to your face, to watch you. It means something, right?"

"It means something," he agreed, and she relaxed against him when he stood, holding her tightly without coming out and lying side by side with her when he placed her on the bed, one of her shapely legs hooked over his hip so they were still connected. "Show me something else," he said in a husky voice, his erection growing bigger by the second when he rolled her over on top of him. She let her knees slide farther apart, slowly felt herself sinking down, taking him even deeper than before.

"Make love to me." He pulled some pillows behind his back, bringing his face level with her breasts, his eyes scorching through her fear as he licked his lips, then pulled one nipple into his mouth. The cool sea breeze tightened the other into a stiff point and she gasped, her legs trembling with excitement and exertion in equal measure.

When she put her hands on his chest, she felt his heart pounding and she pressed her hips down, gritting out a moan when her sore inner muscles clenched around his shaft. "Ooohh…mmm, that feels…crazy," she grinned down at him so he would know it was the good hurt again. His eyes said he already knew how much she liked the exquisite ache. He cupped her breasts to distract her and his abs rippled while he pressed up to pinch and taste her nipples again.

It felt good to grind around on him, this way, that way, in a figure eight. Spreading her legs wider still and leaning back, her arms on either side near his knees, she discovered her clit was wide open to him because he took full advantage, stroking her sensitive flesh with his fingers. Soon she was lost in the feeling again, the sensation of clenching in her belly, when he shifted his hips and palmed her breasts, thumbing her nipples. Somehow he managed to use his cock to massage that spot inside her at the same time, the one that made her spin totally out of control.

"Okay, time to come again, beautiful, you're so hot leaning back like that, let me watch and feel you come again." *Why is it so hot when he tells me to cooommmme?* Her orgasm rippled out from her core, hips and inner muscles bucking and grasping, a shaky moan bubbling up from somewhere as her urgent little sounds got softer and softer. Leaning down, she gave him some kisses, grazing his neck and his chin, lingering on his mouth. Wrung out, she came up straight and looked in his eyes, wondering if she could even move.

He looked at her and she couldn't look away when he wrapped his arms around her, his long fingers splayed out on her ass. *I guess the answer is yes, I can move some more.* All the way up she went, guided by his strength, leaving just the tip inside her sensitive channel, and it took forever, forever. Cole was slick with sweat, so careful and intense, and then boom, he guided her down then, and again in long, slow strokes.

"Too soon, too soon," he moaned and grasped her hips, holding her still again when she raised her arms to toss her hair back. The way her breasts swayed when she did it seemed to energize him. Sexy sounds escaped from her throat, but she wished she could return his words, words of encouragement and praise like *perfect, so good* and *amazing. Yes* was about the best she could muster.

"You are the sexiest woman I've ever seen," he breathed and bucked up into her as she writhed above him, breaking free of his grip and slamming her hips down hard on his. When his big hands possessed her, his fingernails marking her skin, she felt her orgasm begin to build again.

She rode him over and over, circling her hips, a new burst of energy moving her while she steadied herself on the headboard. "Fuck me, fuck me, uh-huh, fuck me," she panted, amazed at her nasty mouth but loving it anyway. She loved how powerful she felt, claiming him this way. He brought out something in her, something she hadn't known she was capable of.

His thumb pressing on her clit to bring her along one more time, he moved her, crashing her down into him. His penis jerked when he let loose a long, low moan of pleasure. Breathing in deep, taking it in, she couldn't help but convulse around him, her gaze locked onto his as they dissolved into one another.

Finally Tania lay next to him, wrapping herself around him, waiting for his breath to slow and devouring him with more kisses. She felt a surge of affection, wanted to kiss him all night long like a teenager in love, but in four hours he had to be up and on the bridge.

"You have to stop kissing me or I'm not going to survive," Cole said in a fake pained voice. Pinning her arms by her sides, he gave her another little love bite on the shoulder, "Or maybe *you're* not going to survive, Miss Trouble. "Maybe I'll take you again right now," his eyes glittered while he held her away from him, his gaze taking her in, "And you'd let me. You would love it."

"I know, *Captain,*" she said, trying again to be cheeky, then sighing, resigned to the truth about herself. "I know I would. When you play with my body, when you lead, I feel free, free to accept and enjoy. It's as if I melt, I melt into you, I feel what you want and I want it too. Why?"

"Because we're into each other and you're...do you know what submissive means?"

"Submissive...like...submitting...like do what the other person wants?"

"Kind of, but...more. I was watching you tonight, letting you lead me, doing what you wanted. But did you notice that you..."

She interrupted, smiling. "I pulled you back in, I put you... back in the driving seat...didn't I? Does it mean something?"

"It might mean I have more experience than you, so you're not confident. But it doesn't feel like it." He smiled and caressed her cheek with a finger. "And it's 'in the driver's seat,' not the 'driving seat.'"

She wasn't embarrassed; she was proud of her quest to master American slang. "Driver's seat, got it. But what does it...what does it *feel* like it means, as you say?"

"I...when we're in the midst of it...I feel like you want me to lead, maybe not want, but *need* me to. Your eyes get misty, kind of faraway-looking. Your body gets hot, like on fire, and yet you go slack...melting, like you say. It's...amazing. Makes me want to eat you alive and at the same time give you all the pleasure in the world." Still holding her, he buried his face in her hair. "Does that sound stupid?"

Her crooked smile wasn't the answer he expected, threw him off guard. "No, it does not sound stupid, but it sounds...like you have some experience with this word, submissive. Is that so?"

It was a gotcha, another of those moments when Tania's agile mind leapt ahead of him. "Uh...yeah. Jack and I have gone to some clubs where dominants and submissives play, and we've...had a good time there." He cleared his throat and looked in her eyes. "There's a sign over the door of this one club saying, 'The things I want to do to you, the things you want to happen—are they the same?'"

"So you're a dominant? And the men do things the submissive wants to happen?"

Now Cole threw his head back and laughed, a magical sound bursting out of him like a gust of wind. "I know you, Trouble. You'll check this out the next time you have internet access and figure it out. And maybe sometime we'll go to a club together. Right now, how about some sleep?" She didn't answer, just nodded and closed her eyes, snuggling into his chest with a soft sigh.

Tania wobbled a little when she woke up during the night and went to the bathroom, her legs and her sex were so sore and swollen. She wore it as a badge of honor, a sign that she was finally a woman, a desirable woman instead of drab Nurse Tania. She'd awakened in the middle of a dream, a fantasy of standing on the deck of the ship holding hands, Cole on her right and Oksana on her left. They were smiling, happy and free. Wondering how and when her sister's cruel reality would crash into her pleasant fantasy, she prayed that somehow a way to help Oksana would be revealed.

When she got back in bed, he mumbled something in his sleep and pulled her back against him, as if they'd been sharing a bed for years. It felt like home. *I'll tell him. I'll tell him tomorrow, the first chance I get.*

CHAPTER EIGHT

MISS AMANDA LEEDS, Khalid's mistress, fell asleep fully clothed in the dark. She knew Ivan was coming to talk—and probably scream—at her. Khalid's bodyguard waited outside her door. Of all the things she missed about her former freedom, what she missed the most, oddly, was her phone. As a college student and sometime call girl, her phone had been her lifeline, an extension of her body so organic she felt incomplete without it. She would've been checking it earlier, killing some time while she waited for Ivan.

In fact, the phone was how she got hooked up with Khalid. Ivan found her through a client, called her, and brokered an amazing one-year deal with the sheikh, during which she'd earn enough money to quit her sex-for-money gig and be a full-time student. The first three months had been fine, kind of fun, actually, with the luxurious hotel suites and the international travel.

But the isolation was killing her. Her contract forbade contact with any of her friends, and she had no phone and no access to the internet. It had been part of the deal, since Khalid valued his privacy and security above everything. And of course Khalid's wives hated her. She'd tried to have a conversation with Hakim, the bodyguard, but he had to avoid any appearance of a relationship for obvious reasons.

Normally not much of a reader, she'd gotten into reading

mommy porn lately. At least she'd been able to learn about sexual bondage and discipline when she got tired of watching reality shows. The sheikh had been pleased with the results of her research, to say the least, and rewarded her with a golden collar like the one described in one of her books.

Her suite was on Deck 9, and her door faced a small lounge near the elevator. Hakim sat there reading his Kindle. Passengers walking by would never know he was keeping an eye on Amanda. He'd smile, nodding and saying "Howzit goin'?" to people walking toward the elevator, and they'd think *He's a young father, hanging out while his wife puts the kids to bed.* When Ivan arrived, keying into Amanda's room without knocking, Hakim merely waited for the door to close and walked away.

"So you're unhappy, Amanda?" Ivan got right to the point, smiling his snarky smile. She was surprised he was being so nice. She'd been expecting an argument from him at best, a beating at worst. "I'm surprised you're unhappy," he continued. "Khalid was so pleased with your recent, uh, activities. The collar he gave you is quite something. You must be a very good little submissive."

Since she was sitting on the bed, her face happened to be right in front of his erection, and he opened his zipper and pulled it out, stroking himself while he pulled her mouth toward him. "Show me what a good blow job you give while I pull your hair, bitch." A distress signal went off in Amanda's mind.

"I don't think Khalid would like it, Ivan. You know he wants me to be exclusive to him." Trembling, she struggled to read the man and wondered how this would play out. Every alarm bell she had rang in her brain, but she wanted to believe she could get out of this unscathed.

"He and I have it worked out," Ivan said and put his cock on her lips, winding his fingers into her hair and pulling until her scalp was on fire. "You can suck it." And she obeyed, knowing, from when she first met Ivan, that he wouldn't last long. And he didn't.

*

After cleaning himself up, Ivan held out his hand to her. "Let's go for a walk on the deck, Amanda. Your note to the captain wasn't even true; you and I have a business deal, nothing more than that, *mon cher*. Tell me what's making you unhappy, all of it." She took his hand and walked out on the deck with him.

There was no moon, and there were no other passengers on deck at three in the morning. Amanda gave Ivan a list of every lonely aspect of her current situation, including Khalid's admission that he found her super-white skin repulsive. "There's nothing I can do about it, though. But I've tried tanning, and he seems to like it a little better."

Ivan was barely listening, glancing around the deck, but he nodded continually and said "Umm-hmm" when she paused in her tale of woe. They strolled along the side of the ship where the specialty restaurants were located, all closed and dark at this hour of the morning, and stopped by the railing.

"He asked you for an English girl, what color did he think my skin would be? Now I have to feel self-conscious about my *skin* for God's sake. What do I do in that case?" Crying, Amanda let it out, all the fear, unhappiness, and anger she'd been keeping inside. "I can't do this anymore. I'll give you back the money, just let me go home. I can't be with him." She turned to Ivan, unhooking the collar. "Oh, and give him this fucking collar for me."

"I'll see what I can do," said Ivan, patting her shoulder while she leaned against the rail. He dropped the collar with a clunk as she handed it to him. "Oops!" he said as he crouched down as if to pick it up, but caught hold of both of her ankles instead, pushed her knees up to her chest and flipped her over the rail. It was over in an instant. The waves crashing against the ship were so loud he didn't even hear a splash or a scream.

Walking quickly to the casino as he tucked the jeweled collar under his jacket, Ivan lit a cigarette and placed himself conspicuously next to an active blackjack table. *These Brits, they're so fucking empowered. It was too soon to turn her over to him,* he thought. *Hmmm. I hope she got caught in the propellers, no body to identify, just chum...or maybe she drowned.* He took a long drag and exhaled in the direction of one of the casino's bubble cameras. *It's a shame, really. Normally I might have shipped her off to one of those nasty dungeons in Asia or used her in films. But so many people here on the ship... too dangerous,* he sighed, grinding out his cigarette in the nearest ashtray. *On the other hand, the ocean provides such a convenient means of disposal. I'll get Khalid covered with the other girl, and the ship has so many other pretty girls and boys from all over the world for me to talk to just in case. No problem.*

CHAPTER NINE

A DAY AT SEA was very busy for the crew. The spa, the gym, the pools, the casino and, of course, the dining rooms were packed to bursting with passengers who were finally getting around to using the ship's facilities—and they wanted everything now, now, NOW! It was routine for kitchen, dining room, spa, salon, casino and retail personnel to work 12-hour shifts, not to mention the bartenders. Everyone knew at-sea days meant the extra tips they needed for their families at home or, for the single staffers, to hoard for their time off between six-month contracts on board.

Around 3 o'clock things slowed down a little while many guests napped or got ready for the evening's big Deck Party Under the Stars to be held around the main pool.

Tania was in the gym watching Cole and Jack while they sat on the machines rowing against each other, quietly trading their filthiest, most outrageous curses, trying to get the other guy to laugh and miss a beat. As she moved mindlessly through the Russian-style exercise routine which had been drilled into her since grade school, Tania wondered again what Cole saw in her. Starting out with running in place, jumping jacks and leg swings to warm up, she progressed to push-ups, dips, squats, and lunges while she, and everyone else in the gym, watched the brothers train.

Their separate personalities were perfectly expressed in the way they moved around the room. It was the first way Tania learned to tell the brothers apart. Jack sauntered into a room, Cole strode in like a heat-seeking missile, arms pumping.

Mr. Carefree, Jack, made working out look fun when he ran for the grab bars on the ceiling and swung like a monkey, pulling himself up and down, soon glistening with sweat, the pack of muscles in his shoulders and arms standing out like a physiology lesson, and completing forty perfect pull-ups in no time. He laughed at himself in the mirror, catching Tania's eye and making *her* laugh, as he roared like the Hulk while pulling heavy weights down with straps in both hands. His biceps bulged, the perfect V between his shoulders strained, and his quads swelled with the effort while he squatted into the difficult pull-down, but he was grinning the whole time. He was leaner and had a smaller waist than Cole, and was lighter in every way, if you'd call such a big, well-developed guy light.

Everything about Cole, on the other hand, seemed ripped from a rock with a jackhammer. Muscles, veins, and bones she never knew existed flexed, tensed, and strained against heavy weights on every rack. There was no question that he intended to maximize every second he spent in the gym.

The hidden truth was, both brothers used working out as a way to self-medicate, to bury the anger they'd learned at their father's knee. No one would ever know the dark side of the twin golden boys, they made sure of it. Making their muscles scream in agony was a handy way to channel their shame and self-loathing into something useful, something socially acceptable.

Watching Cole, Tania was unaware of the brothers' legacy of anger, but she felt an undercurrent of…sadness or pain. No one argued with the result, though. Cole could have been a fitness model.

Focusing intently on the business at hand, his nostrils flared, his earbuds blasting house music into his brain, he alternated intense weight training with full-out running on a treadmill elevated to the steepest incline. When he moved from machine to rack to treadmill, his stride, as always, resembled a panther stalking his prey.

Cole's hair was curlier than Jack's, and when it was soaked it hung almost to his shoulders, giving him the wild appeal of one of those hunks on the cover of a sexy book. He looked so amazing, so strong and sweaty and intent, that every woman—and every man—in the gym was riveted.

Nool, odyn, dvah, try, Tania counted to herself in Ukrainian while she went down for her fourth set of push-ups. No weights, nothing fancy, using her own body weight and lots of repetition to stay fit. When she finished with sit-ups and stretches, she was amazed to discover she'd attracted her own audience.

"Hey, I like this old school boot camp you're doing," said one of the buff young exercise instructors, showing his note pad to Tania. "I took some notes, but I noticed when you finished those leg swings, you…" She laughed while they talked and leaned over the notebook, the instructor trying to write down her routine as if it were the latest thing instead of the same old calisthenics every Ukrainian school kid learned.

A shadow fell over them when Cole came over with those yard-wide shoulders of his. He put his arm around Tania, saying, "Sorry I'm so sweaty, babe. Is Blake taking notes on your form…or noticing your form?"

She thought it would be fun to play along. "Oh, I think both, am I right Blake?" she said, touching the young man's hand on his clipboard while ignoring Cole's possessive arm. Blake smiled and looked up, not realizing until that moment that it was the Captain staring a hole into his forehead. The color drained from his face as he very formally shook Tania's hand, put his clipboard under his arm and said, "So nice to meet you. Thanks," before scurrying off.

Cole pulled her closer while they ambled out of the gym,

growling in her ear "That was not a very nice thing to do to the poor young man, you little tease. I thought he was gonna faint."

"Maybe, maybe so. Might be just me, though. I was going to faint watching you do your workout. Me and every other woman and man in this place. Blake has...how do you say? He has no clue."

"You think men are watching me too?" he asked, slowly raising one eyebrow while sliding his hand to her butt.

"Oh, yes. How do you feel, knowing men are watching you too?" She fought so hard to be cool and keep a straight face, but as always, the flush spreading up from her chest gave her away.

"Well, I don't know. How do *you* feel about it, by which I actually mean, does it turn you on?"

"Huuuh!" she whooshed out a big breath. "You really think I'm a dirty girl, don't you?"

The way she said it, *duhty guhl*, cracked him up even further, and they stopped in front of one of the shops while he finished laughing and composed himself.

"Hey, Bebe!" he said, walking into the shop, hand extended toward the tall, regal, brown-skinned woman hanging up dresses in the ship's ladies' clothing store.

She held out both arms and folded him into a motherly hug instead. "Oh, Cole, how are you, my friend?!" They patted each other's backs and smiled, genuinely happy to see each other.

"Tania, this is Bebe. Bebe and I took management training with SunShips at the same time." He took the sparkling red dress Bebe was holding and held it up to Tania. "What do you think, will it fit her?" he asked.

"Yes, but I have a better one," she said, and came out with a simpler but somehow sexier one. "This would look great on you, Tania."

"No question. Would you charge it to me, Bebe?" Cole's face was excited, like a little boy at Christmas.

Tears in her eyes, Tania thanked the woman and looked at Cole. "Thank you, but you made me cry again. Why are you doing this? This is like a princess dress."

*

He wanted to tell her he had noticed she only had the one black dress and a few other well-worn clothes. He wanted to tell her he noticed her hands were chapped from so much hard work. But instead he smiled and said, "Well then, wear it like a princess. I can't go with you to the Deck Party tonight since I'm on duty, but I want you to enjoy wearing it."

"He's a good boy, isn't he?" Bebe said to Tania and gave him another affectionate peck on the cheek. Tania hugged the dress against her chest, ran her hands over the lovely fabric, and sighed.

"Do you want some time alone with your dress, Tania?" Cole quipped, and they laughed. "Go ahead babe, put it on. I have to be on the bridge in an hour." While Tania walked away, practically skipping, Cole slipped Bebe a wad of cash and said "Would you mind buying her a bunch of stuff at our next stop, some jeans and workout clothes? Her sneakers are an eight and a half."

"No problem, Cole." She patted his hand. "You are either a very kind man or one who is very in love. Or maybe both."

Catching up with Tania on the stairs, Cole imagined sharing a shower with Tania, got hard at the thought, but decided to let the woman heal up a little.

Who is this guy inside me? What happened to the Party God of cruise ships? he wondered. *Is it me who's different, or is it her? If I wanted to get in the shower with her, she would say yes, oh yeah. She loves to say yes. If she gives me that look before she showers, all bets are off.*

But his wet dream apparently didn't occur to her while she used her key card and hurried into her room to shower and put on her beautiful new dress.

Sitting at the work station outside his room later, he looked up from the screen when she came out of her room. The dress was killer, very sheer, hugging her in the right places, including her curvy butt. He was glad he was sitting behind the desk, because his reaction would have been very plain to see, she was so damn sexy and at the same time...fresh and sweet.

The one-shoulder red gown cut across her chest, showing enough cleavage to make him realize that, once again, she was not wearing a bra. She'd swept her hair up, showing off her luscious neck, a few dark wisps of hair escaping onto her bare shoulders. A deep slit in the side of the dress made it easy for her to stride across the room in her shiny heels, twirling around like a little girl playing dress-up.

*

But she didn't feel like a little girl, not while Cole was looking at her like he wanted to devour her.

Being with this man does not happen to women like me. Yet here he is, pulling me in for a kiss, his breath on my neck. He smells so good, not like cologne...good, like fresh air. And those lips...mmm. Tasting him makes me feel confused, like I'm lost. And I am.

"I'm pissed at Bebe," he murmured, holding her at arm's length. Now she was really confused. "She picked out this dress for you, and now I have to let other guys see you in it while I'm at work. At least come up to the bridge with me so I can show you off."

They walked onto the bridge quietly and stopped, watching

Jack scrolling through the screens on the console's vast bank of computers. He ran his fingers through his thick, sandy hair and Tania smiled when she saw Cole absentmindedly do the same thing.

In a loud whisper, Cole gestured at his brother and said, "Godlike, isn't he?"

"That's Mister Godlike to you, douchebag," said Jack, without turning around. "And Tania, just for the record, am I? Am I as much like the King of the World as my brother to you?"

"Oh absolutely!" she said, laughing. When Jack turned and saw her, his eyes widened and he let out a long wolf whistle.

"All right, all right, you're the fucking king, bro," he muttered in mock defeat, as he winked at Tania. "You got the princess, for sure."

She sat at the back of the room when Cole went to work alongside his brother. No words were needed; a nod, a gesture or a glance were the only communication while they planned navigation protocols for the next day at sea. Last night, Cole had told her when they were little they'd even had a secret language, a twin gibberish no one else understood. They got in a lot of trouble back then, climbing on top of each other to escape from all manner of protective enclosures. Picturing them as chubby toddlers, Tania felt tears in the corner of her eyes and a sudden dryness in her throat as she thought of her sister Oksana.

CHAPTER TEN

THINKING ABOUT COLE and Jack's twin language brought back memories of childhood summers with her sister, Oksana, days of picking berries and riding on a load of melons in their grandpa's wheelbarrow. Their grandparents' farm was a magical place of early summer mornings eating a huge breakfast, doing chores, and splashing in the Dnieper River. In the heat of the day, the girls would read books and practice speaking English and French, preparing for another grueling year at their public school in Odessa.

During the school year, they took care of each other and their mother, who was often too drunk to go to work. Luckily, she went to work often enough to stay employed. The young sisters talked for hours about their plans to go to university, live in the city, and trade potatoes and cabbage for sushi in chic cafes.

But it was in one of those cafes where Oksana met a handsome Russian guy who promised to solve her problems, problems which began when the sisters took the state exams for postsecondary school.

The sisters took the exams together because Tania had skipped a grade. When Tania got a perfect score in chemistry and biology, her teachers recommended her for a scholarship in America. Oksana barely passed and faced an uncertain future until the Russian told her he would get her into modeling school.

"Go! Go to America, and you will visit me in Paris," said Oksana. "Yury is taking me to Paris to be a model!" The prospect of the lovely Oksana becoming a model wasn't so far-fetched; two girls from their high school had gone to London and appeared in British *Vogue*.

Tania soon settled into her new life in New Jersey, but she hadn't liked Yury, didn't trust him to care for her sister, and definitely didn't believe her sister's "official modeling website" needed to include so many naked or nearly-naked photos. There was only one thing nude photos meant, and her fears were confirmed by Oksana's emails. She imagined her beautiful sister in a dingy internet café near her Paris apartment, typing away, initially full of hope.

> *"Paris is expensive, so Yury got me a job talking to men on the phone. Today I read a script about going on a train ride, going faster and harder, feeling so hot from the motion of the big locomotive. Ha,ha! I think they are touching their big locomotives while I'm talking."*

Tania wrote back: "And what job is Yury taking? Is his job sitting in a café and smoking expensive French cigarettes? Come to New Jersey, visit with me until we can get you a work permit!"

> *"I'm now working in a nightclub and meeting lots of interesting people. It's called The Red Light, and it's, like they say here, OOO-la-la! One of the other girls is teaching me how to dance and get lots of tips. You know I love to dance, little sister, and Yury thinks I will do well."*

"Oksana, please think once, twice, and again. Is this what you want to do, dance for tips, or is it Yury whispering in your ear while he sits on his lazy ass? At least do this, big sister – hide some of your money from him, keep some for yourself. Don't tell him how much money you actually make, and hide it somewhere just in case."

"You wouldn't believe how much money I'm making doing what I love to do! I fly across the stage and spin around the pole and men throw money at me. I love the music and the lights and Yury takes me to beautiful restaurants to show me off to his Russian friends, he's so proud of me and happy he can buy me things. The other girls want me to show them, and I go early to the club and help them plan their dances. But I'm doing what you said, I'm hiding some money behind the picture of us I keep on my dresser. I want to come there and take a picture with you in your nurse's uniform, I'm so proud of you!

Tania chuckled when she recalled her sister's nurse's uniform comment; unlike the Ukraine, nurses in the US wore whatever comfortable, colorful scrubs they felt like wearing, along with sneakers or clogs. She sent Oksana a photo of herself with some of her nurse friends, but it was months before Tania heard from her sister again. After dozens of worried emails, she sent a prepaid phone to the Paris address her sister had given her, but received no call or email. The phone was returned to her marked "*retour a l'expediteur*, return to sender."

Then came the tearful phone call that brought her to this ship.

"Tani, Tani, it's me!" Oksana whispered, her voice wobbling. "I'm on someone else's phone, listen! I'm on my way to England. In a month I'm going to be on a ship called *Sunset*, and I don't know what's going to happen. He gave me away, Tani, Y-Yury s-s-sold me, he gave me to a man for money!" Still trying to be quiet, she was struggling for breath between sobs. "I saw him give my passport, take the money and walk awaa-aay!" She wailed louder over the awful betrayal, and Tania heard a man's voice.

"Give me the fucking phone, bitch!" the man said in Russian. Tania heard what sounded like a slap and a struggle and the call was gone.

*

Cole was looking in Tania's direction, one eyebrow raised. "Everything okay?" he asked. When she met his eyes and considered what to say, an officer in an area opposite the bridge shouted, "Guys! Get in here! You've got to see this!" The brothers went in to check out the security screens in Officer Ewan McGrath's command center.

Ewan's official title was Chief Communications Officer, but in fact he was in charge of the ship's vast network of camera surveillance and digital safety alarm systems. The system was installed after 9/11 to assess risk potential and monitor security-related incidents. Crew areas, power supply, the Promenade, pool, public rooms—Ewan saw everything. Jack had stuck a crude sign on the door naming the place Sunset Secret TV.

"What's going on, Big Brother? Is some guy fondling his wife's tits while they look out over the ocean?" Cole asked.

"Ohhh, sooo much better than that, Capitano!" Ewan grinned while he gestured at the screens. "Check this scene out! Unbelievably hot!" The brothers leaned in to one of the larger screens. They saw Emile Strauss, the German from the Sky Suite, in a darkened corner behind the closed Wine Bar. Strauss watched as two men, passengers, stood on either side of his beautiful girlfriend. Eyes cast down, a sad, confused expression on her face, it was easy to see the young woman's legs shaking as one man pulled down her dress and was sucking on her nipple while the other kissed her with his hand up the hem of her dress. Primo the bodyguard stood looking away, scowling, at parade rest with arms crossed, scanning the room, presumably for possible interruptions.

One of the men on the screen undid his pants and put Oksana's hand on him while the German nodded and smiled. The other one put his hand on her shoulder and gestured for her to kneel on the floor. The girlfriend looked at Strauss, upset and obviously frightened, but he gestured to her to follow the man's directions.

Tania clearly saw the screen from where she stood and she wobbled, suddenly chilled and nauseous. She trembled and felt as if her heart would leap from her chest. It was her sister Oksana at the center of the action on the monitor. Tania stumbled backward onto a chair. The situation was much worse than she'd thought, and she wondered how to help her sister get away from this man who'd kidnapped her. *Why doesn't she run, scream, why is she going along with this? She's upset and frightened. Is she a slave, is she drugged, do they have something on her?*

When Tania looked up, Cole was there, a hand on her shoulder, his face concerned. "What's going on, are you okay?" She shook her head, unsure how much to say. He crouched next to her and tilted her chin up with his hand. "Just tell me." His voice was cool and commanding, a tone she hadn't heard before.

"That's…that girl. That's my sister in the blue dress. I think she is a…like a slave. She doesn't want to be doing this, I can tell!" Her voice shaking, she looked away from him, dreading his reaction. Would he be angry at her for involving him in this mess?

He walked back into the surveillance center and picked up a phone. "Armando, are you near the Wine Bar? Yes, I know it's closed. Walk over there, we need you to bust up a situation, okay? Yeah, yeah, here's what we need you to do. Talk to the big bald guy, yeah, nice and polite, and point out the camera on the wall in front of him. Right, show him the camera, point to your eyes, and then point behind him as if you don't speak English. Don't get into a big discussion."

The phone still up to his ear, the bartender Armando appeared on the screen and did his pantomime with the bodyguard, who turned and spoke to Strauss. The German threw up his hands, alarmed, and spoke to Oksana who, eyes wide, pulled up her dress and walked away, teetering down the hall on her high heels with Strauss close behind. Cole smiled when Armando shooed the two lover-wannabes to the men's room. "Nice job, my man, nice job!" he nodded, a grim expression on his face. "Thanks for your help."

Walking back over to Tania, he pulled her arm through his and walked her back toward their quarters. "We need to talk. Right now. You need to tell me everything."

Slamming the door behind him when they walked into her room, he stood facing her, fists at his sides, veins bulging in his neck. "I feel lied to. Why didn't you tell me what was going on with your sister the first night? It's the reason you're here, isn't it?"

She nodded and told him about Yury, Paris, the phone call, everything, even the note she gave Primo. Tears trickled down her cheek when she saw the sucker-punched expression on his face, a look of uncertainty and…fear? Vulnerability?

"So the German got her from the Russian guy, and she's scared to run. Have I got it right?" Cole's words were like bullets. Tania nodded, too upset to say more. It made her sick to her stomach when he spoke so sharply, and he had been vibrating with anger since they left the bridge.

He hadn't spoken to her in such a way before, and she was confused. He hadn't seemed like the kind of guy who lectured, bullied or raised his voice to get his way. "So is this why you came with me the first day," he continued, his tone harsh, bitter. "Why you had sex with me... with us? Was it only to help your sister?"

The hurt in his voice struck her like lightning. *No, no, no! I'm falling in love with you! That is not how it was!* But before she could say it out loud, he dismissed her, gesturing toward the elevator. A grim look had settled on his face.

He was strung tight, hands balled up, until he pointed a finger at her. "Go down to the party and try to talk to your sister. We'll keep an eye on you using the cameras." Eyes blazing, Cole stalked toward the elevator in silence.

I knew I would screw this up. A sob hitched her breathing, but she swallowed it down, choked it off. Her instincts urged her to sit him down, talk him through the hurt feelings. Everything seemed to be moving in slow motion as Cole walked out and the door slammed shut.

But Tania Shevchenko was an expert at self-control, and knew how to shrink her feelings until they fit into a little box to hide away in a corner of her mind. She stood, numb and alone, and carefully took off the beautiful dress and hung it up. *No one saw me wear it except the guys on the bridge, so maybe Cole can take it back.* It was amazing the way her thrifty habits kicked back in the minute the stars were kicked out of her eyes.

Her mouth was dry and, strangely, so were her eyes. She'd cried so easily the last couple of days, everything was so intense, but now it was on her again. Her sister—the only person who really cared for her, it now seemed—was a prisoner, a... sex slave, and Tania had to return to her old persona. It was time to be practical Tania, plain Tania, I've-got-a-plan Tania. Not the dreamy Princess Tania in the red dress, the one kissing the prince in the white coat.

Yearning for Cole's laugh, his approving eyes, his lips on her neck, she felt sick to her stomach when she put on her old black dress again. *I want to look nice, but I want to blend in with the crowd.* Instead of her usual ponytail, she let her hair fall over her face, hoping no one would notice the resemblance when she stood next to her sister, praying no one would notice the two girls with the same laugh who had supported each other their whole lives. She hung the dress on a hook next to the door to his room.

CHAPTER ELEVEN

EVERYTHING AROUND THE *Sunset*'s main swimming pool was red. The twinkling lights were red, the crew wore red, the drinks were red, the banners, balloons and flags were red, even the water in the swimming pool had been dyed red, with red candles glowing on silver floats. The band played red drums and guitars while the waiters circulated with sumptuous appetizers displayed on silver trays trimmed with red flowers. The effect was stunning.

The passengers danced and partied, enjoying the elegant setting, the stars above, and the moonlit waves below. Couples drifted into the dark corners, seduced by the cocktails and the sea air into taking some sweet, sexy time with their partners. But Oksana sat stiffly at the table she shared with Herr Strauss, while Primo leaned against the wall nearby. She had always loved to dance, but she was painfully aware that she could not join the dancers on the floor without Strauss's permission.

A waiter brought a tray of raw oysters, and Strauss sucked each one down noisily, belching and wiping his mouth when the plate was empty. His foot tapping off the beat, he patted Oksana's hand when the passengers, mostly women, formed up for a familiar line dance. "Go, little bird, dance mit da ladies, haf a goot time."

Patting the pocket where she'd tucked the note from her sister, she moved to the back of the group, looking around. A hand touched her shoulder, and there was Tania, standing next to her and smiling politely, as if introducing herself to a stranger. They moved together to the music, left, right, forward, back, and leaned in to talk over the loud music, keeping their smiles pasted on.

"I love you, I'm so glad to see you!" said Tania in Ukrainian, opening with her affection instead of her fear.

The calm and confident Oksana was long gone, and her lips trembled while she struggled not to cry. "I love you sooo much, and I am sorry to…sorry I'm in a mess." Her eyes were huge and frightened.

"I am here for you, I want to hug you so much right now. This is strange. We're pretending like we used to be friends, we went to the same school, that's the story, okay? So what is Strauss like, and Primo, the bodyguard?"

"Primo's okay, very nice, really. Emile…he…he says he's going to buy me an apartment in London, help me get a job. He…doesn't hit me or anything. But he…he likes to…"

"I know. I saw. The officers upstairs, they have cameras, and I saw you. He gives you to other men. He likes to watch."

Oksana looked away, her eyes filled with tears, and nodded. "Fucking Yury. And fuck-fucking scary Ivan, the g-g-guy he sold me to. Ivan gave me sleeping pills, and he fucked me when I was s-s-sleeeeping." She was swallowing a major crying jag, and it came out as a teary, low wail. "I didn't even know where I was or who else was th-there. He says he has…" with a hiccup, she whispered, "…he has terrible pictures of me."

"Ivan!" Tania's eyes went wide, but she steeled herself, remembering to keep the fake smile on. She took Oksana's hand, both to comfort her and turn her away from the bodyguard who watched their every move. "I met that *zhopa* the first day. He thinks every girl like us is a DUB, we're nothing more than dumb Ukrainian bitches to him, just off the boat from nowhere. He is the boss?" She took Oksana by the arm and guided her over to the buffet tables where the food was beautifully displayed.

As they walked, holding hands, they fell into the comfort of their old roles. Tania was soft-spoken and focused, a low-key dresser who was always planning the sisters' next step…and the next and the next. Oksana, laughing too loudly and talking too much, would sweep into a room and capture everyone's attention with her colorful clothes and dancer's grace. Though she was far from her usual flamboyant self, she still drew the eye of any male on the ship still breathing without an oxygen tank.

Oksana stared straight ahead, hiccupping again, her jaw set as they moved down the table, taking bits of food they both knew they wouldn't eat. They spoke in low voices, still nodding and smiling for Primo's benefit. "Not only the boss, but Ivan is the…the killer… how you say…the executioner as well. On the way here, there was a girl, Cara from Vietnam. She tried to get away from the hotel one night, and Ivan and the other Russian guy…" Her chest and shoulders shook while she tried desperately to suppress her sobs, letting her hair fall over her face. "The things they did to her, I dream of it at night, I wake up crying. Compared to that, Emile is nice to me." Her weeping subsided and Oksana wiped her eyes, straightened, and looked her sister over, as if seeing her for the first time. "How are *you*, my dear sister? How is your pain?"

Tania was touched that, even in the midst of this horrendous situation, Oksana remembered her problems with agonizing abdominal pain with her periods. "I had surgery for it, and it is much, much better. It was something called endometriosis, and lots of women have it." Smiling and nodding, she didn't tell her sister the scary side effect of her condition—Tania was probably infertile. There would be plenty of time to cry over such things later. For now,

Tania wanted nothing more than to hug her sister again and tell her everything would be all right. Instead, they would smile and pretend to be acquaintances.

"Let's not cry, big sister, we will fix this. It's going to be okay," Tania said, giving her sister's shoulder a squeeze. It might not be true, but it sounded good. "Primo is right behind us, watching, so act happy. Go to the show tomorrow night, and I'll meet you during intermission in the ladies room. I don't have a plan yet, but I will. "

Tania wanted to tell her about Cole and everything that had happened, but why? Her deception had turned him off, angered him, so his help seemed unlikely.

Still, she had never before felt the need to hold anything back from her sister. The two of them always revealed every little anxiety and regret to each other, sharing their cares and their dreams, imagining their magical endings together. But this was too big, too important for the sisters to be vulnerable with each other. *Eyes on the prize*, as Tania's college friends would say.

The line dance was over, and other musicians joined the steel band when they played a funky version of the swing dance classic *Boogie Woogie Bugle Boy*. Prowling the crowd looking for partners, one of the ship's handsome dancers grabbed Oksana's hands and pulled her into a wild jitterbug. His smile grew as he realized he'd hit the jackpot with Oksana's natural dance ability. She picked up the fancy footwork right away, inspiring others in the crowd to live in the moment and kick up their heels. Even Emile Strauss was caught up in the energy, clapping and smiling with pride while a dance floor full of passengers competed with Oksana and the dancer to show off their craziest gyrations.

*

Happy to see her sister smiling, if only for a moment, Tania blended back into the crowd and entered *Sunset's* lofty glass reception atrium, the center of the ship. Three or four generations of a large family posed on the gleaming marble staircase for the ship's photographer. The group was gathered around a smiling dressed-up couple who looked to be in their 80's, holding a sign reading, "Joe and Regina's 60th Wedding Anniversary."

Like my grandparents, Tania thought. *I have always wanted to be like my grandparents, living and working with the love of my life, having a family. Does it even happen in today's world?* For the first time since Cole's angry outburst, the tears crept up on her and she ducked into the ladies' room to wipe her eyes. *He's so angry. And he doesn't even know my other…secret.*

Removing the makeup from below her eyes with a paper towel, she looked in the mirror and remembered the day she'd been diagnosed with endometriosis. "We can help you with your pain, but women often have problems becoming pregnant with this condition," the doctors said.

After years of being doubled over with pain during her period every month, she'd had good results from the surgery. She knew she was better off, able to live a fuller life instead of being in agony for a week out of every month. But what would a man think of a woman who couldn't have a child? She hadn't given it much thought until she met Cole and started having silly forever daydreams. Still, feeling unworthy, the feeling of being less of a woman lurked in her heart.

When she left the restroom, she straightened her shoulders and pulled a piece of paper and her ID out of her purse while she gave her best imitation of walking confidently over to the registration desk.

"I have lost my key. Can I get another one for room…" she looked down at the paper, "…252, please?" Her polite smile was firmly in place as she showed the clerk her passport. She was still so proud of her American passport.

"Uh…there must be a problem in our system. We have no record of you checking in, Ms. Shevchenko."

"Oh, uh…what do we do, then?"

"Well…you are still registered for the room, so the problem must be on our end." The clerk swiped her a new key card and handed it to her with a smile. "Enjoy the rest of your cruise, ma'am."

Upstairs, she carried her things out of the room next to Cole's and winced when the door closed behind her with a click. She felt a stab of regret while she folded that room's key into the note she'd written for Cole and slid it under his door. She'd written:

Dear Cole,

After many changes the last few years, I have been awake but asleep, walking around in my life and hoping someone would take my hand and help me feel alive. You did that. I did not want to face the problem with my sister, and kept putting off telling you, and it was not honest. I am sorry. I have checked back into my original room, and I hope you'll forgive me and know that I appreciate everything you did for me. Thank you, Tania

CHAPTER TWELVE

OR TWENTY MINUTES, Herr Strauss listened intently to the guy who'd danced with Oksana while she and Primo stood watching the band. Strauss's eyes were wide, his face pink and sweaty as he nodded eagerly. The dancer's name was Lucas, a long, lean, badass-looking guy with dark skin and hair. His amazing Brazilian butt was solid muscle, along with every inch of his wide shoulders, narrow hips and an eight-pack of abs, if there is such a thing. While they talked, Lucas kept glancing at Oksana, licking his lips like a predator ready to pounce.

Lucas and Strauss walked toward Oksana, Lucas much faster, gliding along until he pressed his body against her back, leaning in to brush his lips across her neck. She tensed and turned to look at him when he whispered, "I was just telling Herr Strauss all the ways I'm going to tie you up and fuck you, Oksana. I'm Lucas, by the way."

Surrounding her with his powerful arms, he thrust one hand into her hair and pulled it back to open her throat to him. With the other hand, he captured her wrists, clasped them together and held them behind her back. He licked and nipped her neck, and when she gasped, fucked her open mouth with his tongue.

Primo took three steps away, his arms crossed over his chest, far enough away to appear professional, but close enough to step in and protect her if he had to. For some reason, he had to beat away the urge to kick Lucas in the balls.

The atmosphere in the elevator on the way up to Strauss's suite was thick with words unsaid and feelings unacknowledged. Strauss, nervous but excited, his pudgy fingers drumming on the wall. Lucas, cocky, alternating between holding Oksana so tightly she could barely breathe and putting his hands inside her shirt. Oksana, several shades paler than her usual golden glow, her breathing fast, her forehead beaded with nervous perspiration. Her eyes darted from Strauss to Primo, hoping for a sign that either man would rescue her from whatever this was, but finally she closed her eyes and took a deep breath, relaxing into the Brazilian's grip.

Every time Strauss set her up like this, she thought of Ivan and the Vietnamese girl who tried to run. After that, running did not seem like a good idea. And she still clung to Strauss's vague promises to set her up in her own place in London after the cruise. In her mind, she was decorating her new apartment, not submitting to... this.

Primo, arms folded even more tightly than before, watched the numbers on the elevator ascend intently. His tapping foot betrayed his agitation, but not enough to reassure her or alarm the other men. Just enough to acknowledge to himself that he felt like a shit for being a part of this ridiculous, unholy quartet. After unlocking the front door of the suite and ushering everyone in, he hurried to his room on the far side, where he paced back and forth, but left the door open to hear if Strauss called him.

At Lucas's direction, Oksana and the German left the light off while they sat on the suite's expansive deck, watching the moon's reflection on the sea. Though it was one of the most private decks on the ship, they heard women chattering in Arabic, probably Khalid's wives sitting on the deck of the neighboring suite.

The sound of the waves did nothing to soothe Oksana, because she had realized Lucas was much more knowing and deadly than the other bumbling fools Strauss had recruited along the way. Lucas had obviously done this kind of thing before, and when he left them standing on the deck, they heard him rummaging through the suite for a few minutes.

When he came back, he held out his hand for her clothes. "Strip," he told her, and she stood and kicked out of her heels, pulling off her dress, bra and panties, and handing them to him.

Her skin crawled with goose bumps, whether from the cool ocean breeze or her fear, who knew? "Put your hands on the railing facing away from me and spread your legs," Lucas said, fingering the bathrobe sashes and other items he'd taken from Strauss and Oksana's rooms.

While the German watched, sitting in a deck chair and clutching his hands together with excitement, Lucas tied Oksana's wrists to the railing and took his shirt off, rubbing up against her and rolling her nipples in his fingers, pinching them until she flinched, hissing "Shit !" under her breath.

"Stop whining, bitch," he growled, and slapped one of the voluptuous white globes of her ass, leaving an angry red imprint of his fingers and palm.

They heard a tiny stampede on the adjoining balcony as the Saudi women hustled into their suite, closing their sliding glass door with a thunk. Perhaps they'd heard these slapping noises before, or maybe they left at the direction of the single pair of footsteps reopening the door and taking their place on the deck in the ocean air.

"Be quiet, Oksana. No noise," commanded the Brazilian. Turning her face away from Strauss, Lucas stuffed a little sock in her mouth, quickly securing it with a scarf tied around her head.

When he bent her over the rail and pulled her legs farther apart, marking the other cheek with a loud smack, Strauss shifted in his seat, worry creasing his brow. Not wanting to piss off the German, Lucas responded by soothing Oksana, putting his hand between her legs, bending over her and keeping her warm while rubbing circles around her clit. Once she was soaked, he trailed his wet fingers up her belly and teased her nipples, which were already rigid from the sea breeze. He stepped back and both men feasted their eyes on Oksana's naked body.

"Do you want to come enjoy her now, Herr Strauss?" Lucas asked, gesturing toward her. Strauss waved his hands no, licking his lips and nodding for the Brazilian to continue. They both stared intently at Oksana, lust burning in their eyes.

"How many times, Herr Strauss? You decide how many swats. Ten? Twenty?" Lucas pressed up against her, his jeans unzipped, grinding into her through the thin fabric of his briefs.

Strauss walked over to Oksana and caressed her cheek. "Only ten, little bird, only ten." He put his hand on her ass where Lucas left his mark, feeling the heat, and handed the dancer a condom before he sat down.

"Would you count for me, Herr Strauss? Here's number three." He delivered another smack, a little harder this time, right at the top of her thigh.

Oksana made a low, guttural sound through the gag, her breathing heavy. "Three," Strauss repeated, his voice tight.

The next swat landed on her butt cheek with a deafening smack. She yelped and tensed against the next painful blow. "Four," Strauss choked out, crossing his arms over his chest. The Brazilian palmed his hand between her legs and then thrust two glistening fingers into her anus, forcing a muffled scream from her when he whispered to her in a fierce voice.

After two more harsh slaps turned Oksana's choked whimpers

into long, keening wails, the German stood and took a few steps back. He watched Lucas take off his belt, fold it in half, and raise his arm to deliver another blow. Oksana braced herself, knowing every line of her body was screaming for help, but Strauss only stared while the belt cracked down squarely across the center of both cheeks, leaving a thick red line when she screamed through the scarf, her body jolting. The smell of leather and fear mingled in the air. Lucas, stroking his cock with one hand while he raised the belt again, didn't even notice as the German rushed back into the suite, right for Primo's open door.

"End zis now!" yelled Strauss, eyes on fire. "I'm afraid da fucker vill kill bot' of us!"

Strauss stood at the door to his own room and watched while Primo moved swiftly behind the Brazilian, whose pants were now slung low around his knees, and flung Lucas, still holding the belt, over one shoulder. The dancer struggled but suddenly found himself out the door, thrown like a rag doll against a wall in the hallway.

"This is over. Don't come back." One of Primo's huge hands completely covered the Brazilian's throat. "Do you understand?" Primo felt Lucas swallow as he nodded, and the dancer hiked up and then adjusted his pants before hurrying down the long hallway.

Closing the door behind him with a slam, Primo strode out to the balcony. "Take care of her," said Strauss while Primo undid the scarf and the sashes and carried Oksana back to her room. "Take goot care of her."

He lay her on her bed, covering her with an extra quilt. Her shivering was incredibly intense, clearly caused by adrenaline and not the cool night air. Primo stood thinking for a few moments. "How about a bath? Can I draw you a hot bath?" She nodded, tears streaming down her cheeks.

*

After pulling out a fresh bathrobe and towel, he went back for her while the tub filled. She hesitated at first, not wanting to get out from under the covers, but finally remembered he'd already seen her completely naked. He'd carried her in his arms completely naked, as a matter of fact. She was anxious to wash off the filth from the dancer, get his stink off of her. Primo held the robe for her and waited patiently when she belted it closed, weeping again when the sash reminded her of Lucas's cruel beating.

And of Strauss's mindless betrayal of … her trust? Yes, it was odd, but he had taken care of her up until now, despite his strange sexual desires. During her journey here, she'd heard stories from other girls about the physical abuse, gang rape and confinement they'd experienced.

For her, it had been a relief to be with the German and get away from Ivan's little everyday cruelties and his daily demand for a blow job. The best part about those blow jobs were that Ivan didn't last long, especially if she moaned and acted excited. *Stupid men. Do they really think women get excited about their ugly-ass huey when they force you to suck it?! Pfft!* She realized she must be feeling a little better, because she almost giggled at her private joke. Giggled. After all that. *What am I, crazy?*

In the bathroom Primo stuck his hand in the water to check the temperature and helped her into the tub, laying her robe and the big fluffy towel on the counter nearby. "Call me when you're ready to go back to your room. I'll be right outside the door." His face was unreadable except for a little spark in his eye.

She was sure she saw it. A spark of …concern, maybe even affection. *Hmmm.*

When he ushered her back into the bedroom, she saw he'd

found one of her nightgowns and laid it on the bed. "Before you go to bed, I…" he paused, his deep voice uncertain. "I have some experience treating bruises, and I have a special arnica cream that will help your skin heal. Would you like to use it?"

Again she nodded and sat on the edge of the bed until he returned with it. Blushing all over, she took off her robe and lay naked on the bed on her stomach. "Would you…mind putting it on me? I don't want to waste it." *Can you imagine? I can still blush like this after everything that has happened to me?* She had the urge to giggle at herself again—*I'm a little hysterical, maybe*—but quieted when she felt the bed sink when Primo sat on the edge.

He dotted the cream on the purplish welt from the belt and she winced. "Please continue," she said when he hesitated. "I will be fine." To ease his discomfort with touching her so intimately, she asked him a question. "Where did you learn how to treat bruises like this?"

He paused, weighing his response. "I was a fighter, so I had to learn to take care of my own bruises after fights. This cream worked the best." He continued to spread the cream on the red spots and rub it in. When he put her hand on his knee to rub the cream onto her wrists where they'd been bound, she noticed he had a raging erection. But because of his tender care, she wasn't frightened of him.

"Boxing? Were you a boxer?" she asked, looking up at him.

"No. Mixed martial arts. Ever heard of it?"

Her eyes grew large while she stared at him, rolling over and handing him her other wrist. "I saw it on TV once. *Bozhe miy,* Primo! It was so scary and violent. How did you survive?!"

Although he was smiling while he continued to massage her wrist, his voice was strained when he answered "I won a lot, that's how I survived. But I won't survive being here if you don't cover your breasts!"

She pulled up the blanket and did as he asked, but smoothed her hand across his cheek. His eyes closed when he took a deep breath and leaned into her. Then he rose to leave after giving her a quick peck on the cheek.

"Primo," she called softly after him. "I have a question for you. Emile wants me to have sex with these men, why did he never ask you to have sex with me?"

A wonderful grin she'd never seen before spread across his face. He suddenly looked like the handsome young man he was, instead of one with the weight of the world on his very broad shoulders. "Oh, he did ask me. But I said no."

She paused, surprised. "You said no?" Her face was stricken, her words trembling a little.

Still grinning, his eyes ignited as he looked at her. "Oh, I want to. And I will. But not the way *he* wants me to, and not with him watching. I'm going to love you right, from the top of your head to the tips of your toes. Good night, Oksana."

She smiled a little and curled up in a tight ball when he turned off the light and closed the door behind him, his words helping erase some of the ugliness from the evening, from the last few months, and from the bad decisions she'd made. Apparently Primo didn't think she was dirty, that she was damaged goods. And if he didn't think so, maybe it might be a little true.

*

Humming a German folk tune, Emile Strauss stepped away from the peephole where he'd watched Primo massage the cream onto Oksana's bruises and kiss her. His mind was racing forward to the time he would watch them make love, from the tops of their heads to the tips of their toes. It sounded delicious, like his favorite pastry, and he knew exactly how to make it happen.

CHAPTER THIRTEEN

"SHE TALKED TO her sister, did you see? They have the same smile." The brothers were on the bridge steering the ship through the open sea to Ireland, and Jack sounded worried, easing into a difficult conversation with his brother.

"Yeah, Ewan played me the clip."

"Did you see Strauss's crew leave with Lucas, the dancer?"

Cole nodded. He'd felt like he was swallowing ashes after seeing it, helpless to resist the knowledge that he now felt responsible for Tania's sister. "The dancer is bad news. Remember the incident in Glasgow last trip?"

"Oh, fuck, yeah," said Jack. "Who could forget Lucas bringing his bleeding girlfriend back from her botched abortion, pretending everything was okay?" Jack shook his head. "Abortions are legal there, but how did it even happen?" Despite the fact that free condoms were available throughout the crew area, they'd had to deal with many staff pregnancy situations.

"Ignorance. Bare-assed, fucking ignorance is the only thing I can think of. I told Jeannette he was bad news, and she agreed, but hasn't found a replacement yet. Don't know exactly what Lucas did in Strauss's room, but this is it. He's out!" Cole spread his hands, leaning on the console across from his brother. "So…uh…I notice you were checking out the girl dancing at the pool party. Again. Man, you got it bad!"

"Fuck you," Jack said, laughing. "And speaking of gettin' it bad, Pot—meet Kettle!

"Yeah, this trip has been unusual that way." Cole shrugged, feeling a little awkward. "I feel a question coming at me here, bro. Out with it."

"What are we doing here, Cole? What's the plan with Tania and the sister?"

"What do you mean?" Tired and in a foul mood, he knew exactly what his brother meant, but he was irritated at the way Jack read his mind. And the fact that Jack figured out before he had that something was up with Tania. He couldn't help remembering Tania's lips stretched around him, her eyes looking up at him, giving him permission to take over her sweet seduction. *Thinking with the little head, Cole, thinking with the little head. Damn those beautiful eyes, looking away whenever I asked about her sister. And what did it mean? Was she manipulating me from the beginning?*

Jack jumped in, speaking low and calm. "You're usually the first to weigh the hot-to-crazy ratio, my brother. I mean, she's hot and obviously into you, but this whole thing with her sister is nuts. You're a little off balance with this one—what is it about this girl? Or maybe you're going through, like, a midlife crisis. You've been off lately."

Cole ignored the rest but asked, "You think she's really into me? Not, like she needs my help so she slept with me...uh, us?"

"Cole, *really?*" Jack chuckled, shrugging. "I was like Santa's ugly little helper that night! She probably imagined I was you the whole time, she was sooo fucking into you!"

Now it was Cole's turn to laugh. "She actually did tell me something along those lines, bro. Sorry to tell ya'."

"You're not sorry at all. And I don't blame you." Jack locked eyes with him. "Bottom line. Where're we going on this? If we're hands off, let me know. If you want to protect her, help her, tell me, and I'm in. We'll ride in on the white horse and make it happen."

He stuck his hand out and Cole shook it and clapped him on the back. "Thanks, Jack. You're the best." They shared a man hug for a few seconds, glad for the umpteenth time to have each other. "I don't have a plan yet, but keep the white horse saddled up. We'll figure it out."

Cole walked away, paused, and turned back to his brother, arms crossed. "By the way, bro, I've, uh…got a favor to ask. The other night when you…when we…uh…were with Tania. I'd like you to unsee it and never, ever mention it again. Got it?"

Jack zipped two pinched fingertips across his forehead. "My mind is sealed already, I swear." He paused for effect, his solemn face erupting into a grin. "I don't remember a thing about those rosy nipples of hers, or her totally spectacular ass!"

Cole lunged for him, but he was already gone, running down the hall to the bathroom, locking himself in and laughing like a jackass until he knew his brother had to leave for an event.

*

After Cole left, Jack strolled over to Ewan's monitors. He had this new…habit. At least, that's what he told himself. MacGrath, poking fun at him, said it was an obsession. Anyway, Ewan could usually find this young woman who was one of the ship's room stewards on one of the ship's camera feeds. Jack liked to watch her, was fascinated by her, in fact.

He'd met Daniella a few times, the first time shaking her hand and welcoming her (and a hundred or so others) at a pre-sail reception for new staff and crew on the ship. Daniella Flores was her name, a curvaceous American college student who'd signed on at the last minute. Smart and articulate, she would normally have been put behind a service desk, but only room steward positions had been available for this sailing.

Born and raised in the states by Mexican parents, Daniella enjoyed fooling people with her gorgeous Hispanic bombshell appearance. From her amazing caramel-colored skin to her silky reddish-black hair, she fit the Americans' bootylicious Jennifer Lopez stereotype. In the reception line where he met her, he saw one of the British officers ask her in a halting, overly-loud voice, "Hello. Do. You. Speak. English?"

She burst out laughing and replied, in an equally condescending tone, "Yes. I. Do. I. Am. An. American. College. Student." The officer had the good grace to blush and apologize, caught with his stereotyping pants down.

When it was Jack's turn to shake her hand, he apologized to her again. "Sorry about that, some of our officers don't get out much." When it turned out she was going to school in Las Vegas, they compared notes about living in Sin City, and he was impressed by her wit and classy attitude. "I apologize that you have to work as a room steward. It's a complete waste of your skills. The passengers would love talking with you."

She had laughed and patted his hand...comforting him? "It's okay, this is what's available, and I'm sure I'll get to know some passengers anyway. I'll probably do another contract after this one so I can start school again with plenty of money next year. Maybe you'll put in a good word for me for my next contract?" She'd looked at him from under her lashes, a little flirty, but mostly sweet.

Daniella's eyes were so bright and full of hope, but he swore he saw the devil twinkling in there right next to the angel. The beauty mark near her mouth drew attention to her dazzling smile and low, easy laugh. And her walk. Her walk knocked him out, her hips tracing sexy circles with each step, effortlessly erotic. Soft curls from her thick hair were already escaping from the bun she wore for work and for boring parties like this pre-sail reception and meet-and-greet for the new staff.

Of course, the entertainment director was bound and determined to make even this low-key staff party entertaining. "As you know," Jeannette said while the DJ cued up some music, "SunShips is in the business of fun. We're going to kick off the fun by finding the hidden talent in this room, and we're offering an extra four hours of paid time off to the winner of our two-minute dance contest!" The DJ played the party anthem "Play That Funky Music," setting the tone for the competition.

For crew members who worked ten-hour days, four hours of free time was a great incentive, but only four bold people volunteered. The first one was a tall guy from the bursar's office whose stiff moves and white man's overbite made him appear to be in pain. A lovely Filipino girl did a very enthusiastic chicken dance. The third contestant was an eager Indonesian fellow who mostly waved his arms, inexplicably ending his routine by sitting in a chair in the middle of the room.

The last dancer was Daniella. He learned later that she was a pretty famous dancer at her university, her natural, freestyle moves a legend on the party scene there. Letting the music tell her what to do, she slowly gyrated her hips while she took the pins out and let down her hair. Whooping and hollering broke out while she found her rhythm, her midsection twitching north, south, east, west, as she glanced over her shoulder at Jack. But Jack knew how to bust some moves as well, and he made his strut sexier as he responded to hers and mirrored her around the dance floor. But when she pushed him down in the chair vacated by the Indonesian, her booty-shaking sort-of lap dance brought down the house, and the two-minute contest was definitely won and done.

Daniella was so addictive, so fresh and eager, Jack would've liked to pull her down onto his lap and kiss her. "I've got a first-class seat right here, girl," he said, patting his lap and smiling while the cheering wound down.

But instead she turned and gave him a salute. "I salute you Captain, for your efforts in creating a positive work environment on the *Sunset*. Thank you."

Jeannette rushed over and slapped her on the back, full of congratulations and raving about her dancing. "Where did you learn to dance? It's incredible!" She turned to Jack. "I have some money in my budget, I'm going to give her some extra duties as a party hostess!"

And that's how his preoccupation with Daniella Flores began.

"Dude, she just turned twenty-one, you know that, right?" Cole said the next day, catching Jack watching Daniella on the security screen for the hundredth time. They were watching Jeannette and two other staffers present a birthday cake to Daniella in the ship's ice cream parlor, and she was blowing out her candles. "Barely fucking legal for you, old man. She might give you a heart attack or something."

"Tell me about it!" Jack laughed ruefully. "She's got my balls in a twist, and I barely know her."

He'd downloaded footage onto his phone of her dancing with passengers at the nightclub and around the pool, and was starting to wonder if watching her on his phone so many times was illegal or a sign of mental illness. Every time he pressed play, he thought about…well, obviously he thought about *that*, sure, but he also thought about going beyond that, really seeing her, being with her.

"The next thing you know, you'll stop being a man-whore and ask her if she wants to cuddle." Cole whispered in his ear. Cole was a little worried when his brother didn't have a raunchy reply. From the look on Jack's face, it seemed like he might actually be thinking seriously about a cuddle.

*

It drove Daniella insane—when she was working, hauling garbage, laundry, whatever—Jack would show up, hanging out, talking to passengers and watching her, his stare so fucking intense it felt like a laser aimed at her lips. Then he would appear at the nightclub or a party, shaking hands with people, his gaze direct and honest, a half-smile on his face. He would come up behind her and stand there, a little too close, nothing too obvious.

After a dance club event with Jeannette, she thought she felt him behind her and turned with a smile, which immediately faded when she realized it was the weirdo Russian guy, Ivan. The dancers were buzzing about him, saying he was so sophisticated or whatever, but he gave Daniella the creeps. "Heeeey, Chica," he said to her, touching her arm familiarly. "I was watching you dance tonight and I wanted to give you my card. I'll hook you up with producers, people who make music videos. Let's talk, I'll buy you a drink."

"Uh, no thanks, and I'm not your fucking chica, okay?" He had a vise grip on her wrist now and pulled her along like she owed him something.

The forward movement stopped abruptly when Jack stepped between them, glaring down at Ivan, his nostrils flared as if he smelled something rotten. "Are you not familiar with the term 'no thanks,' Mr. Fedorov? It usually means the young lady doesn't wish to accompany you." Ivan stepped back, cursing under his breath, and shuffled away. A group of passengers asked the captain to pose for a picture and Daniella mouthed thank you to him while her friends pulled her over to the bar.

It was so confusing. One minute she felt Jack's breath on her neck, making her tingle where he murmured something too close to her ear. "Hey, you are so fucking hot tonight," he whispered one night, so quiet no one else could hear. Moments later he'd be talking and laughing with a passenger, focusing solely on that person, whether man or woman. She was bewildered and felt completely off balance from his mood swings, seemingly indifferent to her one minute and intensely sexual the next. *Fucking player. Well. I can play too. I think.*

It was fun to "not see" each other in public, at her dance gigs; it held a secret danger for both of them. Dressed in something sexy she'd borrowed from Jeannette, she wore little or no underwear, so her curves did their natural, undulating thing when she was dancing. She wore an insanely sexy perfume from Ivanka which she knew drew him close to her neck, beckoning that sexy body of his ever so slightly toward her when he worked the room with his considerable physical size and dazzling personality. It troubled her to think of the ladies he'd been with (including Jeannette), versus her own pathetically limited experience, but…might as well start at the top, eh?

Daniella was leaning against a pillar in the atrium lobby, sucked into a full-on Jack fantasy when she felt someone next to her.

"A zillion for your thoughts," Jeannette said, giving her a hug and a peck on the cheek, not really expecting an answer.

In Daniella's flustered state, a shrug was all she could muster. She was happy to shake off her dizzy infatuation with the captain when they hurried off to eat a quick lunch together before returning to their grueling schedules.

CHAPTER FOURTEEN

THE FIRST TIME Tania sat by herself in the dining room, she overheard a tall, blonde member of the wait staff cursing exquisitely in Russian. She smiled to herself at first, hiding her amusement at the contrast between the woman's nasty language and the quiet clinking of glasses, murmured conversations in English, and the bland elevator music playing on the sound system. But she couldn't hold it in, and soon her entire body was shaking while tears of laughter ran down her cheeks. After the emptiness of waking in her own little bed without Cole, it felt good to be overcome by the need to laugh.

When the woman suddenly appeared next to her, eyebrow raised, Tania was startled. "*Ya dumayu, vy ponyali, chto ya skazal, da?*" the woman asked.

"Yes. I understood everything you said and you said it… extremely well!" Tania laughed and offered her hand. "Hi, Tania Shevchenko. From the Ukraine, but now American." She looked at the Russian's badge. "Happy to meet you, Ivanka."

Ivanka shook her hand, sat herself down across from Tania and stared, cradling her chin in her hand. She seemed intrigued by Tania, a friendly homegirl who was a passenger, not staff. "These *debils* I work with are driving me mad. Are you here with your husband or boyfriend?"

"No, I'm here enjoying the cruise. I'm a nurse."

"Ohhhh," said Ivanka, leaning back and giving her a knowing glance. "So you're *looking* for a husband or boyfriend!"

Tania blushed and laughed again, patting Ivanka's hand. The woman reminded her of her best friend in high school, funny and fearless. "Aren't we all, Ivanka, aren't we all? But meanwhile, do you ever have any time to hang out? Or do you have to work all the time?"

"I'm a housekeeping manager in addition to working some meals, but we're having a big staff party tonight. Really, really late, like two in the morning! Do you want me to sneak you in, *podruga*?"

"Absolutely!" Tania giggled because Ivanka was calling her *podruga* (girlfriend) already. Everything about this outspoken Russian was unexpected and hilarious. "Can't wait. What does a housekeeping manager do, by the way?"

"Oh, I supervise the *bednyye dushi*, the poor souls who clean and supply the big suites, the rich people up on the top of the ship! Have you seen the sheikh and his wives, with their stupid veils on? Some of them are very pretty under there, I saw them. He has a mistress on my floor, too, but I haven't seen her lately."

"You know everything, don't you, Ivanka? Hey…" Tania said, leaning forward. "What about the German guy, are you in charge of his suite? I met the Ukrainian girl who is with him last night. She went to my high school."

Ivanka was clearly enjoying gossiping about her passengers. "Ohhh, Oksana? Uch, the poor kid. I don't know how she puts up with that *ubulludok*!"

Tania laughed again, tickled by Ivanka's talented mastery of Russian insults. "I kno-ow! She does not seem too happy, does she?"

"I have to get back to work," Ivanka stood abruptly, rolling her eyes. "My *glupo bossa*, the head waiter, is giving me the stink eye. What do you want to eat?"

"Bring me whatever you think looks good," Tania said. "All this food looks great to me." It was a big change from the economy diet she'd been on for years, ramen noodles, apples and cereal when she ran out of paycheck. Feeling good for having made another contact with access to her sister, Tania enjoyed brunch and walked off the ship to explore the city of Cobh, where they were docked for the day.

*

Imagining she was walking with Cole, her hand engulfed in his, she wandered aimlessly for a while until she fell into step with Ellora Lind, the author and lecturer whose photo she'd seen on posters around the ship. After exchanging the usual passenger pleasantries, they decided to share the day. The older woman was warm, friendly, and impossibly enthusiastic, inviting her along on a drive to nearby Kinsale, a beautiful little village with loads of history.

"Hey, looks like you and I are the single girls out for a day of fun, eh?" Ellora said, as she pulled Tania with her toward a waiting cab. When Tania hesitated, Ellora added "It's already paid for, don't worry about it! I'm thrilled to have your company."

Everyday Ireland flew by while the cab driver pointed out sights along the way, while explaining that the Emerald Isle is so green because it's favored with warm trade winds and lots of rain. A sparkling bay with hundreds of sailboats bobbing in the sunshine was bordered on one side by the charming village of Kinsale and the other by quirky hilltop homes and the seventeenth-century Charles Fort.

Smiling, their hair whipping in the wind, the two women had the cab driver take their picture next to the fort. It was the first time Tania had ever experienced the freedom people were supposed to feel on vacation, the joy of being away from everyday responsibilities and indulging in new experiences. During her day in Normandy with Cole, she'd been consumed by learning everything about him, feeling happy, but driven to understand and communicate with him. This was different, completely carefree. She imagined for a moment that Oksana was with her, and resolved to bring her here someday. *What was Oksana doing right now, this minute?*

When they got back in the cab to return to town, they sat quietly for a while. "Who were you thinking about back there?" Ellora asked, patting her hand.

"I was…how did you…I was thinking about my sister." Tania answered, tears burning her eyes.

"Well, I don't know her, but I wish she were here as well, sweet girl." She paused. "I'm a therapist, remember? It might have been windy, but your feelings hung in the air."

Tania nodded, but appreciated that Ellora didn't ask her anything else. She didn't want to tell another half-truth, like she'd done with Cole. Half-truths are lying in the end. She was getting better at discretion, at choosing what to disclose, and allowing herself to feel things without explaining. It felt like progress, somehow, like growing up.

She and Oksana had grown up without a role model for these things. Grandma was the old-fashioned silent type, and their mom was only interested in where her next drink was coming from. *It is amazing how much you don't know that you don't know until you need to know it,* Tania thought.

While the two women wandered among the brightly-colored shops and restaurants, their guide regaled them with stories of the important battles and political struggles which had taken place in Kinsale. They stopped for fish n' chips at an outdoor restaurant, and Ellora kept the Harp lager flowing for both of them.

"I saw your book is about sex therapy," Tania said, feeling herself blush hotly. "Can I ask you a question?"

Ellora chuckled. "Your blushing is absolutely adorable, dear girl. Even the part in your hair is red!" They both laughed and Ellora leaned across the table. "So in any case, most people have at least *one* question to ask me. Fire away, darling!"

"Why would a man..." Tania swallowed and took a deep breath,"... share his woman with another man? I don't understand it."

"Oh, my! Well, that's an advanced question with many, many answers. What do you know about BDSM – bondage, discipline, sadism, and masochism?"

"You mean, like, tying up, spanking, that kind of stuff?"

"Yes. That kind of stuff, exactly." Ellora leaned even closer, her chin resting on her hand, searching Tania's face, and then blowing out a long breath before launching into her explanation. "Soooo... some people, be they a man or a woman, have a strong need for control in a sexual relationship. Others enjoy giving up control to a dominant person. When these two types find each other and agree on the rules, they can be very happy, and everyone involved may *want* to share with others in some way, just for fun.

"But then there are the men, mostly men, who *pay* to have someone to submit to them. They offer money to make it happen. They don't care if the person is willing to submit or share, maybe even like it *better* if they don't want to, they simply pay for it and demand it. Our sheikh on board the ship is one of these types, he doesn't give a flying fuck what anyone else wants, he just wants to be in control. And I don't think he would *ever* share. Have you seen the guy?" Ellora shrugged, her feelings about the Saudi prince evident.

"Yes, actually, it's like he *wants* to be seen that way, right?"

"Right. He gets off on it, excuse the expression. Now there's another type, kind of unusual. Have you seen the older German guy with the blonde girl and the big bodyguard?"

Tania studied the placemat to hide her reaction. "Yes. Uh…I know who you mean. The bodyguard sat at my table one night, along with some other people."

"Now…" Ellora was staring off into the distance, thinking and sipping her beer, "…of course he's paying for it, too, the German fellow, but I hear from some crew members who've been approached that he only wants to watch his girlfriend with other men."

Her fingers tapped on the table, and she appeared to be accessing some information stored deep in her brain. "Now *why*, you may ask? Well, I can't be sure, but my guess is he likes to show off, like 'see this lovely toy I have,' and it gives him a sense of power and control. And maybe it's important to him because…" Ellora paused for a long moment, thinking and drinking. "Maybe because… the man is not well, he can't have sex himself for some health reason, perhaps, so he gets off on doing this instead. It's my theory, anyway. Was that the source of your question?"

"Yes, actually, how did you know?" Tania was happy Ellora didn't inquire if her question had personal significance.

"Oh, my dear, the whole ship is abuzz with it, all sorts of speculation flying about. Everyone stares at the first class passengers, the ones invited to the captain's table. Discussing *that* makes my job a lot easier than addressing people's very real and complicated personal problems!" She chuckled a little, tilting her head to one side, her eyes questioning. "I feel like you have another question, Tania. What is it?"

Tania cleared her throat, leaning forward over the table. "So… this…BDSM you talked about, bondage and all that. People who like to do it…is there something wrong with them? Are they bad people?"

Her eyes wide, Ellora said, "No, noooo," and she laughed. "When both partners consent, when they enjoy it, when it's used to make sex more intense and pleasurable, then I think it's perfectly okay. When there's pain, lack of consent or if sex isn't part of the deal, then, at least in my experience, it may be a symptom of a disorder, you know?"

Tania shrugged, quiet again. She had another question. "Then… the people who give up control. Do they really want to be punished, do they…want to be prisoners or something like that?"

Ellora looked thoughtful, her fingers drumming on the table again. "People like to say so, to believe it, don't they? It's the Freudian shit that's out there, you know, 'my daddy didn't like me so now I have to act it out.' No, it may be true some of the time, but not always. For some of my patients, it's a game, a power exchange, a way of forcing yourself to live in the moment." Looking right in Tania's eyes, her mouth twisted into a sly smile. "Which is certainly how I've used it in my own sex life."

Tania nodded, blushing again, and Ellora picked up her cell, calling the cab to pick them up. "Let's go back to the ship and take our naps, shall we?" Tania thanked her for the wonderful day as they got in the cab, and Ellora immediately began her nap, snoring pleasantly on the way back to the ship.

*

Later in the evening, when Tania walked into the ship's expansive theater, the house lights were already dimmed, and the dancers and singers were performing their medley of current Broadway favorites, complete with elaborate sets and costumes. She deliberately sat in the very last row, near the exit and the restroom where she planned to meet her sister. Three different servers stopped and asked her if

she wanted to order a drink, but she waved them away politely, trying to appear intent on the show.

When a glitzy production number seemed to be leading into
intermission, she went to the ladies' room and busied herself with
washing her hands, fixing her hair, and hiding out in a stall for a
while, checking for her sister's feet while women came and went.

Finally she recognized her sister's shoes and came out. Oksana
still wore the little silver heart necklace Tania had given her at graduation. They stood at the sink, greeting each other like acquaintances
and washing their hands together, waiting for another woman to
leave. When she did, Tania embraced Oksana as she'd longed to
last night and kissed both her cheeks before noticing the red marks
around her wrists.

"What the hell!? Who hurt you, Oksana?" she asked, hugging
her even tighter and staring in her face, trying to read her feelings.

"One of the *chortiv* dancers. Emile invited him, the *mudak*!"

"Are you okay?" Tania's mind expanded and she suddenly realized every added day could bring terrible harm to her sister. She was
amazed at how resilient and cheerful Oksana seemed in spite of it.

When they looked in the mirror and smiled at each other,
Oksana as blonde as Tania was dark, as golden-skinned as Tania was
pale, the resemblance between the sisters was still unmistakable.

Oksana blushed and took her sister's hand, kissing it affection-
ately, and said, "I am so blessed to have you for a sister, Tania, that
you would come and be here, in this terrible situation, for me." And
then, amazingly, Oksana smiled, and said, "But the thing with the
dancer was good in the end because Primo threw the guy out and
took care of me. And he told me he likes me."

Tania rolled her eyes, annoyed at her sister's latest crush. She'd
always been this way, throwing her whole heart at her latest boyfriend. "Let's not count on any man, not completely, okay? We

should have learned *that* lesson, hey? And I made friends with a Russian woman, she's in housekeeping in your section."

"Ivanka. She talked to me. Nice. A little *fou-fou*, though."

The sisters laughed knowingly, because Ivanka reminded both of them of their nutty high school friend. They hugged again, and Tania said, "I want to get you off the ship, but not until we get to the mainland, to Liverpool or Glasgow. And find out where he keeps your passport, because you will need it."

One last hug and Oksana was out the door. As it swung wide, Tania saw Primo leaning against the opposite wall, watching. His eyes went wide and then narrowed when he saw Tania behind his charge, and he stood straight, nodding in her direction. *Is he nodding at her or at me? What does it mean?*

No matter, it was time to go back to her room and sleep before meeting Ivanka. Not sure what time zone she was in at this point, she wished she had warned Oksana not to talk to Ivanka yet, but... *whatever*, as her American friends would say. *Whatever.*

∗

Ivan waited at the stage door for the dancers to come out after the show. He was dressed to the nines and looking his usual dapper self. Struggling, starving dancers were his bread and butter, the source of most of the call girls he booked with his wealthy clients from around the world. A few of the dancers from the ship's troupe were on his hook, ready to swallow his bullshit about how easy it is to make a bunch of money as a "companion," enjoying international travel, luxurious accommodations, and an unlimited clothing budget.

Dancers wanted to dance, so he lured others with the promise of being their agent and placing them in high-profile shows, naming names familiar to anyone in the theater. Of course he had no intention of doing any such thing, choosing dancers who had few friends and weak family connections. He'd talked to a few of the pretty Indonesian room stewards as well. Once he had their passports and took away their cell phone, they would disappear into the dark world of sex trafficking and never be seen again, moving from strip joints to brothels before descending to the dregs of the sex trade.

Taking a deep draw on his cigarette, Ivan felt good. He looked forward to closing a deal with two of the dancers tonight, buying them drinks, and then sampling the merchandise personally.

He was startled when one of the ship's fierce-looking Gurkha security officers tapped him on the shoulder.

"We're watching you," the Gurkha said in his gravelly voice, pointing to a camera on the ceiling and handing Ivan the twenty or so business cards he'd given to vulnerable young people on the ship. "All these people have been warned about you. Stop talking to our staff. Now."

Sputtering, speechless, while the performers shouldered past him quickly without looking his way, Ivan wilted, glaring at the camera and at the bristling officer who stared at him, arms crossed.

Ewan and Cole, observing the exchange from the bridge, whooped and hollered at the sour, defeated look on the Russian's face.

CHAPTER FIFTEEN

N O ONE COULD deny it could be fun being a passenger, but the staff and crew threw the wildest parties. Those events took place in the wee hours of the morning, on the crew deck, and in the maze of hallways, bunks and public rooms on Deck 1. After smiling their faces off and working 12-hour shifts, most crew members are ready to drink themselves into a stupor. The younger ones were often looking to get laid, the quick remedy for being far away from loved ones.

The women come to the party dressed in skimpy club wear, ready for action. From cruise management's point of view, the mindless hookups often caused more stress than they soothed, because the number of women leaving the ship to have babies in their home countries was high.

Asian, Indian, eastern European, Caribbean, many of the female crew members were away from home and earning money for themselves for the first time. Which was why Tania's new friend Ivanka was dancing like a sexy dervish to the driving music accompanying the party on the crew deck, her hair and clothes drenched with sweat while she pulled Tania in to join her feverish, dirty grinding.

"I only dance with staff, no crew!" she yelled over the music into Tania's ear. Crew were the waiters, busboys, maintenance, and the like; staff included the officers, management, and entertainment and spa vendors.

"Why?" Tania yelled back.

"Most of the staff are married, and I don't want to get involved with single guys. They want to marry me and take my money!"

Tania could only laugh; Ivanka's reasoning was twisted, but oddly sound. Both women responded to the thumping beat, the sultry night air, and the mass of writhing, gleefully drunk bodies around them.

At the center of their little all-female group, Jeannette and Daniella were grindin' up on each other in a daze of alcohol, lust and laughter. The giggling increased when Daniella started twerking—bending her knees and bouncing her butt up and down while somehow jiggling her butt cheeks at the same time.

Daniella was flat-out hot, but when other women tried to imitate her it was really funny. Already wobbly on their four-inch heels, the ladies were happy to fall into each other's arms when twerking turned out to be beyond their capabilities. The falling led to groping, which led to kissing and general girl-girl experimentation.

None of the partiers knew Tania was a passenger. What passenger speaks four languages and chooses to hang out here? Within minutes, she was bouncing around with the rest of the crowd, singing along, dancing her heart out. When she raised her arms, the tiny dress Ivanka loaned her might have exposed her thong, but so what? It was okay to be wild here, to be young and crazy. She had almost missed this kind of twentysomething mindless fun, she'd been working so hard to earn the necessary credentials and begin work. Yet here she was, under the half moon, dancing like a wild thing.

Tania felt a tingling along the back of her neck, a sense of someone's eyes burning through her skin, watching her. Searching the shadows off the dance floor, she locked eyes with Cole. He nodded, his expression neutral, watching her with his baseball cap pulled down, his arms crossed, looking very sexy in his jeans and a thin grey T-shirt hugging his powerful arms and muscular chest.

Catching him while he watched her made something hitch in her chest, and her skin flushed hot all over. Dancing for him lifted her like a leaf on the wind, and she felt carefree, energized, and desirable. She closed her eyes and lost herself in the music until Ivanka put her hand on Tania's shoulder and yelled that she was off to fuck a friend of hers.

True to her declaration, Ivanka began gyrating suggestively against one of the giant casino guards, a tall, handsome East Indian staffer with a wide, white smile. Tania blew her a kiss and went toward the dark corner where Cole waited. Unsure of his reaction, she was glad the music was too loud for meaningful conversation.

Her breath caught when he touched her cheek while he looked her over appreciatively. "I'm sorry I got so angry. You didn't deserve it," he said, leaning close to her ear. His hand lingered, brushing her hair back, his fingers warm against her neck. "I've missed being with you."

*

Cole couldn't remember ever *needing* to touch someone the way he needed to touch Tania. He remembered the first time he'd seen her, the spark in her big, brown eyes, the resolve in her long, athletic stride. Her ponytail was always swinging along behind her, her shoulders back and straight, looking like she was ready to take on the world. The pouty lips and the sweet ass…well, those were icing on the cake.

Maybe that was why, when he'd gotten the impression she didn't really care, that she might be using him, it had upset and angered him so much.

She nodded and pecked his cheek, seeming to accept his apology.

He let out a long breath, surprised to realize he'd been holding it. He'd been so anxious after she moved out of the room next to his, wondering if it was a permanent separation, emotional as well as physical. But now she was touching him back, soothing him, moving around behind him, putting her hands on his waist and peeking over his shoulder, making him shiver when she exhaled against his neck. Every move was a little tentative, as if she was unsure of him or feared he would snub her.

Cole fought to stay loose, although he was pissed at himself. *I fucked up the easy way we were getting to know each other, and of course she doesn't trust me now. I have to get us back to the way we were.*

Standing on her toes, she spoke over the music. "I met Ivanka at breakfast. She invited me to this party." There was an unmistakable question in her voice, asking if she'd made a mistake by coming here.

Cole felt a twist in his gut, a sick feeling. *She's scared of me.* Her confidence in him was gone, shattered by his stupid outburst. Clearly she'd had some experience with anger and dysfunction, like he and Jack had when they were teens. *Maybe I can distract her. If I can get the heat back in her eyes, maybe I can make her forget what an ass I was.*

Turning his head, he took her hand and brought it up to his lips. He kissed each knuckle gently, and then turned her hand over and kissed the palm and each fingertip. It was strange the way she fit perfectly against his back, her chin resting lightly on his shoulder, cheek resting against his neck. Her nipples, erect and hard as glass, pressed against his shoulder blades, and he felt the swell of her belly and her hip bones against his ass.

"I loved watching you dance. Especially when you raised your arms. Every man here saw your little red thong, the curve of your sweet ass. Did you like knowing I was watching you?"

"Yes." There was a little hiss at the end, as if she wanted to emphasize how much she liked it. His eyes went wide and he jerked a little when she lay her shaking palm across the zipper of his jeans. She curled her fingers around him, tracing the shape of his cock and his balls when he arched into her hand. Her voice quivered when she whispered "I could tell you liked it, even from across the deck."

Her body molded even more tightly against his. He felt her tension when she stood on her toes and kissed the side of his neck, breathing him in. Her courage humbled him; she was trying so hard to overcome her hesitation, the fear he'd stupidly created.

The music became so loud they were both vibrating while Cole fought the urge to drag her into a corner and ravish her. Reaching his hand back to touch her cheek again, he tried to gentle his voice, though he had to raise it.

"Wait. Stand here a minute. Watch." Cole knew there would be plenty of sexual shenanigans going on at this party, with a bunch of young, attractive, enthusiastic staffers reveling in their freedom, many of them living for the first time without strict boundaries. Hopefully they would make use of the big glass bowl full of condoms sitting in plain view on the bar.

While techno music pulsed, Ivanka and her tall casino guard began circulating among the crowd with cans of whipped cream, squirting cream on the nipples of any woman who would take her shirt off, and inviting everyone (of any gender or nationality) standing nearby to lick it off. What a way to ramp up a party! The music morphed into a sexy Brazilian samba, and the topless women formed a conga line, snaking through the party, with frequent stops for more whipped cream and energetic licking. The line got shorter and shorter when people paired off and moved into the shadows, moaning and sighing in the universal language of sex.

When a slow, seductive song came on, couples put their arms around each other. A beautiful gypsy woman with curly red hair worked her sexy moves, totally topless, her jeans unzipped, a tiny whisper of red pubic hair peeking over the bottom of the zipper.

"Whoa, it's red. It's really red!" said one of the two men she was dancing with. They paused and put their hands down her pants to expose the fiery red pubic hair.

"The carpet matches the curtains!" laughed the other man.

The redhead leaned back and pushed her chest forward while the men began noisily sucking and licking her nipples until they were wet, pink and erect in the moonlight. They pulled her pants down and off; one knelt at her pussy, spreading the lips wide with his thumbs and licking her clit, while the other continued to play with and massage her tits, kissing her roughly with his hand fisted in her hair.

*

Over in the shadows Tania and Cole chuckled over the carpet/curtains comment. She stood behind him watching the orgy, sliding her hands up under his shirt and exploring his chest. Sifting the hair on his chest between her fingers, following it down those rippling abs to his navel, teasing her fingertips under the waistband of his jeans, she felt a wave of pleasure when she saw the dimple in his cheek. Standing here, doing this where others might see, felt incredibly intimate, and her mind whispered the *love* word again, but she pushed it aside, staying in this erotic moment.

His breathing got faster, heavier when she undid his belt and the button. He didn't help, but he didn't stop her, either.

A couple swayed, the woman's hands down the front of her partner's pants, while Tania did the same, her lips against his ear. He closed his long fingers around hers, showing her how tight to hold him, how fast to stroke him, how to cup and roll her palm over the thick bulb at the top.

It thrilled her when he guided her hand, feeling it brought them closer somehow. As if he was letting her crawl into his mind. She'd done the same when he touched her, sometimes surprising him with how rough she wanted him to be, other times coming with a jolt at his first gentle touch.

His response was predictable, moving inevitably from one response to another, like a flow chart. Tania knew her reactions were as unpredictable as following Alice down the rabbit hole. She resolved to take him to Wonderland as often as possible. And to avoid worrying about what might happen when the voyage was over.

"I love touching you; I love fucking you; I love having my mouth around your cock," she whispered, breathing into his ear, feeling his erection swell, feeling the weight of him in her hand. For now, she would only tell him how she loved *doing* things to him. But the love word was in her brain every time she looked at him. *No! Silly, silly girl, don't be crazy. This isn't a fairy tale.*

The heat flared between them, humming low in her belly until he returned her touch. Then the heat spread everywhere, erasing everything but the urge to make love. His fingertips reached back and curled around the back of her neck, pulling her around in front of him, facing away from him. His pants were slung low, and his velvety dick slid up and down on her lacy thong under the dress, lazy, unhurried. It was torture, but they loved torturing each other.

Rolling his hips to the music, his lips on her neck, he slowly pushed against her, driving her nuts with his touch. His hands under her dress explored, grazing the sides of her breasts and stroking her thigh, making her shudder and laugh at herself a little, which triggered his laugh.

She turned her head, her voice husky and low. "I have never laughed so much. You make me laugh all the time."

"You've never fucked so much either, have you?" he smiled into the back of her neck.

Giggling, she answered "You know it is the truth." Tania had never liked dirty talk, used to be offended by it in any language, but everything Cole said thrilled her. His laser-like focus on *her* made her dizzy, disoriented. He wasn't a big talker, but she admired so many things about him, every time he talked to a waiter with respect, every time he praised a fellow officer, even his take-no-prisoners attitude in the gym.

She'd come on this ship to save her sister from hell, but found herself in heaven. Living in the hookup culture with her college friends, no man—not one—had ever tried to get to know her, shared himself with her, or wondered if she should become a doctor. No one but Cole. The fears and confusion which had made her withdraw after his outburst were evaporating, burning up in his flesh and heat and arousal.

Attraction was buzzing around them, buzzing louder than the music. Surrounded by sweaty bodies, but feeling like they were the only humans on the planet, their mutual focus was a fierce, live thing. He nipped a little spot on her neck with wet lips and then blew on it, triggering a delicious shiver.

It was clear he wanted to take her back to his room, but she had other ideas, naughty ideas. Though she was still a little hesitant, she turned to face him, this solid wall of man. His scent surrounded her and she felt the familiar ache between her legs when she pressed her lips into the notch at the base of his throat. It vibrated against her mouth when he put his face down into her hair and breathed her in, exhaling with an *ahhhhh*.

She walked him toward a table in the shadows, pulling his T-shirt up and off and palming his bare chest with both hands, answering his uncertainty with her furious lust. Stroking him, running her thumbs over his nipples, sliding both hands under his waistband and down the back of his jeans, she dug her nails in as she squeezed his butt cheeks, pulling them apart. "Mmmm, I love to touch you...and I like that someone might see me touch you," she whispered.

*

A sexy thought, yes. But Cole looked over her shoulder, his eyes darting back and forth, to make sure no one *could* see them before he turned her around and unzipped her dress, letting if fall to the floor. She was naked, skin gleaming in the humid night air, except for her thong and shoes.

"Just sit there, sexy. Spread your legs for me, those amazing legs of yours," he rasped, lifting her onto the very edge of the table.

"Are those the captain's orders?" Her voice was teasing, but breathy with need and anticipation.

"Yes. Wider. I want to stare at you and smell your sexy smell." He pulled her legs apart and knelt between them, pulling the wisp of fabric aside and licking her slit. "Oh, there you are, pink and so, so wet," he murmured. "God, you're beautiful."

Tania used her hands to pull her thighs apart impossibly wider, the scent of the moisture gleaming on her delicate tissues filling the air. Then he ripped the thong apart with both hands and held it up to his nose before shoving it in his pocket.

Licking her bare thighs, he ran his big hand between her legs, then rubbed her juices on her nipples while his mouth dove back into her fleshy sex lips. He kissed her, tasted her, caressing her long, smooth legs, her sounds of pleasure urging him on. She hissed when he held her clit between his teeth, trembling when he gave it a tender nip.

She came to the edge in a mad rush, his hot breath sparking her wet flesh, his day-old whiskers scratching her thighs. Her orgasm built quickly, his insistent tongue commanding everything between her legs while he plunged first one, then two fingers into her, stroking her inside where she liked it until she let loose a keening cry. "Cole!" she moaned.

She was getting panicky now, beyond her limit, in a breathless, mindless state of need, needing to come and come NOW.

"Show me your whole pussy," Cole groaned roughly before he drove his tongue into her, curling it, thrusting, sucking her clit. "And come, Tania, please, baby, come for me!" She leaned back and spread even wider, her legs trembling, and then put one hand up to pinch her own nipple, hard, gasping as her body convulsed, her hips thrusting, and her orgasm rippled through her while she moaned his name in a low voice.

Are those stars in the sky, or behind my eyelids? she thought, tightening and shuddering, knowing he was staring at her pussy while she came. Wondering why, instead of embarrassing her, his stare turned her on and made her want to go again. He stayed still while her orgasm subsided, waiting while she caught her breath.

"That was so fucking hot...when you pinched your nipple. And I..." he stood, murmuring into her neck, holding her close. Absorbing every last shudder of her pleasure, he confessed in an even lower voice, "I love hearing you cry out my name when you come."

"Of course you do, *Captain!*" She was suddenly vividly aware that anyone could walk over and catch them in the act. *What was I thinking, making love again with this amazing man? Ah, well. After you've had lobster, can you go back to cabbage and potatoes?* She felt woozy, kind of drunk on the intensity of her orgasm—and the thought of more to come.

"You're so hot, Miss Trouble." She smiled against his shoulder. When she relaxed against him, he asked "Will you come...back to my room with me?"

His handsome face was twisted, hope and his uncontrollable need written there. Crazy Tania wanted to take him again, right now, right here, in this dark corner. But he *was* the captain. Best not to push it.

"Captain's orders?" Tania licked her bottom lip, part of her wanting bossy Cole back instead of this more subdued version.

"No. Captain's urgent request." His eyes were bright, his voice husky, while they searched each other's eyes. But Princess Tania had returned, and she nodded graciously, holding out her hand for the dress he'd scooped up when he put his cap back on.

*

They wound their way to the elevator through the couples swaying or lying in every position. It was almost 5 a.m., the music was quiet, but groans of sexual ecstasy came from all directions. The words were in every language, but the sighs and moans were understood no matter where the partners were from. After a night of drinking, couples would often have sex in plain view on the crew deck, but they could only be seen if the moon was out. Since the crew deck was directly below the ship's control room and bridge, there were no lights to obstruct the officers' view of the ocean.

Up on the bridge, Officer Ewan MacGrath, of course, used night vision binoculars to closely monitor the orgy below. "Wow, I never knew a woman could actually do that," he said to no one in particular. The rest of the officers had apparently decided to give the lovers on the crew deck some privacy, maybe because they had visited the party themselves at one point or another.

Ewan saw the captain's familiar Phillies baseball cap winding through the crowd, Tania behind him, and put down the binoculars, bringing up a screen showing the work station in the captain's quarters. He switched the screen to an elevator lobby view when he heard

Jack talking to someone close behind him. But MacGrath's curiosity, it seemed, knew no bounds, extending even to officers' quarters.

"Hey, Captain," MacGrath said to Jack as he strolled in. "Did you notice a certain lovely young lady at the crew party?"

"Daniella? Really? Show me the clip."

*

Loud music blared from the console while Ewan zoomed in on the clip of Daniella, hands high, hair flying, crushing her sweaty curves against Jeannette while they laughed and kissed passionately. "Looks like they're more than girlfriends, eh?" Ewan said, a lecherous smile on his face.

Jack wanted to wipe Ewan's smirk off, stalk away, and pretend he'd never seen the clip, but he couldn't stop watching, especially the part where Daniella shook her booty like a zany fiend. He even laughed when the other women tried to imitate her. Shaking his head and trying to cover the fact that he was struck stupid by Daniella's lethal hips and phenomenal breasts, he said to Ewan "She's young, look at them, booty clapping and kissing each other. Interesting."

"Jeanette's not so young. She's been around," Ewan countered. "I'd say she's a man…er…uh, a woman with a plan!"

Jack shrugged, sauntering away, looking as indifferent as he could manage. But he was seething inside, wishing Daniella had danced with him instead of Jeannette, had kissed *him*, was hungry for *him*. She might like Jeannette, but he definitely felt a spark from her as well. *Every man can have a plan, even a guy like me who usually doesn't give a shit. My dating skills are a little rusty since I don't usually have to date. Then what's my plan here?*

CHAPTER SIXTEEN

COLE PULLED TANIA into his arms when the elevator doors slid shut, pressing hotly against her, and she savored the feel of him, all warm and muscular and male.

"I was out of it last night and yesterday, feeling like I'd lost you," he whispered. "You have been...so...so great." He stood there, looking uncertain. "Before you came, I was losing it, working and...like you said in your note, sleepwalking through my life. I mean, Jack keeps an eye on me, but I was...I wasn't even hooking up with anyone, although I know you think I was."

Her breathing deepened as she processed what Cole was saying. "It seems like people kind of expect you to. Why didn't you?"

He reached for her, slipping his hand around the nape of her neck. *Before you came...*she tried not to read too much into it, shoved the hope aside. She thought maybe she had walked into his life at the right moment, but had never thought he might actually *care* for her. How was it possible? He was always meeting such beautiful women!

When they got off the elevator, he pulled her behind him into his room and shut the door. Remembering the last time they were together, she shivered when he sat in the same chair and pulled her into his lap. "It wasn't fun anymore, hooking up made me feel..." he closed his eyes and pulled her close, wrapping her tightly in his embrace.

After leaning back and scanning his face, she kissed him softly again, throwing out a word to complete his unfinished sentence, something she'd felt herself. Her voice was unsteady. "Lonely? Hooking up made you feel lonely?"

He nodded and her emotions surged again, so she put her arms around him. "I know, because I felt the same. Not because I have done it so many times like *you*," as she pursed her lips and gave him her best pissed girlfriend look, "but because my friends were doing it and they were mostly sad."

Chuckling, Cole added, "And I think you were scared to get with someone because of your boyfriend. What happened between you two?"

"He…his name was Petro. We met through friends. He would work all the time, in computers, and not call for a week, and then he would just show up, sometimes in the middle of the night. No explanation, he'd knock on my door, and then he expected me to sleep with him."

She paused, tears clouding her eyes. "I…gave him my virginity. It was important to me, and to him it was like…nothing." swallowed hard. "Can you imagine if you saved something, something precious, and then you gave it to someone and they threw it away?" Cole dragged her even closer, rubbing her back, trying to make her hurt go away.

Gazing out the window, where the moon created a silver trail on the ocean, she continued. "I heard him talking to his mother sometimes, and he had plenty to say to her. It was the most I ever learned about him, when I heard him describing his work, how he was feeling. Nothing about me, he told her nothing about me. We never went out, not to a movie or anything, and yet he expected me to cook for him."

"Like his mother, right?" Cole laughed and she joined him,

feeling his chest shaking against hers. It was amazing how easily and often he'd make her smile through her tears.

"Yes, like his mother. I talked to him about going out, meeting his friends or my friends, but he wasn't interested. It went on for a long time, and I had nothing to compare it to. My mother, uh…my mom had boyfriends but her real boyfriend was a bottle of vodka."

Cole stared up at the ceiling for a moment. Rolling his eyes back down to her, he murmured "It all comes back to our parents, doesn't it? We carry their shit around on our backs like dead weight."

She nodded and held him tight while she continued her narrative. "When I got to be better friends with girls at school and then at work, I didn't want to be with Petro anymore. I moved in with some girls, into a different apartment, and I got a new phone and a new number the same week. I wonder what happened when he knocked on my old door and someone else answered it!"

"I hope it was a big, ugly gangbanger who scared the shit out of him!" Cole said, and she cracked up again, both of them picturing Petro confronting some giant ogre of a guy instead of scoring another booty call.

*

It was the first time Cole really understood how lonely Tania must be at times, missing the anchors of her sister, her family and friends, living in a new country, not having opportunities to speak her native language, tearing down her life one week and beginning a new one the next. It touched him to know she was so strong and yet kind… and sexy as hell.

"Speaking of scaring people." He shifted under her, moving her out onto his thighs, away from his heart. "I understood your note, related to it, like I said." His lips were pressed thin and he had that unfamiliar dark tone in his voice. "But I have to tell ya'. Please don't run away from me like that again, like you're abandoning me. Taking your stuff the way you did."

He dropped his chin to his chest, and she ran her fingers through his hair. "I have a history with that kind of crap." When he met her gaze, his blue eyes blazed right through her. "Before you walk out, talk to me first about…whatever it is. Please."

"Okay. I will. I understand." She lowered her eyes, looking ashamed.

He tipped her chin up, locking her eyes in his, and put his hands, fingers spread wide, on her shoulders. "I hate the feeling I get from you sometimes, like you think I'm better than you, like you're not good enough. That sucks, it's wrong, and it also makes it too easy for you to walk away."

Pulling her back in close again, he rested his cheek on her chest. "I know it's only been a few days, but I hope you'll stop buying into this bullshit of yours. It's like you feel like you're second rate, like we're not on the same level. My brother and I were lucky enough to be born in the U.S. to parents who were…well, who had it together at the time, anyway. But that's our only advantage."

He looked up at her again. "Yesterday Jack pointed out that you've actually had a better education than we have, and you speak four languages. Remember *that* the next time you feel second-rate and you want to escape. And I know I'm a demanding bastard most of the time, I know I have to change, but I think you can help me. Just…do you *want* to help me?"

*

She ruffled his hair, releasing the fragrance of his shampoo. Then she leaned back a tiny bit and slid the dress off over her head again, putting his hands on her breasts. She felt the whole hard length of him beneath her, like hot metal burning through his jeans.

"I want to help," she murmured, laughing softly while she smoothed her hand down his chest and over his zipper again. "I want you to handle me, and I want to handle you, demanding bastard."

She leaned in and nipped his neck, a whiff of sweat and aftershave rising when she pulled him back for a kiss, tugging his hair as he'd done to her. His chin was rough with stubble, but she knew those lips were soft, smooth, and sure. The touch of her lips was an invitation, and he dove in, stoking the fire in her, exploring her with his tongue, framing her face with his hands and going deep and urgent.

Her excitement built when he moaned and shifted his hands beneath her ass, leading her hands down below the waist of his jeans. His kiss was so intense she felt she could no longer inhale on her own. He swept her into his arms as if she weighed nothing, and the room went by in a blur while he carried her over to the bed.

She surprised him by rolling over and pressing him down onto the mattress, never releasing her grip on his cock while the other hand fumbled with his belt. "Wait," he gasped, and took her hand away, kissing it and grinning, flushing a little, signaling that her touch might finish him off. *He likes it when I come back at him, when I challenge him. It is like a dance, a mutual agreement to surprise and delight as we caress the secret parts of each other.*

*

Groaning when her hands stroked his thighs, Cole reached up to crush her against him, to brand her with his need and heat. It struck him, as he felt her pulse against his skin, how close she'd come to staying away, to remaining frightened of him. "I'm going to study you now, Tania," he whispered.

She nodded, smiled slyly, and said "Didn't you study me out there?"

"Oh, no, that was only one delicious little part of you!" he growled. "I'm just getting started. I think I'll resume my study with…your perfect ass." He licked his lips while he turned her onto her stomach, moving her hair out of her eyes so she could watch him over her shoulder. He left little love bites on her ass while he stroked that fine, firm flesh. It was cool the way she gave herself to him, letting him take over so sweetly, it made him want to give her everything.

He continued to explore the sexy curve of her hips, pausing every so often to strip off more of his clothes, needing to feel her skin on his. He was torn between wanting to touch her everywhere at once and impaling her with his cock, pulling her hair while he— *Focus, you dope. This is about her, winning her back.*

Going with the touching her everywhere option, he got her to relax, watched her sink into the bed while he took his time, massaging her, dropping little kisses all over her behind, darting his tongue into the forbidden fold and blowing on it, making gooseflesh break out on her back and the backs of her arms while she sighed and moaned. So sexy, her little sounds in Ukrainian. He made a mental note to ask her exactly what she was saying.

"I love feeling how perfect the back of your neck is, your long, beautiful neck, and your hair…your hair is like silk." He held her glossy mass of hair in one hand while he kissed and licked, his hot breath leaving a trail of shivers down her neck and onto her shoulders as he traced and rubbed every curve and muscle with his lips and fingers. Pulling her hair a little, he took a deep breath and inhaled, brushing the silky drape against his face.

"You smell so good, Tania, so amazing." Skimming the sensitive skin between her shoulder blades, he trailed his tongue along her spine, then kissed his way down. A rosy flush bloomed on her skin, exactly the way he liked it, evidence of how the heat and pressure grew between them. He hoped his whispered compliments and playful attitude in bed were infectious, freeing her to accept the gift of his slow hands and even slower mouth. Still, Cole felt her squirming, desperate for friction, especially when his cock would drag along her skin.

His lips lingered again on her ass, on the sexy mounds of flesh, so white and firm, before he moved on to kissing and caressing the crease at the top of her thighs. When he saw the contrast between his dark, tanned hands and her intimate flesh, his cock jerked painfully. The contrast of dark against light made him think of opposites, of his experience versus her innocence and fresh excitement. Maybe sharing with her would make his skills actually mean something.

Sliding off to the side, he ran his stubbly chin down her legs, raining down kisses while he nipped and licked the skin behind her knee, then blew on it. She'd turned to him, biting her lower lip, her nails digging into the bed when her squirming turned into thrashing. *I like that thing she does where she looks directly at me when she's turned on, not closing her eyes.* "Oh, you like that, don't you Trouble? Here, let me do the other knee."

More thrashing, this time accompanied by a groan and a request. Her face and neck were flushed scarlet, and her breathing fast, when she looked at him and asked, "May I please turn over now, Captain? And would you please, please not touch my feet, because I'm...ticklish?"

Cole did his best imitation of looking solemn and thinking it over. "Well, I hate to miss a spot, but since you asked so nicely..." He slid his hand up to her hip and let out a long breath while he nudged her over onto her back. He forced himself to ignore her luscious breasts, instead kneeling over her and dragging his lips across her collarbone and up to her mouth, exploring every inch of her lips with his.

Moving her hand from his waist, he kissed her wrist, tracing the veins with his tongue and tasting the palm of her hand. Then he closed his eyes and moved her hand down to his raging erection, pressing her fingers around it and holding her still. "This is what you do to me, Trouble. I want you so bad."

*

"Please, please," she whispered, her voice thick with desire, wanting him inside, a part of her, right now. Arching her back, feeling his dick swell in her hand, she let loose a low moan of pleasure. *So beautiful, this man. Mine, mine!*

His sweet loving and his blue eyes pierced through the shield of her rational mind to the raw emotion, to her love—and it was love, or becoming love, it was true. But his sensual lips, now grazing her breasts, made her want to stay in the now, pushing away thoughts of the future. *To be with a man like this? Too big to think about. How wonderful he makes me feel, how wonderful he is!*

"Did you know when you arch your back it means you want me to play with your breasts?" Cole flicked one nipple with his tongue while he captured the other between his thumb and forefinger, tugging and rolling until she let out a wailing cry.

"I could make you come doing this, but I'm going to do this, too." He was stroking her clit with his cock, gliding back and forth, first fast and then slooowly over the sensitive little bud, spreading the wetness from her slit with his free hand. "Show me how much you like this, Tania."

Her eyes wide, she pushed up onto her elbows, loving his dirty talk, watching his velvety cock push open the lips of her slit and glide over the last, most tender nerve in her hypersensitive jewel. She licked her lips at the sexy sight of him sliding over her and she felt the familiar sensation building down low.

"Fuuuuck, this is killing me, but it feels so good. Are you ready to come, beautiful girl?" he asked, pressing harder and faster against her, the slick friction of his erection setting off stronger and stronger tremors in her belly. When he took her breast all the way into his mouth and then pulled back, biting her nipple sharply, it sent shock waves through her body, waves that burst through her, rolling down her spine and exploding into a shuddering, low cry that seemed to come and come and come.

When he kissed her and spread her legs, putting two fingers inside her, she wanted to push him away. *It's too much, it's enough, I cannot come again.* Her thighs shook with a thousand little aftershocks and she jerked when he circled her clit with his thumb. When he pulled away to sheathe his cock, she saw his eyes go dark and shiny, but as soon as he touched the head of his cock to her opening, she began trembling so hard she couldn't see anymore, finding herself—unbelievably—ready to come again. She was scared she would fall apart, completely lose it…and then *hoped* she would lose it, and bring him with her.

*

It was a relief when he finally lay on top of her, warm skin to warm skin. He'd touched and teased her for so long she was like a firecracker with the fuse lit, ready to go off again at any moment. Taking both her hands and weaving their fingers together, he brought their hands over her head while he kissed his way up her chest, her neck, her cheek before opening his mouth over hers. He went deep with the kiss, with his tongue, and with his cock inside her at the same time, feeling her contract around him, squeezing any thoughts away except filling her completely.

"Cole," she exhaled, and they locked eyes when she lifted her legs, her warm thighs gripping his hips as she pulled him in completely. "Oh God, oh God," she said in a husky voice, closing her eyes and pushing into his slow rhythm, in and out. She squeezed their linked fingers, moaning, saying more hoarse words in Ukrainian, her voice low. Sucking and biting at her chest, playing with her body until she arched off the bed again, he went faster and harder, grunting when his hips slapped against her thighs.

"Huh. Huuuh, so sweet, fuck!" he cried while her body bucked and her legs gripped him, begging for more. He saw the telltale flush start on her chest and smiled, releasing her hands when she raised her hips to him. He slid his hand between them, rubbing her clit, and her cries spiraled higher and louder.

She was so fucking hot, her whole body tense, her nipples tight. "Tell me what you like sweet thing, do it," he growled, reaching around and smacking her beautiful white ass cheek, his hand flat. "You like it rough like this, don't you?" Her eyes widened at the hot sting and she nodded. "Say it, tell me you want me to fuck you hard."

"Yes, yes, I like it when you fuck me hard," she rasped and he saw her eyes grow heavy as she came apart, her mouth open in a round "Oooohhhhaahh," before she went limp and soft beneath him.

"Do you want to see it, do you want to see me come, Trouble?" he asked, his voice tight. His hand stung from the slap, sending him even closer to the edge. So close, but he loved her curiosity and passion, and he wanted to surprise her. It was fun to show her things.

Her energy renewed by his offer, her eyes flew open as she propped herself on her elbows. "Yes, I want to watch," she rasped. She stared intently, her eyes flaming when he pulled out of her, took the condom off and stroked twice, the length of him jerking and pulsing cum onto her belly again and again while his orgasm tore out of him. He closed his eyes for a few seconds, breathless, shuddering, and when he opened them again she was still looking at where he'd come on her, apparently fascinated.

"I love that you liked it, that you like to watch," he said, collapsing next to her as he leaned on his elbow, watching her. "I like that you're so brave and you want to…you want to try everything, every damn thing I think of." He rubbed a little towel on her belly, another between her legs, moving reverently while he inhaled the musky smells of their lovemaking. Taking a deep breath, then letting it out with a long sigh, he sank into the pillow, facing away from her.

*

Giggling, she turned to him, wanting to snuggle and share her warmth. "And I love when you tell me what to do, when you tell me what you like. I think I am kind of *like* you, liking sex a lot, only I'm…I guess women like it in a different way. I like to make you happy, because you make me so happy." When he didn't respond she listened and realized he was asleep. She heard a door close in the hall and wondered if Jack was going to work.

Shifting carefully up and over him, to his other side, she watched Cole sleep. She pictured him as a boy, his long eyelashes fluttering in time with his dreams. It was hard to reconcile this languid man-boy with the irate male who was so angry with her days ago, making her feel like a wayward child.

While Tania was growing up, her mother had been kind of a happy drunk, either sloppily affectionate, melancholy, or sleepy. Some of Mom's boyfriends, on the other hand, were mean, raging drunks who thought it was okay to hit people and throw things. Tania and her sister developed a keen sensitivity to loud voices and anger, and would freeze their feelings and be sure to keep a physical and emotional distance from the irrational goings-on. It had given them a sense of control, protecting them from the pain and chaos of life with an alcoholic. Oksana liked to say they were the Invisible Lizards, blending in with their surroundings. Laughing to herself and yearning to be close to her sister, Tania fell asleep again.

The next time she opened her eyes, Cole was still asleep, but pulling her tightly to him as slivers of sunshine leaked through the window shade. His sleepy embrace brought tears to her eyes, he seemed to need the drowsy hug, the closeness, so badly. He'd seen parts of her she'd never seen herself, he'd kissed her everywhere and been inside her, but this peaceful embrace somehow was even more intimate. She planned to wake him up later in the most delightful way…but fell asleep again thinking about it.

When she finally did wake up, he was gone. He'd left a note on the pillow, *Work. See you later?*

CHAPTER SEVENTEEN

THE HEAD WAITER escorted Tania to a two-top near the window and cleared the place setting from the other side, smiling and bringing a vase of flowers to the table along with her menu. The sun shining over the ocean awed her, and she was happy to be sitting there, enjoying it…until she smelled Ivan's fucking Russian cigarettes. Of course the head waiter was trying to pair them up, and had placed Ivan's menu so he was facing her, only a few feet from her at the slightly separated table. Ivan walked behind her with that slimy forced friendliness of his, hands on her shoulders, kissing both cheeks from behind in the French manner.

"Tania," he said, nodding while he sat. *"Comment allez-vous?"* Dressed in a grey cashmere sweater and elegant grey slacks, he wasn't his usual impeccable self. Instead he was sweaty, his hair a mess, his eyes red. He seemed agitated, strung tight as a bow.

"Bien, et vous?" She could handle the exchange of how-are-you-good, because she'd heard about how frustrated he was by ship security. When he ordered a bottle of wine and directed the sommelier to pour it for both of them, she thought, *Sure, asshole, let us drink to you not ruining any more lives on this ship!*

But she decided to get right to the point. "Ivan, why are you sitting here? I'm not one of those Natashas you can turn into a slave, and you're not going to be my pimp, my *mamachki*. So what do we have to discuss?"

"Are you always so direct?" Not expecting an answer, he let out a long breath and wiped his brow with the crisp, white napkin. "Let's talk about your sister." When she flinched, the smile on his thin lips wasn't reflected in his eyes. "Yes, I know Oksana's your sister. I fucked the chambermaid, Ivanka, and she told me everything while she was sucking my cock."

He enjoyed sticking the knife of fear in and twisting it, it showed in his eyes. "Don't worry, I won't tell your boyfriend the captain what you're up to, my pigeon, trying to use him to rescue your sister." Leaning closer, he hissed, "Or maybe you're getting both of them off, both the brothers, is that what you're doing little *blyat*?"

"Maybe I am, Ivan, maybe I am," Tania said in a low voice. Ukrainians love a good insult, and she gave as well as she got. "Ivanka told me how small your dick is, so what can I do? I had to move on. And then when they saw you trying to recruit the pretty dancers, they had to zoom in on your cock with the camera because it's so tiny." She pushed her chair away from the table and stared him down, pointing two fingers to her eyes, then one finger toward him. "They're watching you, *zhopa*, hoping to throw your ass off the ship at the next stop!" After she turned to walk away, she smiled a little smile and gave Ewan a thumbs up, knowing he was probably watching the whole exchange on one of his cameras.

A loud crash and the sound of breaking dishes made her turn around again. Waiters rushed toward Ivan, who was passed out on the floor in a tangle of tablecloth, wine and flowers. Tania's nursing training kicked in and she rushed to kneel down next to her enemy, noting the perspiration and burning heat coming off him when she checked his pulse.

The head waiter met her eyes. "You think virus?" he whispered. He'd apparently seen it before. She nodded and he stood, shooing the passengers away, wrapping up everything Ivan had touched in a tablecloth and making the staff who'd waited on him accompany him to the medical facility. In case this was a possible Norovirus outbreak, the staff was trained to quickly quarantine and disinfect anything related to it.

*

"*Chert poberi!*" Ivanka cursed God and everyone around her while the smell of bleach filled the air. She didn't care who heard her, and who except Ivan, Tania and Oksana understood Russian anyway?! She'd spent an evening with that Russian idiot Ivan, but she wasn't sick. She almost wished she was, though, because now she had to triple clean her entire section of ship's cabins with bleach.

Ivan was tested in the clinic immediately after his collapse. Unfortunately, he was positive for the Norovirus, the second most common illness in the world after the common cold. Then he was isolated back in his suite.

"What do you think," Ivanka said to Dr. Santos when she came to the clinic for him to test her, "I kissed that *mudak*? No, I give him a two-second blow job and he says he's going to introduce me to a millionaire. He told same thing to every girl on the fucking ship!" Santos blushed and shook his head, but hey, it was Ivanka, what could you expect?

"Hah! I've heard that one before!" continued Ivanka. "Every Russian girl thinks she's going to marry a millionaire, how many millionaires can there be? Pfft! I accepted a diamond bracelet from Ivan, my buddy Marisol in the jewelry shop made sure it was real, then I flick him off like a bug! Pretty good dancer, though," and she laughed harshly. "So why are we cursed with this shit virus Doc?"

"It's not just the ship," Santos replied. "People catch it in any group setting, whether an airplane, a sports arena or a school, and spread it through touch. Then they go home and get sick, not knowing where they caught it. Unfortunately, while you're on a cruise it *is* your home, so the illness is more apparent, though very few passengers ever get it."

After Ivan tested positive, a low tone was sounded on the ship's sound system, almost imperceptible to the few passengers on board that time of day, but very significant to every member of the crew. The tone was a signal to drop everything—put down the fork with your lunch, stop moving the deck chairs around, declare last call and close the bar, fold your last set of sheets, put down the mop, end the endless serving and preparing of food, and close the doors on the fitness center. When the tone stopped, the first instruction was to STOP, stop and think for three minutes.

It was so strange to see the entire crew, from the guy stocking the freezer to the captain, standing there thinking. Normally, the place was like an ant colony, with furious effort at all times. And what was everyone to think about? Anyone, passenger or crew, who might be sick, anyone who'd complained they weren't feeling well, who wasn't eating, who was feverish, who seemed sleepy, achy, or chilled—and certainly those with diarrhea and vomiting.

Whether it was your roommate or a passenger in a dining room who was pale and not eating, it was essential to report those who were sick before they infected everyone else by touching stair railings, elevator buttons and poker chips. Catching it at the beginning might cut the contagion rate in half or more.

Passengers were warned to step up the hand washing and sick passengers were asked to stay in their rooms for a few days to avoid spreading the virus, which was at its most contagious now. Many wore gloves and masks, and the cruise line offered them a free in-room medical visit and special room service treatment for themselves and those they were traveling with. If they chose to get off the ship and go to the hospital at the next stop, a portion of their cruise was refunded. Crew members who were ill were also confined to quarters, and arrangements were made to cover their tips and salaries so they wouldn't be tempted to work and spread the illness.

When the tone sounded again, the staff reported anyone they thought of and went into the "enhanced cleaning" mode, dumping food and continuously and intensely cleaning everything people touched. The staff was very proud of their speedy health monitoring system, and maintained the lowest contagion rate in the fleet.

Still, a few people were going to suffer through some uncomfortable days.

CHAPTER EIGHTEEN

THE HANDCUFF CLOSED around Oksana's wrist with a click. Strauss put the key in his pocket and patted her head before he turned to leave. She wanted to ask him why he was leaving her like this, one arm manacled to the headboard, why he used an unfamiliar real handcuff instead of the usual red leather ones, but she'd learned not to ask.

Earlier, she sensed something was different when he told her she needed to use the bathroom because she was going to be bound here while he was away for a few hours. Speaking to Primo in the next room, she heard Strauss say he'd be visiting a friend in Waterford. "Vould you go now und bring back sometink for her to eat? I don't vant room service poking around." Shortly after she heard the door open and close, she quelled her anxiety in her usual way. She fell asleep.

The room seemed smaller and more intimate when she woke up to find Primo standing over her, holding a tray of food. His sheer size seemed to gobble up the space in the room, and she felt a prickle of excitement looking up at him, remembering their conversation. *I'm going to love you right, from the top of your head to the tips of your toes.* She was turned on remembering his words and his deep voice and wide smile.

Right now his sexy lips were pursed in confusion, probably wondering how she was supposed to eat with her right wrist fastened to the bed. "I'm sorry, Oksana, I didn't know you were handcuffed like that, or I would've asked for the key. Herr Strauss is gone for the day. Are you right-handed?"

She looked down while she swung her legs off the bed, very conscious of wearing only a short, sheer nightgown. She saw his huge cock stir along his thigh when he realized it as well, probably because he'd seen her dark nipples through the transparent material. Dragging the nightstand closer to her, he set the tray down and handed her a fork. Everything seemed doll-size in his hand, and she looked up at him as she accepted it, giggling a little.

"What? Why are you laughing?" he asked, flushing while he jiggled the handcuff, hoping to slide it off the headboard somehow. He pulled on it, trying to unbolt it off the wall, even rip it off.

"I...the fork seemed so small in your hand. Can you get it off?" she asked, and then laughed again when she realized the double meaning of her question. "Get the handcuff off is what I mean."

Now his deep, hearty laugh joined hers and he pulled up a chair, cutting up the chicken, potatoes and vegetables on her tray for her. She took a few awkward forkfuls using her left hand and then scooted a few inches from behind the nightstand, licking her lips, her right arm extended in the cuff. "Would you feed it to me Primo?"

*

Quirking a smile at her, he picked up the plate and fork and leaned toward her, putting a piece of spicy chicken in her mouth. He thought he could handle this and stay sane, but when she licked the sauce off her lip with her little pink tongue the second time, he knew he was done for. Oksana's nipples and a sweet tuft of pubic hair showed clearly through the veil of her nightgown. The silver heart locket she always wore drew his eyes where he knew they should not be.

After a few more bites, followed by more lip-licking and Oksana's luscious breasts swinging as she leaned forward, Primo stood and let out a long breath. "Uh…I don't know if I can keep doing this," he said, his swollen erection at a painful angle in his trousers. "Can I get you something to drink, water or juice?"

*

Oksana stared at his bulge, knowing he really wanted to leave the room so he could adjust himself in his pants. She had been in all kinds of sexual situations recently, feeling absolutely nothing sexual. Kneel down, suck this, spread your legs—did they have any idea how, in her mind, she was far away, imagining her freedom, and not one of them had a face or a name, the *prydurkys*? Each of the six assholes Strauss had selected so far thought of himself as an unfor-gettable stud, but she refused to even meet their eyes. They were reasonably attractive, but she was being treated like garbage, so she returned the favor, all the while pretending to be turned on so they would finish faster, the idiots!

But her need had awakened now, roaring back with a bang. "Is there any vodka? If it is cold, I will take it without ice please." Oksana never drank when she was with strangers, fearing that one of Strauss's scenes would turn violent as it had with Lucas. But she felt safe with Primo, transformed by her crush on him, changed back into the sexual creature she used to be, dancing and swinging on a pole in Paris.

Of the two sisters, Oksana was by far the more sensual, begin-ning with her first boyfriend when she was fourteen. She sometimes envied Tania's detachment, her ability go without sex and not crave a man's touch. Still…with this beautiful man, for a little while, she'd let the bird out of its cage, eh?

When Primo returned, he'd recovered his composure but still had a hooded, drunken look in his eyes, drunk from lust perhaps. He set the glass down and stepped back, looking surprised when she downed the whole glass in one gulp. "Are you still hungry? Do you want me to keep feeding you?" He was sweating and the cords in his neck stood out as if steeling himself for another round of horny frustration.

"Actually, I am hungry…from the top of my head to the tips of my toes." She smiled shyly up at him and saw his eyes widen before he smiled.

Oksana saw him tighten his jaw and swallow, trying to cover his reaction. "You…uh…remembered."

She paused, giggling again, this time aided by the vodka. "I remembered?! I've thought of nothing else since you said it, beautiful man. I thought about it so much I couldn't even look at you. And now Strauss is gone and he can't watch you."

"I wondered why you seemed so shy. I thought you might've been upset by what I said. I guess not." When the big man came over and sat next to her on the edge of the bed, he was so heavy she almost toppled over when the bed dipped beneath his weight. To steady her, his left hand quickly caught her square in the chest while the right circled the back of her neck, the long fingers almost reaching the front.

From there, it felt so natural for him to pull her to him, his mouth hungry on her neck, his hand cupping her breast and splayed wide all the way down to her belly. He took another deep breath, inhaling her hair and skin, and when his hand went exploring under the flimsy nightie, she moaned, sending the vibrations through her lips and setting fire to her brain. Her free hand stroked up his crisp white dress shirt to his neck, feeling his pulse throbbing madly.

The hand around her neck gently turned her face to him, willing her to look him square in the eye while he pulled her away a little. His face was kind, so kind and concerned. "You're sure about this? I can't get the handcuff off without ripping the headboard out of the wall. If we do this, and talk to the captain, Emile will involve Ivan, and he's a mean son-of-a-bitch. Ivan'll come after us, and he's armed. But I'm game if you are. I'm not letting anyone else hurt you...*ever*."

Oksana stood, eyes wide with surprise, twisted her handcuffed arm around, turned toward him and shooed him over to the spot where she'd been sitting. He gasped when she climbed into his lap and buried his face in her breasts, planting little kisses on his forehead. She ripped his shirt off with her free hand, most of the buttons flying across the room, and threw it on the floor while he touched her through the nightgown. "We don't have to do that, be in danger, Primo" she said. "Help is coming. Right now, I just want you to love me right, from..."

*

"...the top of your head to the tips of your toes." Primo finished the sentence, his voice rough, lost in the valley between her breasts. Offering her body like this, her daring in the context of everything that had happened to her, made him want to drop to his knees and worship her.

He wanted to be systematic and start at the top, but he couldn't resist taking a brief detour, sucking a stiffened nipple right through the fabric of her nightie, moving the slight stiffness of the wet fabric across the crest of her breast with a skillful tongue as a whimper leaked out of her throat. Drawing her between his lips, his tongue memorized every little bump around the edge of her areola before he nipped the center into a hard little button and she hissed with pleasure. She thrust her chest out while he raised the nightie and left it dangling on the handcuff, grazing the stiff peaks of her breasts with his teeth.

A sexy, surprised cry burst from her lips when he reached between her legs and stroked her wet, creamy flesh. Her excitement galvanized him as he raised her off his lap and pushed her farther onto the bed, backing her up to the headboard so she was not straining against the handcuff. They were both kneeling, their bodies molded against each other, nuzzling and grinding and touching each other like teenagers making out, just as they'd longed to do since they met and boarded the ship.

Primo put one hand over her manacled wrist and his other hand high on the wall behind her, leaning into her and possessing her with his kiss, with his whole huge body. While he pressed against her she looked up at him, returning his kiss, her tongue welcoming his…but her eyes were open, not closed in pleasure, experiencing him like he wanted her to.

I'm dominating her like those other guys, she's unsure, I have to back off, he thought. If he was being honest with himself, seeing her restrained gave him the wrong cues and brought his cock close to the edge. But he had no intention of pleasuring himself until he'd made her wishes come true. And maybe a few wishes she hadn't thought of yet.

"I can't start at the top or at the bottom 'cause I can't wait to taste you," he said. "Lie down here." He put some pillows behind her so she could watch him between her legs.

"Taste me?" she asked as she settled on the bed. She looked so genuinely confused, he wondered if it was a language problem.

"Spread your legs. I'm going to taste your pussy. With my mouth."

She still looked bewildered. "Why?"

"You don't...you never...you've never had oral sex?"

"Oh, baby, you know I can suck you off. I wish you had not, but you have seen me do it."

"No, I mean...I'm going to lick you and make you come."

Her green eyes were huge, unbelieving. "I have only ever... when I'm...I have only ever made myself come. You would...it sounds...so hot." She blinked rapidly, processing the idea. "I almost came when you sucked my breasts."

His dick jerked when she talked about getting herself off, but thank God he still had his pants on. His cock throbbed, feeling like a hot poker trapped in his briefs. Remembering her reaction when he touched her there, he swallowed thickly and said in a low voice "Go ahead, show me. Show me what you do and I'll show you what I do."

Spreading her legs wider, he played with her pink-tipped breasts again, the handcuff making her arch her back, and he touched her clit with his fingers. Each time he did she flinched, but it did seem to give her permission to spread the lips of her sex and caress her pussy, displacing him and moving her fingers in a circle.

He couldn't take his eyes off her, the cream on her labia making his mouth water as it glistened on her fingers. Running his fingers through her soft pubic hair and inhaling her scent, he lost himself in the warm, satiny world between her thighs. He opened her even wider, at first letting his tongue ride along with her fingers, occasionally gliding over the sensitive kernel of flesh until she gasped and her fingers pulled away, wanting him to caress her clit with his tongue.

"Primo!" she cried out, and her whole body started quaking when he opened his mouth wide, covering her whole pussy, gorging on her sweet juices and stabbing at her clit with his tongue or sucking gently until her breathing became ragged. Closing his eyes, he ran his tongue around her slit and plunged it inside again and again as she gasped and cried out, begging him to let her come while whimpering desperately for him to fuck her at the same time.

When he sucked her clit between his lips and teeth, her body went rigid as she screamed in delicious climax, her body trembling. Coaxing every last whimper out of her, he showed no mercy while he continued to eat her with savage lust, putting two fingers inside her and making little circles on the cushy g-spot he knew was waiting for him to awaken. She gasped his name again, gushing and marking his shoulders with her nails while he pressed her apart with his hands, forcing her to accept his face buried so intimately in her sex. Though she was bucking and thrusting her hips, he continued to lick, press and stroke her inside and out, sending shivers through her and making her scream until she exploded again.

Finally he moved up, lifting his head and lying it on her belly, running his hands from hips to ribs to breasts, learning the feel of her. Watching her face and body react was like watching a flower bloom, and her erotic sounds almost put him over the edge. It thrilled him to give her this gift, an experience that she'd never had before, but when he looked at her face he saw tears.

Placing his knees on both sides of her hips, he leaned over her and wiped her tears away with his thumbs, placing a sweet kiss on her lips. "What?" he asked, always uncomfortable with a crying woman. *Those lips, those lips...*his cock swelled even bigger when he looked down at her.

"Men do this?" she asked, her voice quavering. "This is something not just you do, other men do this?"

Oksana was so sad and serious, Primo tried to contain his amusement, but instead his body shook like he was having a seizure and he fell sideways on the bed next to her, convulsing with laughter. Spreading his hand on her chest and lightly stroking her breasts, he sobered enough to answer her, a shit-eating grin still lighting up his face. "I can't speak for every man in the world sweetheart, but lots of men do this, yes. When they care for somebody, lovers do this for each other."

"Maybe it's Ukrainian men and Russian guys, maybe they don't do it." She still seemed puzzled. Wiggling under his hand, she murmured, "Ooooh, you make me ready to come again when you do that." Shifting a little to face him, she ran her free hand down his chest and tried to undo his belt after sliding her fingers under the waistband of his pants and touching the tip of his straining erection. "Too many clothes, too many fucking clothes Primo! Take your pants off and kneel over me again, show it to me." Desire glittered in his eyes while he removed his pants and briefs.

She gasped when she saw what was under his zipper.

"It? What's it?" he teased as he kneeled over her again. His enormous rigid erection bobbed up and down when he settled over her and she couldn't curl her fingers around him fast enough, starting at the base and stroking upward with a firm grip. "Oksana, for God's sake," he moaned through gritted teeth.

"I want to touch you so bad, touch you all over, play with you and pump your cock and…and…hold your balls…and…" She was thrashing around, energized by her amazing orgasms, still stroking him but frantically pulling on the arm handcuffed to the bed.

"Hey, shhhh, it's okay," he held both her breasts in one hand and stroked the side of her face with the other. "This is supposed to be about you, remember?"

"Mmmmm…mmm…yes, now it's me. And I want to taste you now. Stand next to the bed right here, I want to show you something special, something none of these assholes know I can do." She rolled on her side, blushed when she looked up at him, raised an eyebrow and licked her lips. "Have you ever had anyone take your whole giant, delicious cock down her throat?"

Primo shuddered at the idea, the muscles in his huge body tensing at the thought of seeing every inch of this thing in his hand disappear down her throat.

"It's not possible." He stood utterly still, his longing for it to be possible roaring in his brain.

"Yes, yes it is, Primo. Now do what I say, beautiful man." Twisting under her manacled arm, she moved her feet facing away from him and lay flat, her head hanging off the end of the bed – as luck would have it – at the same height as his throbbing dick. "I'll hold on with this hand to the back of your thigh. Don't worry about your balls, I will love your balls." She saw his hesitation. "I won't move when you're there, you have to pump and…and…come here, my *kokhany*," she said softly.

Suddenly self-conscious, he moved closer and nudged her lush lips with his cock. He leaned forward and stroked the velvety skin on her chest, his two hands overwhelming each of her full, firm breasts. He groaned when her tongue came out, wetting the tip as her lips closed around it, and inched closer to the bed while she sucked him in, nearly finishing him off with each wet, swallowing sound she made. She cried out around his thick cock, her tongue thrilling him, her mouth so hot as she pulled the back of his thigh even closer.

"Are you okay?" he murmured while he watched more and more of him slide in, more than he'd ever, ever experienced. And he *was* pretty experienced, since word of his…abundance had always managed to spread in high school, college, and the years after. Women always took Primo on as a challenge and, though he was selective, he wasn't immune to their enthusiasm, either.

Oksana nodded, her eyes bright and her breathing slow and

focused. She moaned softly and he clenched his jaw tight while he felt the vibrations through his cock and all the way up his spine. Jolts of pleasure shivered through him when he literally felt her swallow him, the clench of her throat all around when she came within one inch of his pubic hair. The process made him want to explode immediately, but he definitely wanted this to last.

As she held him inside her, her tongue stroking him up and down, surrounding him with her heat and massaging him with her throat muscles, he reached down and ran his fingers over the folds of her pussy. Lightheaded and lost to everything but the sensation of her wetness and the sight of his cock surrounded by her mouth, he felt her arch her back, and wiggle into his hand. When she jerked in reaction to his touch, he found his nine inches, impossibly, all the way in.

Her hand squeezed the back of his naked thigh, signaling him to thrust, and he bit his lower lip and quieted his hands, desperately seeking control over this sharp, strange pleasure. Improbably, when he looked down, he saw her throat moving around his cock! "Holy fuck, oh my God!" He had to close his eyes and stop thinking about that twisted, erotic sight. Shaking so damn hard and fighting to keep his strokes in the space between too little and too much, he realized it was over. When he opened his eyes his vision had gone white, sparks jolting through him while his heartbeat drummed in his ears.

Going fast and furious to the finish, feeling her suction and stroking and lips stretched over teeth, Primo's entire body went rigid when his slamming orgasm overcame him, a groan of pleasure escaping from his throat. "Oksaanaa, uhhhh, ohhh fuuuuck!" There wasn't a question where his cum would go, there was nowhere but in, and she didn't even have to swallow, it was beyond that.

He'd never felt anything like it before, not even close. Body shaking as he fell forward, clutching at her thighs, he felt a hot flush when the pressure drained out of his muscles, as if every bit of ecstasy and desire he'd ever felt was pumping into her. The hard, demanding pulses of his release slowed down and he struggled to catch his breath, her gift melting his brain. She slowly slid his length out of her mouth, standing and turning herself, tucking him between her legs so sweetly, keeping his cock warm against her pussy.

When he opened his eyes, she was standing pressed up against him, steadying him with her free arm wrapped around him, nuzzling his chest. It was insane, what she'd done for him, and he resolved to pamper and pleasure the other parts of her body the next time they were alone.

Normally a quiet guy, he suddenly had so many words to fill her up with his feelings. He couldn't tell her enough how beautiful she was. "Oksana, I love the golden color of your skin," while he tenderly cleaned her up; "Holy fucking God, your tits are perfect," as he pulled her nightie back down; "Your curls on the pillow, so soft. You're like an angel;" and, "I can't stand to leave you like this, so sexy, for him to touch," when he brought her a glass of water and tucked her in.

That last really got him, and his jaw was clenched tight at the sight of her lying there, already asleep, as he crawled around finding the buttons from his shirt. *Get rid of Ivan and we can get this done without hurting anyone. How should I do this, who do I trust?* He got a text from Strauss to pick up some packages at the gangplank and his mind snapped shut. She was okay for now.

*

"I want that. I want that thing she can do," Khalid whispered when he and Strauss stepped away from the wall where they'd been watching Oksana and Primo devour each other. Taking his phone down from the ledge where he'd filmed the whole encounter, the sheikh looked intently at Emile Strauss, considering whether to just take the girl or get the German's permission.

Strauss shook his head, his eyes wide with alarm. "Did chu not see dat ve're not supposed to know dat she can do dat? Ve can't, dey vill know ve're vatching, und I like to vatch."

"Oh…yes, right, then." Khalid paused, changing tactics. "It was brilliant, chaining her to the bed so we could see them clearly. I enjoyed it thoroughly, thank you." Khalid's English education was obvious from his accent, and he shook the German's hand with quiet formality. "What do you think she meant, though, when she said 'help is on the way?'" Strauss shrugged, seeming unconcerned.

Before he let himself out of the suite, Khalid paused in the door and saw Strauss sit on a chair in Oksana's bedroom, watching her sleep. It was obvious Strauss was actually fond of the girl. It wouldn't deter Khalid, though. When he wanted to sidestep opposition of any kind, he changed the subject…and then did whatever he pleased.

Staring at his phone while he lounged on his private patio, he played the recording of Primo and Oksana over and over again, their sighs and cries loud in his earbuds. Completely aroused, he was turned on by the mechanics of it and completely missed the point—that this was what people might do when they really wanted to know and enjoy each other.

Khalid had been taught from birth to care only about himself, his power and his wealth, in that order. Relationships and laws were something to work around, to be aware and careful of while doing whatever the hell he wanted. He would always see sex as an exchange of power, his possession of power versus her lack of power (whoever *she* was). Period.

Feeling certain the day would come when he would look down and see Oksana swallowing his dick, he would wait like a spider for the chance to touch her golden skin whenever he wanted to. It was only a matter of time and opportunity.

*

Later that night, Emile Strauss got sick. He went down hard and fast. One minute he was drinking an expensive bourbon at dinner and the next he was running a fever and spending a lot of time near the toilet. Mrs. Santos came up and checked Strauss, asking him about his medical conditions after noting his grayish pallor. She had him on a transport stretcher down to the clinic in no time, hurrying to get him on an IV. Khalid leaned against the wall in the hallway connecting their suites and asked her about his condition.

"This is bad," she said to Primo and Khalid. "It may aggravate his heart condition. Don't stay in his suite until they clean it, Primo, and bring Oksana into the clinic. We'll check you both out. Did you have any personal contact with Herr Strauss, Mr....uh...?"

"Just call me Khalid, Madame. No, merely a nodding acquaintance." He heard opportunity knocking when he looked at Oksana's lips before she turned and followed the nurse down the hall.

CHAPTER NINETEEN

THE CITY OF Liverpool, England worked hard to raise its tourism profile above "the birthplace of the Beatles." Yes, the cabs still lined up on Liverpool's Albert Dock to take travelers to The Cavern Club, Penny Lane, and John Lennon's birthplace. But now the city sported a beautiful new museum, amazing shops and restaurants, and a festival of music, food or crafts pretty much every weekend from May through October.

When they docked in Liverpool at 6 a.m., Jack and Cole were accustomed to seeing festival vendors building carnival rides and food tents along the waterfront. But the van from the National Crime Agency, complete with flashing lights, piercing sirens and a contingent of local police, was something they'd certainly never seen before.

"Uh-oh," said Jack. "It looks like they're waiting for us. That's the new British version of the FBI. What the fuck do they want with us?"

Cole ran his fingers through his unruly mane of hair. "Maybe they heard we're fighting a flu outbreak. Would they get involved in that?"

Ewan, joining in the conversation, said "We've been in touch with National Health Agency, and they're satisfied we're taking appropriate measures. Some of their blokes will be eyeballing passengers as they get off, looking for symptoms, standard stuff. Those other chaps, NCA, they only get involved with criminals who're foreign nationals. I believe we might have a few of those, unfortunately."

"And speaking of foreign nationals, there goes Khalid. Wow, he's on the move early today, 6 a.m.," Jack observed. "Maybe he's a big Beatles fan, eh?" Now it was his turn to rake his fingers through his hair and let out a long, worried breath. "Prob'ly not. Shit, I get the worst vibe from that guy."

Khalid, his bodyguard and one of his wives, shrouded in her long black burka, were the first passengers to hustle off the ship toward an expensive-looking sedan parked across the broad Liverpool dock.

"Beatle's fan? Doubtful." Cole felt a tingle at the back of his neck. He'd get one sometimes, whenever there was a shit storm gathering at the edges of his life. Through painful experience, he learned to heed the feeling and go looking for trouble and head it off before it found him, unaware and unprepared. "I'll go down in a few minutes and talk to the NCA guys."

The NCA officers eyeballed Khalid's little ensemble, and the tallest one greeted Khalid, bowing a little and shaking his hand. The encounter seemed pleasant enough to Cole, watching the tall guy show the sheikh his badge and appearing to chat him up.

"Ooohhh, will you look at that," crooned Jack. "I read in *The Examiner* that Khalid is on some kind of blue ribbon panel to 'create better trade relations' between the UK and the Saudis." He'd air-quoted the *Examiner* euphemism, rolled his eyes and chuckled. "That's code for 'lower crude oil prices.' So now the Brits are kissy-kissy with Khalid."

There was a woman with the officers who stopped and said something to Khalid. The sheikh drew himself up, shaking his head, and the woman in the burka appeared to stumble while the little group hauled ass to the black sedan. Khalid put a briefcase in the trunk and they drove away.

Cole made it down the elevator as the officers stopped to show their identification to the employees at the ship's gangplank.

The woman with them looked more and more familiar as Cole approached the group.

"Miss Leeds, isn't it?" Cole extended his hand and they shook, taking each other in. Cole was confused. *Why was Khalid's mistress, Amanda Leeds, boarding the ship with a crowd of cops? Shouldn't she be going the other way,* getting off *the ship?* It couldn't be good that she looked terribly thin, beat-up, bruised and really, really angry! "Officers, I'm Cole Carleton, captain of this vessel. How may I help you?"

The tallest of the British officers smiled politely and held out his badge and a photo. "Philip Gorman, nice to meet you Captain. We're here to arrest one of your passengers, Ivan Fedorov. Can you tell us where this fellow is?"

"Unfortunately," Cole replied, "I know exactly where Mr. Fedorov is. We have an outbreak of Norovirus on the ship, and he's infected and confined to his room. May I ask what the charge against him is?"

Amanda Leeds stepped forward and strode onto the ship, nodding at Cole and the officers to follow her. "Attempted murder," she pronounced angrily. "Ivan threw me off the ship around 3 a.m. Wednesday morning. What he didn't know is I was captain of the long course swim team at my high school."

While they walked through the ship's lobby, crew members in surgical gloves and masks were busy cleaning every available surface, attempting to keep healthy passengers safe from the spreading virus. Gesturing to the swarm of workers, Cole said "You folks should wear gloves and masks as well, and I'll have our doctor escort the prisoner off the ship, but you'll then be exposed to an infected person." Everyone including Amanda gloved up and donned a mask.

"Strong woman, this one," said Gorman, gesturing at Amanda as the glass elevator doors closed. "Some fishermen found her on

Bishop Rock, a tiny island off the Isles of Scully. She was helicoptered to hospital on the mainland." Turning to Cole, he asked, "I'm assuming you have surveillance on the ship?"

"We do. But we don't monitor from two to six in the morning, we record and review if the situation demands it. Would you like us to review and see if we have a record of the incident?" asked Cole.

"That would be fantastic!" Amanda was relieved to learn they'd likely filmed the incident, so it might not be just her word against Ivan's. "We were on the deck next to the specialty restaurants, but of course not another soul was there at 3 a.m."

"If it's not too much trouble, we'd appreciate any images of interaction between Mr. Fedorov, Ms. Leeds, and others on the ship as well, Captain." Cole called Ewan and relayed Gorman's request. When they got off on Ivan's floor, Gorman added "Let me knock and enter the room first so I can witness any reaction Fedorov may have when he sees Ms. Leeds, all right?"

He knocked. "NCA Officer Gorman, Mr. Fedorov. May I come in?"

A man's faint voice answered, "It's open." When Gorman entered the expansive suite, he recognized Ivan from the photo, though the Russian was coming out of the bathroom in his pajamas. He was pale, sweaty, and apparently as ill-tempered as he was sick. "I hope you're here regarding this ridiculous plague?" Ivan demanded peevishly. "There must be something you can do, the staff here is incompetent!"

Gorman smiled tightly, playing along. "Well, perhaps I can. I *would* like to see your passport, Mr. Fedorov." Ivan's passport safely in hand, Gorman motioned Amanda into the room. "Actually I'm here to charge you with the attempted murder of this English citizen, Ms. Amanda Leeds."

Cole and a few other agents followed close behind her and they were greeted with one very surprised Russian pimp, so surprised he staggered backward and fell full-out on the bed, muttering nasty-sounding phrases in Russian when he banged his head on the wall.

He rubbed his eyes as if he thought he might be hallucinating and stared wide-eyed when Amanda crowed "Hello you bleedin' arse-hole. Surprise!! I'm back from the dead!"

Ivan knew enough to remain silent, but blanched when Gorman added, "Oh, by the way Mr. Fedorov, I speak Russian. I heard you say, and I quote, 'I thought I killed you.' Did I understand correctly, or is there more?"

Hands flying to his mouth, the Russian gagged and scuttled to the bathroom. "He's armed, by the way," Amanda said, and one of the agents stepped in front of Ivan in time to have his shoes coated with vomit.

Apparently the agent was one of those guys who has a total aversion to the smell and has to puke immediately when confronted with the stuff. Retching and flinging barf from his shoes as he ran out in search of a hall bath, the agent cleared the way for Ivan to shuffle in, close the door and suffer privately in his own suite's restroom.

Gorman, Amanda and Cole stood helplessly in the middle of the suite, not knowing whether to laugh or cry over the stench of the puke fest. While Cole called housekeeping to clean up the mess, the bathroom door slammed open and Ivan staggered out in his flannel pajamas, sweaty and miserable-looking, waving a gun.

"I told you he was armed!" Amanda muttered and ducked onto the sofa.

"Sit down next to her," Ivan said, motioning to Gorman and Cole with the gun. "Give me my goddam passport. I'm getting out of here."

Gorman pretended to reach into his pocket, one eyebrow raised. "That's all very well, but what about those blokes behind you?"

When the Russian spun around he lurched forward, dizzy, and

the gun went off. Fortunately the mirrored bar at the entrance to the suite was the only casualty, shattering into a thousand pieces while Gorman got Ivan in a chokehold and dragged him to the ground. "Hard to believe you fell for such an old trick, eh, Fedorov?"

"Hey, you're fucking hurting me, you *mudak*!" Ivan cried sharply.

Gorman pulled a glove out of his pocket, put it on, and slid the pistol out of Ivan's hand, handing it to an officer who'd burst into the room when the gun went off. "Let's run ballistics on this and see what else we can learn about Mr. Fedorov, shall we? Oh, and, we're adding assaulting an officer to your charges, sir."

"Ow!" yelped Ivan when Gorman gave Ivan's neck another rude shove with his knee, pinning him down before handcuffing his wrists snugly atop his flannel jammies.

As the officers packed up Ivan's things, Amanda added, "If you need an even tidier case against this dodgy bugger, check around for a really posh gold collar necklace. He took it from me right before he dumped me overboard."

"Right 'ere!" said one of the officers, pulling the collar out of a suitcase. "And this too!" The officer's eyes widened as he displayed a dismantled rifle in a silver hard case. Cole's eyebrows shot up and he rolled his eyes. He didn't even want to *think* about how the Russian got it through the ship's luggage x-rays and metal detectors.

"Ha!" laughed Amanda, smiling at Ivan as she flipped him the universal fuck-you sign. Stepping toward him, she staggered a little, her ordeal finally catching up with her. Sprawled on the floor, the only thing he could move was his head, and he turned it away from her, probably hoping she'd evaporate. Realizing Gorman and the other officers were preoccupied, she quickly snatched a camera and a small electronic box on a shelf and shoved it, cords and all, into her bag.

"Can we talk outside?" Cole asked Amanda, offering his arm to steady her as she wilted before his very eyes. She lurched out of the room, stuffed the electronics farther into her bag, and melted into a chair near the elevator.

*

Cole stopped short as he ran into The Great Wall of Primo outside Ivan's room. Primo was agitated, a wild look in his eyes. "Captain, it's Oksana—she's gone. I was helping to take care of Emile Strauss in the medical center and when I came back she was gone. There was overturned furniture, she must have struggled, and this necklace was on the floor, broken. She wouldn't go anywhere without this necklace! I thought she might be with Tania and when she wasn't, we searched everywhere."

"You know about Tania?" Cole asked.

"He figured it out," Tania said, coming up behind Cole.

Cole opened the necklace's locket and inside was a picture of Oksana with Tania. It was a lightbulb moment. "Fuck! Khalid! Did Oksana have any contact with the sheikh?!"

"He…uh…tried to talk to her a few times, and Strauss…uh…" Primo fizzled, ashamed of his inaction.

"Primo, yeah, we know, did Strauss offer her to him?" Now it was Cole's turn to be agitated.

Before Primo could reply, Dr. Santos arrived with a wheelchair. The Russian was wheeled out of the room while the officers inside gathered his bags. Ivan's wicked laugh was loud enough so the lawmen heard. "Oh, Oksana, poor thing. She's under new management and you'll never see her again! Too bad!"

Amanda came back to life, hissing, "Thaaat fucking arsehole! Of course! The woman in the burka this morning, she had sneakers on. It must've been this Oksana you're talking about! The security guard had a tight hold on her."

Tania launched herself at Ivan's chest, pulling his white, clammy face up to hers by his pajama top. "Where!" she shouted. "Where did he take her?"

Ivan smiled faintly and shrugged her off while the doctor wheeled him away. Gorman and the other agents followed close behind, their arrest complete. "Do you need a minute, Ms. Leeds?" Gorman was apparently expecting Amanda to accompany them back to London.

"Yes, sir. However, I'd appreciate it if I could have a moment with the captain." Amanda raised her eyebrows at Cole and pulled up her pant leg, showing him her ankle monitor. She was a prisoner, though the feds seemed to need her help. "I'll meet you on the dock in a few minutes, if it's okay Officer Gorman."

When they left Cole rubbed the back of his neck, thoughtful. "I guess the authorities have problems with your former relationship with Ivan…and for that matter, with Khalid?"

Amanda quirked a sad smile. "Are you asking if I'm being charged with soliciting and prostitution?"

Cole nodded. "We don't want to get you in any more trouble than you're in already."

"No problem there, Captain, I'm awfully good at doing it by myself. The Bobbies slapped me with a lesser offense 'cause they've been wanting to get Ivan on some other charges. But I appreciate you asking." Amanda looked up at Cole. "I tried to talk to them about Khalid, but the cops couldn't scarper away fast enough! Bugger's connected, unfortunately."

"Yeah. I also wondered…now that you brought him up," Cole leaned back, unsure. "I wondered what you said to Khalid on your way in today."

"I told him I'm coming after him next!" she hissed, pounding her fist into the palm of her other hand.

"He was a prick to you?" Now Tania and Primo were as interested in the question as Cole was, waiting to hear how bad the situation with Oksana was going to get.

"A prick? Khalid is a hideously mean, violent, narcissistic, sociopathic bastard. And I want to help you to get your Oksana away from him."

Amanda's voice shook with fury until she took a deep breath and leaned back, her eyes wide. "I know where the wanker is!" whispered Amanda when they all leaned in. "I'll bet he's going to London to the Savoy. I was there. Khalid has a permanent suite."

While they got on the elevator, Tania propped herself against the wall, arms slack, her brown eyes wide in her pale face. Cole hadn't seen Tania like this. She absorbed Amanda's anger and fear and, her shoulders hunched, the humor and sass drained out of her. It made him want to jump in a car and chase Khalid to London, but he forced himself to be rational and ask, "Should we talk to Gorman?"

Amanda shook her head, her laugh bitter. "Did you see Gorman suck up to him on the way in? The wheels of justice spin slowly when it comes to Khalid, so no, I don't think you should involve Gorman or the cops yet. They'd bodge it up, and Khalid will have Oksana out of the country in no time." Amanda held up the black box she'd lifted from Ivan's room. "You'd be certain of where Oksana is if you get this thing to work. And you might want to be careful of what's on this camera, you might see something...uh...on the jungle telegraph." She thrust the camera at Cole.

"The...what?" Cole turned the camera in his hands. These British expressions were a mystery to him.

Tania whispered in his ear, "Oksana told me Ivan has horrible films of her, so don't give the camera to anyone, guard it closely."

By this time, they were at the gangplank where Ewan stood waiting. "I found the footage of Ivan throwing you over, Ms. Leeds. E-mailed it to Gorman already. It clearly shows Ivan's identity." Ewan beamed with smug efficiency. "And what's this interesting device?" he asked, nodding at the black box.

"Oksana has a tracking sensor under the skin of her forearm, like you would use to find a bloody stolen car or a dog. I had one too, but they dug it out for me at the hospital. This box shows the location of her sensor." The concept was so weird; Tania and Primo joined the conversation and they looked puzzled. "You familiar with LoJack tracking for cars? Ivan referred to this set-up as his HoJack." No one laughed, but Amanda added, "Laugh riot, eh? Can you get this receiver to work wirelessly, Mr...?"

"MacGrath, Ewan MacGrath, Ms. Leeds. Absolutely, I can hook the receiver up and make it sing," said Ewan, shaking her hand (a bit too enthusiastically) and ogling her cleavage while accepting the receiver. "Give me an hour or so." He had a gleam in his eye, and a vibe that said he was thrilled to be in the middle of something so potentially titillating.

Cole walked Amanda over to Gorman and shook her hand, wishing her luck and exchanging cards with Gorman, offering to help with Ivan's prosecution in any way possible. "You're right, you know," he said to Gorman. "Amanda told me the story of her survival, and she *is* extremely brave. I know there are...circumstances, but in the end she's simply a university student trying to pay for everything." When he shook Gorman's hand, he shrugged, "I hope you'll deal leniently with her."

CHAPTER TWENTY

A S COLE WALKED away, he called Jack and explained the situation, ending with an apology. "Listen, uh…I'm sorry. I know Khalid is a big shot, and I might go down in flames for this. I might get fired. You might, too. I don't think so, but you never know. This isn't your problem, and I'll say you weren't involved."

"Let's cross that bridge if and when we have to, bro. Ivan's clearly implicated, he fired a gun at law enforcement on our ship, and we have plenty of film of Khalid talking with him. We're covered, and you're doing the right thing. Good luck!"

Cole took the driver's seat when the rental car pulled up to the ship. His heart was hammering and his jaw set as he gripped the wheel, attempting to hide his anxiety from Tania. *A nurse, a ship's captain, and a bodyguard. It sounds like the beginning of a bad joke on late night television. It certainly doesn't seem like much of a rescue squad, does it?*

Primo held the passenger-side door open for Tania and stuffed himself in the back seat. She sat silently, her body rigid. Cole turned to them and delivered his best pep talk. "It'll take us around four hours to reach London. When we get to Birmingham, we're nearly halfway. Then either Ewan will get this sensor thing going or we'll go to the Savoy Hotel. Khalid's got some time on us, but we'll get there."

They looked at each other in a kind of a what-the-fuck group

stare. Can people achieve an objective like this, an outcome so out- ·
side their experience, just because they love someone? Can a few
determined amateurs get around trained security guards? They
would soon find out.

First, Cole had to survive driving for four hours on the wrong
side of the road. *Tania's counting on me; it's time to man up in every
way. Yeah, common sense says to tread lightly with Khalid. I've gotten
to be such a polite pussy in this cruise gig. But fuck it! What's right is
right.* He was thankful Jack had at least ordered a car with auto-
matic transmission.

Primo, knees sticking up in the back seat of the compact, fingers drumming on the armrest, looked somewhere on the contin-
uum between fidgety and panicked. Tania squirmed in her seat, her
chest rising and falling as if she was breathing through something, a
pain she couldn't escape. Her eyes darted here and there, unfocused,
while the English countryside flew by.

When Cole reached out and combed his fingers gently through
her long, silky hair, she blinked, coming back from whatever hellish
mental place she'd been visiting. Caressing Cole's cheek, she spoke
in a hoarse whisper, "This is…this is like a bad dream. Thank you
for being here, for doing this with me."

"You say it like I have a choice," he answered with a grin, trying to keep his tone light. "Like I would let you go without me."
Reaching over, he squeezed her hand and struggled with what to say
next. He felt her pull away, put him at a distance.

*She's doing that thing again, she's making it seem like this has noth-
ing to do with us, like I don't have feelings for her.* Was she putting him
on a pedestal again? Out of her reach? He felt the uncontrollable
anger threaten, the rage he wanted to bury so deep it would never
rear its ugly head again.

"You do the right thing, you always do the right thing. You're a good person." She patted his shoulder with a trembling hand and gave him a shaky smile.

Cole focused on the road, relaxing his neck, then his hands, letting his anger go, an even better strategy than burying it in his gut.

Primo leaned forward, head in hands, his elbows on the backs of their seats. "Cole, I should've talked to you on Wednesday about Oksana, I wanted to. Strauss went ashore for the day, and I was alone with her. We discussed busting out of this whole situation with Strauss, but she didn't want to get me in trouble. She said help was on the way." Looking at Tania, he added, "I guess she meant you." Burying his face in his forearms, he confessed, "But that's not an excuse. I'm sorry I didn't act sooner. I'm ashamed."

*

Tania was surprised by the emotion in his voice, his obvious feelings for Oksana. "None of us put this together quickly enough," she said. "I told her we would try to do something today, when we were back on the mainland. We couldn't know Khalid would do this. What does he want with her? Doesn't he have enough wives?"

Primo's mouth twisted into a grim smile. "What he wants to do with Oksana has nothing to do with wives, I'm afraid. Wives are for alliances with other families and having children. His other ladies are for whatever his current idea of fun might be."

"Oh." Her voice was small, her mind filled with frightening pictures again.

Primo put his hand on her shoulder. "I'm sorry, I didn't mean to scare you. And Oksana...I don't know her very well, but I do know she can be strong. We'll get to her in time."

In time for what? None of them knew. Yet.

"Uhhh. I'm not so sure right now." While they rolled to a stop, Cole replied to Primo's hopeful assurance they'd get there in time. South of Crewe, traffic on the M6 motorway came to a complete standstill, red brake lights blinking for miles, as far as they could see.

When they got out of the car in the stalled traffic, Cole's cell phone beeped. The cruise ship was a refuge from the constant avalanche of information from cell phones, and it felt strange being back in the digital world. But in this case, it was a blessing. Ewan had the signal from the HoJack hooked up to Cole's phone, which showed as a blinking red dot in something resembling a Google Maps universe.

He placed the newly-rechristened locator on top of the dash and reached across to borrow Tania's cell. "Yeah, Ewan, I didn't know if I could make a call without disrupting the system. Right, okay. And where's that? About eight miles ahead? Hand me off to Jack, okay?"

The rental car made some ominous groaning noises and settled, creaking, low on its wheels when Primo climbed onto the roof to see if traffic was moving further up the line. "Jack, do you know why the M6 is stopped? I'll wait."

For a guy who was six foot five and 225 muscular pounds, Primo looked pretty nimble as he scrambled down. "Nothing's moving, and there are police cars on the shoulder and the exits. Looks like they're not letting anyone cut ahead or get off."

*

Tania watched Cole's face fall while he listened to Jack's explanation of the huge jam on the highway. Blowing out the breath she'd been holding, she stared straight forward, listening, the dozens of dangerous, scary scenarios she'd already imagined replaying in her mind. Suddenly the German guy, who'd seemed like such a threat yesterday, took on a grandfatherly aura, a much safer bad guy than the apparently vicious and well-connected Khalid. There were goose bumps on her arms as she imagined the consequences of failure and the unlikelihood of success.

Cole played a bulletin from the BBC on her cell so she and Primo knew what was ahead. "A chemical tanker exploded on the M6 near the motorway junction for the town of Fenton today, filling the air with hydrochloride gas," the announcer's voice-over continued while they broadcast images of terrified drivers abandoning their cars by the hundreds and running from the toxic fireball. "Firefighters have set up an exclusion zone, encouraging motorists to remain where they are until rescue services allow traffic to proceed."

"I'm leaving you in charge of keeping Jack informed, babe," Cole said, handing her the cell. "Primo, Oksana's tracker shows her still on the highway, stuck about eight miles in front of us. Jack says traffic will start moving in around an hour. So...how're your running skills these days?"

Primo grinned, stripping off his jacket, revealing his gun in its holster. Stuffing the gun in his pants and the holster in the rental car, he growled "I can dust you, old man!" and took off down the shoulder.

*

Cole grabbed his phone and followed at a steady pace, his arms pumping higher and higher while he picked up speed and the car with Tania disappeared behind him in the snarl of stalled cars. He quickly discovered Primo had the right idea about running on the shoulder.

A car door opened right in front of him, too late to dodge. He turned and shouldered the door with an *Oooph,* startling the tiny white-haired lady who climbed out. By bending his knees and push-ing up, he managed to stay upright and off the pavement, and to spin around the door to the other side, rubbing his shoulder while he walked a few steps, checking himself. *No bones sticking out, no blood, and Primo's five car lengths ahead, dammit!*

Now safely on the shoulder, Cole had a prime view of Primo's rapidly diminishing backside. The big man really moved. His rapid strides and tall torso, leaning slightly forward, spoke of an experi-enced, educated runner.

It took Cole back to high school days, when he and Jack joined the cross country team to get away from their dad's drunken bullshit. It was the only sport where the brothers could train long hours unsupervised without having some coach yelling at them. Their dad, known to most people as 'the Admiral,' had gone straight down the tubes after he retired at Commander rank from the Navy. The brothers experienced more than enough yelling at home and didn't need more at school, thank you very much.

They'd work in the local diner for two hours after running, eat a free meal, and fall into bed in a near-coma, deaf to the old man's angry ravings.

Knowing their father would usually be sleeping off the effects of the night before, Jack and Cole would get up early to shower in the locker room at school and do their homework in the library. The Admiral barely noticed if his sons slept at home or not, and they'd long ago learned to sign their own permission slips or it would never get done.

With the race course spread out over miles of forest pathways, cross-country was also the only sport where others didn't notice or care whether your parents showed up to root for you. The night before every track meet the team would gather at one of the runner's houses for a big spaghetti dinner, surrounded by that kid's caring parents and siblings. On those nights, the twins would remember bitterly how warm and organized their household had been when Mom and their sisters were still around and their father was still in the Navy, posted in some blessedly faraway place.

Cole and Jack would watch other dads embrace their sons when picking them up from practice and wonder what it would be like. *But that crap happened right after Mom left... This's the first time I've thought of it in years. And hopefully the last.* His mind snapped shut and locked the memories away when he poured maximum effort into catching up with Primo.

When they ran back in high school, Cole had been stuck watching Jack's backside for hours until he discovered how to pull some extra energy—some magical endorphins, he guessed—out of his butt at the end of a race, and pass the other exhausted runners. He planned to do the same with Primo in five miles or so, when they got closer to where the tracker indicated Oksana was located, apparently still stuck in traffic with Khalid.

His lungs burned and his legs felt like lead, but the miles flew by and he began to notice drivers leaning against their cars, smoking, eating, talking on cell phones, and soothing crying children. They didn't appear to be frightened, just bored. A young couple ground into each other, openly making out on the hood of their car.

Relax your face, breathe in for three paces, out for two. Cole had a good, even cadence going, but they were going to have to go all out to make it eight miles in less than an hour.

Once traffic started moving, this opportunity would become nothing more than a good workout and an exercise in frustration. They needed to get this done now, because in London they were more likely to run into lots of guns, professional muscle, and high-tech, low-success situations.

Feeling his legs get lighter and his head clear a little, Cole pulled up next to Primo, and the two men ran side by side. "Call Tania, I don't want to lose the signal on my cell," Cole huffed out.

"How's it going?" Primo asked Tania, putting her on speaker while they surged forward, faster still, pacing each other.

"Jack saw an aerial shot on the BBC. The explosion will be cleared up sooner than expected, they say probably in twenty-five minutes. The police are still parked on the shoulder right now, so I can't drive forward and pick you up. Sorry."

"Don't be. We're flyin'."

And they were. Babies crying, lovers loving. Breath searing lungs, arms reaching, legs pumping, the Admiral yelling, Mom leaving, it was going by a lot faster now, hurting a lot less. Except for that last one.

CHAPTER TWENTY-ONE

"CAPTAIN GORMAN."

The officer cleared his throat politely, attempting to wake his superior, who was asleep in the passenger seat. The National Crime Agency van with Ivan in custody was stuck in the traffic a short distance in front of Cole, Tania, and Primo's rental car. Everyone in the NCA van was asleep except the officer driving and Amanda, who tapped Gorman on the shoulder.

"Captain Gorman," the driver repeated. "Look at the man running up behind us. No, wait, there are two men, one of them very tall. Aren't they the Captain and the other man from the ship? They're running as if they're chased by demons!"

Gorman and Amanda lowered their power windows in time to feel the *whush* when Cole and Primo flew by, directly to their left on the shoulder. "Go!" Amanda cheered, sticking her head and a fist out the window. "Go get that bloody muthafuckaaahh!" Cole gave a little backwards wave, since they were already four cars further along.

*

The runner's high. Every runner had heard of it, but Cole knew how to tap into it, to make love to it. Apparently Primo did too. The two men ran easily, companionably, matching each other stride for stride.

Yes, they were sweating, their shirts now tied around their waists. And the acrid smell from the chemical explosion was inside their heads now, stripping their nasal passages and beginning to create a pain right between the eyes. But when Cole pulled out the phone and they saw the red light beeping right in front of them they felt the high, the surge of energy, the euphoria that makes the body seem to float on a cloud, above the pain.

The endorphins flooding the brain while running created a sense of freedom and power that was amplified by one urgent fact: around them, cars were being cranked up, ready to move. Cars were flowing forward, freed from the 70-mile backup created by the accident.

When they finally sighted Khalid's black Maybach sedan, the engine was already running, brake lights indicating it might be in gear, ready to go. They saw the back of Khalid's head, his longish hair and stylish jacket. But most important, they saw Oksana's blonde curls, thankfully freed from the heavy burka that would have made it impossible for her to run away.

Surprising Cole, Primo ran to the driver's side and stopped, leaving Cole to pull Oksana out of the back. Oksana's mouth formed an O when she saw the captain, but he couldn't hear a thing from inside the car. She appeared to be screaming and struggled to open the manual door lock, but Khalid saw him and snatched her hand, shoving his phone into his pocket.

It was like watching a silent movie until Primo wrapped his shirt around the gun and used it to smash the driver's window. Once, twice, three times with the strength of a big man in love, and the window shattered onto the driver's lap as the bodyguard reached for his gun, stuck in the center console of the luxurious vehicle. "Do you really like Khalid that much?" Primo asked, his gun inches from the driver's face. Apparently the guy spoke English, because he put his hands up in surrender.

But before Primo snatched the pistol from the console, Khalid got out of the car, running toward a nearby exit ramp. He stumbled, leaving his fancy loafers on the road while he disappeared to the left at the top of the exit. Traffic was now streaming past them, the cars behind the Maybach merging into the next lane while drivers blared their horns, scowling at them as they passed.

Cole helped Oksana out of the car, and when she threw her arms around him, apparently unhurt, he relaxed a little, their mission all but completed. She went limp, relieved, and then jumped back, her arm outstretched. "Khalid! You have to get him! He has a film on his phone of…of Primo and of me."

Oksana was still pointing up the ramp when Tania drove up on their left, finally freed from the police block of the road's shoulder. "Khalid! Up the ramp and he ran to the left! Get him!"

Without even braking, Tania gunned the car up and around the corner, tires squealing. Cole ran up after her like he'd been shot out of a cannon, worried she might kill the guy—not that he wouldn't like to do the same thing. But that meant too many complications.

He got to the top of the ramp and ran down the deserted road in time to see Tania following behind Khalid with her brake lights on, a little to his left side. She stepped on the gas and opened the driver's side door just enough to bang him hard in the ass, knocking him down, and quickly closed it again, braking and putting the car in park just beyond where he lay sprawled on the pavement.

When she scrambled out of the car and sat on Khalid, her hand fisted in his hair to hold him down, Cole completely lost it and laughed like a lunatic, tears running down his face while he caught up with them. Her beautiful face was so flushed and determined, like a kid in a playground fight. Guts and common sense. Tania's combination of the two was potent and, at least to Cole, sexy and funny as hell.

"Let's check his pockets," he choked out, still laughing. Khalid looked up at him, eyes wide, trembling, while Tania found Oksana's passport in his jacket pocket. They left Khalid's passport and wallet on the pavement but took his phone.

The video gallery icon was already open so Cole tapped it. A vivid image of Primo, balls deep in Oksana's mouth, came alive on the phone. "Oh shit, you fucking asshole!" Cole bit out as he pitched the phone against the rental car and it shattered on the pavement. He willed himself to erase the image from his mind *forever*. Tania mattered too much for him to let it lurk anywhere in his memory. For good measure, he strode over and ground the phone to dust with the heel of his shoe and scooped up the pieces, scattering them in the grass by the side of the road.

His hands were bleeding from the sharp plastic when he placed his shoe on the back of Khalid's neck and pressed down. "Do those images exist anywhere else, you jerk-off? Tell me the truth now, or I'll crush your fucking neck!"

"No, for God's sake, no!" Khalid bleated in his clipped accent, while his hands and legs shook uncontrollably.

"You looked away, prick, you're lying," Cole said, beginning to enjoy the feel of Khalid struggling under his foot, and getting grim satisfaction because Tania was still pulling his hair and riding his back, determinedly holding him down.

"Keep him down," Cole instructed her, removing his foot and searching through the rest of Khalid's pockets. "Nothing. Let's get out of here." *His car! I saw Khalid put a briefcase in the trunk. Those images will likely be on there. And they'll be history when we get our hands on it.*

Tania held out her hand to Cole and he helped her up. They got in the rental car, spun around, and drove straight for the sheikh as he stood and dusted himself off, laughing when Khalid threw himself over the side of the road and rolled down an embankment. They paused long enough to see him blubbering, looking up at them from the bottom.

When they reached the top of the exit, Cole leaned out and yelled, "Guys, come on up! We have to drive to Glasgow since we missed the ship. Get Khalid's briefcase with his laptop out of the trunk and let's drive north instead of getting back into this traffic!" Primo sheathed his gun and kept the bodyguard's for safekeeping while he popped the trunk and yanked out the briefcase. He and Oksana ran up the exit and jumped into the back of the car.

The M6 North would get them most of the way to Glasgow in four hours, but it seemed shorter because of the laughing, kissing, and canoodling going on in the back. Cole even let Primo drive for a while since Oksana and Primo had reminded him how much fun you could have in the back seat of a car.

CHAPTER TWENTY-TWO

JACK WAS ALL smiles on the phone, listening to Cole's account of the rescue. "Sounds like you guys got a good workout, bro, so sorry I missed it...NOT! Seriously, though, great work, really. I got it covered here, no new cases of the flu, and everyone except the German is feeling better. Strauss is doing badly, Doc says he needs to be admitted to the hospital in Glasgow. Yeah, pneumonia," said Jack as he stood outside the theater on the *Sunset*. "He asked for Oksana and Primo several times...Yeah, I know, weird, but...maybe he wants to apologize." He paused, listening. "No, Strauss told the Doc there's no family to notify. See you soon."

It was *Dance with the Captains* night on the ship, and Jack was wearing his white dress uniform, ready to waltz around with the winners of the ship's dance contest and give them their trophies. The ship's professional dancers had been teaching and partnering with passengers, and putting on ballroom dance shows like the ones on TV. Entertainment director Jeannette and some of the ship's officers served as judges, and they led the whistles and wild applause when Jack walked onstage to announce the winners.

*

Every woman in the ballroom stared at those broad shoulders and the way the short jacket tapered down to his trim waist. Jack's pants hugged his amazingly perky butt (also highlighted by the deliberately short uniform jacket). Which made Daniella, who was sitting in the front row with some other staffers, smile. First, a guy had to have a good self-image to be able to dance with lousy dancers, make them look great, and rock that too-stylish Italian uniform at the same time. And second, it was how she differentiated Jack from Cole—Jack's derriere gave new meaning to the term "high and tight." Not that Cole's was anything to sneeze at, but still...

Daniella was enjoying both her rare night off and the sight of Jack filling out his uniform like it had been made for him...which, come to think of it, it probably was. Watching Jack whirl around with the contest winners, she remembered the two captains' handsome faces and light brown hair were the same, though Cole seemed to let his hair get a little longer before he had it cut. Their adorable dimples were on opposite sides, Jack had one on his left, Cole's was on the right.

If only I'd studied for my college courses the way I've studied our adorable twin captains. Sigh. *I'd have my degree by now!* The truth was she *had* studied, hard, but she simply...ran out of money. Which brought her to this cruise gig, in this theater, hoping Jack's intense stare was really aimed at her. It seemed to be. *So why would he, the captain, a big shot, be interested in a nothing like me? I clean people's toilets and make their beds.*

Cole's blue eyes were really, really blue; Jack's were a little on the grey side, mysterious. A little cold, some would say. But not Daniella. She felt a special heat from Jack's fierce eyes, eyes now reaching across the stage to her. His sharp focus made her imagine taking off those tight pants of his and pressing up against him, holding one of his perfect ass cheeks in each of her hands. *And feeling his giant erection pressing against my pussy, feeling his rough kiss, feeling him hold my breasts and thumb my nipples. Yuummm.*

An elbow to the ribs from a coworker woke Daniella from her

reverie. "Daniella! They're calling you! Go up on the stage." Jeannette was gesturing to Daniella while she talked to the crowd, urging her to run up there.

Wearing jeans and a thin white tank top, Daniella definitely didn't feel dressed for whatever this was when she stood there in the bright lights. Jeannette put her arm around Daniella and announced, "Tonight we have one more award to give out, an award suggested to me by many of you who've attended our parties and visited our dance club, La Bliss. " She held her hand to her ear and said, "Who gets the sexy dancing going on the *Sunset* like no other, people?"

"Daniellaaaaa!" was the cry from all assembled. Passengers in the audience hooted and stomped their feet until the theater seemed ready to vibrate loose from the ship and slide into the sea. Jeannette gave her a hug and a trophy. When Daniella held out her arms in a big I-love-you audience hug, the room erupted with even louder screams, rebel yells, and hollering. Gradually the room went quiet.

Winking at her buddy in the DJ booth, Daniella waited while the DJ cued up something for her, and smiled when she heard the rhythmic opening chords of a naughty Britney Spears tune. The audience started yelling again as Daniella let her head hang and her body go slack, as if she was in a trance. Moving her hips slowly, milking the beat for all it was worth, she raised her arms while Britney sang *I'm a Slave 4 U*. When Daniella's belly button ring peeked out from under her shirt, a low rumble spread through the crowd. Her lean torso circled as the song got sexier, urging her to "dance up on ya."

Jack, captain's hat on, took it as his cue to bring a chair out onto the stage and pat his legs, beckoning her to dance up on *him*. It seemed he was hoping for a replay of the staff party lap dance. The crowd roared its approval while the DJ changed the song to the Pussycat Doll's "Buttons." With Jack in his white uniform, the scene definitely had an *Officer and a Gentleman* feel to it and everyone, young and old, was riveted.

Daniella let her power loose for all to see, strutting across the stage like she owned it, tossing her hair as she put on Jack's hat at a jaunty angle while she lip-synched the words to the song. The crowd hummed its approval when she ran her hands down the sides of her body, hips swaying to the music, breasts swinging under the nearly transparent T-shirt. People in the room spoke at least a dozen different languages, but Daniella's moves needed no translation.

"Loosen up my buttons babe," her lips moved to the song as she slammed her foot between Jack's spread legs, missing his junk by inches. Jack took his hat back and placed it over his crotch, laughing and pretending to be scared of her.

The audience couldn't get enough of the whole thing, howling with laughter. When she finally sat facing him on his lap, her legs wide, her arms circling his neck, the laughter turned to a steady purr of "OooOOooo!" It was fantasy fulfillment at its finest for the ladies in the audience when he put the hat back on her head, framed her face with his hands and pulled her in close for a long, super-hot kiss. This was as close to sex as they could get with their clothes on, and the crowd seemed to alternate between holding their breath and breathing heavily at the erotic scene. "Kind of like the end of *An Officer and a Gentleman*," whispered one of Daniella's co-workers to the other, "but hotter and dirtier!"

Jeannette started clapping, signaling the lap dance—and the smooch—should end, but Jack had Daniella in a tight grip, devouring her in a deeply passionate kiss. The crowd did clap, but together in a loud rhythm while chanting, "Go, go, go, go, gooooo!"

*

What the crowd didn't know was her mouth was surprisingly sweet and soft on his, lazily stroking his tongue while he responded by pulling her in even tighter, his big hands spread over her behind. Hoping to get with her somewhere more private—immediately, if not sooner—he finally ended the kiss, his lips against her forehead as he whispered, "Do you know where my cabin is?" She nodded, her lips trembling, but winked at him as a show of bravado, an invitation.

As if he needed encouragement. His senses were filled with her scent, the taste of her lips, the lush feel of her ass in his hands. If touching and devouring every inch of her in front of these people was the only way to have her, he might just do it. He was frantic, wanted to get her naked and tell her how beautiful she was, to caress her cinnamon skin and find the secret spots on her curvy body.

The crowd streamed out of the theater while Jack shook a few hands and considered his exit strategy. In his current mindset, the distance and time between this theater and his bed seemed endless. Picturing himself alone in his room, waiting for Daniella, he decided to wait backstage and see if she came that way.

When she did, he put his arm around her and slowed their steps, separating them from her friends. "Good night ladies, hope you enjoyed the show!" he said, unleashing his most dazzling smile. Women of any age were helpless when confronted with his seductive grin and its disarming dimple.

Her friends giggled, waved, and ambled away, certain of the captain's intent, taking Daniella's consent for granted. "I mean, who wouldn't wanna get with that guy, riiiight?" one of them said to the other, and Jack and Daniella cracked up, dissolving some of the tension between them.

Still laughing, Jack leaned into her, his voice raw and low. "So, is this a date? Can I buy you dinner or a drink?" She chuckled again and shook her head. "How about a cheesy pick-up line?"

Pursing her lips and blushing, she squinted at him. "Give it your best shot, Captain."

"Hmmm....how abouuuut...I don't have a library card, but do you mind if I check you out?"

"Oh, shit," she snorted, laughing in spite of herself. "Hmmm... how about can I take you back to my room and show you my etchings?"

Facing her, he tipped her chin up toward him with one finger. "Ooooh. I like it. So....can I?" Daniella nodded, speechless, her big brown eyes hazy with a potent mix of lust and anticipation.

He pulled her close in the elevator, and was stunned to realize she was trembling. "Are you cold?" he said, rubbing her arms with his hands. In fact, he now realized she was nervous. *Nervous?! How could this blazing hottie be nervous?* He had to say something to bust through her panic attack.

"I know a lot about you, you know."

She peered up at him, looking puzzled.

Laughing again, mostly at himself, he admitted he'd looked at her personnel file. "I know you're a college student in Las Vegas, you speak English, Spanish and Portuguese, you work hard, and you've charmed the hell out of everybody on the ship."

She smiled a shaky smile when they got off the elevator, and he decided to really go for it. "Everything in the public areas of the ship is on camera. You know that, right?" She nodded, her eyes questioning.

When he pulled her into his room and closed the door, he handed her his phone and pressed play on the file of her dance clips he'd strung together. Ewan was right; he was obsessed with her. And something made him want to show her his obsession, show her how he saw her, how he couldn't stop looking at her.

Eyes wide, she stared back and forth from his phone to his face, her lips parted, amazement on her face. "Stalking a little, hmm?" There was sarcasm in her voice but her lips tugged into a grin. It was obvious she was enjoying his agitation.

Facing her again as she watched, both his hands on her hips, he asked "Who's the real you, Daniella? The sweet, serious girl who gives away the two cents you make to anyone with a sad story?" Her eyes got even wider. "Yeah, your supervisor told me you gave some money to your idiot roommate with the gambling problem. Is she the real you?"

He paused to sit on the bed and pull her onto his lap. "Or are you the wild child, blowing everybody's mind when you dance? Where did you learn to dance like that?" He rubbed circles on her back with one hand and spread the other hand, wide and still, on her belly, holding her tight. Feeling a little like a slightly creepy Santa Claus, he wondered if he should tell her what he was going to give her for Christmas. The difference in their ages was definitely messing with his mind.

Letting out a long breath, she closed her eyes, oblivious to his insecurities, and gave him the phone back. "It...the dancing thing, it just," she shrugged, "... bubbles up inside me and comes out. I don't even see it before I do it, I see it *as* I do it. Do you understand?"

"I think so. Kind of," he murmured. *You want to dance? I'll give you the dance of your life, darlin'.* Of course it wasn't real dancing he had in mind right now, it was the horizontal mambo kind. There were some pins left in her hair, so he picked them out, then tangled his fingers through the glorious mass, pulling it to the side to kiss her neck and breathe her in.

"I like your hair, your wavy hair. I like that you don't make it flat and straight like the other girls," he breathed into her ear. He got a smile out of her when he added, "Let's face it, you're not flat and straight like the other girls. And I like that a lot." He pressed his face against her neck, feeling the drag of his stubble on her skin, then kissing it away with loose, moist lips.

Her low whimper vibrated through him, making him feel a little light-headed as she pressed her luscious booty against his erection. *What the hell?! I'm not sure who's leading who here.* Little goose bumps popped out on her skin, and she tilted her head, eyes closed, inviting him to continue kissing and touching her. *Whatever. It's all extremely, extremely good.*

"I understand one thing really clearly, Daniella. When you dance, I want to fuck you till we're both totally wrecked and happy." Finally she opened her eyes and looked at him, a smile twitching at her lips. "Me and everybody else with a pulse, right?" He shrugged and added "But I'm better than they are, because I also want to fuck you when you smile, when you laugh, and when you stare at me like that, like I'm insane." Now they both laughed and she turned to face him and put her arms around his neck, her lips light against his.

But light didn't feel right, not to Jack. He seized her mouth and devoured her little gasps and moans while he explored the sensitive corners of her mouth with his tongue and nipped her full lower lip until they were both breathless, greedy, their hands lingering at the clothing, the buttons, the zippers blocking their entrance to paradise.

He felt her straining up to him, grasping for his kiss, her hands in his hair, answering his question with her body—yes! She brushed her hand over his jaw, opening herself up to his kiss and kissing him back, running her fingers under his jacket, even sexier and more passionate than he'd imagined she would be.

She shuddered when he caressed her breast, his finger outlining her nipple through the thin fabric. Easing her off his lap, he stood with her, running his hands down her arms like he had in the elevator. She was trembling again. "Too many clothes, don't you think?"

he said in a low voice, and took off his jacket and the T-shirt he wore underneath. "Need help with yours?"

Daniella nodded yes but didn't take her shirt off, running her hands over his chest, up over his shoulders and stroking the muscles in his back as she pressed up against him. Her wordless begging almost killed him when she buried her face there on his chest, running one finger around his nipple the way he'd touched hers. She seemed to be touching him into her memory, her hands shaking when she pressed kisses to his skin.

He felt her breath on his chest, and when she looked up, saw a glint of single-minded lust in her eyes. When she took his hand from her shoulder, she cupped it around her face, inhaling his scent from his palm and slowly pulling his thumb into her mouth.

"Mmmmm," she moaned, her mouth vibrating around his finger while she sucked and swirled her tongue around it, looking at him through her eyelashes and leaving no doubt in either of their minds what she really wanted to put her mouth around. It was Jack's turn to shiver when he fantasized what it would be like to possess that talented mouth of hers. To adore her sweet pussy with *his* mouth. The anticipation was killing him.

She tried to undo his belt but he gathered the bottom of her shirt and pulled it up with one hand while he undid her bra with the other, throwing the flimsy clothes on top of his jacket. *She's so beautiful! Doesn't realize I'm keeping my pants on so I don't lose it when she touches me.*

"That's better isn't it?" he asked, trying to sound calm but really, truly desperate to have her, to claim her. Cupping a breast in each hand, thumbing the nipples, he gazed down at her while her brown eyes burned fiery and dark. He took a nipple in his mouth, licking, nipping, and drawing on it while he rolled the other in his fingers, then he sat on the edge of the bed while he unbuttoned and pulled down her shorts so she wore nothing but a thong. *I love her little noises, wonder if I could make her come just doing this. And what an amazing view!*

When he put his hand in her thong, she was so wet he felt his dick lurch. Crying out in pleasure, she spread her legs when he circled the fingers of one hand over her clit, using the other to pull her thong to the floor.

She braced herself and dug her fingers into his shoulders when he spread her pussy lips with his thumbs and swiped her clit with his tongue, back and forth, up and down as she arched to welcome him. He didn't wonder if Jeannette did this better because he didn't care, he couldn't get enough of Daniella's moans, her gorgeous breasts and her sweet honey.

Covering her with his mouth, he lapped at her as if her sex was the most natural, delicious treat in the world. Her cries urged him on, her legs shaking as she looked down at him, both his hands on her hips now. He held her captive that way, his tongue mastering her sweet button, making her orgasm build, making her tingle and burn and buck against his mouth.

"God, you're so beautiful, so wet. I could do this all night, Daniella." Orgasm crashed into her like a hurricane, and he kept licking her saturated folds while she stiffened and shook and cried out his name. When she kept jolting and moaning he stood, letting her fingers scratch his arms while she came and came, gasping for air. He held her, a warm place for her to fall after flying so high, his face in her hair, his lips trailing down her neck, his hands spreading her ass cheeks wide, holding the soft flesh he'd fantasized about while he watched her on his phone.

Fear flickered through Daniella's eyes when he kissed her again, and Jack saw it clearly. He paused, jaw clenched as he reined himself in, reminding himself again that she'd just turned twenty-one.

"You okay?" One hand held the back of her neck, holding her still for more of his scorching kisses, the other explored her pussy again, fingers touching exactly right as her wet sex pulsed into his hand. "Do you want to stop?" Inwardly, he groaned. *I hope the fuck not! Her tits, those hips, that luscious ass…she's driving me nuts!*

Eyes bright, she shook her head. "I want you. I…I want you inside of me." Her fingers fumbled at his zipper and she rubbed her lips over his stubble as she reached down into his pants, enclosing his cock in her fist. Jack felt it pulse in her hand, seeming to have a mind of its own, mostly erect but hanging down one of his thighs at an awkward angle. "Can I…can I move it?" she asked, looking up at Jack, her eyes curious and wide.

"Yes," he smiled, tamping down a laugh at her serious request. "You can move it, it won't break. You can stroke it or kiss it or lick it, whatever you want." He undid his belt, button and zipper and pushed his pants and briefs down to his hips as his erection swung free. *Whoever she was with, maybe they just…fucked her. Maybe she hasn't done the foreplay part,* he thought.

The no-foreplay idea seemed unlikely when she kneeled and massaged his balls while she ran her tongue up the underside of his cock, finishing by licking and sucking the big bulb on top. Her eyes were bright although she was a little awkward, but she licked her lips and smiled up at him as she explored. He groaned and his legs trembled a little; she was surprising and he wanted her so much.

*

Jeannette had certainly taught Daniella a lot about orgasms, both giving and receiving them. The woman's touch was soft, generous, luxurious even, but tonight Daniella was hypnotized by Jack's flinty possession of her. That sultry place low in her belly was yearning to experience the maleness of him, the full force of his desire, and the rough feel of his hands on her.

And for the first time, Daniella really wanted to know what it would feel like to have that giant thing inside her, filling her. A while ago at school, when she was upstairs at a party with a guy, his cock had seemed ugly, bringing back a scary memory. She had been too frightened to stop him, and she almost let him fuck her mouth, tears running down her cheeks. He hadn't noticed her tears, but luckily it was pretty much over before it began.

Yes, technically she was a virgin, never having had a man inside her. And her natural oral skills, the curiosity of her tongue, fooled Jack into believing she was experienced.

The corners of her mouth tilted up in a smile, she was giggling inside while she sucked and licked and fondled him. Jack kept smiling and telling her how beautiful she was, how good her mouth felt, stroking her hair and letting her take the lead. He didn't seem nervous or urgent like other guys she'd made out with, just…enjoying himself. How exciting to taste and feel the maleness of him, to explore this wonderfully huge example of amazing manhood! She was discovering how much fun it was to feel the power a woman has when she holds a man in the palm of her hand, when she's in control of his pleasure. Swirling her tongue around the top like she was licking a lollipop, she pumped him with her hand. She caught him staring down at her, his blue eyes blazing while he watched her eager lips around his cock.

"Oh, fucking God, you have to stop, I'm not going to last, gorgeous. We can come back to this, I hope we will. Let me get inside you, you said you want me to, right Daniella?

Spiraling her tongue around him as she reluctantly slid him out, she stood. Pretending to be puzzled, she said "I did say so, didn't I? Do you think we should, Captain?" She ran her tongue around her lips, trembling a little. There was a sharp yearning inside her she tried to hide with her smartass remarks.

"You're so beautiful," he whispered, flashing his sexy grin and covering her breasts with his hands. She wondered if he felt her heart pounding while he kissed her again, tracing his finger along her jaw, down her neck. Working his way down her heated skin, his tongue left sexy little tracks he would then blow on, his breath hot. She felt the goose bumps break out everywhere he went, and she whimpered with need, wanting this and wanting more, wanting everything.

She moaned and opened to him when he nipped, sucked and licked her sweet bud, his fingers circling, finding her wet and ready again. Almost immediately, a husky cry came from somewhere inside her when she flew apart and tensed against him, pushing against him and panting.

*

Ready? She's so ready I barely have to touch her. Jack scooped her up and laid her gently on the bed, where he leaned over her on his hands, his knees between her legs, which were spread wide for him. Everything about her called to him, made him want to put his stamp on her, claim her. "I want to get deep inside you, stretch you," he said, and she answered by lifting her hips greedily to him.

Hissing through clenched teeth, he put on a condom and entered her, just one hot, wet inch. She felt like a vise, incredibly tight, but it wasn't only that, she... something was wrong. Maybe he hadn't aroused her enough, there was resistance. Yet she was slick for him, her nipples pinched tight as she bobbed her hips against him.

"It's okay, Jack, don't make me wait." Reaching down between them, she wrapped her fingers around the base of his cock. "Fuck me, I don't want you to stop. Just do it."

He kissed his way back down to her pussy, working her precious little knot again, getting her all loosened up for him. She was beyond wet, writhing beneath him, moaning and begging. He took a deep breath and held her steady as he pressed the thick head of his cock against her entrance again. When he exhaled and flexed his hips into her, he went nowhere because she seemed to resist him again. Sweat broke out on his forehead, something felt...off, not quite right. She moaned shakily, opening her legs wider, grinding against him while she dug her fingernails into his ass.

"Daniella?" His voice was strained, desperately struggling for control, watching her carefully. "Are you okay?"

"Perfect, I'm perfect," she gasped. "You're perfect." She appeared to be drowning in sensation, melting into him, her little whimpers and cries getting more intense when she pulled him in closer, sliding her hands up to his neck, threading into his hair and pulling on it. He drew in a shaky breath as he pressed the tip inside her creamy slit, her grasping friction blowing his mind.

Both hands tightly clamping her hips, he drove into her in one strong move.

Her eyes flew open and she let out a cry that sounded like... pain, not pleasure. She stiffened and thrashed around, her pussy like a vise around him but her upper body said no, no, no! Jack froze. He remembered his first girlfriend, back in high school, who'd given him her virginity. *That's what this is.*

"Daniella, you're a...?" His question had an edge to it as held himself back, fighting the overwhelming urge to continue tunneling down into her skintight, velvet channel. Pulling out a little, he saw a bit of blood on the condom. Calming himself, he stayed inside her (no way to do otherwise) but rolled them onto their sides.

"I mean, you never...?" She nodded, one tear rolling down her cheek when she answered his near-incoherent question. He stroked and comforted her, realizing he wasn't on edge, just...regretful.

What did he regret? For her, he regretted she felt she had to deceive him. He would've gotten to know her better, gone a lot more slowly, made it special for her. She deserved his care, the best he could offer. His inner voice said, *Uh-uh. She saw who you are, player, knew you'd run from a challenge. You ain't Mr. Right, just Mr. Right Now, and she decided to overlook it. Lucky you.* Suddenly, he wasn't so sure.

"I'm so sorry, I didn't know. Why didn't you tell me? I would have done it differently so it wouldn't hurt you," he crooned, whispering in her ear, trying so hard to control his erection, still throbbing inside her. For himself, he regretted he hadn't gotten to anticipate being her first, to plan how to relieve her of her innocence, to lead her consciously down a sensual path to her first time. Instead, he'd just…drilled her. Well, not really, but still. *I mean she is only 21, but how…how does a woman with a wicked, talented mouth like that, a woman who could rock your fucking world when she swings her hips…how on earth could she still be a virgin? And what the fuck do I do now?*

*

Looking up at him, she almost wanted to laugh. The big tough guy, the player with no heart, looked gobsmacked, totally taken by surprise. *The player's been played, huh? But it doesn't help with this throbbing between my legs.* She felt herself pulsing, clutching him inside her pussy again and again, and she saw he felt it too, closing his eyes, growling from deep in his throat. Yeah, that first thrust was a sharp pain, but it'd faded, and she wanted to feel him deeper inside her, find out what all the fuss was about.

"How do I feel?" she asked Jack in a throaty voice, helpless to keep from clutching his fullness again and again. She felt his lips on her neck, his hand cupping her breast, but he was surprisingly sweet, asking for nothing but direction from her.

"So fucking good, you're so tight," he choked out. His tender kisses reassured her, told her she was in charge. "And the squeezing thing you're doing? Holy God! What do you want me to do, sweet thing?"

She reached down between them, her fingers touching her clit, fondling his balls. "Make me come again, Jack," she pleaded huskily, "Show me how this works, *Papi*." His fingers nudged her aside on her hot little button and she started panting again, then sighing and finally letting out passionate cries in Spanish, calling him *Papi* again and using some other words he wanted to research later, like *duro* and *mas*.

*

Rapido was one he figured out for himself, and he got her stirred up again, gritting his teeth the whole time because the muscles inside her were still gripping his dick so tightly he was in constant danger of losing it. When she was close to coming again, he could feel she was unbelievably soaked and much looser and softer inside. He watched her face, ready to stop if she winced while he pressed deeper inside her, inch by aching inch.

"Look at me, look in my eyes, I want to see how you're feeling," he whispered. Her eyes opened and she smiled when he filled her completely, her eyes going wider when he put his fingers in his mouth and let her watch him suck her juices off them.

"Jack!" she gasped, shocked and apparently turned on by what a naughty boy he was.

"Mmmm, delicious," he said, his voice a hoarse purr. He began to pump, stroking deep into her, slow and deliberate. "How does this feel, inside, I mean?"

She answered by digging her heels into the bed, throwing her head back and writhing, circling her hips into him and whimpering, "Please, please, please." She probably wasn't sure what she was asking for until he laid her down, bent her legs back at the knees and lifted her hips again. He found her sensitive spot with the tip of his cock and surged forward again and again, rubbing against it until she was shrieking, "Oh, fuck yes! Yes!" and moaning Spanish words again.

He angled into her center, pounding into her when she froze, closing around him as she came, her pussy burning and clutching, crying out his name and taking him over with her as he groaned long and low, jerking inside her.

When she continued to pulse around him, gripping his cock as if she would never let go, he couldn't see, couldn't even think anymore, and collapsed on the bed, kissing her frantically. He wanted her to stop now, but at the same time he didn't want her to stop—ever. The pleasure was so fierce, he could swear he saw stars.

His hands on her trembled while their breathing slowed and he lay next to her, caressing her, his forehead pressed to hers. Finally she went limp and calm, her tight cunt releasing him. He'd thought it would be a relief, but he suddenly felt as if he'd lost something, as if part of him was missing.

CHAPTER TWENTY-THREE

THIS WAS USUALLY Jack's cue to disappear into the bathroom and make himself scarce, but he stripped off the condom and kept kissing her, touching her, holding her. *What the fuck? I'm cuddling, for God's sake. Who am I all of a sudden? And now I want to lie here and talk to her.* For the first time in his life, he wanted to be more; maybe he even wanted to be everything to a woman who was this sexy, funny and real.

His impulse was rewarded immediately. "I liked it," she said with a sly smile, her eyes shining. "And I like that thing," she purred, stroking his dick and bringing it to throbbing, instant life again. "It's pretty and smooth and…well, you know."

Jack laughed. "Actually, I don't know, at least not from your perspective. And what you're doing feels…" he let out a long breath, "awesome, but you have to let me keep my hand warm between your legs while you do it to me." He palmed her pussy, feathering her with his fingers, kissing her again and then locking his eyes with hers. "But I was…surprised. I guess you figured that out. Your hips don't, uh, speak virgin, you know what I'm sayin'? And your booty language, well, I guess you know it doesn't need translation."

He chuckled and took a deep breath, pressing into her. "You are so sexy, how did you get to be twenty-one," he paused, and his cock swelled in her hand as he circled her clit with wet fingers, "and still be a virgin?"

*

She wanted to look away, to flip him off with a sarcastic remark, but instead she was shaking, quivering inside and out from what he was doing with his fingers and the way he commanded her, compelling her with those eyes and those lips to give him an honest answer. He was like a drug and she, unbelievably, wanted more and wanted it right now.

"I…I…never met anyone I wanted to, you know, really be with. People wanted to, guys and girls, but I…stayed away. If they asked, I would tell them I was with someone else." Her mouth was dry and she wanted to stop talking so badly, change the subject, force him to make love to her again, but his hand on the back of her neck gently held her steady.

"So you were afraid. Why?" *How does he know, dammit?* He seemed genuinely puzzled, increasingly alarmed, slowing those magic fingers, stopping her hand on him.

When her tears came, he stopped touching her, pulling her in close instead. "Tell me, just tell me, get it out."

"I don't…I don't ever…I don't want to talk about it." She tried to pull away and he let her, but never took his eyes off her face. Her shoulders sagged when she realized she needed to tell this story to someone, and…well, here he was, asking. "It was an elderly uncle who visited us. I was nine."

"Oh, my God, Daniella, I'm sorry." Jack was sober as a judge now. "I…are you all right? Are you sorry we—? I'm so sorry."

The floodgates were open now, she wanted to tell him. "Don't be sorry. You were perfect, absolutely great, the way I always…hoped it would be with a man. Not like then." She sucked in a deep breath, staring at the floor. "The whole thing took probably ten minutes, is all, when he did it to me. I was alone in the house with him, and he touched me…you know, down there…and he made me put my mouth on him. It was over in a few minutes, and I never told anyone, even my mother. But every time a guy touched me, it would come back. I felt like a scared kid again."

*

Jack had never listened so carefully in his life, trying to rub her back enough to comfort her, but not to overwhelm her. He'd never listened and talked with any woman the way he was with Daniella Flores, had never stuck around long enough to hear anyone's story.

"Jeannette figured it out. She said she figured it out by the way I reacted when she touched me," she continued with a sigh. "It happened to her too, years ago. She opened me up, kept telling me how beautiful and smart and sexy I am. I guess I started to believe her. I *want* to believe this, to put him behind me. She opened me, like a flower."

Daniella, her eyes glittering with desire, put her hand on him again, slowly stroking him up and down. "And now there's you, telling me the same things and showing me all about you." Pressing herself against him, her arms around his neck, she was kissing him and touching him again, needy and emotional, hot and willing to go another round.

And now there's me?! thought Jack. *There's me, the asshole who's getting hard again because you're naked and you're beautiful, even though I'm horrified by your story and I want to twist your uncle's dick off.*

"Is he…the uncle…is he still alive? Can I kill him?"

She giggled then, but it didn't stop her from driving him nuts with her hands. "He passed away a long time ago. But I'm alive, and I feel like I'm just beginning to really live. I don't want to remember him right now and I don't want to think about him ever again, okay?"

Jack nodded, incapable of intelligent speech. She was turned on and passionate enough for both of them.

Hmmmm," she purred, lying on top of him, swiveling her hips against him, "and you can help me with that, make me feel alive."

"Are you sure? You're not sore?" He couldn't stop thinking how magnificent she was, her mane of dark hair tickling his chest, her lips swollen with kisses, and her cheeks and chin red from his stubble. She was moaning and panting above him, grinding on him, and her husky sex sounds were his new favorite things, especially mixed with her Spanish murmurings. When she called him *Papi* again, he lost it, his brain froze and he was gone, lost to anything but feeling her touch him, want him.

He rolled her over onto the bed, his mouth on her breast, taking as much of the soft, beautiful mound into his mouth as he possibly could, swirling her nipple with his tongue. Literally gasping when he released it, her spectacular breast wet from his mouth, he held both tits up like a feast, flicking and nipping her sensitive brown nipples until she started writhing and growling his name.

He quickly covered her mouth with his, trying to muffle her cries, but loving them at the same time. "Your skin, fuck, you feel so good," he moaned, kissing her neck and breathing her in the way he'd been wanting to. "You have no idea how many times I've imagined this while I watched you dance on my phone."

When he rolled on the condom and was inside her, she pushed back at him with no hesitation. Feeling her excitement jacked him over the edge and he stopped holding back, pumping harder than before, pressing her clit with every stroke until she shuddered and came with a hoarse cry, as out of her mind as he was, and he let himself go with her.

He kept his eyes open the whole time so he wouldn't miss a thing—her throaty cries, the goose bumps he saw wherever he trailed his lips, how she threw her head back and went stiff when she came, her sweet trembling while she came down from her orgasm. Why was it he felt…reverent, worshipping her and kissing away the dampness on her forehead and her upper lip while she went limp and still beside him? Sure, the virgin thing felt like…he wasn't sure. A gift, a responsibility?

"Why do you speak Spanish when you…uh…you know, when you…" he was curious, but now he just felt stupid.

*

Daniella arched a brow at him and pursed her lips, definitely cracking up that the big, bad lady-killer couldn't just spit it out. "When I get turned on, when I come, you mean?"

"Yeah, then." He was even blushing a little.

"I guess it's because it was my first language, my mother's language, so it's the language of emotion for me. It's weird though, I think in English. Spanish is for when I'm outside my head, when I'm not thinking." She pushed his hair back. "And you make me not think. You make me feel. I can't believe you got that story out of me by…touching me, making me want to tell you about my uncle."

Jack looked thoughtful, stroking her hair. "I'm honored you told me. And I want to keep…making you feel alive." They both laughed at the hidden meaning, and he let himself ask, "Did you call your dad *Papi*, and why do you call me *Papi*? I don't know why, but it turns me on. The way you say it, I guess."

"Actually, I never called my dad that, but my mom did call him *Papi*. Weird, right? I guess in our family it was more a term of affection, like 'honey' or 'who's your daddy' or something. I don't know, maybe it's an East Los Angeles thing. It's where my dad grew up."

Kissing his cheek, she leaned in further and whispered in his ear, "Don't freak out, but I've never called anyone *Papi* before."

"Okay. I won't freak out. I like it. Keep doing it, a lot, and by that I mean…"

"Yeah, I know what you mean *Papi*, now maybe we should get some sleep."

*

Back in bed with her after they took turns going to the bathroom, he lay awake, spooning her. "When do you have to be back at work?" he whispered. He was amazing himself again, inviting her to sleep in his bed. "And by the way, don't freak out, but I've never invited anyone to actually sleep in my bed before."

"4:30," she sighed, giggling and yawning. "I brought my uniform but the other stewards get all the clean bedding if I don't hop to it." It was 1:30. "And I love….uh…staying here like this." She burrowed her sweet ass into his belly, snuggling and going still, seemingly oblivious to the reawakening of his erection.

"Maybe we shouldn't bother sleeping, maybe keep the good times going," he grinned evilly against her neck, but he was greeted with quiet, steady breathing. She was naked, asleep in his arms and he was…enjoying it. Reaching over her to the nightstand, he set his phone to go off at 4:05, barely enough time for them both to put on their uniforms and get to work.

*

When the dreaded alarm bleeped, they jumped out of bed like scalded cats. Jack stared at Daniella's instant transformation from a cuddly sex kitten, warm and soft, to a macho domestic, her uniform starched and buttoned up to the neck, her hair back in the severe bun. She took the bottom sheet with her when she got ready to go out the door, but he pulled her in for a kiss, a question in his eyes. *He is…different. Unexpected sometimes. I can't put him in a category and be done with it.* Impatient to get going, she grinned. "Okay. What is it?"

"Two things. One, why do you dress so butch for work? And two, why are you taking my sheet with you?"

He looked so serious, she wanted to laugh. He kissed her neck while she answered and his busy fingers were threatening to take the pins out of her hair. "Two answers. One, do you know how many passengers sneak up behind me while I'm making the bed and try to molest me? This look is meant to discourage that." His head jerked back in alarm, his jaw tight with anger. She smoothed her hand over the side of his face. "Yeah, it does happen to the ladies and a lot of the young guys, too. And the mind-fucker is, each stalker thinks he's the only one who ever thought of it!"

"That just...sucks. We men are pigs, aren't we?"

She thought he was joking, but he was dead serious. A hint of a smile tugged at her lips. "Uhhh...there's no good way for me to answer you. But the answer to question two is, I know where to dispose of this sheet, since it has the blood on it, I don't want the person who makes up your room to gossip on Deck Zero about why you had blood on your sheets." It wasn't often Daniella blushed, but this topic was making her face hot.

Jack let her go, looking thoughtful. "Huh. You have to protect your badass reputation, eh?" With a wicked smirk, he followed her out the door. "Now there's something a pig like me can totally understand."

CHAPTER TWENTY-FOUR

A T FIRST LIGHT in Glasgow, Jack and the entire contingent of officers on the bridge were greeted with the comical sight of Cole, Tania, Primo and Oksana staggering onto the ship. The Fantastic Four had gotten rid of Khalid's briefcase; after running it over with the car several times and making sure the laptop was destroyed, they'd dropped it into the ocean.

The heroic quartet was exhausted, still wearing their rumpled clothes from yesterday morning, and buzzed from touring a good number of Glasgow's charming all-night drinking establishments. They'd first tried to rent hotel rooms, but the city was packed with tourists attending Glasgow's popular music festival Summer Sessions. They had finally passed out in the rental car at Bellahouston Park until the cops rousted them out of a deep sleep and out of the parking lot at 1 a.m., which was when their pub crawl began.

"Jack! Jack, we did it!" Cole said to his brother, hugging him and gesturing grandly to Oksana, newly free and arm in arm with her sister. Primo grinned, not nearly as drunk as Cole, and winked at Jack.

"Yeah, yeah, bro," chuckled Jack. "How 'bout if we get up to your room now, good buddy. You're a little...uh...ineeeebriated at the moment, and you need a nice, long nap." Motioning to the other three to follow, he handed out key cards. "Maybe you guys should crash in our quarters too. Strauss is so sick they're keeping him in the clinic. I'll have some people disinfect his suite thoroughly before you go back in there, okay?"

Tania, charmed by Jack's affectionate care of his brother, gave him a peck on the cheek and slung Cole's other arm over her shoulder while they half-dragged, half-staggered to the elevator, the others following, up to the captains' quarters. Tania snuggled in with Cole, but Primo took up every inch of Jack's bed. Oksana blew him a kiss and let herself into the other room, flopping onto the bed with a sigh. In minutes, the silence was deafening.

CHAPTER TWENTY-FIVE

I SHOULD BE ANGRY at this man, I should hate him.

Instead Oksana found herself sitting at Strauss's bedside, smiling at him during his rare moments of consciousness. The virus had hit him harder than anyone else on the ship, aggravating an existing heart condition and progressing to pneumonia. When Oksana and Primo woke, they went down to the clinic and sat with the elderly man for a while.

Emile Strauss looked small and grandfatherly, his silver hair mussed by the pillow, and every time he looked up at them he patted her hand and seemed to be trying to say something to both of them. The ship's doctor looked in after he checked his other patients and motioned Primo and Oksana to sit down with him out in the waiting room.

"When he was brought in yesterday, he told me you were his next of kin. Is that correct?" Dr. Santos asked, looking back and forth at both of them.

"We…uh…we work for him. And we've developed kind of a relationship, I guess." Primo wasn't sure what to say. *Why kick a guy when he's down?*

The doc nodded and checked his clipboard, looking uncomfortable about what he had to say. "He made a few phone calls yesterday and asked my wife, who's the nurse here, to fax some documents for him to his solicitor in London. He was getting his affairs in order."

Santos let out a long breath and his shoulders relaxed. "It turns out it was a very good idea. His immune system is compromised, and he has pneumonia on top of the virus."

"Last night, he took a turn for the worse, advancing into heart failure. His lungs are full of fluid, his legs are swollen and he's very weak, plus his heart isn't able to supply his organs with the blood they need. When we talked to him about transferring to the hospital in Glasgow, he refused. We don't expect him to make it through the night, and he knows it, so…here we are. We're managing his pain, and the end-of-life preparations are done. His solicitor is expected to arrive here shortly and wishes to speak with you, Miss Shevchenko."

"His lawyer wants to talk…to me? Why?" Oksana was surprised and a bit scared, wondering if she was going to be charged with something. Primo held her hand, letting her know he was ready to support her if anything seemed strange.

"Actually, you shouldn't worry, I think it's a good thing. I think he wants to leave you some money." Santos smiled a little, registering their astonishment. "It's what the documents he gave my wife indicated, and he asked me to tell you today it was what he was doing."

Dr. Santos left, and when they were back sitting with Strauss, Oksana asked Primo, "What do you know about him? All he told me was he lived in Berlin."

"I did a background check and checked out his company on various securities sites before I consented to work for him. It was when I started working for him years ago, and I swear he never did any of this weird sexual stuff until now." Primo ran his palm back and forth on his shaved head, something he often did when he was puzzled or frustrated. "He inherited his aluminum fabrication company from family, and sold it last year for big bucks. Seemed like a solid guy, definitely lonely. Never married. Last year, the third time I worked for him, he went to restaurants and the theater in London, alone, as usual. Then he went to this club called Torture Flowers, a BDSM club. I think it's where he met Ivan…but since I waited outside for him, I'm not sure."

A very stiff-looking fellow rapped his knuckles on the door frame, barrister's briefcase tucked under his arm. "May I come in?" he asked. Extending his hand to Primo, nodding to Oksana, he gave each of them his card, which identified him as Irwin Lewis, Solicitor, with an address in the swanky South Kensington section of London. "The chaps at the entrance gave me quite a time coming onboard until the captain came down and escorted me here. How is Herr Strauss doing?"

It was obvious Irwin Lewis, Esquire had no intention of getting any closer to Strauss's bed, fearful of catching the Norovirus. Which was understandable, since so far it had caused two crew members and ten passengers to be taken off the ship and quarantined in hospital rooms in Glasgow. There'd been no new cases but still, it was clear there was no such thing as too careful in the solicitor's world.

"He…uh…he's not doing well," replied Oksana, surprised at the twinge of sadness she felt for the lonely, peculiar man who'd recently handcuffed her to her bed. Still, she took Emile's hand in hers, squeezing it once in a while to reassure him he wasn't alone. He was no longer looking around or trying to talk, but once in a while she could have sworn he moved his fingers or his eyes tried to flutter open. She couldn't be sure.

"That was my understanding," said Lewis crisply, opening up his briefcase and taking out some documents. "Dr. Santos tells me his condition is worsening. Yesterday, Herr Strauss dictated his will to Mrs. Santos and asked me to read it to both of you, in addition to verifying…certain…other arrangements."

He drew himself up officiously and began reading. "I, Emile

Strauss, an adult residing at 10-10 Ackerstrabe Street, Berlin, Germany, being of sound mind…"

Primo interrupted. "Of sound mind… was Herr Strauss of sound mind when he did this paperwork yesterday?"

"Actually, sir, yes, absolutely. Mrs. Santos had him read the first paragraph aloud while she recorded it on her phone and then sent it to me. Any challenges to his mental fitness would be easily rebutted by that recording. Allow me to continue."

Lewis droned on and on, through the "I appoint Irwin Lewis as my Personal Representative," through "pay the expenses of my last illness, all estate taxes," to "cover the cost of end-of-life preparations."

The next section had them both staggering up out of their seats. Handing each of them an envelope, Lewis read, "To Peter De Luca and Oksana Shevchenko Strauss, I devise, bequeath, and give a check to each of them for $100,000 United States dollars to cover their expenses over the next two months, until such time as my residuary estate shall be free and clear of enforceable claims, taxes, and charges."

"Who's Peter De Luca and when… why did you say my last name is Strauss?" Oksana blurted out, her expression equal measures puzzled and upset.

Primo threw his head back, laughing, taking both of her hands in his. "I'm Peter De Luca. It's my real name." They'd been through so much together, it was shocking to realize how little they actually knew about each other.

Lewis was twitching, looking very awkward at this point. Stooped over his papers, he peeked over the top and squeaked "Inheriting Herr Strauss's considerable estate is contingent on Miss Shevchenko marrying him today, right here in this room. The ship's captain is qualified to perform the ceremony, and Strauss's previous written instructions to me will stand as *prima facie* evidence of his informed intentions."

CHAPTER TWENTY-SIX

COLE AND TANIA slept for nearly five hours, and went down to the ship's ice cream parlor before he had to report to the bridge. They sat across from each other in the booth, both tapping away on their tablets. It felt...comfortable, like hanging out with a friend.

Cole thought, *Are we friends? I've never done this shit before, how can you tell this stuff? Like right now, I'm trying not to stare at the fringe on her cut-off shorts against her thighs. Those thighs. But I'm also curious about what she's typing, what she's thinking.*

Cringing inwardly when he remembered how drunk he'd been when they boarded earlier, he wondered if he'd looked foolish to her. She drank pretty much anyone under the table, including guys twice her size. Spoke languages, saved lives, and, man, was she sexy! He often found himself wanting to make a good impression on her, not just sexually but in every possible way.

"What?" she looked at him, eyebrow raised, her dark hair stark against her pale skin, pale as fresh cream. Beautiful white skin is sexy, and she had miles of it.

"I was wondering if we're friends. You know, in addition to... uh...along with being..."

"Lovers. Yes." She paused, considering the idea.

Tania could be very direct, kind of like a dude sometimes. *Maybe it's a Ukrainian thing, but I like it.*

She continued. "My friends from nursing school, they look out for me, we look out for each other. They know what I'm thinking, they *care* what I'm thinking. My sister, too. When we danced on deck, it was like we had never been away from each other. When I met you, when I saw you, I felt…my life will change now. My life will get better. Is that being friends?"

"Like when I stood between you and Ivan, is that the kind of thing you mean?" Cole asked.

"No, I saw you, I watched you, leaning against the wall. Before you saw me, you were looking around, hiding under your hat. You seemed sad. But I…I knew before we spoke, I knew before you walked across the room. Something would happen, I would get to know you."

Still processing what she'd said, Cole picked up his tablet and slid onto the seat next to her, brushing her shoulder. "Here is the test of friendship. Can I sit next to you and not start messing with you?" After a minute, they looked at each other and burst out laughing, as his hands skimmed down her arms, caressing her and pulling her closer.

*

He turned a light on inside her when he was like this, when he was playful and carefree. She pulled away a little and searched his eyes, smiling. "I feel like when I told you about Petro, about my sister and grandparents, you wanted to know me. You really listened, as friends do. Only one thing is missing."

"Really? What's that?" His face, his expression was wide open.

"You haven't told me of your parents, about you and Jack growing up. I want to know you that way." Her voice trembled a little when she saw his tension, saw his eyes shutter.

"It's…it's a bunch of negative bullshit." Cole's shoulders grew rigid, and his hands bunched into tight fists. She saw how awkward he felt. "We should sit down sometime and let Jack tell you, he's more rational on the subject."

Tania pushed back a lock of Cole's hair with gentle fingers. "That is a good plan. I like it. And maybe in ten years we can stop touching each other every minute. Maybe not. Maybe I'll still be sucking your face all the time."

He laughed again and she blushed, the heat blooming on her chest and spreading up to her face.

"Did I say it wrong?" she asked, pressing her hands to her flaming cheeks.

Shaking helplessly, he shook his head to reassure her, but could not stop laughing. It was the first time either of them had discussed the future, and for some reason it felt *good*. After yesterday's adventure, she felt that he *saw* her, really saw things in her no one else ever noticed. Maybe in ten years...

Ewan sat down across from them. "You pair are having way too good a time. Get a room, why don't you? We have three thousand on the ship." It was obvious he hesitated to break up their affectionate touching and steamy conversation.

Cole pushed his tablet aside and leaned forward, smiling and raking his hand through his hair. "How can I help you, Officer MacGrath? What's new and exciting on *Sunset* Secret TV?"

MacGrath looked at Tania. "It's about your sister, I must tell you, as well as the Captain," he said, clearing his throat noisily. "You didn't answer your page, and you may be needed to...uh...perform a wedding ceremony, actually."

Tania went from giggling to upset; anything involving her sister had that effect on her.

Cole looked at his watch and back at Ewan. "At 2 o'clock in the afternoon, while everyone's on shore? Ooookay, lead on Officer

MacGrath," Cole said, standing and raising an eyebrow while he offered Tania his arm. Bowing a little, he helped her out of the booth and asked, "Would you care to attend an emergency wedding with me?"

CHAPTER TWENTY-SEVEN

I N THE END, it took a dream and a donation to convince Oksana to marry $30 million.

Primo had done some checking, wondering if there would be some kind of unintended outcome if Oksana married an unconscious Emile Strauss. First, did the man have any debts she would have to assume? Lewis produced very official-looking paperwork disputing that notion.

Primo called Strauss's London bank, pretending to be a real estate agent, and a bank manager chuckled when Primo asked if Emile had any debts, afterward assuring him Strauss was as debt-free as a person could be. They'd already retrieved Oksana's passport from Khalid, and even found her birth certificate in the safe in Strauss's suite, making the marriage an even more viable possibility.

But what if the man lived? What then? Dr. Santos assured them Emile Strauss had only hours to live, and then showed them the copy of the statement Strauss had given to the solicitor saying that he wanted Oksana to marry him and inherit his fortune.

Still, Primo wondered, *there's no road map for this kind of thing. It's so bizarre and unexpected, who wouldn't search for the catch in this little scheme? If we stopped now, we'd still be $100,000 richer. Each. Maybe we should be happy with that.*

Oksana, still sitting at Strauss's bedside, was in a panic of indecision when Cole and Tania got to the clinic. "Oksana, *yakoho bisa*?!" Tania put her arms around her sister, asking what the heck was going on. She wasn't sure whether to scold or congratulate her, because she mistakenly believed the captain had been summoned to marry Oksana and Primo. Still, after a lifetime of dealing with her sister's impulsive decisions, she'd learned that a cold blast of criticism wouldn't change her sister's mind. Listening without judgment was a better bet.

Primo took Cole and Tania aside and filled them in on the terms of the agreement and Strauss's proposal of marriage. He explained the solicitor's repeated reassurance that the marriage was the only way anyone would benefit from Strauss's money. There were no relatives, not even a brother or sister to inherit it. Oksana sat near them, slumped in confused misery, wringing her hands.

They were still in port and Cole googled some quick research on his phone. Eventually he said to her "Oksana, a bunch of the money is already going to go to the German government for taxes, about thirty percent, but if you inherit the rest, you could also do some good with some of it." He scrolled through a screen, reading out loud. "The Polaris Project is a leading organization in the fight against human trafficking and modern slavery."

Reading further for a while, he sat next to her and showed her his phone. "There are stories in here about women who were drugged, abducted, beaten up, threatened, and lied to just like you, more than twenty million all over the world. You could help other women by donating some of the money. Does that help you decide?" She nodded, suddenly looking a bit dazed instead of miserable, her mind obviously spinning from the possibilities.

Tania took her sister's hands. "Yes, consider helping women who've suffered as you have, and… how about your dancing, Oksana? You could teach dancing or…"

Cole looked over at Emile Strauss, lying unconscious on the

bed, and suggested, "Hey, this feels a little strange. Let's take it out to the waiting room here."

Moving to the other room seemed to relieve Oksana a little bit and gave her the strength to dream out loud. "I could donate and help women, and I could dance in a show." She smiled a shaky smile, meeting her sister's eyes.

"Dance in a show?" Primo laughed. Oksana had told him about some of her dancing dreams on the drive up from their Khalid adventure. "How about financing your own show and do the kind of dancing you've always wanted to do?" He looked thoughtful for a minute. "And Mr. Lewis here says in around six months, after everything is settled with Strauss's estate, you could marry…uh… mmmm…someone else." He shrugged. "Like me…or someone." For a guy who didn't talk much, the big guy sure had a way of summing things up.

"Is that a proposal? Are you asking me to marry you Mr. Peter De Luca?" Oksana was smiling, but her eyes shone with tears.

"Uh…yes." His answer was simple and direct, but he lowered his head till she couldn't see his eyes. "But maybe you should get used to being a rich lady first, before you decide what you want to do." When he looked up he was holding back a laugh again. "And I'm okay with that."

He held out his arms for her and Oksana jumped into them. The difference in size was comical, Oksana's arms wrapped around this giant redwood of a man, as if she would never let go. He took her mouth in a deep, hot kiss, all the emotion of the last few days contained in that one moment. Cole and Tania could only smile and do likewise.

Everyone's feelings were expanding and multiplying until the room fairly vibrated with them. There were no words for what was happening—the excitement and happiness in the room were too big. Tania and Oksana threw their arms around each other, squealing and jumping up and down. Then, remembering Strauss, the sisters calmed themselves, subdued by the sad state of the man in the next room, yet still quietly elated by the possibilities awaiting them.

Irwin Lewis consulted with the doctor again and watched the sisters, his expression unreadable. "Let's take a short break, go for coffee or a walk," he said. "If we're going to perform this marriage, we need to do it within the hour. The doctor has informed me Herr Strauss is experiencing..." Lewis paused to clear his throat, "...ahem, end-of-life respiration."

*

"By the power vested in me by the General Registrar of Scotland and the Interfaith Foundation, I now pronounce you husband and wife." Cole caught himself before adding "you may kiss the bride." Of the thirty-or-so weddings he had performed on cruise ships, this was the most unusual. They'd agreed Oksana and Primo would stay with Strauss after the ceremony until the end. The solicitor would take over afterward, as arrangements for Strauss's cremation had been made through him. It seemed thoughtless to break out champagne. Maybe tomorrow.

CHAPTER TWENTY-EIGHT

"THANKS FOR TAKING care of Daniella's virginity problem, Jack. I knew you'd do a great job," Jeannette drawled.
"I was sure you would make it...special for her." She'd sat
down opposite him in a section of the dining room where the officers often stopped for a quick meal.

Ohhh, fuck. What the heck is this merry little get-together about?
He was startled by her brazen smack talk and, for the hundredth
time, cursed himself and his brother for last year's ménage with her,
since they had to work with her so closely.

"Well...it seemed a shame to bust her cherry with a dildo, didn't
it?" she continued. "When I found it, I thought of you, to save her
for you."

Normally he'd have a sarcastic reply, but this was a conversation
about Daniella, which made it a very different matter. Jeannette's
cold, clinical words made him angry.

"I can't believe the way you said that. It's...harsh. Weird. And
she cares about you. Why would you talk about her this way? I
don't get it." The irony wasn't lost on him, hearing himself accuse
a woman of typically male horn dog behavior, behavior he'd been
guilty of too many times.

"Oh, *you* totally get it, Jack, *the* guy who likes to share! What
the fuck are you talking about?! You and your brother enjoy double-
teaming all the time. You've got a great routine worked out, and

I enjoyed every minute of it. You think it's different because we're two women?"

No it's different because... in his mind he said, *because she's special.*

Suddenly every bit of mindless sex he'd ever had was coming back to haunt him, reflected back on him with Jeannette's words. "No, it's not about that, it's...I care for her. She's...I want to be with her, spend some time and see where it goes. The difference in age may be a problem for her, and I don't know what she wants. Maybe she wants to be with you. What's your deal?" Jack was kind of amazed to hear himself describe something that sounded suspiciously like a relationship.

*

Jeannette leaned back, laughing, getting a kick out of the obvious struggle going on in Jack's mind, and his libido. The guy was used to getting exactly what he wanted from women, a fact she knew intimately from her ménage with the brothers. "Hey Jack, she's clearly attracted to you, too, but she and I have a good thing going. We're going to Vegas, so why don't we...share?"

Jack's face looked like she was making him suck lemons. "Oh, come on, you like to share," she repeated. "Why don't you and I share?" Pausing she made a low, purring sound in her throat. "I would like it a lot, actually. I like you, you like me, and we both like Daniella. She's young, smart, and wants to learn about sex." She shrugged. "What could be better?"

Jack leaned forward, agitated, but curious. "I don't get it. Do you like men, or do you like women?

"Why do I have to choose? Let me give you a metaphor here, bear with me a minute. Do you like pizza?" He nodded. "How about a good cheeseburger?"

Jack shrugged, "Both. Of course."

"What if I told you that you couldn't have both, only one or the other? You wouldn't like it, would you?" She leaned back and gave him a steamy smile, stroking the inside of his thigh under the table with her bare toe. "Well I like both, cheeseburgers and pizza, men and women. I always have. Let's share. What do you say?" Enjoying his breathtaking face with its cute dimple, she was filled with lust at the memory of that face between her legs. The brothers had been very generous with her, and they'd definitely shown her some of the hottest sex of her very active sex life.

"Honestly, I'm surprised about this, and I'm very uncomfortable with the idea." He put her foot gently down on the floor, not wanting to antagonize her. "Like I said, let's see how it goes."

He felt awkward when he stood to leave, not knowing if he should close this bizarre negotiation with a firm handshake or a hug. Jeannette took the initiative and gave him a squeeze, patting him on the back to reassure him.

She walked away from him with a wave and reassured herself, *There's nothing bad here, we'll have some fun, he'll get bored, and I'll take care of her over the long haul.*

Jack didn't look back, striding away with his jaw set, thinking, *Daniella is mine. I'll let this thing play out for a bit while I work on winning her over to the hetero side, specifically the Jack side.*

CHAPTER TWENTY-NINE

P LEASURE. I KNOW so little about pleasure. But this feels wonderful. Tania had never once tried sunbathing in her twenty-
six years of life. Do you have to do something extra to deserve
pleasure? If you don't accept it right away, will it somehow go away?

Back home, winter in the city was school, summer on the
farm was work. Where would sunbathing have fit in? And in the
Ukraine, it was mostly foreign tourists who sunned themselves by
the Black Sea.

She wasn't really tanning, though; she'd slathered her pale skin
with sunscreen. But she was truly enjoying the way the sun warmed
her muscles and emptied her mind of everything that had happened
or might happen. The whole thing with Oksana made her anxious,
of course. Pretty much everything about her sister made her nervous, but the feel of the sun on her skin was lovely. The colorful
bikini Cole bought her was comfortable and she almost fell asleep
on the luxurious sun lounge, the sun lighting up her skin and making her feel…horny? I guess this is why honeymooners go to the beach.
Lying in the sun makes you feel sexy.

And speaking of honeymooners, the couple on the lounge next
to her should probably go back to their room soon. The girl was topless, like many of the European women on this exclusive sunbathing
deck. Her man kept kissing her nipples or tweaking them with his
fingers, and those fingers had a way of sliding into the crotch of her

bikini and making her, to put it delicately, restless. The buff young man was wearing a white Speedo, and there was absolutely no doubt he was responding to her little cries and whimpers.

Tania, of course, thought of Cole, wishing it was the two of them torturing each other on the sun lounge. She wondered if she'd feel more or less aroused if she took off her top. *Hey, everyone else is.* But when she reached around to unhook it a shadow fell over her— Cole, in his casual work clothes.

He shook his head, raising an eyebrow and pointing to a spot on the wall to her right. She smiled and nodded at him when she saw the round bubble covering a camera lens. "Ewan is enjoying the show, then?" she whispered, waggling her fingers hello at the camera.

His lips on her neck made her shiver. "When I saw him looking at you, it made me insane. And I refuse to allow him to see your tits, so…"

He gave her his hand when she stood, standing on tiptoe to whisper in his ear. "Hmmm…jealous. Bossy. I like it! But I'm sure Ewan was more interested in this lovely couple next to me."

Flipping the bird at the camera, Cole pulled her away from her comfy sun lounge. "If that was true, I'd leave you here enjoying the sun, but I'm sorry. My friend Bebe has excellent taste in bikinis, but I think she may've chosen one that's too small." Looking down at her, he licked his lips. "I'm sorry you're by yourself, and I have to work. But, indulge me? Jack and I have to catch up on stuff, but I'll see you later, okay?"

"What are you saying Cole? Are you telling me you don't want me to lie here because it makes you…um…angry, or uncomfortable?"

Raking his fingers through his hair, he looked down. "Uh, yeah, I guess it's what I'm saying." Kissing her on the cheek, he added "I guess it makes me sound like a dickhead, so…enjoy."

Giggling, she lay back down on the lounge, this time face down.

"Is this better?" The luscious globes of her butt spilled out of the tiny triangle of the bikini bottom.

"Not really, but go ahead. I'll just suck it up." Tania chuckled again, this time at his interesting choice of words. He turned and went back to the bridge, his hands clenched at his sides. Looking at him striding away, she knew the camera would go dark as soon as he got to the bridge. *I love when he tells me what to do in bed. But what is this about, does he not trust me? I'm starting to trust myself, why is he like this? He seemed carefree at first.*

CHAPTER THIRTY

EMILE STRAUSS LAY so peacefully, Oksana and Primo didn't even realize when he took his last breath. They were still sitting by his bed when Mrs. Santos came in, took his pulse and pulled the sheet up over his face. "I'm sorry dears, Herr Strauss has passed on. Your job here is done. The people are here, the people the solicitor hired to care for his body. Are you okay?"

They nodded, standing next to the bed. Oksana kissed Strauss's hand and tucked it under the sheet. Each said a little prayer, Primo crossed himself, and they walked hand in hand out of the health center.

When they got back to Strauss's suite, the cleaning crew had just left. The smell of bleach was so strong they opened the windows and sliding glass door and decided to go for a walk while the place aired out. Waiting in the hall was a lovely dark-haired woman wearing a head scarf. "Hello," she said, smiling but not holding out her hand. "I'm Nasrin, staying next door to you." She watched their faces, letting it register that she was one of Khalid's wives. Addressing herself to Primo, she asked, "You work for Herr Strauss as a bodyguard, is that correct?"

"I did, yes ma'am, but Herr Strauss just died of pneumonia, complications of his heart condition, and the flu."

Her eyes wide, she gasped and her hand went to her mouth. "Oh, I'm sorry! Please, don't let me bother you, then."

"It's okay, ma'am." Primo's voice was soft. "How can I help you?"

"Well…I….we…," she adjusted her scarf, visibly composing herself. "We hoped you might help us, thought we'd ask Herr Strauss's permission to hire you, use your services."

"Is anything wrong? Do you need protection Madame?"

"Oh no, nothing like that!" Nasrin laughed softly, smiling at Oksana. "Khalid has been detained by business in London. We'd like to leave the suite and eat in the dining room, see a show, even perhaps arrange some private time in the spa. Would you help us?"

"It would be my honor, Madame, but you don't have to hire me." Primo smiled and pulled Oksana even tighter to his side. "I'm a bit of a free agent right now. If you don't mind, I'm going to involve the ship's concierge in your care. Would you be all right with that?"

Nasrin nodded, blushing a little. "You're right. I didn't think of the concierge. I actually went to university in London and used to make my own arrangements, but I'm a little out of practice. Thank you."

*

Later in the evening, Khalid's wives enjoyed a lovely dinner in one of the special dining rooms, wearing colorful head scarves and dressed in modest, elegant clothing instead of their somber burkas. They mixed excellent English with their Arabic chatter and their laughter tinkled through the dining room. They were having such a good time, the head waiter approached the table. "I haven't seen you lovely ladies before this evening. How do you know each other?"

The women exchanged smirks and raised eyebrows but Nasrin answered solemnly, "Oh, we're sisters." And they laughed again.

Oksana and Primo sat at a table across the room, enjoying the relaxed atmosphere. Oksana covered his hand with hers and leaned across the table. "I know why you wanted to help them make these arrangements," she said in a conspiratorial whisper. "You knew how angry Khalid would be if he knew!"

Primo chuckled and squeezed Oksana's hand. "Yeah, and it's a sweet, sweet revenge, isn't it? It was obvious Nasrin had no idea why he stayed in London, by the way, or that we were involved in what happened." He leaned back and crossed his arms, pretending his feelings were hurt. "Do you mean you don't think I helped them because it was right for them to enjoy themselves?"

"Definitely. It was your second thought, I'm sure, beautiful man."

CHAPTER THIRTY-ONE

"VEGAS! MY DANCE show will be in Las Vegas, in Nevada of the United States! Primo's father lives there, Cole and Jack live there, and soon my sister and I will live there, right, sister?" Oksana's arms were crossed and she was beaming, looking like her mind was happily made up and there would be no changing it.

"But I...I work in New Jersey, I live in New Jersey," sputtered Tania, realizing as soon as she spoke how ridiculous it sounded in this context.

"Work? You think I will allow my beautiful sister to work now I'm a millionaire?! No! I need you to help me, to work with me now." Apparently she'd gotten quite used to the idea of being rich in the twenty-four hours since Emile Strauss died, and was planning her future like a general gearing up for war. "Primo showed me online that in Vegas, dancers even dance sometimes with no tops on, beautiful girls with big feathered hats, and lots of people love to come and see sexy dancers there. Perfect for my new show!"

Tania smiled, walking arm in arm with her sister to the dining room to celebrate and discuss the future. *They need nurses in Las Vegas, I'm sure, so I can always get a job.* Cole was working hard, catching up on the paperwork and other drudgery which had piled up while he was off the ship. "If I'm going to quit my job and work with you, you have to promise me one thing, big sister, will you do that?"

"Whatever you need, my sister and savior." Oksana pecked her on the cheek.

"Promise me you will not spend any money, you will not give any money away, hire anyone or sign any papers without checking with me first? Okay?" She stopped and looked Oksana right in the eyes. "You have a big heart, sometimes too big, and I don't want people to take advantage of you. Agreed?"

"Agreed." Oksana was bubbling over, she was thrilled to have her sister on her arm, to have her freedom, and to explore her new relationships with Primo and money. Especially Primo.

The sisters asked to be in Ivanka's station for lunch, and the Russian asked what their excitement was about. Oksana looked down at the table, unsure how much to reveal, so Tania squeezed her sister's hand and answered, "Oksana just inherited some money. And she has a wonderful new boyfriend! "

"*Uchh!* Let's celebrate." Hustling back with three shot glasses and two bottles of Russian vodka, Ivanka sat down with them and poured the icy liquid. "*Za Zher-sheen.*" she toasted, and Tania and Oksana answered with the translation, "To women."

"*Budmo,*" declared Tania over the second round, and the other women raised their glasses, saying "We shall live forever!" It went on that way, more toasts in more languages, until their food came and they giggled, feeling absolutely no pain when they slammed their empty glasses down on the table.

Ivanka seemed unfazed and went back to work, but Oksana wobbled when they wandered into the casino after lunch. Tania, always a better drinker than Oksana, offered her arm and kissed the top of her sister's head.

"Oh Tani, I stink at these games, but you can play with my

money!" The sisters stood watching a blackjack game for a while, and after about ten minutes Tania sat on one of the stools and began playing. "Do you know how to play this game?" Oksana whispered in her ear while the dealer shuffled and dealt.

"Yes, I learned from my nurse friends, they play sometimes when a night shift is very boring or we have a night off." Soon Tania had a big pile of chips in front of her, having won three out of the last five hands.

"How are you doing it Tani? I do not get how you win."

Not sure of the protocol at the table, Tania stood slightly and whispered in her sister's ear. "I'm watching the cards on the table, and if they are low, especially a five or six, it means the dealer may take a card and be over twenty-one. And not many aces or tens have been played so I might get a blackjack or close."

"Ma'am," the dealer was annoyed with Tania's inattention. "Would you like a card?"

She paused for a minute, assessing, and took a card. She won that hand and the next four.

The tall Indian casino guard Ivanka danced with at the staff deck party tapped Tania on the shoulder. "May I speak to you privately over here for a moment, ma'am?" Gathering up her chips to leave the game, Tania blinked up at him, concerned. "You are too skillful for us, mademoiselle. We're going to have to ask you not to play blackjack in our casino, since it seems you are counting cards. It's considered cheating."

"Doesn't everyone have to count in order to play, in order not to go over twenty-one?" Tania was genuinely confused.

"I believe the problem comes when you are counting to know the numbers still left in the deck, mademoiselle. This is when the house asks you to discontinue play." He bowed slightly, indicating the conversation was over.

Oksana, scared from her recent experiences, was looking at the cameras around them. Tapping her sister on the shoulder, she took off her high heels. "My feet are hurting, dear sister. Maybe it is time for us to go, anyway." Tania kept her eyes down, still thoroughly confused, when she cashed in the chips and the sisters scuttled out of the casino as fast as their feet would take them.

They arrived on the main deck when Jeannette was organizing the Hairy Chest Contest, a hilarious event where men who should never dance or take off their shirts in public did both, aided by waaaay too many cocktails. "Okay, we've got our contestants, now here are our first two beautiful judges, the lovely Tania and her sister Oksanaaaa!" Jeannette smiled while she worked the mike, gesturing toward the sisters.

The sisters weren't sure if they were more surprised by how drunk Oksana still was or by the roar of the crowd gathered on deck for a beautiful day at sea. Before they had a chance to escape, chairs were placed under their butts, two other ladies were seated next to them, and ribbons with the word JUDGE were draped across their chests. Tania blushed scarlet, of course, and managed a shy wave while Oksana stood and did a little cha-cha while music played.

Jeannette held the microphone up to the other ladies, and the taller one introduced them. "Hey, we're Alexus and Alicia, and we're sisters too!" The sisters had bodacious boobies with colorful tattoos fully displayed by their low-cut dresses when they smiled, wiggled their butts and threw their hands in the air.

"All right ladies," Jeannette said, addressing them but really talking to the crowd, "Our contestants are going to come across the deck and show us some sexy dancing and prancing as they take their shirts off for you. I want you to check out their chest hair, inspect their back hair, but know this! We are not only judging them on the hair, we are judging them on the FLAIR! May the best booty-shaker wiiiin!"

Gesturing to the crowd, she added, "And I hope you capture it on your phones because what happens on *Sunset...*" she said, while she held her hand up to her ear waiting for an answer.

"...ends up on YouTube!" the mob yelled, holding up their phones.

"Yeah!" Jeannette fist-pumped the audience and did a little jig with her phone when the music blared for the first contestant. Getting people to post outrageous, ridiculous videos on YouTube was an important goal of the SunShips' marketing department, and Jeannette was excellent at reminding passengers to do just that.

A big, hairy guy with American flag swim shorts and an undulating beer belly drew a roar of approval from the crowd when he ripped his shirt off, swinging it in big circles as he skipped down the aisle toward the stage. He sang along with *I'm Too Sexy* and gave each judge an enthusiastic booty shake and a kiss on the cheek.

Tania shrugged and smiled at her sister while they pretended to take notes on the dancers. The energetic response from Alexus and Alicia more than made up for Tania's restrained smile when the next guy let out a Tarzan yell and beat his hairy chest, grinding his hips left, right, forward and back to the delight of all assembled. Another guy with long hair and zombie tattoos began with a cartwheel and ended with one-arm push-ups. With each dancer, Alexus and Alicia waggled their breasts more provocatively, inviting the last couple of guys to give them lap dances at the end of their big moment. Oksana and Tania took a preemptive approach, standing and shaking the men's hands as soon as they came in for the close-up.

"Hey ladies, our judges up there!" said Jeannette, "Let's keep those hands north of the border, you know, like touch the guy only above the belt in Canada! Anyone here from Canada?" A hundred

Canadians let their presence be known with a yell as everyone else laughed and continued filming the event with their smartphones.

Unfortunately, Jeannette forgot to tell the dancers not to touch the judges. The last two contestants copped a good long feel of Alexus and Alicia's breasts and lunged for Oksana and Tania, hoping to score another grope and a real kiss. Given Oksana's tipsy condition, the Ukrainian sisters didn't make it to the exit quickly enough to totally avoid the attack, but luckily Jeannette arrived shortly to distract the bare-chested crazies by raising their arms high and declaring them the official runner-ups. Not realizing they'd actually lost, they did a victory lap through the crowd while the guy who did the Tarzan yell was declared the official winner and gifted with dinner for two in one of the ship's upscale restaurants.

Cole, disguised in his jeans, T-shirt, and Phillies cap, helped Oksana and Tania down from the stage, his mouth set in a tight, grim line. He put his arms around both of them, guiding them briskly toward the elevator and up to Strauss's suite, their new unofficial hangout. "How much did you ladies actually have to drink? It smells like vodka in here." Cole waved his arms, trying to disperse the smell in the elevator. "And congratulations, by the way. You cheated at cards and the images of you being drunk and disorderly and of those guys fondling you will be on the internet...hmmm, well, let's sayyyy...forever."

"I did not cheat at cards! Why did they say that I did? I was only counting the cards already on the table and guessing what was left! And Cole, we were just..." Tania sputtered, speechless and shocked by his angry words.

A sleepy Primo answered the door to the suite in sweats, confused when the ladies rushed in and Cole turned and marched briskly away down the hall without a word. "What's...why does Cole seem pissed?" he asked Oksana. She shrugged, her face filled with regret as they heard a bedroom door slam behind Tania. When they knocked and asked if she needed anything, she answered with a simple, tearful, "No."

"What the hell?" Primo was thoroughly confused.

"It's what we do," Oksana said wistfully. "When someone's angry, we hide and become an Invisible Lizard.

CHAPTER THIRTY-TWO

J ACK KNEW BETTER than to talk to Cole when he was slamming drawers and striding around like an agitated tiger. But since they were alone on the bridge, he did anyway. "I watched you walking them to the elevator and wondered what the fuck?"

"Yeah, what the fuck for sure," growled Cole, his face rigid.

"So you're pissed…because Tania was partying? Because she figured out how to win at blackjack? Because they got trapped in the middle of something stupid? Because they were drinking? What? I don't get it." Jack took a deep breath and put an arm around his brother's shoulder. He paused, thinking. "All of this is new for you. For us, actually, since I've never felt any of this shit about a woman before either. Is it because you feel things are out of control?"

Cole considered for a minute. "Yeah, that seems right. I guess I hate to not know about her, can't stand to see her in a situation…in something potentially…'"

"Where something might hurt her? Where you don't know the outcome? Where she could run out on you?" Jack squeezed the back of his brother's neck. "Cole, she's good people. So super-smart she can count cards at blackjack half drunk and without breaking a sweat. Helluva drinker too, she'd had five shots by the time she hit the casino. You can't control everything that happens, people gotta do their thing. And not everyone is like Mom, not everyone is going to walk away. I honestly don't get where you're at here."

Cole winced, his stomach spinning at his brother's words. *Damn brother who knows my shit.* "I don't get it either. I just get these feelings. I don't know what to do to protect her. And stop talking about it."

"Jesus, Goose, how 'bout some truth, here? You finally care for someone and it started out with some scary shit, and now you can't tell her what to do. We've got issues. We're afraid to trust, blah, blah, blah."

"I know it's Dad's crap coming out of my mouth." Cole stalked across the room, posture stiff with rage.

"Fuck that! Get your head out of your ass and give Tania the respect she deserves. She's had shit to deal with too, and look at her—she goes for it. She's never had anyone to care for her. I've never seen you act like this. Stop blaming it on Dad and stop being a pussy!"

"Are you calling me a pussy? You? The guy fucking a girl who's so young she won't call you on any of your man-whore shit?" There was a bitter, cold tone to his voice and his chest was heaving.

The voices went quiet when the fighting started. Jack threw the first punch, pissed at Cole's comment about Daniella. Even though they both knew it might be true. It was kind of a shove, kind of a jab to the chest. Cole fell against the radar console and launched himself forward, butting into Jack's stomach. "Ooooph!" Jack let out a burst of air and they both hit the floor.

When Cole rolled over and pinned him, raising his fist, both of their eyes were flashing, their nostrils flared and jaws clenched in anger. After a few tense beats, Jack shielded his face and laughed. "Leonardo, stop the training! The Shredder has a thermite grenade. Turn me loose, we must fight against him!"

Cole went limp, chuckling at the Ninja Turtles speech, an oldie but goodie from their younger days. Before they were Maverick and Goose, they were Leonardo and Michelangelo, swinging their nunchucks around. After a long, heavy breath he relaxed. "Sorry Michelangelo, you're right. I suck sometimes. I'll fix it."

Officer Ewan MacGrath leaned over the console, puzzled by the two men lying on the floor laughing and playfully punching each other in the arm. "Taking a little stretch break there, eh?" Four blue eyes and two opposing dimples greeted him with more cackling and punching, continuing to roll around like puppies and act like they didn't have a care in the world. Which, once they gave it some thought, turned out to be pretty close to the truth.

*

Cole went back to his exhausting schedule, losing track of where Tania was and what she was up to on the last day of the cruise. They would dock tomorrow and…he didn't want to think about it. He wanted to ask Ewan to keep an eye on her today, but knew he'd better stop stalking her, because he had too much work to do. Still, he felt restless. It was like a part of him was always somewhere else, with her. *I mean, what the fuck? I don't date women like this, nice, hard-working girls who want me to toe the line. I date party girls who know the score, women who don't hang around long enough for me to lose my temper. She's seen me lose it, but let me back in the first time. Maybe this time was it.*

When he went to a director's meeting in the ship's theater, Jeannette sidled up to him and signaled that she needed a private word. "Have you heard?" she said, her voice barely above a whisper. "About Vegas?"

"What about Vegas?" He could tell she was thrilled to be in the know and a little surprised he wasn't.

"Oksana's starting a dance show there, renting a theater and everything." She lowered her eyes, looking a little coy. "You know, with the Strauss money."

"And you heard this...how?"

"From Daniella. Do you know her?"

"Uh, yeah, the dancer-slash-room steward. And how does *she* know?" He left out the part about Jack being infatuated with Daniella.

"She and I will be roomates. We're going to live together in Vegas during my three-month leave, and Oksana recruited her for the show. I offered to help out as well."

He kind of knew the answer before he asked, but he had to ask anyway. "And Oksana's sister Tania. What're her plans in all this, do you know?"

Jeannette seemed surprised again, amazed to find he wasn't connected to this story the way she was. "Oh, she's coming, too. Quitting her job in New Jersey and helping with the show." She ducked self-consciously, obviously swallowing a question about his plans. *Awkward.*

*

Cole felt his blood begin to boil and marched toward the room next to his, hoping Tania would be there alone. The entry door was open and he found her sitting on the balcony, looking out to sea.

Cole stormed in, slammed the door behind him and crossed his arms, fists clenched tightly over his chest. Then he yanked the desk chair around and sat backwards in it, his position aggressive.

When she came in and sat on the bed across from him, it reminded both of them of the night he found out about Oksana. He was like a tornado, sucking in the good feelings and spitting them out as bad, dangerous flying debris that could take someone's head off. When he stared, taking in her packed bags and her departure forms lying on the bed, his eyes narrowed, his face in an expressionless mask.

"Are you angry again?" she asked, her eyes confused.

He snapped. "Hell yes, I'm angry. Jeannette told me you girls are going to Vegas, and you know I'm going there for my furlough. Why wouldn't you tell me that? Why did I hear it from fucking Jeannette?"

"I...I didn't want you to think I expected anything from you, especially since you have been...apart from me a lot."

"Would you please stop deciding what I'm thinking? Would you ask me before you think you know my answer?! So you're just going to walk away and not say anything." Faced with Cole's heated words and belligerent posture, Tania looked at the floor, seeming passive and defeated. "You are fucking doing it again, thinking you're not worth it, thinking you'll walk away from me before I walk away from you, right?"

Tania's posture was closed to him, her manner defensive, as if she was ready to run out the door. This relationship was going to shit faster than he could spit his angry words out. What he really wanted was to hear her say she loved him, hear her say she wouldn't leave him. *Leave him like* she *did. Like my mother did.*

His brain knew she couldn't say anything good when he was scalding her with his fear and frustration, but his response was a reflex, learned at his explosive father's knee. Cole fought to dial down the anger in his voice but failed, the anger still bubbling up inside him. "What do I have to do to make you fucking trust me, even a little?!"

Surprisingly, she stood and faced him, trembling but drawing herself up tall. Confronting his tirade was costing her. She had a history with other people's rage, and any fool could see it. She lowered her chin as if she expected a slap, but looked him right in the eye.

"How about if you say…some words. You haven't said one thing about how you feel about me. You haven't said what happens next." A tear escaped from the corner of her eye, but she swiped it away. "Yes, we're all going to Las Vegas. What does it mean to you, that I will be there? I know you're a good guy, and you do right things *because* they're right things, not because you have feelings."

She was very still, like a pond with no visitors, no ducks, not even a leaf. And she was perspiring. She appeared to be exerting a huge effort to force herself to stand there, her arms at her sides. "I have poured my feelings into my body, put aside my fear so I can love you, but you… you say nothing about the future, and make me remember Petro."

It was a standoff, two stubborn, smart people in a stupid situation. "Petro!? How can you put me in the same sentence as that asshole?! The more time I spend with you, the more I let you in, the more you pull away from me." His anger was palpable, heating up the air in the little room until it seemed it might explode.

Walking toward the door, she opened it and turned. "My whole life, I had to do everything without help. I had no one to worry about me, and I learned not to get close to people, only my sister and my grandparents. Everyone else made us sorry after we trusted them."

She pulled her shoulders back and shifted from one foot to the other. "You know, I talked with Jack a little. I know where your anger comes from, I know about your father, the Admiral. I want to hear the rest from you. And I want to trust you and I want you in my life. But I won't talk to you when you're like this. I'm going to be with my sister now, and you should talk to Jack. He knows about our plans. Then I will talk with you."

The door closed behind her with a quiet click. *It's easier for her to talk to Jack than to me? That fucking sucks.* Almost immediately, he answered his own question. *Yeah, because I'm an angry asshole.*

Though he collapsed on the bed like a deflated balloon, he continued his irritated argument in his mind. It was like a freight train he couldn't stop, though it seemed to slow and lose steam as each minute she was gone ticked by. *Anger fades when it has nothing to explode against, that's what my mom finally figured out. Jack and I did too, yet here I am being a jackass again.*

But the freight train was still roaring in his head. *It fucking hurt when she put me in the same sentence with Petro. Haven't I done right by her? Just because I didn't puke out my feelings doesn't give her the right to walk away. Think about what I've done, what I'm doing! I'm not her sister or her girlfriend, I'm her...*

Who am I...what are we? What. The. Hell. Was I thinking? The thought stung. Suddenly he realized he didn't know how to describe what he was to her. And if *he* didn't know, surely *she* didn't know either. What was their relationship, exactly? They'd talked about being friends as well as lovers, but the freight train came to a complete, dead stop when Cole rubbed a hand across his face. It would take a lot more than that to rub away the guilty feeling burning the pit of his stomach. *People need to know where they stand, idiot. Women especially. Fuck me and my angry bullshit...again.*

A while later, Jack knocked and let himself in. "I heard you yelling," he said. "The Admiral is fucking up your thinking and spewing out of your mouth again. His bullshit has actually been rolling around my head lately as well."

"So...you told Tania about the Admiral. How much of...you know." Cole wanted her to understand him, not pity him. There were some things about family, about the past, he didn't want to share, not ever.

"Just general stuff. Shouting, name-calling, staying out of the house. Nothing about the big incident. Nothing that explains why you and I have the emotional maturity of 15-year-olds."

"Good."

"Why good? Why not get it out of the way? If you want to be with her, you'll have to tell her at some point."

"I'm not ready."

"Did she tell you about her and Oksana being the Invisible Lizards? You know, like chameleons? It's how they describe how they used to hide from the mother's drunken boyfriends. Sound familiar? Anyway, my point is, Tania can handle it, bro."

His brother was right. He and Tania could discuss it. It was okay to tell the whole story, she'd understand and call him out on his reactions. She, after all, had made similar decisions in her own life. It was comfortable and uncomfortable at the same time, knowing she would get right in his face if he was on the wrong track.

She would challenge me, she's the only one who ever cared enough to do it. Other than Jack. And they're both singing the same song—full disclosure...or die. Probably better to spill the beans. Fuck. I sound like a lovesick teenager.

CHAPTER THIRTY-THREE

PETER DE LUCA, otherwise known as Primo, was having the wet dream to end wet dreams. Soft lips slid down his body, and then a hot, wet mouth surrounded his dick, tasting the tip, swirling around the top, hungrily exploring the whole damn thing. Delicate fingers fondled his balls, pulling them away from his body and massaging them, then gently scratching them with fingernails. The increasing speed and pressure on his shaft had his whole body quivering so wildly that when the curious fingers rubbed the sensitive spot behind his balls, his shuddering moan woke him and he realized it wasn't a dream, it was Oksana.

He looked down to see her pretty blonde curls bobbing up and down and he touched her shoulder, gasping her name. Her face flushed, her lips swollen, she looked up at him while twisting her hands around his cock, keeping it warm and ready.

"Condom?" she asked, licking her lips and raising an eyebrow. "I'm loving your beautiful cock, but I want to put it in me and then I can love the rest of beautiful Primo." She reached over him to the bedside table and found a selection of condoms. Tearing it open with her teeth, he could've laughed at her enthusiasm but didn't, counting backward to himself while she rolled it on.

"Why do you keep calling me beautiful? I'm not beautiful." He was panting, determined not to lose it until he was finally inside her. In spite of everything they'd been through together, he still hadn't penetrated that silken channel of hers, hadn't claimed her from the inside out...yet.

"You *are* beautiful, and not only to me. Every pretty girl wants to climb up on Primo, like *this*!" Oksana straddled him and tried to lower herself all at once onto his monumental cock. "Aaaoh-oh!" she winced, her stunning face twisted in surprise and discomfort.

"Oh, baby, sweet baby, I'm sorry. Let me kiss you loose!" Once he had her flipped and pinned to the bed, he felt her relax as his hungry lips kissed her there, and there, and there and THERE, the sweet, magical button guaranteed to drive her insane, as she writhed beneath him. Now she was ready when he thrust deep inside her, then stayed still, the low rumble of a growl rumbling up from his depths. She wrapped her legs around him, her hands flexing on his ass every time he pushed, his strokes deep and slow.

He raised her hips and hitched up a little, hitting the cushy little spot inside that made her go rigid and whimper "OhGodohGodohGod!"

Smiling and matching her pace as she pushed back against him, he held her hips tight and took her mouth in a kiss, watching her as she stiffened and arched into him. "Let go Oksana, let go baby, yeee-aah." Jerking and trembling, her inner muscles milking him, her lips parted, she looked into his eyes as she shattered beneath him. And to think he was the first man on earth to see that gorgeous sight! Getting to watch her lose it like that? Well, there was nothing to equal it.

In the process, she closed around him with a grip so intense, he felt his own climax build, burning through him and firing all his senses at once. The scent in the air, the air heavy with sex and sweat, the sounds of her pleasure, the feel of her skin—he felt his heart would explode with the passion he felt for her. Stroking long and hard, his hips pounding against her thighs, he'd never felt a woman answer every thrust the way she did. She'd been lost in her orgasm but she snapped back, totally present with him and for him. Totally real.

Primo was unsure how to tell her, couldn't explain it, but when he was with her like this he replayed the times he'd seen her with other men. It was hard not to say aloud how he'd felt her pain and her shame, but he didn't want to bring up those bad memories. He'd known she was pretending, trying to survive. He wanted to tell her he didn't pity her or think less of her, he *admired* her for her strength, and it turned him on. And here, now, with him, she was not pretending and it made all the difference.

Especially when he reached between them and pressed perfect circles on her clit. "Eh, eh-oooh," she gasped, "I…Iiieeeee…" She seemed to wait for him, wait for his permission.

"It's okay, you can come again, do it little girl, do it for me," he gritted out, his teeth clenched. Pounding her furiously now, he felt her bow up into him, trembling and going tight, so tight and then soooo loose. "Fuck, fuuuuck!" he hissed, finally collapsing on top of her, searching for her mouth and kissing her, breathing her in and losing himself in the wet paradise of her mouth.

She kissed him back with such intensity she seemed insatiable, as if she wanted more. Relaxed inside her, he woke himself up by wandering down to her breasts, flicking and lingering on this one, then giving the other equal treatment. When he sucked a little love bite on her neck, she gasped, "More, please," and started moving on him, circling her hips, pressing up and down until he was hard again, thrusting slowly, while she sucked in her breath and made her sexy moans and whispers until the pleasure burst through them once more. Each of them knowing for the first time what it was like to trust someone with your body, to let them take a peek at your soul, they curled into each other, sweaty and thoroughly at peace.

CHAPTER THIRTY-FOUR

"I HEAR YOU'RE GOING to Las Vegas to dance in the show and you're going to live with Jeannette, right?" Jack tried to sound casual but knew his tone was terse, irritated. He'd practically stalked across the lobby toward Daniella, like a lion chasing down its prey. He had all the patience in the world when it came to counseling his brother about Tania, but it was a whole other story when he had to confront a situation himself.

Daniella pursed her lips and gave him a shrug when she turned to walk away. "Why? Did I have another offer?" she asked, her sexy high heels clack-clacking on the marble floor. Suddenly she found herself pinned against the wall, his arms caging her in while he pressed his big body against hers.

Jack had all the invitation he needed when she licked her lips and he took her bottom lip between his teeth and nipped it, getting a slow, hot kiss started when she tipped her head back. Shackling both her wrists behind her with one hand, he felt her hips answer his as he pressed against her. She trembled and kissed him back, but he pulled away a little, enough to see her eyes. "Does Jeannette make you tremble when you kiss her? Does she make you blush and get your nipples hard like this without even touching them?"

Daniella let out a breath and looked away, getting herself together to answer. "She makes me happy and makes me feel... safe. And yes, she's very sexy, too." When she finally looked back at him, there was something edgy and needy there. "But why are you going all Neanderthal on me like this? Are you making me an offer? I know you live with your brother, so I assumed…"

"You assumed what? We have bunk beds and there's no room for you?" That visual—the hunky, formidable brothers sharing a bunk bed—broke the tension, and they both grinned at the unlikely image.

"The truth is, I don't know what I want." Blushing, she ducked her head. "You of all people should know that. I haven't lived enough to know yet."

Jack's arms relaxed, sliding down her arms and hips until his hands came to rest, clamped possessively on her ass. A sexy, slow grin spread across Jack's face when he remembered for the millionth time what *he* was like when he was twenty-one, and he took a deep breath. His father's anger problem was peeking out from under his usual easygoing nature, and he was determined to shake that crap off. "Okay, no more caveman shit. I'm listening. What do *you* want to do, and what do you want *me* to do when we're in Las Vegas?"

Daniella had her smart-and-resourceful hat on despite being very aware of his hands on her butt. Jack liked that about her, actually. "Jeannette has a sublet on a two-bedroom apartment twenty minutes from the strip. I'll have my own room, and we'll be working hard for a few months to get the show set up and we'll…see what happens."

He wanted to tell her about his conversation with Jeannette, how heartless she'd sounded when she discussed Daniella's virginity and how cold she'd seemed when she proposed a ménage à trois arrangement for the three of them, sharing this sweet young woman's sexual education.

But if he did, he'd have to reveal the intensity of his feelings for her. Frankly, he didn't know if his feelings were reciprocated, and he was afraid to put himself out there, to expose the rush of emotion he was feeling. She might think he was nuts, a grasping older guy who was cramping her amazingly provocative style. *There's the age thing again, I'm fucking fifteen years older than she is. She can do better. On the other hand…. Jeannette's no spring chicken either, so game on, ladies, game on! What happens in Vegas is I'm going to make this girl mine, for as long as I can hold on to her.*

Out loud, consciously segueing into his sexiest drawl, he said to her, "That sounds great. Let's see where it goes. But right now… where are you going, looking so nice? Can I monopolize your time? Your body?"

Daniella's amused smile was overshadowed by a dark, hungry look in her eyes. "You're so direct. You…you get me worked up, did you know?

"I do know because, as you can see," he glanced down briefly and rolled his eyes, "you have the same effect on me. I want you naked, I want to work you up and make you wet and ready for me to fuck you. Now where did you say…?"

"I'm going where you're going, of course. To the closing night show and party. And you are breakin' hearts in your tux, by the way."

His mouth twisted into a rueful smile. "Backatcha, lovely lady. You look amazing in the almost nothing you have on." He marveled again at the way her skin was the same beautiful brown color all over, from the brightly painted toes peeking out of her sandals to her shapely shoulders and graceful neck. She had a natural flush on her cheeks and wore nothing but mascara and lip gloss on her pretty face.

"I'm helping Jeannette, and then I have to go to work in two hours. I can't…" her flush got a little deeper, her eyes a little dreamy, "you know, uh, be with you. Though I'd love to take your uniform off you later."

The comment was awkward, kind of cheesy, but the combination of her shyness and obvious desire was a turn-on. "You never know what can happen in two hours, do you?" He kissed the beauty mark next to her mouth, then her mouth, and walked into the ballroom with her on his arm. He was happy that everyone, including Jeannette, saw his claim on her. Even if Daniella didn't get it.

Jack kissed her hand with exaggerated formality as he left her and joined Cole on the stage. They stood there in black Armani tuxedos custom-designed for them, switching it up from the white uniforms, dazzling everyone who laid eyes on them. A few tasteful medals decorated their breast pockets, giving their tuxes the right captain feel. Jack saw Cole search the crowd, looking for Tania, and finally finding her sitting with Oksana and Primo in the back of the room.

With a great deal of fanfare from the band, Jack and Cole introduced each of the ship's officers with words of praise and warm handshakes, gesturing to the crowd to clap longer and louder. Recognition—babies cry for it and men die for it, and these hard-working officers were no exception. The brothers worked hard to show they were genuinely grateful for their crew's loyalty and expertise.

When the band played some familiar oldies, Jeannette, Daniella and the ship's dancers joined a few sluggish passengers and got them movin' and groovin', working the crowd like pros. The passengers were dressed casually in travel clothes for early departure the next morning, their luggage already packed and outside their doors to be gathered on the dock for them in the morning.

Jack and Cole joined in the dancing, charming old ladies and little kids as they talked and twirled around the room, posing for pictures. Their personalities shone larger than life, commanding attention, and Daniella and Tania both stared, along with everyone else in the room, wondering what it would be like to truly be a part of these guys' lives, to actually "be with" these impressive men. It felt like a silly crush, like wanting to be with a movie star, but when the lights dimmed and the band played Madonna's *Crazy for You*, both women walked onto the dance floor and into the captains' arms.

Cole was surprised but welcoming, pulling Tania in tight, swaying to the music with her. "I'm sorry, really sorry," he murmured. "I want to talk more later, but I hope you'll forgive me. I know you've heard this before but please…hear me out one more time." She flushed with pleasure at his humble sincerity. Her ear to his chest, she heard his heart racing, telling her this meant as much to him as it meant to her. Knowing it gave her peace of mind and the courage to hear him out.

Her eyes went wide and she leaned back, looking at his face. *I have known him a week, why does he have to explain anything? Yes, he has anger and wants to control, and what kind of life would that be? But then he makes me laugh…is it too soon to decide?* For now, it was fun to sway in his arms, to feel him kiss the top of her head, to imagine they could share more than anger and sex, be a real couple like she saw in movies.

*

"It's time for you to go, isn't it?" Jack asked Daniella, tapping his watch while they danced.

"I have a few minutes." She snuggled into his chest like a tired child, even though the song was over. "Oh, and again, you totally rock that tuxedo." He was so sharp and clean-shaven, looking like a young god, she just had to muss his hair. His jaw tightened and his eyes went dark and intense when he looked down at her.

"Tell Jeannette you have to go. Leave through that door." He jerked his chin toward a door at the back of the room, one leading to a quiet forward deck.

"Uh...oh...okay." From the corner of her eye, she saw him walk out that door before she spoke with Jeannette and headed out.

"Hey, it's me," said a familiar voice as a pair of strong arms pulled Daniella into a dark corner of the deck where lounge chairs were stacked for the night.

When she saw it was Jack, his shirt unbuttoned, his jacket hanging on a chair, she smiled. "I don't have time for this, I have to go to work!"

"This is going to be quick, and you're going to remember it. Captain's orders." His grin was mischievous, knowing. "You've never been fucked standing up, have you?" It was dark but she felt one of his hands on the back of her neck, pulling her in for a possessing, bone-melting kiss. She gasped and kissed him back, panting and enjoying his scent, soap and something a little spicy.

"You know I haven't. But I know you'll make it good." She heard the rasp of the zipper on the back of her tiny dress and then felt the sea breeze on her skin, making her nipples stand at attention. His hands roamed her body, caressing, squeezing, pinching. His mouth followed, licking and nipping, wild and sexy, like he could never get enough of her. She liked the feeling she got from him, like he was starving and wanted every part of her at once. Goosebumps rose on her skin and she trembled, feeling close to coming already.

"Mmmm...you like this, don't you? The idea that someone might see, that someone could walk over here and watch. You might even like it if another man was here, touching you, wouldn't you?" He pulled down her thong and palmed her pussy, thrusting two long fingers inside her, his thumb rubbing her clit. His other hand held her chin, making her face him. "When people watch you dance, it turns you on. You know they're imagining they're fucking you, putting their hands all over you like this. Tell me you like it."

She paused, then nodded, her eyes glittering. "I like it. And I want you to fuck me right now."

He backed her to the wall and ripped her thong off before pulling a condom out of his pocket and opening his pants until they hung loose over his hips. She put her hand on his cock, felt it pulse as she looked over his shoulder, her eyes wide with the reality of what they were doing. Startled, she threw her arms tightly around his neck when he lifted her, his arms under her knees, spreading them wide open. Totally exposed, there wasn't a thing she could do except hold on.

"Look at me." He watched her face when he positioned himself and then drove in, filling her while she gripped him tightly and moaning as she felt his teeth press into her neck. "Does Jeannette do this for you?" he growled into her ear as urgent pressure built inside her.

"Please," she whimpered when she bounced up and rolled her hips, taking him deeper. The sound of flesh slapping against flesh was punctuated with his grunts, bursts of pleasure as he moved, fast and urgent.

They heard voices when a door opened and he put one of her feet on the ground, putting one hand over her mouth to still her cries. He left her other leg lifted, her pussy open while he continued to thrust, hard and slick, every sensation as sharp as a knife. When it was quiet, he kissed her again, devouring her, nailing her to the wall, every stroke building that feeling in her belly when he pinched her nipple, hard, and moaned, "Ooooh, Daniella, you are hot." When he bit and sucked a love bite onto her breast, she was done for.

Heaving against him in a frenzy, she had to close her eyes and clench her teeth to keep from screaming her release. He was there to catch her while she came, continuing to plunge into her over and over, rubbing every sweet spot inside her, and, unbelievably, she trembled and came again, holding onto him for dear life when her ragged moan joined with his, his fingers digging into her flesh, his dick pulsing inside her as his orgasm rolled through him. She knew Jeannette would see the love bite on her breast, and she knew Jack knew it, too.

Her legs shook when he released her, setting her on both feet and stroking her hair, his kisses suddenly warm and tender. "Mmmm, think of me, sexy girl, and I'll see you in Vegas. We are gonna be some crazy band of cruise gypsies, aren't we?" Daniella looked up at him, a little surprised by his comment, and saw a question in his eyes.

"What?" she asked, stroking the side of his handsome face. "There's something, what is it *Papi*?"

He nuzzled into her hand, clearly enjoying her touch, and cleared his throat. "I…uh…wondered if you'd like to…uh….be exclusive with me, at least as far as men, I guess."

She giggled and kissed his jaw, standing on tiptoe, enjoying his discomfort. He continued. "I'll get tested. I want to be inside you without a condom."

"I'd like it too. Yes." Smiling into his lips, she was the aggressor, a low hum spilling from her mouth into his. His lips coasted down her neck, ready to consume her again, but she dug her hands against his shoulders, realizing she had to stop the direction this was going in. "*Papi*, we can't, not right now. You know I have to work."

He closed his eyes and took a breath. "Yeah, and I know you're leaving early." Handing her a handkerchief from his pocket to clean up, he helped her pull her dress on and zip it, his lips grazing the back of her neck. Picking up her thong and putting it in his pocket, he said "I'm starting a collection of these. Where do you think I should keep them?'"

"In your nightstand, right next to your bed. I'll think about you looking at them, touching them." Her voice was husky and low.

Jack laughed at her, noticing her crimson flush. "You naughty, twisted little girl, holy shit! You're imagining me masturbating with them, aren't you?"

Lowering her eyes, she nodded.

"Fuck, Daniella, you are going to kill me. Just for that, I'm going to make you watch while I do it." He pulled it out of his pocket and dangled it. "Even better, I'm going to make you touch yourself while I do it." Shaking the horny out of his thoughts and adjusting his pants, he looked toward the door. "I'll leave first and I'll clear my throat if everything's cool, okay?" Once inside, he held the door for her and stole another kiss before she hurried away.

*

There was a moment in every party when staff didn't have to push it anymore, it had its own momentum, and they'd reached it by the time Cole worked his way to the back of the room. He hugged Primo and Oksana and sat with Tania, hanging his jacket on the back of the chair to signal others he was off the clock. She smiled at those hugs; Cole hugged men and women easily, he was a hugger, such a contrast with the angry guy he had been yesterday. Primo grabbed Oksana's hand and they walked onto the dance floor while some upbeat techno music sent a rush of adrenaline through the crowd.

Tania shivered at the sad, unfamiliar expression on Cole's face. Her heart squeezed at the misery evident in his tense posture. "Are you ready to look behind the curtain and expose the wizard?" Cole asked, his fingers drumming on the table.

"Here?" Looking around, she realized there was no one interested or near enough to hear them.

"Yeah. This is good. I have to keep my mask on here. That way I can't unload on you and hurt you."

"Okay."

"Okay. Just okay?" He looked puzzled.

"I don't want to say anything to stop you or...upset you."

Cole sighed, a crooked little smile bringing out his dimple. "You're being an Invisible Lizard."

Her lips curved in a bit of a smile. "I am. It is safe for you to talk now. And safe for me to listen."

"Okay." He blew out a big breath and took both her hands in his. "My dad, the Admiral, was always pissed about something. My mom held her own, sassing him back. But for us kids, he'd yell about how you made your bed. What you ate or didn't eat. If you coughed or rolled your eyes. From the time we were little kids. When we were six, we were in a soccer league, hyper little dudes running all over the field. The Admiral would scream and belittle us, make us run around the block ten times and practice with us, hip-checking us to the grass and stealing the ball. He cursed the refs and yelled at the kids on the other team.

"When we got older and called him on his bullshit, he always had a rational-sounding reason, and you would doubt yourself, think maybe part of what he was saying was right. Then we'd wonder if we did *anything* right. His raging would silence us, we'd freeze, like you talked about.

"And now here I am, yelling and doing the same shit. I'm learning it's really hard not to blow up, because it's what I grew up with. It comes out of nowhere, like...anyway, back to the story.

"I think in another profession, the Admiral would have been out on his ass, but in the military they reward people who can control and intimidate others. I think he would've stayed in the Navy forever, but he must've pissed off the wrong person, 'cause he retired all of a sudden.

"We moved to Las Vegas, my mom got a job, and things went from bad to worse. He got fired from three part-time security jobs, no mystery why, and hung out with other ex-military guys, drinking all day. They started hanging around the house, and out of the blue my mom moved out with my sisters, leaving Jack and me there with the asshole."

He paused a moment, blinking as if he was fighting tears or swallowing a bitter pill. "We were fifteen. His bullshit continued, and we worked with our guidance counselor, even drafted a fake letter from the Admiral to our congressman so we could go to the Coast Guard Academy." Laughing bitterly, Cole rolled his eyes. "Man, did that piss him off! He would never tell his Navy friends his sons were joining what they called the Sea Scouts."

She was still squeezing his hands, her long fingers twined through his. "Any idea why your mom left, why she didn't take you with her? Did you ask her?"

He kept his head down; it was obvious this part of the story was tough. "She moved into a cheap little place just big enough for the five of them. When we asked, she said we'd be fine where we were."

"I'm sorry it happened. You should maybe talk to her again someday. The answer might be different today than then, you know?" Tania felt a lump in her throat, longing to weep and tell him that she loved him. But she fought it and spoke in a voice that was only slightly shaky. "I want to keep seeing you, but I...what will you do about being angry? You need to learn about it, how to—I don't have the right to tell you what to do. But I can't wonder every time what mood you will be in."

"I guess I have to talk to someone, isn't that what you say when you're a fucking head case like me?" He sounded more bitter than angry. When he stood to walk away he caught himself, put his hands around her face, kissed her on the nose like a child, and sat back down. "And there's something else." When he exhaled again, it sounded like pushing the air out of a ball. "When Mom left, the Admiral started hitting. He'd wait until one of us was out of the house, then pick a fight and punch the other one. One time I came home and Jack was at the bottom of the basement stairs; he'd fallen, hit his head and passed out. Dad didn't even remember how it happened."

Cole left out the part where he beat up his father that day, gave him a black eye and a broken jaw and called an ambulance. The hitting stopped. And he left out the times he couldn't describe, the time when they were little and he called them idiots for putting their shoes on the wrong feet, the time when there was no money for the school graduation trip 'cause he drank it all.

"After that we were never home without each other. Good times, huh?"

"Not good at all." Tania nodded and kept holding his hand while they walked out of the ballroom. "My sister and I did the same thing when Mother's boyfriends started being…interested in us. We stayed together and became invisible. We have a lot in common, you and I."

He turned toward her and pulled both her hands up to his mouth, kissing her knuckles, his gaze tender. He couldn't remember ever discussing feelings this way or having the stakes be this high. "You've been through a lot and you're so good. It amazes me. You've forgiven your mother, haven't you?"

She put her lips where their hands were linked and kissed him back, nodding yes, looking into his eyes. "My grandmother talked to us about it, and Oksana and I decided together. Forgiving made us feel free. You might like it."

He ducked and ran his fingers through his hair, his voice soft and low. "I know you're right. Well, I want to believe you're right, and to believe I deserve to let the old shit go." Kissing her hand again, he whispered "I want to deserve *you*. You make it seem easy and logical to do the right thing."

He saw she was still wary of him, skeptical that he would handle himself differently in the future. *I have to be okay with it, I'll be with her wherever she's at. Even though I want more.*

A nurse from Ukraine via New Jersey was making him look like a whiner. Abused and neglected, Tania and Oksana had nevertheless turned into resilient, independent women. *So what's my fucking problem?* He'd always thought he had it together, but apparently not. Shaking off his anxiety, he felt energized and a little ashamed of himself. For the first time in a long time, he was kind of looking forward to seeing his family in Las Vegas.

"You give me hope, Tania Shevchenko."

CHAPTER THIRTY-FIVE

"WE CAN PAY our own way, you don't have to do all this." When the stylist turned her toward the mirror, Tania gasped. She could hardly believe the glamorous face in the mirror was actually hers. Her hair pulled to the side with a silver clip, eyes vamped-up with subtle false eye lashes, the only contrast to her pale skin was a slash of bright red on her lips and nails.

Her sister jumped up and down with excitement, waving away Tania's protest. Oksana had insisted on the four of them getting dolled up for a night on the town in London. She'd made reservations at a snooty salon in Mayfair, but Tania cancelled them after looking up the prices online. The adorable salon and funky boutiques she'd found tucked behind their hotel in Kensington had worked out fine.

The edgy black-and-white dress Oksana bought her was tuxedo style, with a plunging neckline and a slit up the side accentuating her curvy figure. There was absolutely nothing under the dress except a tiny thong. Sexy black and white pumps made her long legs look impossibly longer. "This is a dress the Queen of the Vampires would wear to a wedding," giggled Tania, pursing her flaming lips and batting her eyelashes while striking a pose at the mirror.

Cole appeared close behind her in the mirror, his voice a sexy purr. "I need a vampire in my life. Pleeeease let it be you!" She shivered when he ran a finger down her spine, which was exposed in the backless dress. She saw his gaze burn a path from her lips down the white skin of her neck to the tops of her breasts, exposed and clamoring for attention in the low-cut dress. "Do you have *any* idea how beautiful you are, Tania Shevchenko?"

Looking in the mirror at the two of them, she marveled that he was still around, despite her Cinderella transformation. When he stepped from behind her, he looked devastatingly handsome in his close-fitting Hugo Boss suit. So much so that the shop girls from the front of the store had followed Cole and Primo and were ogling them from the doorway. Cole's hair was cut in a new way, the front still a little too long, the back razored into some kind of cool rocker thing.

On both Cole and Primo the right amount of 5 o'clock shadow completed the bad boy look. It was tough to find a jacket to fit Primo's massive shoulders, but he was totally rocking a pair of elegant grey slacks, a crisp striped shirt with sleeves rolled up and a vest. Oksana's blonde mop was in a messy, wispy bun and her shiny strapless green dress brought out the intense green of her eyes. Taking tiny steps in her high-heeled gold sandals, she snuggled into Primo's side to signal the gaggle of shop girls that he belonged to her.

The four of them were grinning like happy idiots, basking in the reality of their new relationships. Being off the ship made it easier for them to pretend they were just friends going out to party, easier to forget the complicated circumstances of the past few days and the life changes yet to come. Jack had bowed out of the preparations but promised to meet them later for a drink.

*

Gliding along London's Regent's Canal holding a glass of Nemiroff vodka, Primo and Cole were really getting to know each other well.

It seemed every one of the other ten guests on the party barge were jabbering away in Ukrainian, but luckily the bartender was bilingual.

"So this is what it's like to be in a relationship!" laughed Primo, slapping Cole on the back. "We get to stand around while *they* have all the fun." But both men were grinning ear to ear, watching the sisters talk a mile a minute with Ukrainians they'd just met on this vodka booze cruise for the Ukrainian brand. Tania and Oksana were so animated and excited, their eyes bright with laughter, that it was an education for the two men new to their lives.

First they noticed Ukrainian was a beautiful-sounding language, kind of a soft mix of Polish and Russian. The pleasant, lilting sound of it floated on the breeze as they drifted down the canal from Kings Cross to lovely, leafy Islington.

"You haven't lived until you've heard Ukrainian hip-hop and folk rock," said the bartender, and they had to agree. He gestured to the group, and then himself, chuckling, "Not to mention that Ukrainians are so damn good-looking." If the music videos shown continuously on the boat were any indication, the people were indeed attractive, and the music was apparently filled with politics and passionate love of country.

"And the vodka is pretty awesome as well!" Cole threw back another flavor and slammed his glass down in the traditional manner.

Watching Tania and Oksana speak their native language was especially revealing. A non-native speaker of English is always mentally translating, Tania less than Oksana, but it was still hard work. "Ukrainian has no articles, words like 'the' and 'a,'" said the bartender. "It's why we sound like dumbasses when we say 'I live in city' instead of 'I live in the city,' and 'I have dog' instead of 'I have a dog.'"

But when the sisters spoke Ukrainian, as they did tonight, they didn't have the translation-hesitation loop, resulting in conversation that flowed more naturally and seemed more intelligent. "We can never break these girls up," Primo said, looking at Cole and slurring his words a little. "You're stuck with me if you stick with her, 'cause I'm sticking with Oksana."

Cole busted out laughing. There were few things funnier than a guy as big as Primo when he's drunk. "No worries, man, you can be the third brother, and we'll be triplets. Did you see that movie with Arnold Schwarzenegger and Danny DeVito?"

"Yeah, yeah, we'll be triplets! You and Jack and me will be fucking triplets!" Primo slapped his thigh, rattling the stool he was sitting on. "How about if we're Ninja Turtles, were you into them? I liked being Donatello, with my big bo staff."

"You know, as a matter of fact...," Cole began, but he was interrupted when Tania came over and put her arm around him, leaning on the rail next to him.

"I'm sorry about this, I did not know everyone would be speaking Ukrainian. Is it...not polite? Are you bored?"

"Actually no, we're..."

Primo interrupted in a too-loud, slurry voice, "We've been talking and I'm a brother now, we're triplets! Or maybe Ninja Turtles!" His lopsided grin resembled an eight-year-old boy who'd found a Cracker Jack prize.

Tania broke out in a full, throaty laugh, her eyes taking in both the sexy man-boys leaning against the rail. "You are both such happy drunks, you know? I love that about both of you."

"Cowabunga, dude," Cole said to Primo, "I'm cutting you off. You've had enough to drink." Gesturing to the bartender, he added "Pour a nice tall glass of water for my friend here?"

When Oksana walked up and folded her sister in a tight hug, rubbing her back and murmuring something in her ear, it seemed like time for her to take a break from drinking as well. When they separated, arms linked and eyes glassy with tears, Cole shrugged and said "What?!"

"I...I...do you know how many times this sister has saved my life?" Oksana asked, the tears now running freely down her cheeks. "...how many times she gave me her money and told me to go to my dance class? Helped me with my school work? Talked to me for hours about this boyfriend or that when she was tired? I owe her everything, I owe her my life." They were both crying now, so Cole sighed quietly and got them some napkins from the bar, handing one to Primo while they tenderly wiped mascara from under their ladies' eyes.

"Well, we know now," said Primo, grinning. "And I'm looking forward to having brothers and a sister after being an only child my whole life." Oksana dragged Primo into a conversation with her new Ukrainian friends. He smiled and nodded, happily sipping his water while they tried out their English on him.

Cole took Tania in his arms and planted a loud smooch. "We actually got a real kick out of watching and listening to you ladies speak your language, not having to think and translate. You seemed very happy. Do you miss it?"

She thought for a minute. "No. Not really. But thank you for asking. I think at least half in English now, and I like being an American, especially now my sister will be there. Someday we'd like to go back and visit, though, see my grandparents and my mother. Oksana will have to work on becoming a citizen first, not easy." She leaned into him, feeling his hand on the curve of her hip. "Besides, I..."she looked down, still smiling a little. "I like American men now, they are..."

"Any particular American man?" he lifted her chin, and she was caught in his intense blue gaze. The dark, exquisite suit he wore, the crisp white shirt with his hair brushing the collar...oh, dear, she was distracted. He was smiling, his obscenely adorable dimple showing. There was an edge though, as if he was remembering his anger, her reaction, and regretting it.

After a quick peck on his cheek, she said "There is this one guy...although actually there's two of him!" Her eyes were innocent and wide, her smile playful, when she added, "I really don't know which one I like better." She *sounded* pleased with herself because she was, pleased to be confident enough to joke about it so soon after their ménage.

Vaguely aware she was being spun around against the boat's railing, she was taken by surprise when he dove in for a kiss, a kiss so long and fierce she had to respond in kind, lacing her fingers through his hair. He nuzzled the side of her face, snarling, "Does that help you decide, Trouble? Because you're driving me so nuts I'm ready to drag you into the river and swim back to our hotel. I'm out of my mind around you."

It occurred to her his possessiveness came from a new place of uncertainty, now that they'd left the ship and had to negotiate their relationship going forward. *Maybe this was the problem all along, with his outbursts toward the end of the trip. He was afraid? Afraid of what?*

"Yes, I've decided I like you the best." She grinned. Smiles were the best weapon against fear. "As a matter of fact, I think I'm...: His talented hands were clouding her brain, one thumb circling her nipple through the thin dress, the other pressing her against his arousal. "I'm...craving you, I am, how do you say it...I'm addicted to you." She felt his body relax slightly, but she murmured softly in his ear, "But I still want to go to the club, dance and hang out with your brother. This is our second date, remember? I want to see you dance."

"With my brother?" He quirked a smile.

She cocked her head at him, eyebrow raised. "You are a bit too smooth for me, Captain, I'm just a nurse out for...a night in the city?"

"A big night on the town?" he asked, and she nodded. "And I think you're overdoing the little nurse thing, Tania, you are by far the hottest woman in London. Every man who looks at you starts drooling."

She took a shallow breath, so dizzy from his praise she was unable to draw a deeper one, and opened her mouth to contradict him.

Instead he pressed a finger over her lips and added. "And I don't want you to dance with anyone but me. Including my brother." Pausing a second, he seemed to edit himself, "Is that okay?"

His question at the end, it was rare for him to ask permission. For anything. But there it was. *He's trying to change. To listen.*

"Yes, it is more than okay," she whispered. There was a lump in her throat she couldn't explain, an emotional feeling of attachment, of safety and at the same time...hope. Hope for a future very different from her past.

CHAPTER THIRTY-SIX

"INTERESTING NIGHTCLUB, BRO. Were you into your second whiskey when you chose this?" Cole held Tania very tightly, dragging her swiftly over to the bar where his brother sat, nursing what looked to be three fingers of whiskey.

Looking a little guilty, Jack shrugged. "Well, you and I came here, remember? We had a good time. And the...uh...DJ sounds great, right?"

The club was called Erotica and posters at the entrance featured nearly naked ladies in shiny black fetish wear and promised, "Your darkest fantasies will be fulfilled." It was no surprise Jack would want to come here, but Cole felt different about the place with Tania at his side.

Still, it was a surprisingly attractive crowd, all ages and races, already dancing and buzzing with energy and excitement. Tania and Oksana generated a wave of interest, the men in the crowd staring at them intensely, but there were plenty of other gorgeous women dressed in everything from formal wear to lingerie. It was hard to tell who worked there and who was a customer, especially when a person's drink order might be taken by a buff young man wearing nothing but shiny black pants or a freaky tattooed lady in full military regalia.

"Jack, Jack, this is great! Fantastico! Perfect!" Oksana was flushed with enthusiasm and toooo much vodka. "Did you see they have a show at midnight, a circus with fire-breathing and dancing?"

"I did see that, thought you might like it. Research for your show?" Jack tipped back a healthy swallow of the amber liquid in his glass. Oksana giggled and moved toward the dance floor, Primo right there with her.

Cole had that shit storm feeling at the back of his neck. Jack didn't usually drink this much. "So...what's up with you?"

Forcing a watery smile, Jack looked up at him from already slitty eyes. "I'm having a wing man crisis. You don't need me anymore, Goose."

"That's insane, man. Go upstairs and get something going with a hot chick, give her a thrill. You'll forget I ever lived." Cole remembered the last time they'd been here. Who could forget? They'd teamed up with two beautiful women, taking advantage of the sexy bondage equipment available for public and private play in the nightclub upstairs. "Have an energy drink first, you look a little schwasted."

"I think I'll do that, my brother. But you might want to rescue your lady from The Terminator over there." He laughed and waved at the dance floor where Tania was reluctantly dancing with a giant, beefy guy in leather pants. It was refreshing for Jack to laugh, really laugh, feeling cheerier already at Cole's stony expression when he marched over to snatch Tania from the jaws of Jaws.

"I want to hold you." Cole's hand was at Tania's back, moving her away from dark-and-arrogant. Terminator looked annoyed but recovered quickly, turning away to dance with a tiny blonde who cut in. "Remember twelve days ago when I told you dancing was an excuse to hold you? Doesn't it seem like a year ago? A lot has happened."

She brushed her fingertips along his cheek and nodded.

Cole continued, "And it's still true. But right now I'm angry, even though I know the guy probably started dancing with you without asking." He moved her smoothly around the dance floor, smiling and confident, spinning her and then supporting her in a poised dip, her long, shapely legs showing through the slits in her dress. "How am I doing?"

*

Tania sighed, a sigh of pleasure, and ran her thumb along his jaw. She didn't see anything or anyone in the room except Cole, conscious only of his strong arms around her. "You are doing great. No one would know your feelings, I see it only a little myself, right here in your jaw. You're…biting your teeth together, very tight."

"I'm learning. It feels good, to learn from my mistakes." He smiled and relaxed a little while they moved across the dance floor. Oksana and Primo were glued together, swaying, barely stirring when Cole tapped Primo on the shoulder. "Dude, thanks for keeping an eye on my girl," he said sarcastically.

Primo's eyes were dreamy, his face blissful. "Sure. No problem, man."

Tania and Cole burst out laughing, ordering energy drinks for themselves and their compadres. They were coming down from the booze cruise and wanted to continue to make the most of the evening.

Lacing her fingers through his sexy hair, Tania pulled Cole in closer as they sipped their drinks. "You feel even better than good. Where did you learn to dance so well? Your sisters?"

"The cruise line insisted we learn to dance." His smile was mischievous. "Jeannette taught us to dance, and her training was very thorough."

Her fingers closed into a tight ball and she had the urge to scratch him, her eyes narrowing into jealous slits. "That's what you did with Jeannette? Dancing?"

"Ha, haaa! Turnabout is fair play." he murmured into her neck, and they laughed, realizing they might both have to learn to be a couple one infuriating step at a time.

"Is Jack okay? Where is he?"

Without thinking, Cole replied "He's upstairs."

Tania picked up something in his tone. "Upstairs? What is upstairs?"

The muscular employee in the shiny black pants stood on a stage at one end of the dance floor and announced that the "depraved erotic extravaganza" midnight show was about to begin. Not sure what Tania knew about sex clubs, Cole answered "Upstairs is a sex club. People…play around and have sex."

*

He was startled when she asked "Is it a bondage club?" They'd talked about it once, but after her discussion with Ellora Lind, she'd done a little research on BDSM.

"I…I saw online the spanking, the handcuffs, the nipple clamps. I was…I am curious about it." She looked down, wringing her hands in her lap.

Her cheeks were pink, and he grinned when the flush spread to her neck and shoulders. "Why? Are you interested?"

She seemed too embarrassed to reply, but nodded. Turning to look at the stage while he digested her reaction, he murmured "We'll check it out after the show."

*

The lights went out and an exquisitely powerful-looking woman hung from the ceiling gripping a wide floor-length red banner. The hunky announcer began to walk in circles, pulling the silky banner while the dancer, wearing only a G-string, posed above him, turning this way and that to the sexy music. Oksana was transfixed, her hands gripped in her lap, while the woman pulled the audience into her trance with her graceful midair dance moves. When the music speeded up, the announcer moved the banner in faster, tighter circles, and the strong, smooth muscles stood out in the aerialist's arms and shoulders as she extended her body straight out, her eyes closed and her nipples dark pink, impossibly erect and long.

When she stopped spinning and the music got slow and sexy, she slid down the banner head first. The announcer jerked the red silk and yelled "Nein!" and she turned over, spreading her legs wide, now rubbing her slit against the banner while she slid down to the floor. He pulled the silk even tighter against her pussy when she stood on both feet, embracing her from behind and playing with her nipples as he sawed the fabric back and forth in a sensuous rhythm. When her eyes went wide and she cried out, the stage went black.

In the next act, two men danced together in a pantomime of fighting, their perfect hard bodies leaping, kicking and tumbling one over the other until they lay exhausted, stretched out on the floor staring at each other.

Two women with wild, curly blonde hair came into the audience with flashing backpacks on, touching the audience with long, thin wands that caused pleasant, exciting sparks on the skin.

The finale was the fire eater, a guy with a body so ripped and athletic-looking he could serve as a walking anatomy lesson. A gorgeous redhead, naked except for her high heels, played saxophone across the stage, her music wailing, howling, and praising the fire eater while he swallowed and touched his body—and hers—with the flaming baton.

When the lights went on, Oksana was sitting on Primo's lap,

his arms tight around her to keep her from jumping onto the stage in her enthusiasm. Tania hugged her sister, trying to calm her and assure her that, no, they didn't have to instantly hire these people and bring them to Las Vegas, and yes, there would be talented people like this when they got there.

"Find out their backgrounds and what they're getting paid, that'll give us some clues," said Primo to Tania when her sister dragged her backstage. "And make sure she doesn't make anyone any promises, *please!*" Tania smiled and blew Primo a kiss, happy to know this man already knew and accepted her sister's enthusiasm and impulsiveness.

Cole spoke to Primo in a low voice. "Tania's interested in checking out the...uh...play area upstairs. Jack's already up there. Do you want to come up or go back to the hotel?"

Primo did the rubbing-his-bald-head thing, a sure sign that he didn't feel good about the upstairs suggestion. "I'm thinking hotel," he said, as something a little like fear flashed through his eyes.

"You're afraid she'll..."

Primo cut him off. "No, honestly, I can't let you blame it on Oksana. I used to go to a place like this and it didn't end well."

"'Nuff said, man. We'll hang out at the bar until you're out the door so she won't feel like she's missing something." Cole smiled and murmured to Tania that they should hang at the bar until Primo left with Oksana, and she nodded. *Another thing I love about Tania. She's willing to go with something and ask questions later instead of digging in and insisting on an explanation up front. So cool!*

Primo started loving up on Oksana, and Cole suspected he was whispering filthy things in her ear about what he planned to do to her back at the hotel. She went all clingy onto his side, her arms almost reaching around him as they left.

*

"I love how Primo is with her," Tania sighed, leaning against Cole's shoulder. "We found out a lot from the performers. It was good, there is a network of people all over the world who do this kind of thing, many from eastern Europe."

"Good," he said, pulling her in, his arm brushing along her chest. "Why do you want to go to this club upstairs? I'm curious."

Of course she blushed, looking down with her cheeks hot. "I love when you...hold my arms and when you...spanked me. I looked at things online. I think I like this and..." she looked in his eyes, "I think you like it too."

His dimple came out as the corners of his mouth curled up, he got such a kick out of her shy desires. "You are right, I would love to do these things with you. There are places like this in Vegas, too. Why don't we just watch for tonight, then discuss it and try it when we get there?"

"That sounds good." To Tania, it sounded good on many levels. He was being thoughtful of her, cautious, like he really didn't want to blow it. And he was talking about the future, the next and the next. Not about forever, which was a silly little girl's dream, really, especially for a woman who was unable to have children. What would he think of that? But "when we get there" sounded good for now.

CHAPTER THIRTY-SEVEN

THE HOSTESS WHO greeted them upstairs did a double take. "You…Mr. Carleton, I didn't see you leave." She looked down at the sign-in book, and seemed to recover her composure. "Well…Welcome back, sir."

Tania turned to hide her smirk. Speaking quietly, she said "I'm beginning to see how much fun it is to be twins. Do you remember the American gum commercial? Oksana and I used to sing it when we were little girls." In a sing-songy whisper she chanted, "Double your pleasure, double your fun…"

His hand gripping the back of her neck, he kissed her hungrily right there in the hall, his tongue warm and wet, opening her, nipping her bottom lip and licking it. "I will double your pleasure, Trouble, and you're about to witness one way I might do it. But let me say something first."

He held her away from him, his thumbs stroking her jaw. "I'm not into the slave thing, a woman who has no opinions, who won't say how she feels. You're so hot because you're strong and smart, yet somehow you like me to take charge of your body. Of your pleasure. If you check out the stuff in this room and hate it, it won't change a thing for me. Being with you is more important. I don't *need* this, it's just fun."

He waggled his eyebrows and smiled. "On the other hand, imagine the possibilities."

Cole felt a wicked tingle of anticipation, but he was glad he talked about the slave thing with Tania before they walked into the play room. Three women and one man around the huge room were mostly naked, tied up and filling the air with their sighs and cries. Whether from pain or pleasure was hard to tell. *Probably both. It's all the same in here, pleasure and pain. At least that's what I found when I spent an evening here with Mistress Kitty. And I learned what it's about. There is a fine line between the two, a line I only want to explore on the dominant side.*

He had been curious when the dominatrix approached him back then, curious enough to submit to a little private punishment session. It'd been an incredible education in safety and on edge play, how it felt to be brought close to orgasm over and over again. Surprisingly, Mistress Kitty didn't make him feel like a pussy; in fact, it felt very manly to experience the erotic pain she was dishing out. He learned the limits of his pain tolerance, and he didn't regret it, used what he learned in his own kinky repertoire. But though he certainly hadn't witnessed it, Jack still teased him about his time with Mistress Kitty. Of course. Cole would *never* live that one down (though he sensed a begrudging admiration in his brother's taunting).

*

There was a couch in the middle of the room facing two dark wood X's, each about seven feet tall. Like a sleepwalker, Tania walked to the couch and sat down, fascinated by the two women whose hands and feet were shackled to the structures. A provocative redhead, her hair cascading over her shoulders, was being pleasured by two men, one pinching, licking and slapping her breasts, the other kneeling at her pussy and eating her with uninhibited hunger. Tania felt a sharp pang of desire vine up her body, swirling at her center, puckering her nipples and flaming her cheeks. Apparently the redhead did too, because she alternated between panting and sighing for more and begging them to stop when she couldn't take any more.

I get it now. Sometimes they restrain you so you have to accept the pleasure, whether you think you want it or not. You accept both the pain and the pleasure. Why do I want to? Even though Ellora said no, I still wonder if something is wrong with me. But yes, I do want to.

Barely aware of Cole staring intently at her, she turned her attention to the other X, where a very curvy older woman with short blonde hair was shackled. The colored lights were dim, casting red and amber shadows on her pale skin. Her eyes were wide open, watching the tall man who stood before her. The man struck her over and over again with a leather whip with dozens of suede strips. With each stroke, her body tightened and she whimpered, closing her eyes but arching into the whip as if asking for more. It didn't seem to leave marks, but Tania wasn't sure, it was too dark.

Would I want it to leave marks? Not blood or cuts. It's so bad, but I...imagine my skin with red marks and it makes me...hot.

"Is this like you imagined it? Like you saw online?" Cole spoke softly, but he wasn't looking at her, maybe trying to be offhand, neutral. He put his arm around her, massaging her neck with his strong hand, and she pressed back into him, enjoying it as always. But he seemed nervous, as if it *did* matter to him what she thought of what they were seeing.

"This is funny, you and me." Tania chuckled softly, leaning sideways and putting her lips on his neck. "You like to be dominant and I like to be submissive...with you. We are each what the other wants, but I sit here wondering if you think I am a pervert for wanting this, and you wonder if I think you are a freak for liking it." She climbed sideways into his lap, feeling his steely erection, knowing he could feel how wet her panties were. "I like this. I see now that other people like this. I want to do it with you. Does that say clearly how I feel?"

Cole was cracking up, looking relieved and grinning like a fool. Tania gazed at him, planting little kisses on his beautiful face, wondering for the millionth time why he cared what she wanted when any number of beautiful women would fulfill his naughty desires without question. Like the ones who stared at him wherever they went tonight and every night.

"Come, show me more," she took his hand and pulled him up, grinning at him when he stood and adjusted his enormous boner. "What is the X thing called?" she whispered when the two men with the redhead unhooked her and bent her over the arm of the very couch Cole and Tania had recently been sitting on. When some vigorous fucking and sucking ensued, it was like watching the hottest thing she'd seen on the internet, only live.

"It's called St. Andrew's cross."

"Seriously? You are joking." She pursed her lips at him and he shrugged.

"Apparently, this is the device used when the saint was put to death." He rolled his eyes. "The name doesn't create the best mental picture, I grant you that."

They walked over to where a brutally gorgeous young man was expertly suspending a beautiful naked young woman from a heavy wooden rack. His obvious physical strength was compelling, his muscles flexing and rippling while he pulled the apparatus this way and that. There was a strength of will about him, an intensity that reminded Tania of Cole.

He used red rope that emphasized the bronze color of the woman's skin, her blonde hair falling like a sunny stream through the maze of cord supporting her head and neck. She appeared to be in some kind of hypnotic state, her eyes open, her body relaxed, her legs spread wide. "Mmmmmuhhh," she moaned softly when he stopped to kiss and stroke the round curves of her ass and beautiful breasts, curves pressed and surrounded by intricate knots. He bit her nipple and she cried out, "Ahhh," her mouth loose with pleasure, spreading her legs wider.

She was at the right height for his rock-hard cock and he paused, panting, rolling on a condom while he positioned himself, his hands grasping the ropes at her waist, fingers digging into her flesh. With a snarl and one swift jerk he impaled her and immediately began filling her with fast, punishing strokes, keeping up the demanding rhythm for a very long time, his arms pushing and flexing as if she were an elegant puppet. Finally he went rigid and yelled, ramming into her convulsively until his orgasm subsided and he kissed her and whispered something before stepping away and taking off the condom.

A tall woman with dark hair and colorful tattoos licked her lips and took his place between the blonde woman's legs, kneeling and worshipping her pussy with tongue and teeth and fingers while two men pleasured her nipples and kissed her. She shivered, trembled and cried out, stiffening and shattering three times in sweet agony as some of the watchers masturbated or pleasured their partners. Tania squeezed her thighs together, so aroused she felt dizzy.

"I know this is a lot to take in." Pulling Tania into his arms and turning them slightly toward the erotic scene, Cole put his forehead on hers, his voice a shaky murmur. "What do you think of the public aspect of this? Doing those things in front of other people?"

Tania felt the delicious clenching of the muscles *there*, her breasts swelling and achy. "It scares me, but it is sexy. It's…is there a choice, though?

"There are private play rooms. Same equipment, but no one watching." He let out a long breath, flexing his hips against hers.

Tania felt her heart beating quickly against his, knowing she would do anything, *anything* he asked. There were places he knew, places she knew nothing about but looked forward to exploring with him. In a soul-deep way, she knew she wanted him to guide her on this journey, wanted to follow him to every sensual, forbidden place there was.

His teeth grazed her ear. "Would you prefer it, being in a private room? I guess people have been staring at Jack and me for so long we're kind of used to it."

"Is that where Jack is, in a private room?"

"Probably." His voice was raw. "I'd like to go back to the hotel now and ravage you, so let's discuss the rest of this later, okay?"

*

When Jack entered the club an hour before, he'd sat down on the same couch Tania and Cole did, watching the redhead and the blonde being fondled, kissed and attached to the St. Andrews crosses. He was a little swimmy from the energy drink he'd poured on top of the whiskey, but he told himself he was feeling fine, fine, fine! An absolutely stunning young Asian woman with dyed-pink hair sat lightly on his hand on the arm of the couch, her velvety bare pussy right there under her glittering silver dress. "Hi," she purred, hitching herself up a bit so he could turn his hand over…if he wanted to. When he did, she smiled and gently brushed against him, inviting his touch. "I'm Suki."

"Hey Suki, you're…lovely. So soft and smooth. What would you like me to do?" His breath hitched, *I mean, hello? Does it get easier than this?*

She pursed her red Kewpie-doll lips and brushed the beaded piercing on her clitoris over his fingers. "Whatever you want baby, whatever you want." Looking in her eyes, he saw that she meant it.

His fingers feathered over her cunt, starting a little circular motion at the piercing, feeling her excitement as he watched her pinch her nipples through the flimsy dress. The redhead on the cross was moaning, the other woman too, and now Suki, her breath coming fast, her nipples hard under her dress. His mind was on fire. But unfortunately not in a good way.

All he could think about was Daniella. He was imagining the women's voices he was hearing were her voice, the beautiful faces her face. Here was this luscious woman, her tight little body already wet for him, and she was right next to him, ready and waiting to fuck him senseless and do whatever other kinky shit he could imagine...and he only thought about Daniella. *She's probably in bed with Jeannette right now, what time is it there, anyway?*

The warmth lifted from his fingers and Suki stood, adjusting her dress and leaning over to whisper in his ear. "I don't know where you are right now, handsome, I don't know who she is, but she's a lucky bitch. See ya." She was pouting, her lips pursed as she walked away.

Jack's head was spinning when he stood, from the drinks and these feelings, emotions he'd never had before. He took a stroll around the room and wondered what alien had taken over his brain. *Why can't I do the things I like to do? Why can't I screw this out of my system?*

It was like an alternate universe, a twisted world where he was being led around by his dick, his brain in a tangle. There was yearning, hot, fire-breathing, out-of-control *wanting*. It wasn't sweet or nice or pleasant. It was way out of his control and it wasn't fun. And dammit, he couldn't wait to see Daniella. He was outta there in less than an hour, chuckling when he noticed his brother and Tania sitting on the couch he had recently vacated.

CHAPTER THIRTY-EIGHT

I T WASN'T UNTIL they'd reached the highest point of London's Millennium Bridge that Jack regretted coming along. He'd never thought of himself as being single or alone until the moment they reached the graceful curve of the old city's newest and most ultramodern suspension bridge. Now he was acutely aware of his status as the odd man out when Primo held hands with Oksana and, more importantly, Cole held Tania closely at the waist.

Who will I hang out with now that my brother's with her? Since the day we were born, we've always been the twins, the boys, Leonardo and Michelangelo, Goose and Maverick. How the fuck did this happen?

Tania looped her arm through Jack's and pulled him into the group while they leaned against the rail, St. Paul's Cathedral in the distance to their left, the Tate Modern art gallery to their right. "Let's be the Musketeers, one for all and all for one!" she said, giving Jack a peck on the cheek. It seemed that she understood his sudden isolation, overcoming her previous shyness toward him.

Primo cleared his throat, taking a gray metal container out of his backpack and handing an envelope to Tania. "You want me to read it?" she asked, surprised.

"You know I hate to read out loud, Tania." Oksana stood on tiptoe and kissed Primo's cheek. "And it turns out Primo does not read out loud, either. "

Cole looked at Tania with a mixture of humor and pride, smiling at the way everyone ended up depending on her. She cleared her throat and said in her most formal tone "Okay, Emile Strauss, let's hear what you have got to say for yourself." Taking a deep breath, she unfolded the page Strauss, knowing he was dying, dictated to the nurse.

"When you read this letter, you will see London's past to your left, her future to your right. My beloved adopted city is the place where I enjoyed the best and most meaningful times of my life. In my sixties, after a lifetime of nothing but going to work every day, I looked for another life, a life where others might see me and depend on me. I guess loneliness suits me best, because I never found friends or a family to share with.

"My proudest accomplishment is the museum to your right, the Tate Modern, a place which expresses everything I am and all that I've seen. I have been a secret patron of the museum since it was only an idea and was proud when it finally opened.

"Burned with my ashes was a letter listing everything in my life that I am ashamed of, including keeping Oksana against her will. My life is an example of what not to do, of waiting and being afraid to love. As you pour my ashes and my regrets into the Thames, remember that many opportunities are lost because you're afraid of what people will think. Don't hesitate. Live your life, make mistakes. I was so afraid to make mistakes, it kept me from living fully. Use the money to live your dreams and create joy for yourselves and others."

Primo turned the urn over and they watched in silence, each lost in their own thoughts, as the stream of ashes scattered in the wind. "Rest in peace in the place you loved, Emile," said Oksana, and they nodded and exchanged hugs.

Like the millions of other people who walked this bridge every year, each of them hoped to live fully and to love well. Their feelings about the future resembled the bridge they stood on — bright, shiny, new…and a little wobbly, swaying in the wind.

*Read on and enjoy the first chapter of the next adventure for
Tania, Cole, Jack, Daniella, Primo and Oksana:*

ROMANCING VEGAS
A CAPTAIN'S ORDERS NOVEL

CHAPTER ONE

"UNDO YOUR BUTTONS," he said, and she watched her hands undoing them one by one in the image in the corner of the screen. That edge was in his voice, the easy authority that made her *want* to do whatever he said. It was so… naughty doing this, seeing Cole's intense blue eyes on her iPad, watching her. But so, so hot.

"Take your shirt off, yeah… that's it." His voice was lower when he groaned, "Ooohh, your skin is so beautiful when you blush all over. I can't…I can't think about anything else when I see you like that. Let me see your gorgeous tits." He'd shipped her the iPad with a simple note, "Can't wait to see you touch yourself."

When Tania put her hands on her breasts and stroked her

nipples through the bra, she forced herself to keep watching him when he took a deep breath and bent forward, smiling and laughing under his breath. It was okay if he saw her trembling, he already knew how she craved his touch. No secret there. Thankful she had on one of her nice lace bras, she sat up straighter in the chair and unhooked it, baring her breasts for him.

His reaction made her feel beautiful and his hands—clenched tight—showed off his sexy biceps and the muscles in his forearms. "Hold them up for me sweet thing, lean forward and show them to me." Pursing her lips for a kiss, she cradled them high and jiggled them a little, smiling when he leaned in, his lips almost pressed against the screen. "You. Are. Killing me." His voice was tight and flat as he sat back, sighing. "I thought you said you wouldn't be good at this."

It was so cool that the screen and camera were essentially in the same place, making it easy to search Cole's eyes. There was a look there she hadn't seen before, a feverish look that inspired her. "They feel heavy in my hands, they ache for you. I wish you were here, squeezing my nipples, they're so hard right now." *Did I just say that?*

Locking eyes with her, he shifted again, his face flushed. "Wet your fingers and put them on your nipples, I know they're sensitive. Roll them and pretend it's my mouth." Enjoying her soft moans and sighs of pleasure, his sexy voice went even lower, commanding her, encouraging her. "Pinch them, you like it when it stings a little. Look at me while you do it."

She obeyed but it was impossible, too intense, to hold his gaze while she caressed and pinched her breasts, longing for his hands and teeth on her. Her head thrown back, she let out a long, breathy moan. "Oh, Cole," she whispered.

"What? Why aren't you looking at me?"

"I...I want to touch myself. I'm so close and I want to come."

Tania's voice quivered. She put a finger in her mouth and drew a slow, wet circle around her nipple.

"Mmmm, fuck girl. You're wearing me down here, I wanted to torture you for a while."

It was one of the things she loved about him, the way he could slow everything down and watch her, focus on every step and put words to the things that gave her pleasure.

"Okay, you've... got me goin' here. Let's do this together Miss Trouble. While you're walking over to the bed, take your panties off and then sit up against the headboard." When she got there, she saw that he was doing the same. Cole's long, sexy legs were slightly bent and she felt dizzy when she saw his cock standing at attention. He had the iPad leaning against something on his nightstand.

"Yeah, put the pad right there so I can see your sweet cunt. Reach down between your legs. Are you wet, so wet for me?"

"Uuuhh, huh, I am." Her voice surprised her, low and breathy, shaking with emotion.

He talked in that bossy tone, the one that drove her nuts. "Open your legs wide, beautiful girl. Run your nails along your thighs, over your belly, around your breasts. Pretend it's my teeth, my rough beard teasing you. Don't touch yourself, not yet."

"Ohh, okay." She was smiling a little, flushed, but Cole looked serious, as if this was hard for him.

"Make your hand flat and put it on your pussy. Move it up and down a little." The excitement in his voice was increasing. "When it starts to feel good, slap it. Yeah that's right, the whole thing, slap it!" She did it and was shocked at how good that felt; she saw him flinch, his eyes wide and glassy. "Keep doing it, quick, quick! Do it!" He watched intently, his chest heaving when he leaned into the lens. "God, look at you, so fucking hot...mmmm, uh, stop, I don't want you to come yet."

"Ehhh, please, I need it so bad."

"Soon baby, soon. Tell me about it Trouble, tell me what I should do now so we can come together."

Tania moaned with pleasure, moving the phone so he could see her face. His hips shifted and she gasped, thinking she might come when he pumped his shaft ever so lightly, running his thumb over the top. There was something achingly erotic about the sight of that, his confidence and power evident as he challenged her to jump in. Her clit ached to be touched, but it was her turn to stroke him with her voice. "You would feel so good in my hand right now, so warm and smooth. I wish I could lick that little slit in the top and roll your balls around in my hand. Imagine how it would feel if I was there with you, naked and putting my mouth on you. Can you feel my tongue circling around the top, wrapped around you when you're all the way in my mouth, when it feels like I'm swallowing you? "

"Ohhh, fuck." He was panting. The first time they tried this, she said almost nothing. It happened that way in the beginning, his rough demands would reduce her vocabulary to two sounds – Ohhhh and Mmmmm. "Look at that little bit of cum on the top, spread that around with your fist and keep it so tight. Watch me, yes, think of touching my tits and my ass and stroke it so tight."

*

"Shit girl," Cole said, "when did you get so good at FaceTime sex?" She seemed to have gotten over her shyness. His mouth tilted in a smirk, and that's the way it was between them, laughter at their missteps mixed with vivid, intimate lovemaking. When he met Tania a month ago, she'd never had an orgasm. Now she was letting her freak flag fly, unleashing the sexy beast within. That low, husky voice of hers was hypnotizing him.

He licked his lips and locked her eyes with his. "I'm watching you, and you look ready to come. Are you ready to come? Put your fingers on that spot, the one on the side of your clit, and feel my tongue there, feel me bringing you so close."

"I'm…I'm close. I want to come with you inside me." Her moans were intense now, her words slurred with desire while she watched him stroking his cock until his legs were shaking.

"Put two fingers in and fuck yourself, push your hand against that sweet button of yours, yeah, yeah…."They were both so ready, hearts pumping, minds open to each other's pleasure. "Think of how hard I'm fucking you, my fingers pinching your nipples, kissing you until we can't breathe. Oh fuck, oh fuck!"

They were totally consumed, arching, hips rocking as they focused inward, each revealing the sensation of coming, exhibiting it for the other to see. After the first peak, they stared into each other's eyes, kept going and came again, not together but close enough. It was hard not to feel self-conscious as their orgasms waned, but they let the outrageous waves of pleasure stutter away slowly and then lay quietly, alternately smiling and making faces at each other.

"Hey," she waved into the phone, her voice relaxed.

"Hey back." Cole stretched out on the bed, holding the blanket up and pulling in a pillow, pretending she was snuggling in there with him. "You sure you don't want me to fly to New Jersey and drive to Vegas with you? You could molest me while I'm driving."

She snorted. "No, I am driving myself across America, foolish man. Waves of grain, purple mountains and all that. It's like…it will be like a sacred pilgrimage for me, Tania Shevchenko the brand new American. I stop in Omaha, Nebraska, and then I'll see you. I can molest you then."

He knew she was proud of the car she bought with her nursing paychecks, so he didn't suggest she just sell it and let her newly wealthy sister buy her a new one. That just wouldn't fly with fiercely independent Tania. "Okay Miss Trouble, see you in two days. Stay in touch and be safe." She started to blow him a kiss when he added, "So, uh...I want to say that...I really think you're brave and I appreciate that you're coming out here." The L-word was on the tip of his tongue but he'd never said it to a woman, never said "I love you" to anyone but his mother and sisters.

*

"You make it easy to be brave but...thank you." Tania paused, nodding and smiling. She knew exactly what he was struggling with but didn't want to deal with it like this. "A-okay!" she said and gave him the thumbs-up, and they both laughed.

You would think she'd sleep peacefully after that, but no—once her engines were revved, she wanted to go, go, go, and she had the sexiest dream. She dreamed of the night she seduced Cole's brother Jack, thinking he was Cole, and how she was kneeling naked on the floor in front of him when Cole walked in and discovered them.

Remembering the panic she felt, the naughty appeal of the offer to make love with both of them, the feel of their hands on her heated skin, their blue eyes hooded with desire. Tania tossed in her sleep, tasting them, hearing their moans and growls of pleasure, their husky voices telling her how beautiful she was, the slap of skin on skin. She sat up in bed when she began to come in her sleep, feeling the slippery wetness between her legs.

The memory of Cole's kiss, telling her he would never share her again, was the last part of her dream to fade. Knowing her car was filled with boxes and her bags packed, she looked around the room and realized she was ready. Ready to jump off the nice, safe cliff piled with everything she'd worked toward for the last eight years. Ready to jump into the muscular arms of the most beautiful, blue-eyed, crazy-sexy American she'd only known for a few weeks.

"Who does this?" some of her nursing friends had asked.

"Me, I'm doing this," she said sticking out her chin defiantly. Her friend Adriana held up her iPad and showed all the nurses the website photo of Tania's boyfriend Cole and his twin brother Jack Carleton, the captains of the cruise ship *Sunset*.

After a gasp, three of the girls raised their hands and asked "Can we come with you?"

KARA KEEN

After a career in public relations and advertising, Kara Keen got tired of writing half-truths and decided to write the whole truth—love is all you need! She wrote two nonfiction books (under a different name) about sex, intimacy, and women's health, and spoke at conferences across the country.

Recognizing that the brain is a woman's most important sex organ, she started writing stories to fire up women's minds about the many ways men and women get together. She enjoys guiding her characters through emotional situations and sophisticated adventures while showing how they can heal each other through wise-cracking humor, honest talk, doing the right thing, and really hot sex! Hanging out with her family in northern Virginia, she's adopted five black lab mixes from the shelter over the years and each one is smarter than the last. Her current canine writing companion is both smart and intuitive—Mr. Spock.

Connect with me online:
My Website – http://www.Karakeen.com
Facebook – http://facebook.com/karakeenauthor
Twitter – http://twitter.com/karakeenauthor

If you enjoyed reading *Captain's Orders* – please recommend it and review it. If you do review the book on Amazon or Goodreads, feel free to email me and let me know. KaraKeen.author@gmail.com

Made in the USA
San Bernardino, CA
23 July 2015